GOLD DIGGER

GILLIAN GODDEN

Boldwood

First published in Great Britain in 2021 by Boldwood Books Ltd.

Copyright © Gillian Godden, 2021

Cover Photography: depositphotos and istock

A CIP catalogue record for this book is available from the British Library.

Paperback ISBN 978-1-80280-048-7

Large Print ISBN 978-1-80280-044-9

Hardback ISBN 978-1-80280-043-2

Ebook ISBN 978-1-80280-041-8

Kindle ISBN 978-1-80280-042-5

Audio CD ISBN 978-1-80280-049-4

MP3 CD ISBN 978-1-80280-046-3

Digital audio download ISBN 978-1-80280-040-1

Boldwood Books Ltd
23 Bowerdean Street
London SW6 3TN
www.boldwoodbooks.com

1

SURVIVAL

The sound of gunshots filled the air, men firing aimlessly into the black night lit up only by the half moon. Two young women were running blindly across a potato field the size of a football pitch, when one stumbled and fell.

Julie was covered in mud and bleeding from the scratches of the bramble bushes used as fences around the fields to stop anyone from escaping. She looked down at the girl on the ground, crying and gasping for breath.

'Get up, Frankie.' Holding her side, Julie stood upright and threw her head back to fill her lungs with air. Her chest felt crushed and she could only speak in between breaths. Every part of her body ached, but fear and adrenalin were spurring her on.

'I can't,' Frankie sobbed. 'I've hurt my ankle and I can't run any more.' Her tearful eyes looked up at Julie pleadingly. 'Let's go back, I can't take any more.' Sweating and crying and smeared with mud, Frankie had given up. They had miles to go yet.

'Are you fucking crazy? This is our only chance. God only knows, they will kill us anyway. We can't go back. Don't you understand?' Panting and breathless, Julie looked around the dark farmland. There was nothing to guide their way, only instinct. 'Listen to me. They are not going to let us get away with this. These bastards do not want troublemakers like us.'

Frankie lay face down in the mud, sobbing. 'Like you, you mean.' Turning her head, she looked accusingly at Julie, who stood over her, her eyes wild with fear. 'Why did you do it? This was all your idea.'

Guilt washed over Julie and she brushed away her own tears while listening to her sister's recriminations. It was true. This was all her own doing, but now she was going to free them from those few months of torture.

'Get the fuck up, or I will drag you. Ankle or no ankle, we have to keep going.' Julie's heart was pounding so much she could hear it like drums in her ears. Her chest hurt from lack of air and the pain in her side made her wince. Half bending over, she gulped in more air. Hearing a noise, she swiftly turned her head to look behind them. It was not just the gunfire and the smell of sulphur in the air; they had let the dogs out, those half-starved, vicious dogs. Now they really were in trouble. Grabbing Frankie's arm, Julie started to pull and drag her sister across the dirty field, both of them breathless. 'Frankie, we have to go, now!' The urgency in Julie's voice brought Frankie back to reality.

'Is that those horrible dogs I can hear? Are they coming for us?' More tears fell down her mud-encrusted face.

'Yes! Are you going to get up and run now? Because, believe me, when they get you, they will tear you apart.' The very idea of those crazed Alsatians and Rottweilers tearing them limb from limb made her panic. Fear gripped Julie and, as much as she wanted to, she couldn't shout at Frankie. In the dark night she realised her voice would echo and give their pursuers a clue as to their whereabouts.

Frankie managed to stand, but winced at the pain in her ankle where she had stumbled on a rock. She was bleeding and her clothes were torn. Taking one more look backwards, Julie could hear the barking getting louder and closer. She took her vest top off and smeared some of Frankie's blood on it, then reached down and picked up a hard piece of mud and gravel. She wrapped it all up into a bundle and with all her strength threw the top in the opposite direction. Then she grabbed Frankie's hand, gripping it tightly. 'That might keep them off our scent for a while. Run! Run for your fucking life!'

In silence, with only the noise of their heavy panting, they ran and stumbled their way through the darkness. Stopping suddenly, Julie pulled Frankie down onto her knees in the mud.

Coughing and spluttering, Frankie gasped for air. 'What is it? Is it the dogs?'

'Lower your voice, you silly cow. No, look.' She pointed into the distance and whispered in between breaths, 'There is the main road ahead, just like Elliot said. I did wonder if he was so off his face on drugs he had imagined it, but no, there it is, Frankie, and there is the truck.' At last, they had a goal. The run had been endless; with all her might, Julie had hoped it was not a wild goose chase.

At the end of the field there was an open truck parked on a side road near trees and bushes. Its headlights were on low beam, but in the darkness it lit their way to the main road. Crawling on their stomachs, scratched by the mud which had been hardened by the sun, Julie watched the sight before them with horror.

Now they were at the roadside, it was just as Elliot had said. There were dead bodies in a heap on the ground and Elliot and another man she did not recognise were being watched over by a guard with a gun while they picked up the bodies and heaved them into the back of the open truck. The smell of the rotting bodies hung in the air and made her want to vomit. She saw Elliot had a cloth tied over his mouth. However, he and the other men had obviously got used to the stench. God knows how long those poor bastards had been dead and the hot Spanish sun hadn't helped.

'What are we going to do now, Julie? That one has a gun. I recognise him from the camp.'

'I don't know, but we have to get into the back of that truck. I can still hear those bastards in the distance trying to find us. Now they've realised we're free they won't stop until they do. Our scent is all over that thorny wall and the dogs will have sniffed it out.'

'They might think we're dead already. If not from the bushes then probably from the fall.'

'True, but they'll need to make sure. It's their lives or ours when the boss finds out. He'll be so fucking angry if he knows we've got away and we could blow the whistle on this farm. Oh well, in for a penny...' Mustering what little courage she had left, Julie grabbed Frankie's hand and took a step towards the truck.

Frankie hung back. 'I haven't gone through all this to be shot. That man will shoot us.'

'Yes, Frankie. But we're women and that man still has a prick. I'm wearing a pair of torn shorts and my tits are bare because I threw my vest in that field. I may be scratched to fuck and bleeding, but we're still young and in better condition than most of the women back there. He's going to think it's his lucky night. He'll probably want to use us first and then kill us when it's time to leave. Either way, it's all we have.' Despondent, Julie held Frankie's hand and walked further into the beam of the truck.

Hearing the noise from the bushes, the guard looked up and pointed his gun. 'Show yourselves. Who's there?' Pointing his rifle in their direction, he stood and waited.

'It's only us. The guards sent us. They thought you might like some company but they wouldn't give us a lift any further. It's been a long walk.' Plastering on her most charming smile despite all the pain she felt, Julie stood in front of him.

Still pointing the gun at them, the guard eyed them suspiciously. He looked around and beyond them for anyone else. Striding forward, he grabbed hold of Julie's hair and pushed her down into the headlights of the truck to see her more clearly.

'Do you know this bitch?' He turned around to a panic-stricken Elliot, who was obviously afraid that Julie would tell the boss that he had left the door open for them. Nodding nervously, he said, 'Yes. She is a new one from the sheds.' He pointed at Frankie. 'That's her sister.'

The guard raised his hand and slapped Julie across the face, making her head bang against the truck. 'Right, you bitch, you can help these two first and then we'll have some fun, eh.' His stale breath in her face made her feel sick. His English still had a Spanish accent to it as he barked orders at them.

Dazed and reeling from the bang on her head, Julie suddenly felt herself released from the grip of the guard. Opening her eyes properly, she saw that Elliot had hit the guard from behind with a plank of wood and the man had collapsed to his knees. Clearly, seeing the guard hit Julie had angered Elliot, who was protective of her. Somewhere hidden in the depths he was still a man and she had become his woman.

Rubbing her head, she looked up and saw the other man who'd been throwing bodies into the truck with Elliot take off into the night. 'We're getting out of here,' she said. 'Are you coming with us?'

'No, you go.' The fight had left him years ago. He was a broken man. The idea of the outside world frightened him more than this, after being institutionalised for so long.

The guard began to stir and tried to get up. Julie saw that

Elliot had picked up the gun and was pointing it at the guard. 'Shoot him!' she shouted, but there was no response. Quickly grabbing it from him, Julie held it towards the guard's head. Although her hands were shaking, she fired it and watched him fall to the ground with a bullet hole in his head. Now she knew their time was limited. Their pursuers would have heard the gunshot.

'Come with us, Elliot. You'll be okay.' She watched as he ignored everything that had gone on and still tried to lift the bodies on his own. He threw one over his shoulder and put it into the truck.

'The keys are in the truck. Bye.' Elliot was sad to see her leave; she had been the only meaningful human contact he'd had in years. He wanted to help her, even if he couldn't help himself.

Rushing forward, she held his face in her hands and kissed him. This time it was for real. She was truly grateful. 'Thank you, Elliot, darling. You do realise they will kill you for this.' When she saw him nod, she knew he welcomed the end. He'd had enough and his body was tired. 'Frankie, get in the truck.'

'But you can't drive.' Frankie was in shock, wide-eyed and staring at her sister.

'Well, I'm going to learn bloody fast. How hard can it be?' Seeing lit fire torches looming towards them, she jumped in. The truck stalled and the gears crunched as she tried to change gear, her haste and fear getting the better of her. She tried again and the truck jerked forward. Putting her foot on the accelerator with all her might, she sped off. Through the rear-view mirror, she could see Elliot waving. Tears rolled down her face, not only for Elliot, but because this nightmare was nearly over for them. 'Get some sleep; I think I'm getting the hang of it now.'

Frankie was now crying, half hysterical and shaking. 'You

killed that man. You could go to prison for murder. What have you done?'

'I killed him before he killed us. We've already been in prison, Frankie, anything else would be a hotel. See if you can grab an old T-shirt for me off one of those bodies in the back then get some sleep.'

As Frankie did as she was told, Julie carried on driving, thinking to herself that this was not the first time she had murdered. However, that was another story...

Opening the windows and breathing in the fresh air seemed like a luxury. Not knowing where she was driving to was the mystery. Julie had no idea what to do next. She had no money and no passport. And there was no one to contact in England to send them the money they'd need to get back home.

All she knew was she had to get as far away from the camp as possible.

Turning to check on Frankie in the darkness of the truck, Julie could see she was fast asleep. They were both exhausted, mentally and physically, but the adrenalin and fear drove her on. With each headlight from other cars she saw on the road, she froze, expecting it to be one of her captors.

With only the radio on low for company, she could hear the quiet. For once, there was no one having bad dreams and shouting out in their sleep, or walking around the hut aimlessly wringing their hands and mumbling to themselves.

During the brain-numbing drive, Julie's mind wandered back to how this nightmare had begun. There had been no real time to think about how they had got into this awful situation. There had only been survival. Each day had been another long, hot day to get through and all she had concentrated on had been the golden opportunity of escape. She had no idea how or when it would present itself. But when it did, she had grasped it with both hands, not caring about the consequences. She had nothing to lose. Escape and survival – that was the key.

2

Spain had been a dream come true. It was everything Julie and Frankie had dreamt of.

'I'm glad you let me come, although I am sorry Sheila let you down at the last minute,' said Frankie.

Julie had lied to Frankie, saying Sheila had let her down because of illness. Poor Sheila had paid for her ticket and Julie had intended to go with her and she would be so angry when she found out Julie had gone and robbed her of her money and her long-awaited holiday. But it had been vital that Julie got Frankie away from their home.

And there was no turning back now. Julie wondered if she had been too hasty in taking Frankie, but she'd had no choice. It would only have been a matter of time before that sleazy, drunken bastard stepfather of theirs had helped himself to her innocence. Consoling herself that she had done the right thing, Julie still felt nervous. Derek had deserved everything he'd got, but in the cold light of day Julie also felt it might have been easier if she had just absconded with Frankie; then, there would always be the opportunity of going home.

* * *

When they landed, the Spanish sun was hot and the beaches were packed with tourists and to Julie it felt like the best place on earth. No one seemed to care about age, or even notice when she took Frankie into one of the nightclubs. They had danced the night away to songs of the seventies without a care in the world.

While walking around the town one day, Julie saw a flyer pasted to a lamppost that was offering jobs picking fruit and vegetables. It offered accommodation and good rates of pay. A thought crept into her head. If they had jobs in Spain, then they could stay here. They were already four days into their holiday and she had nearly spent all her money. Thankfully, some of the men in the clubs had paid for their drinks when chatting them up, but they were running very low on funds. And in a few days, they would have to leave their hotel, which Julie dreaded. The horrible memory of Derek loomed in her mind. They simply couldn't go back to England.

Clutching the flyer in her hands, it seemed to be the answer to her prayers. She saw a telephone number at the bottom and when she dialled, it was answered instantly. Again, she was told of the opportunities and money she could earn. She asked if there were enough vacancies for herself and her sister, and they said they welcomed another pair of hands, stating that the farms where they picked the fruit and vegetables were large, and the more the merrier. The woman on the other end of the telephone informed Julie that they had a pickup point in the centre of town where the coach collected everyone and took them to the farms and accommodation. *Thank God*, Julie thought, putting her hands together in prayer. Everything was going to work out for the best.

'Shouldn't we tell someone where we are?' asked Frankie.

'Why?' snapped Julie. 'Do you think they've even noticed we're not there? Mum and Derek will probably think we're staying at Gertie's. No, we have jobs, Frankie, and that means we can stay in Spain. Imagine it, a job where we live in the sun and spend our days off on the beach.'

'It sounds great. When do we go? I can't wait.' Frankie was excited at the prospect of her new home and job. At last, their luck was changing for the better.

A few days later, Julie and Frankie made their way to the pickup point to look for the coach. Once Julie had spotted it, she saw there was quite a queue to get on and she hoped there would still be enough room for them both.

A lot were students and backpackers who just travelled around from one place to another, picking up jobs on their way. Quite a few were Spanish, obviously locals who were looking for work. They were all excited as the driver put their cases into the boot of the coach and welcomed them aboard, after giving them homemade badges to write their names on and pin to their tops.

The long coach drive was tiring and the further away from the city they got, the more an uneasy feeling came over Julie. She looked around the coach. Everyone was introducing themselves and looking forward to their new jobs, but Julie had a nagging feeling. Maybe Frankie had been right. They were going into the middle of nowhere and no one knew where they were. She felt she had been too hasty in her decision and should have found out more about it from the receptionist at the hotel. Maybe the locals could have told her more... but there were locals on the coach, too. Doubt was creeping in and, call it gut instinct, suddenly she had the urge to get off.

Walking down the aisle of the coach, Julie stood beside the driver. 'Will we be going to the accommodation first?' she enquired. She wanted more information. 'It's been a long journey and it would be nice to freshen up a little.'

The coach driver shrugged and made out that he did not understand her. Pointing his thumb back to the seats, the distasteful look on his face told her he wanted her to go and sit back down.

Her anger rising at his snub, Julie turned to everyone else on the coach. Did no one feel the same about this situation or was she just being paranoid? 'Do any of you remember this driver speaking English when we got on the coach? Well, I do. But it seems he has been struck dumb now.' No one answered her. In fact, they seemed embarrassed that she was making a fuss. Turning to the driver, she shouted at him, 'Oy, stop this coach! I've changed my mind; I want to get off.' Banging on the doors of the coach to make him understand, Julie's face was flushed with anger. What's more, no one else on the coach gave a shit. They were all ignoring her outburst and looking out of the windows.

The driver gave her a sideways glance, not wanting to take his eyes off the road. He beckoned her with his finger and Julie moved closer to him. 'Sit down, you mouthy fucking bitch!' Shocked by his manner, her face dropped; her suspicions were confirmed. Something was definitely wrong.

Julie sat back down beside Frankie. She wanted to remain calm. Once the coach stopped, she would tell the managers she had changed her mind. They hadn't signed any contracts.

'Is everything okay? You seem angry. What did the driver say to you when you shouted at him?' Frankie was used to Julie's outbursts. She had witnessed them all her life.

'I'm just bored, and he's an ignorant bastard.'

Thankfully, half an hour later, the coach stopped and Julie breathed a sigh of relief. She had mulled over in her head what she would say when they stopped and now she was going to have her chance. She was definitely going to report that bloody driver!

Some of the other passengers had dozed off and were woken by the coach stopping. Julie was itching to get off, but again, the feeling of foreboding engulfed her. As she stood up, she looked through the window and could see three men. One was in a suit and the other two were dressed in trousers and shirts, holding clipboards.

The afternoon sun was high and shone brightly. It had been hot and stifling on the bus. Breathing in the fresh air, Julie shielded her eyes from the sun and looked around. For miles and miles, all you could see was farmland.

'Stand in line, please,' one of the men shouted at them all, gaining their attention and stopping their chatter.

Julie stepped forward and looked directly at the man in the suit, determined to get his attention. He was talking in Spanish to the other men with clipboards. She stuck her chin out stubbornly. 'We've changed our mind, mister,' she said. 'Can we jump back on the coach and get a lift back to civilisation?'

He looked up, angry that she had interrupted his conversation, and calmly walked down the line towards her. The stinging blow across her face made Julie stagger backwards.

A young male passenger stepped forward. 'Hey, mate, there's no need for violence. Leave her alone or we'll all leave.' A loud bang filled the air and he fell to his knees, then flat out on the ground. He was dead.

Horrified at what they had just witnessed, everyone looked at each other in stunned disbelief. Before they could say anything, two more gunshots were fired into the air by the man in the suit. 'Everyone shut up. You're hurting my ears. Not one word or you will be next!'

Shaking and terrified, everyone looked down at the lifeless figure of the young man on the ground and then back up at the man in the suit. No one dared to say a word. The next gunshot could be them.

The man in the suit walked arrogantly down the line, inspecting everyone; he looked disgusted. He pointed to one of the men in the line. 'This one is too old. Shoot him,' he said. Another gunshot was fired and the man slumped to the ground, before he had even had a chance to beg for mercy. Now everyone was terrified and crying hysterically. Some fell to their knees and held their hands together, praying and pleading for their lives. Julie held Frankie's hand tightly and shook her head to stop her from doing the same. She knew begging to this heartless bastard was useless.

Julie was shaking inwardly and felt her legs go weak as the man in the suit walked up the line towards her and Frankie. Grabbing Frankie by the jaw, he pulled her forward and inspected her more closely, then nodded to one of the other men, who started writing something on his clipboard. 'I have another camp for a young girl like you. You're wasted here,' he spat out and pushed her back into line beside Julie. There was a cold, evil look in his eyes and, as he looked Julie up and down, she could tell he already disliked her. 'You, lady, need to learn some manners and to speak only when spoken to. I have met trouble-makers like you before, I have broken their spirits, and I will soon break yours.'

Biting her tongue and holding back the tears, Julie nodded. This was a time to hold her temper, before she joined the two men on the ground, leaving Frankie to this merciless bastard. 'Can I ask a question, sir?' She lowered her eyes and showed the man the respect he required.

He gave a smug, satisfied smile and looked at the other two men with him, then turned back to Julie. 'That's better. Go on, ask your question.'

Julie pointed at Frankie. 'This is my younger sister. I would like to stay with her, if possible, please. She is a bit slow and will need my help to understand your orders.'

He looked at Frankie and then back at Julie, then nodded. 'Very well, as long as you do as you're told and keep that mouth of yours shut. Any trouble and the deal changes. It is up to you whether you both die or not.' His words were cold and heartless. These people meant nothing to him other than slave labour.

Although her blood was boiling inside, Julie needed to keep her head for now. It made her cringe having to be polite to this cold-blooded murderer. 'Thank you, sir,' she said, then reached out and took Frankie's hand and squeezed it. She knew Frankie wasn't the slow-minded idiot that she had made her out to be, but she also knew Frankie could not cope alone. The only way to keep her safe was to abide by his rules, for the time being, at least.

'Now, let me show you who rules the roost. What is your name?' he enquired.

'Julie, sir. My name is Julie.' She was bargaining for her sister's life and realised subservience was the only way.

Ignoring her smile, he said, 'Well, Julie. English, eh?' He nodded. 'Let me show you who is the boss around here and how fragile your life is. You're nothing to me so don't even bother trying to charm me. As I have said, you can stay with your sister for the time being, to keep her in line. But let me show you how quickly deals can be broken.' Pulling Frankie forward, he turned to one of the other men with him. 'Rape her,' he commanded.

'No! Leave her alone,' Julie shouted, much more loudly than she'd intended.

Numb and still in shock, Frankie stood wide-eyed with fear. Stepping forward, the man ripped Frankie's blouse, revealing her bare breasts to the people in the line. Frankie screamed and tried to hide herself with her hands, but the man ripped at her blouse again and slapped her, then started undoing the belt on his trousers.

'Please, sir!' Julie shouted. 'We won't give you any trouble. Just leave her alone.'

Satisfied, the man in the suit held up his hand to stop the assault on Frankie. 'Next time I won't be so generous.'

Stepping back and ignoring Frankie's cries, he addressed the rest of the line. 'Right, listen up. You're all here to work. I want no slacking or the supervisors will make you speed things up a bit. I want your passports and your wallets. Open your cases. You may take extra clothing, but everything else goes back on the coach.' Everyone proceeded to do as they had been told. The line of people was silent as they each handed over their belongings. It was obvious they had all been tricked. This was slave trafficking. Everyone had heard about such things, but this was real. An open-back truck drove up beside them. 'Get in,' the man in the suit barked at them all.

They were taken to a wasteland with a few large wooden sheds, hidden behind an overgrowth of bushes and weeds. Julie felt her heart sink. There were some people milling around; they looked almost like ghosts or zombies. Thin, skeletal, they were wearing dirty, torn shorts and vests. You could not tell if they were men or women. Between the huts was a fire with a tripod over it. Hanging from that was a large cooking pot. Julie looked into the pot as they were led past it. It held brown, disgusting filth. The man stirring it with a large ladle looked up at her. 'You don't get any, because you haven't worked yet. If you don't work, you don't eat.'

Frankie was crying beside her as they walked through the camp. Julie felt helpless. There was nothing she could do. The wooden sheds were empty. They were told to find a spot on the hard stone floor, somewhere amongst the dirt, and to sit down. Although it was a dark, foul-smelling shithole, Julie and the rest of them were glad to rest their weary legs and get some shade from the sun. They were all in shock after the shootings, but too afraid to show any emotion for fear of repercussions. Guards walked around with rifles. They did not speak. You were not a person, just someone to be worked to death until the next coachload of fools turned up, and then disposed of.

Days turned into weeks and Julie started to lose track of time. The hot sun burnt their skins as they trudged along the fields each day from sunup to sundown. Picking and digging up potatoes with small trowels was hard work, but if you didn't meet your quota by the end of the day you were punished.

Although it was disgusting, the soup they served filled their stomachs. But Julie quickly realised there was something not quite right about it. The headaches it gave her and the way she passed out after eating it told her that they were drugging it to keep them quiet. Everyone she had seen on the coach that day seemed to have turned into a zombie who just followed orders. That was when she decided not to eat any more of the soup. She needed to keep her wits about her.

One day Frankie waltzed into the hut, smiling.

'What have you got to smile about?'

'Do you remember that man when we first got here; you know, the one in the suit?'

'Of course I bloody remember him. How do you forget

someone who killed two innocent people in front of you as a welcoming gift,' snapped Julie, feeling too exhausted to listen to Frankie's ramblings.

'I was called to the big caravans where the guards live and he was there. He was very nice this time. Well, he said he wants me to move to another camp, a better one. He thinks I'm pretty and should be in the movies or a model. Something like that.' Frankie preened.

It was the first time Julie had seen her sister smile in a long time, and her naivety shone through.

'What other camp? Where?' Julie felt the panic rising inside her. This was what she had feared. 'Did he mention me at all?'

'No,' Frankie stammered, 'but I'm sure he will. I bet he wants to see you next.'

'Are you fucking stupid? This isn't Hollywood! I have a fair idea about the movies he wants you to star in. It's porn, Frankie, love.'

Julie was afraid if she let them take Frankie now, they would never see each other again. She had to do something, and quick. God knows when that bastard was going to come back for Frankie.

The wild, faraway look in Frankie's eyes confirmed Julie's suspicions. 'You have been eating that shit again, haven't you?'

'I'm hungry, Julie. I can't eat any more tomatoes and raw potatoes; they make me sick. I needed something else. Something warm inside me.'

'I told you, you bloody fool. It's drugged to keep everyone in line. Look around you – they're all fucking dead.'

'We're going to die soon, so we may as well die off our heads. I can't stand it any more. That person is offering me a ticket out of here and I want to take it. I'm sick of fields, the sun burning my back and the stench in here when everyone has to shit in the same buckets.'

'Okay, sweetie, I know. I'm hungry, too, but we have to be strong. I will get us out of here, I promise.'

'You've been saying that every day since we got here. Nothing has changed. We're still here!' Frankie shouted at her.

Julie felt beaten; there was no clear way out. Her only hope was Elliot, an institutionalised trustee. The time to take their chances and flee this godawful place was now. What did it matter if they were killed in the process? They were dead, anyway. And Elliot had given her an idea. But most of all he had given her hope.

Elliot had been at the camp so long even he had forgotten who he was. He had no memory of his former life. Now in his fifties, he had become a kind of trustee for their jailers. The bosses knew he was not a threat; his spirit had left him long ago. He had given up on life and accepted his fate. He plodded along, full of emptiness and desperation.

Elliot showed all the newcomers where to go and what to do, and did all the fetching and carrying for the bosses. It didn't exclude him from their torment, he still had to work from sunup to sundown, but he got certain privileges, mainly cigarettes and better food, although it was still laced with drugs to keep him quiet. Everyone was addicted to drugs. No one would ever think of running away because they had become so dependent on their jailers for their fix. However, they were still locked in the sheds at night, like caged animals.

Elliot helped put the padlocks on the large wooden doors and secured them to keep the workers in, convincing everyone it was for their own protection from the dogs and the night patrollers.

It was obvious no one had spoken kindly to Elliot or shown him affection properly in a long time. Julie noticed he had an old cigarette packet and when the bosses gave him two or three as payment, he kept topping his packet up. It seemed to be his only possession and his prize one. Each cigarette he had was half smoked and he kept all the stubs to save the tobacco to make new ones.

Julie walked over to him while he sat in his own corner, smoking, and smiled. 'You got a spare one of those?'

Grasping the packet close to his chest, he stared at her through glazed eyes.

'I'm Julie. I want to be friends. I don't have anything to share with you, though.'

Elliot eyed Julie suspiciously while she reached out and stroked his crotch. She had watched him and instinctively felt he was her link to freedom. The thin shorts he wore left nothing to the imagination. Maybe she did have something to share after all. Slowly he handed over the cigarette from his own mouth.

Elliot never spoke or answered her; he was like a scared rabbit caught in the headlights. First, she had to earn his trust. He knew everything about the camp, and even the guards ignored him. After a while, he would walk over to her and sit beside her, offering her cigarettes, and Julie would masturbate him. Well, almost, because he could not manage a full erection, but he enjoyed the intimacy of it. One day he had given her a piece of chocolate from a bar he had hidden under his makeshift pillow.

Puzzled, Julie had looked at it and smiled. How did he have his hands on a bar of chocolate when there was nothing nearby? Just rows and rows of fields. It was then Julie realised that Elliot must leave the camp at some time. The very thought of that piece of chocolate gave her hope and Elliot was the answer.

Frankie looked at Julie with disgust. 'I don't know how you can sit and talk to him. He's filthy and disgusting. He has no teeth and he stinks.'

'Haven't you noticed, Frankie? You stink, too. We all do.' Julie raised her arm and sniffed her armpit. 'There is nowhere to wash here. Elliot's okay, he's a bit weird, but then so are you.'

As frustrated as Julie was at her younger sister's whining, she loved her. Frankie had always been her little doll. She had been four years old when Frankie was born and she had fallen in love with her instantly.

Julie walked over to Elliot and sat beside him, nudging him playfully with her elbow. 'Come on, Elliot, love,' she whispered in the darkness. 'You can tell me, we're friends. Where did you get the chocolate from?' It was nearly black in the hut, now. People around them were snoring. Others had nightmares and cried out.

'I get it for helping them with the bodies. I help put them in the truck and bury them. I get extra treats for that.' He sounded almost childlike as Julie sat there, stunned.

'You get rid of bodies? How?' Although she was stunned, she was intrigued.

'When they die,' he whispered, and reached for her hand and laid it on his crotch. Julie started to stroke him gently while pushing him for more information. She knew she had to treat him with kid gloves and be gentle. Elliot put his finger to his lips. 'We can't let anyone find them. We have to get rid of them. Give some to the dogs.'

Julie's blood ran cold at this revelation. She was glad it was dark because her smile was forced and weak.

'A special truck comes sometimes to take them away. I help

them. I get chocolate for it.' Elliot seemed very proud of his status as chief gravedigger. So this was how he had survived all of these years.

Julie did not want to stop pushing for more information. She had managed to get Elliot talking and she did not want him to clam up. 'So, where is this truck? I've never seen one around here. Go on, you're just kidding me, aren't you?' She laughed playfully and continued stroking him. They were both sitting on the floor in 'their' place.

'On the main road about ten miles from here. Past all those fields.' He pointed in mid-air, almost boasting about his secret. 'You can't see it because of all the thorn bushes. Very high, they are, and painful if they scratch you.' Like a young child, he showed Julie some old scratches that had healed on his arms.

'Here, let me kiss those for you to make them better.' Her voice was warm and soothing as she kissed his arm. 'So, when does the truck come?'

Holding up his fingers, Elliot indicated two days. Julie secretly jumped for joy. She wasn't sure what to do yet, but now was the time to hatch a plan.

'You know what, Elliot, darling, and you are my darling, I think you should leave that side padlock undone for when you get back. You will have worked so hard... maybe we could sneak out and have a cuddle without all these people watching us.' Julie paused, waiting for it to penetrate his brain. When she saw his puzzled frown, she thought she had gone too far. Maybe he would turn on her and tell the bosses. 'No, that was a daft idea.' She shook her head and smiled reassuringly. 'I just thought we could be alone when you get back, but you will be tired. Anyway, you would have to make sure the padlock wasn't on so I could get out and meet you.' She knew she was walking on thin ice, but she could see him thinking it over and for now, that was enough.

* * *

Nervous and anxious, Julie lay beside Frankie on the floor and waited until the two days were up. She wasn't quite sure what she was going to do, but she was determined to get out of this hell-hole. There was no time to lose.

Julie kept a close eye on Elliot, not daring to take her eyes off him for one minute, and in the early hours of the morning she heard a bang on the shed door. She feigned sleep as Elliot looked around at everyone, then got up and opened the shed door. Not daring to breathe, she realised that she had not heard the usual chilling, depressing noise of the chain being put back through the padlock. She heard it rattle, but nothing else. She waited for what seemed an eternity, not daring to breathe in case the guard came back with Elliot.

Eventually she stood up and slowly climbed over the sleeping bodies on the floor in the darkness, then tentatively pushed the door with her finger. Stunned, she realised it wasn't locked. Somewhere in Elliot's foggy brain, the idea of being alone with her had seeped through. Pushing a little further, she saw the thick chain drop to the ground.

'Frankie, wake up,' she whispered, trying to shake her sister into consciousness. 'We have to go. Quickly now, this is our chance.'

Bleary-eyed, Frankie yawned and looked up. 'What are you talking about?'

The glazed look in her eyes confirmed to Julie she had been sneakily eating that bloody soup again. 'Be quiet, get up and follow me.'

It was taking time to rouse Frankie into some sort of consciousness. Julie did not know how much time she had, so gave Frankie a good slap across the face; it seemed to do the trick.

After creeping out into the fresh air, Julie was surprised that there was no one around. Holding her finger to her lips, she linked her arm through Frankie's and, slowly, they both crept away from the shed.

Feeling her way in the dark, Julie tried to fathom out which route to take. She had looked around over the last couple of days but all the fields looked the same. When they were safely out of earshot she pulled on Frankie's arm and they ran towards a maze of bramble bushes. Long thorns stuck out everywhere, like barbed wire. It was overgrown and twice their height. This is what hid them from any authority's suspicion.

Frankie's heart sank. 'We can't get through there, we'll be torn to shreds, it's impossible.' Horror filled them both as they looked at the overgrown wall.

'Bollocks. I would rather die in there than back in that rathole. We are going to have to climb it. I don't know how thick it is. Pick the lowest bush you can and don't cry out, for God's sake. It is going to be painful but fuck it. Do you want to go home or not?'

The thorns bit at their flesh, which stung as they tried parting the bush with their hands. As they tried to climb over and through, it felt like electric bolts through their bodies. It was agony and they were bleeding; their hair was tangled up in the bushes and nearly being pulled out by the roots. At last, they managed to get through the middle of it. Turning towards Frankie and nodding, Julie hissed, 'Jump!' They did, and hit the hard ground on the other side with a thud.

Out in the darkness, Julie picked Frankie up off the ground. 'We're out now, though God knows where we are. We have to run as far away as possible until we find the road Elliot told me about. Where there are roads there are cars. Come on, Frankie, I need you to be strong.'

* * *

Now, after putting her plan into place, Elliot had come up trumps for her. Here she was, battered and bleeding, driving through Spain with a truck full of dead bodies in the back. But they were free.

'Come on, Ralph, mate. It's quitting time. Bloody hell, do you want to spend all of your days in this quarry? All you think about is dynamite and blowing up stones. Ireland has more to offer than that. It has pretty women, good Guinness and bare-knuckle fighting. Are you ready for tonight?'

Tired after a long shift at work, Ralph Goldstein wiped the sweat from his brow. 'Yes, I'm okay, and money is money. I want to go home first and see the wife and little Shaun.'

'Why? You know what they look like. I thought we could go for a drink first and rustle up a bit of gambling money.'

Taking a deep sigh and stepping over the quarry rocks, Ralph straightened his denim dungarees and looked his best friend, Paddy, in the eye. 'Paddy, mate, I've been out of prison for six months. My son was one year old when I went inside and now he is five. I like to see him. Is that okay with you?' Again, he wiped the sweat from his face with the back of his hand, then turned his head as the long-awaited whistle blew, informing the workers that the shift was over.

'Well, that will teach you not to drop your pants with a good

Catholic girl in Ireland. Best shotgun wedding I have ever been to.' Paddy's boyish grin crossed his face and he winked at Ralph. 'You should have gone to the synagogue that day, and just masturbated like the rest of them. Not exactly a common Irish name, is it? Goldstein.' Paddy laughed aloud and kicked some of the stones near him like a football, sending up clouds of dust and nearly blinding himself.

'My father is Jewish, and my ma is an Irish Catholic. Now shut it.' Ralph laughed as he saw Paddy wincing and rubbing his leg. 'Did that rock hurt your foot?' When he saw him nod, he was satisfied. 'Good, then don't kick them.'

'Oh, don't get cross, mate. We shared a cell together, eh? That makes us lifelong mates. Drink first, and then you can visit that sprog of yours. No funny business with Irene tonight, though. Not before a fight, it weakens the legs!'

The coolness of the pub was a welcome respite after a long day. Ralph was hot and sweaty. Songs rang out from the jukebox and the days of war seemed to be behind everyone. This was a new era.

'Here you go, Ralph, nice and cold, just how you like it. Get that Guinness down you. Full of iron,' the barman joked. Not impressed by the landlord's flippancy, Ralph picked up the pint and took a sip. He knew what the landlord wanted. Ralph had a reputation for bare-knuckle fighting. He had fought most of his life, and especially in prison where it had been dog-eat-dog. He'd kept himself fit, and working in the quarry lifting rocks day in and day out kept his muscles firm and solid.

This was bare-knuckle fighting and tonight there was a match. Although bare-knuckle fighting wasn't illegal, this was a fight with no holds barred, no restrictions, apart from weapons. Ralph was a known scrapper and always pulled a crowd. His opponent was the favourite, a man with a hard-earnt reputation he was desperate to defend. This pub landlord wanted the fight held in his pub to bring in the customers, but the location was always kept under wraps until the last minute, when Paddy spread the word.

The Garda, as the Irish police were known, seemed to know all about the illegal gambling and vicious fighting. That was how Ralph had ended up in prison. Grievous bodily harm, they had called it, even though both fighters had agreed to it and accepted any consequences. He hadn't meant to crush the other guy's jaw, it was part of the fight, but he had been charged when the police had burst into the upstairs room at the pub. It was beginning to be an occupational hazard.

However, this last prison sentence had been very productive. He had shared a cell with a man who had been an explosives expert in the war. He enjoyed telling his wartime stories. Even though it bored a lot of the others, it intrigued Ralph. This man's knowledge was endless. Everyone called him Bandit, after the gambling fruit machines with one arm, because he had blown one arm off when he had cut the wire on a detonator. But he was good company and Ralph liked him. Once Bandit realised Ralph was interested in his tales of unexploded bombs, he had told him all about explosives. Lying on his top bunk bed, Ralph listened intently, amazed when Bandit told him how to make them.

With all that knowledge, it had been easy to get a job when he had gone down to the Labour Exchange. His prison record went against him but Ben, the supervisor at the quarry, had given him a chance. Out of bad can sometimes come good.

Once Paddy started spreading the word about the fight, people turned up in their droves. Even Ralph had to admit to himself that despite all the secrecy leading up to the event, Paddy wasn't very discreet when it came to announcing where it would be and at what time.

In the upstairs room of the pub was a pall of tobacco smoke, making Ralph's eyes sting as he walked in. It was stifling hot, but no windows could be opened because of the shouting and cheering of the men watching the fight. Men sat around on wooden chairs drinking their pints of beer, waiting for the fight to start, but Paddy wouldn't let that happen until he'd taken all the bets. They made a good team, although Ralph didn't trust Paddy an inch.

Dropping his braces and taking off his shirt, Ralph stood bare-chested in his trousers and boots. He spied his opponent. He was a big man and carried a lot of weight, but Ralph saw that his belly was soft and most of it was fat. He was losing his edge, past his best, and Ralph fancied his chances of winning.

Paddy started the countdown in the middle of the amateur square ring he had roped off and the fight got underway, much to the pleasure of the onlookers. After four long, hard rounds, the other boxer's friends stepped forward and threw the towel in the middle of the ring. Ralph had taken a punch to the eye and blood streamed down his face and he realised the other fighter had a razor blade between his knuckles. Much to the annoyance of the baying crowd, the friends of the other boxer shouted, 'Enough! Enough! It's over.' Sweat poured from Ralph's body and he realised his nose was broken again. Another occupational hazard.

Angry jeers came from the crowd; they wanted more than this. They bayed like a pack of wolves waiting for the kill.

'He can't carry on, you bloody idiots!' the opponent's friends shouted at the baying crowd. 'His arm is broken.'

Lying on the wooden floor, howling in pain, was Ralph's opponent. His face and knuckles were bloody and grazed, and his arm lay awkwardly at his side. Someone threw a pint of beer over him to bring him back to semi-consciousness.

'Ralph here is the winner!' Paddy shouted, holding Ralph's

arm up in the air. He pulled up a wooden chair and sat Ralph down, then gave him an old bar towel to wipe his face. 'Time to collect your winnings, guys, if you were smart enough to put your money on him.' He removed the Woodbine from his own mouth and gave it to Ralph, along with his whisky.

Paddy walked around the room, paying out the winnings from the wad of notes he was holding. It wasn't getting much smaller, which was making his smile wider than usual. The upstart challenger had won this time. Looking over, he gave Ralph a thumbs up. As the crowd started to head back downstairs into the pub, they walked past Ralph's opponent lying on the floor. Showing their disgust, they gave him sly kicks with their boots and called him a loser. Some had spent half their wages on this fight in the hope of winning some back. Now they had to explain to their wives where the rest of the housekeeping money was.

Ralph rubbed his aching shoulder. Looking through the sweat and blood running into his eyes, he saw teeth marks clearly imprinted in his shoulder, where his opponent had bitten him. Thankfully Ralph was still wearing his steel-toe-capped boots and had raised his leg and kicked the man mercilessly in the balls and yanked at his arm. That was when it had broken. He had heard the snap and then twisted it in return for the razor-blade trick. The bastard could have had his eye out.

'Fifteen quid, Ralph, mate.' Paddy waved the money in the air before Ralph's face.

'Hand over the rest, you fucking weasel. You took more than that. I might have a swollen eye but I can still see and count!'

The smile slowly disappeared from Paddy's face and was immediately replaced by a frown. 'Did I say fifteen? Oh no, that is all your cut, less expenses for the room and good marketing to get the men here.'

Sulkily, Paddy handed over the money. Ralph knew he had

not paid anything to use the room at the pub. In fact, he had probably taken a backhander for filling the pub full of customers. *Expenses, my arse!* he thought.

'You sort this lot out, Paddy. I'm going home.' Ralph picked his shirt up off the beer-drenched floor and then walked downstairs and out of the pub doors into the fresh air. His heart was pounding and he was pleased it had only gone four rounds. He was exhausted and hungry.

Entering his mother's small, two-bedroomed, barely furnished house with its peeling paint and coal fire, he shouted out for his wife. 'I'm home, Irene.' As he leant over and kissed his mother on the cheek, he secretly handed her two pounds. 'I know, I know. It doesn't look good, but I'm okay. Get something nice, Ma.'

Stroking his battered face gently, his mother smiled. 'Are you really okay, son?'

Nodding to reassure her, he sat down. Ralph loved his mother. She had always stood by him and never judged him. She had known the hardship of World War Two and for the first few years of Ralph's life, until his father returned from the war, it had only been the two of them.

Irene came rushing through from the kitchen. 'Oh, darling, you're hurt. Have you been fighting again?' Knowing not to ask any more, she disappeared back into the kitchen and returned with a bowl of warm water and disinfectant. 'Here, darling, let me clean you up,' she said, and began washing away the blood from his hands and face with a flannel.

Ralph was too tired to resist and welcomed the warm water washing away the blood from his cut face, even with the sting of the antiseptic.

Ralph reached into his pocket and put ten pounds on the table before her, and watched the smile appear on his wife's face.

Ralph liked his wife, Irene, but it had never been love. After a couple of dates at the local dance hall, she had told him she was pregnant. He had no choice but to do the right thing by her. They were both young and stupid at the time, but she was a good woman and she was loyal. Worst of all, he knew she was grateful he had saved her from shame. She had settled for the hand that fate had dealt her.

Irene had caught the bus to Dublin on a regular basis to visit him in prison and had looked after his mother, now that his father was dead. There were no other family members to step in: when she, a Catholic, had married his father, a Jew, both sides had walked away.

'Do you fancy some good old-fashioned Irish stew to make you feel better?' Irene said.

Although Ralph was hungry, he wanted to go to bed. His body ached all over. He walked to the bedroom and almost collapsed on the bed, then looked up at the ceiling in the darkness. There had to be more to life than this. He was a young man with a prison record as long as his arm and he was living hand-to-mouth in Ireland, with no future. The only certainty was death. No, this was not good enough. He wanted more. There had to be more than this.

4

HOME AT LAST

Julie was exhausted and driving to God knows where, when she noticed she was running out of petrol. She knew she had to dump the truck somewhere discreet. After all, it still had half a dozen dead bodies in the back of it.

Yawning, she nudged Frankie with her elbow. 'Frankie, wake up, love. We have to go.'

Half-asleep and with spit dribbling out of her mouth, Frankie opened her eyes. She was surprised to see that it was early morning, and the sun was rising. Rubbing her eyes and sitting up, Frankie looked out of the windows. 'Where are we?' She didn't recognise any of the surroundings.

'We're near the docks. I don't know, exactly, I can't read the signs. We need to dump the truck. We can't be found with those bodies in the back. We're going to have to run for it.'

Walking along the quayside, Julie knew from the looks on people's faces that they both looked a fright, with their scratches and bruises. She felt the heat of the Spanish sun as it warmed her bones. All around her were cargo ships, unloading and loading. Men were everywhere and the quayside seemed to be getting busier and busier. Men came pouring out of the dock cafés and pubs as they heard the trawlers and cargo ships blowing their horns as they entered port. Julie and Frankie looked on in awe. Suddenly the dockside had become a hive of activity. People were everywhere, shouting and bumping into them as they pushed past to wave at their old shipmates.

As brave as Julie was, she realised she actually felt nervous being surrounded by so many people at once in a confined space. The noise was deafening.

Suddenly, Julie began to shake. Whether it was from shock after the previous night or the awful realisation that she had unintentionally become institutionalised, she didn't know, but even after only a couple of months, the outside world seemed loud and daunting. No wonder Elliot felt it was easier to stay put, she thought to herself. She hoped he was okay, although inside she knew he was probably dead. He would have taken the blame for everything.

Pulling herself together and dismissing Elliot from her mind, Julie saw some apples on the ground that must have fallen out of a barrel. She picked them up and handed one to Frankie. Taking a bite of the green, juicy apple felt fantastic. It was the first proper food she had eaten in a long time.

Looking along the quayside at the ships gave Julie a thought. Shielding her eyes from the sun, she looked up at the huge trawler before her. She could see that it was being loaded with cargo. That meant it was leaving port.

'Where are you going?' she shouted to one of the men standing on the ship. He was waiting for the crane to lower some cargo.

'Back to England, girlie. We're going to Liverpool. Sounds like you been there, too,' he shouted, acknowledging her accent.

Relief washed over Julie. They were English! 'Where is your

captain? Is he around?' The Spanish sun blinded her as she looked towards the man. She heard him shout to someone and a tall black man wearing a red jumper, jeans and a flat cap leant over the side of the ship and looked down at her.

The sight of him made Julie smile. In all of this sunshine, he was wearing a jumper. Definitely from England. Everyone else she had seen lately wore vests and T-shirts.

In his thick Jamaican accent, the man shouted to her. 'I the captain, miss. This is my ship. What do you want?' His smile was broad and genuine.

'Just a quick word, please,' Julie said hopefully. She felt nervous, not really knowing what to say. She'd have to think on her feet. She gave him her best smile, even though she knew she must look a sight and so thin.

This was one hell of a chance she was going to take, but what choice did she have? She needed to get as far away from there as possible.

'Okay, I'm coming down. But if it's money you're wanting, tell me now and don't waste my time. I have work to do. Here.'

Julie and Frankie watched him throw some coins towards them. Julie scrambled to pick them up and shouted back to him, 'I know you think that we're beggars, but I want to talk to you about something else.' She beckoned to him.

Again he smiled, then grabbed one of the ropes from the ship and swung on it like Tarzan, landing on the ground before her.

Noticing his puzzled expression, Julie pulled him to one side and looked around furtively. It was time to make her move. 'My sister and I need to get back to England,' she whispered. 'We've lost our passports. It's a long story. I just need to get home. Any chance of a lift? We're willing to work for it.'

Shaking his head and adjusting his cap, he smiled. 'Why don't you just go to the police and report it? You wouldn't be the first

tourist to lose their passport. I ain't no passenger ship.' Looking at
her dishevelled appearance more closely, he said, 'You on the run,
lady?'

'Kind of, but not from the police. Got in with the wrong
company, you know how it is. They have our passports, we had to
leave quickly, and now we need to get away from here.' Julie
looked at him pleadingly, tears almost brimming in her eyes. 'I
need to get my sister home. She's ill.'

The captain turned to look back at his ship and then looked
at Julie and Frankie properly. They looked half-starved and feral.
They were covered in cuts, scratches and dried blood. Bruises
were beginning to appear on their skin. Taking out his cigarettes,
he offered Julie one and then lit his own.

Inhaling on her cigarette, which she needed badly, even
though it made her feel dizzy, she said, 'We can work our passage,
Captain.'

A curious frown appeared on his face. 'How do you propose
to work your passage, lady? We already got a chef.'

Swallowing hard, and fighting back the tears, she felt she
could trust this man. Her gut instinct was to like him. He seemed
friendly and easy-going.

'Well, you have a chef, which is good because I can't cook. But
I bet you don't have entertainment. Those sailors of yours don't
have a lot to do in the evenings, apart from play card games, do
they?' Julie saw that familiar glint in his eye and knew she had his
interest. Sex was always a bargaining option and it was all she
had to offer. She stood with her hand on her hip, feeling a little
more confident now he hadn't laughed in her face and walked
away. 'All those guys on your ship, cooped up with each other day
and night. You must get arguments and fights.' Seeing that he was
going to interrupt her, she stopped him and carried on. 'I know a
big man like yourself will easily sort it out, with those big muscly

arms of yours, but if they had a little light entertainment, something to look forward to...' Stroking his arms, she winked at him. She knew they were both talking the same language.

The cockeyed smile on his face convinced Julie she had made her point. Men were men all over the world and working away from home made them miss the 'benefits' of home even more.

Eyeing her up and rubbing his chin, deep in thought, the captain lowered his voice to a whisper. 'We leave at two, on the afternoon tide. If you sneak on my ship at the far end where the ropes are without anyone seeing you, how would I know?' Reaching into his back pocket, he took out a couple of pounds. 'My name is Roland. Captain Roland.' His broad, proud smile showed a row of white teeth. They each knew what the other meant. He had just told her how to get onto the ship without actually giving her permission.

Taking the money, Julie nodded. The smile dropped from her face. It was still early and she knew they needed to stay out of the way, in hiding. God only knew who was on the lookout for them and their first thoughts might be to check the docks. Their captors knew they couldn't catch an aeroplane. Quickly making mental notes, Julie decided that she needed to find a public toilet where they could get cleaned up, so they looked a little more respectable. She needed to be able to blend in more. It was going to be a long day.

'Wait!' Roland took off his cap and scratched his head. He was troubled and deep in thought. 'How old are you?'

'I'm twenty and Frankie, that's my sister, over there, is sixteen years old. Why?'

The pair of them looked over to where Frankie sat on the pavement of the quayside with her back against the wall. She had almost fallen asleep.

'I got a daughter her age and...' He let out a huge sigh,

followed by a roguish Jamaican laugh, then he smiled. 'She looks like shit, if you don't mind me saying. She been smoking the wacky baccy, eh?'

Julie was desperate. It was no time to lie, so Julie told the captain the truth. 'She has been given worse than that to keep her quiet. That is what we are running from. Full story another time, eh, Captain Roland.'

'Go and stand at the far end of the ship, way over there.' He pointed to the spot and Julie turned her head to see. 'I'm gonna throw you some clothes. Maybe if you were dressed like one of the men you could get on the ship sooner. Especially if you were carrying something, eh?' His deep Jamaican accent felt as warm as the sun on her back. He wanted to help without putting himself in jeopardy. He had built up a fierce reputation, but he also had a heart.

Julie knew she was taking her life in her hands. Once on that ship those sailors could do whatever they liked with Frankie and herself. They were both taking a gamble; the only difference was that Julie had no choice. That old rust bucket Roland was so proud of was going to take them back to England as stowaways, to her hometown of Liverpool. Sweet Jesus, she'd never thought she would see the place again.

In a nearby alley, they quickly changed into the old dungarees and hats Roland had thrown from the ship. Julie pulled Frankie along and, amongst the hustle and bustle of the quayside, no one seemed to notice them walk onto the ship. They made their way below deck, where Roland was waiting for them.

'This is the chef, Paul; he'll make you something to eat. Then you wash and sleep. The men are going to be busy for a while yet sorting the loads, so you can get some rest. I must be fucking crazy!' Shaking his head and giving Paul a high five, he left the room, deep, warm laughter ringing in his wake.

As crazy as the situation was, Julie did not feel threatened. For the first time in months, she felt safe. She was tired but she couldn't sleep. Her mind was already in Liverpool. What would she find when she got there? Out of the frying pan and into the fire!

She had left in such a hurry, not even thinking of the consequences of her actions. As far as she had been concerned, she was off to Spain in search of a better life and never going back to England. That was only a couple of months ago, but so much had changed since then. Now she was a stowaway on a cargo trawler, on her way back to Liverpool. She could be arrested on the spot. It was worth it, though, to get Frankie home. She needed to be at home with their mother. And Julie had to go home and face the music, whatever that was. At least that drunken stepfather wouldn't be there; she had made sure of that.

Julie's only concern now was Frankie. She was starting to have withdrawal symptoms from all of the drugs she'd had and was pale and couldn't stop vomiting. Bathing her sister and putting her into one of the bunk beds with clean sheets was a luxury in itself.

5

GUILTY EMOTIONS

Relief washed over them both as the ship docked. It had been a good few days, considering they had worked their passage keeping the men on board happy. But they had been fed and treated well, and it had been straightforward sex. They ate with the men and had a few beers with them when their shift was over, and then they would depart to their cabin. Even Roland agreed it lightened the mood. Some of the men didn't have sex but had enjoyed the female company. Others took full advantage.

'Julie.' Roland beckoned her to his cabin. 'The customs people will come aboard as soon as we drop anchor. They will want to see our papers and stuff. You need to get off here as quickly as possible. If you are caught, as much as we have had a lot of fun, I will deny you as stowaways and I have told the men to do the same. No offence, I like you and I know you have both had a hard time, but back to reality, eh? It has been good knowing you. If you're ever in need of a captain, you know where to find me. Take this money. The guys have had a collection; you've earnt it. Good luck, pretty lady.'

Understanding what he was saying was without any malice,

Julie felt there was real warmth in his goodbye. The wad of cash he gave her was more than generous. 'Thank you, Roland, love,' she said. She kissed him on the cheek then winked as she left his room.

'I cannot believe we're really home, Julie. I never thought we'd make it. I'm sorry you had to do all the work because I haven't been well, but I promise I will make it up to you.'

'Frances, darling.' Julie cupped Frankie's head in her hands. 'I got us into this and I was determined to get us out of it. Don't worry. Come on, once this ship slows down we're going to jump and run like hell.'

They jumped off the ship as it docked at dawn, then they both ran. Instinct told Julie to turn around. Doing so, she saw Captain Roland standing on the deck. He raised his hand in a sort of wave and she blew a kiss. *Goodbye, Captain Roland, God bless you*, she thought to herself. Then she grabbed Frankie's hand and ran with all her might, as far away from the docks as possible.

Julie bit her tongue and ignored the stares of the people on the bus as they tutted and whispered about their appearance. They were wearing dungarees rolled up at the leg and large T-shirts. It was a lot cleaner and better than they had started with. *Fuck 'em. Fuck them all*, she thought, as she glared back at them.

As the sisters linked arms and walked towards their council estate, a sense of foreboding filled Julie. The grey high-rise tower block surrounded by others made her nervous.

'Oh, Julie, we're home. We're home.' The elation in Frankie's voice filled Julie's ears, but she still felt dubious about what might be waiting to greet them.

'Shit! Nothing much has changed here. The bloody lift still isn't working. Twelve bloody floors of stone steps to climb.' Julie stopped and lit two cigarettes and handed one to Frankie before starting nervously up the stairs.

Estate trash, that is what they were known as. It was the worst estate in Liverpool, more like a ghetto for every drug dealer and pimp around. There were always fights and loud parties. No one had a job. No wonder their mother had turned to alcohol once Julie's father had left. She'd made an occupation of it. It was no secret that their mother was an alcoholic and she'd met and married another alcoholic, Derek.

As she knocked on the familiar front door, Frankie was beaming and couldn't contain her excitement, whereas Julie felt like a failure. She had gone full circle.

They heard the bolts being pulled aside, and the door eventually opened. Both of them stared at the strange woman who stood before them, a baby in her arms. The security chain was still across the door to stop them from entering. *Much good that would do if some druggie decided to kick it in*, thought Julie to herself.

'Who are you? Where's Mum?' Julie asked, presuming this was one of her mother's new drinking friends.

'I have no idea what you're talking about. Now, if you don't mind, I'm busy.'

'We live here,' Julie shouted, and she tried pushing the door, but the safety chain across it prevented her from opening it.

The young woman shrugged. 'You must have the wrong flat. I've lived here for a month. Now, bugger off and leave me in peace.' With that, she slammed the door in Julie's face.

Tears filled Frankie's eyes. 'Mum!' she shouted at the door. 'Mum, it's me, Frankie.' The door didn't open again so she turned to Julie. 'What's happened? Where's Mum?'

'I don't know, love. This is some homecoming. Come on, we're going to find out. Let's go and see old Gertie, she'll know what's going on.'

Four floors down, Julie knocked on the door where their mother's friend, Gertie, lived. She had been their permanent babysitter when their mother was down the pub and was more like a grandmother to them.

'Julie. Frances, my love. Come in, come in. My, it's good to see you both.' The old woman leant forward and hugged them. She must have been in her late seventies and for some reason always had her hair in curlers, although she never went anywhere. 'Where have you girls been?' The warmth of old Gertie's flat felt good.

'Where's Mum, Gertie? There's someone else living in our house.' Frankie seemed confused and distraught.

'Let me put the kettle on, Frances, love. You sit yourself by the fire and get warm.' Exchanging glances with Julie, Gertie walked into the kitchen.

Leaving Frankie to sit by the fire, Julie went into the kitchen and stood at Gertie's side while she filled the kettle. 'Where is she, Gertie? What's happened?'

'She's in prison for murdering your stepfather. I didn't know where to contact you. After you left for Spain, there was no forwarding address... sorry,' she whispered.

Julie walked across the room and shut the kitchen door. Frankie was shattered and the safety of Gertie's home and the warmth of the fire was just what she needed.

'I don't really know all the facts. No one does. Your mum came out of the flat screaming and shouting. Her hands and clothes were covered in blood. When the neighbours ran in to see what had happened, they found your stepdad sitting in his armchair with his throat cut. She was arrested and charged with his murder. Well, I think it's manslaughter, because she was drunk.'

Julie stood and listened to Gertie's hushed whispers as she told the tale while making a pot of tea. She wanted to scream out and shout, but thinking about the living room where Frankie was dozing off by the fire, she tried to remain calm.

'You know they always had violent arguments and so hearing her screaming didn't raise the alarm, but when she ran up and down the corridors and down into the streets covered in blood, it was the only explanation. Your mum must have done it.' Gertie shrugged, not knowing what else to say.

'I need to go and see her. Where is she, do you know?'

'Oh, yes, love. I've been to see her a couple of times, myself. She's doing okay.' Putting her hand on Julie's and patting it to reassure her, Gertie smiled and nodded. 'Really, Julie, she is doing okay. You look shattered. Take this tea, go to my bed and get some sleep. I'll look after Frances.'

Taking the china cup and saucer, Julie walked to the bedroom. Her mind was all over the place. Her head felt like it was going to explode. This was all her fault. After putting the cup and saucer on the bedside table, she sat on the bed and let the tears flow. It had been the first time since the night of the escape that she had been able to relax. Her whole body ached and she couldn't remember the last time she had slept properly. She was tired of being strong. This had all been her doing and now her mum was in prison. Lying back on the bed, she pulled a blanket over her and let her mind wander back to a couple of months ago. Even though she had blocked it from her mind, now she was back in England, back in this tower block where it had all started, she remembered that night very well.

6

Bouncing into the flat with a big smile on her face, Julie waved her new passport in the air. Each day she had waited for the postman and at last he had come, bringing her saviour.

'My passport has come, Frankie, love. I am off to Spain for a week. What do you want me to bring you back, honey?' She had been excited at the prospect of going to a foreign country, flying on an aeroplane like the rich and famous.

'I'll miss you. I don't want you to go.' Frankie pouted, blinking her eyes to let tears brim on her eyelashes.

'Oh, come on, my little baby doll. I won that competition honestly and I'm going to claim my prize. It's only for a week. I have my wages from the factory and here's some for you, to keep you in chips and Bay City Rollers records until I get back. I tell you what, when I get back, I will buy you a pair of those tartan trousers they wear. You'd like that wouldn't you?' Guilt washed over Julie. She loved Frankie, but she just wanted this grown-up time on her own. She'd rarely spent any time during her teens on her own. She had either looked after Frankie or put their drunken mother to bed. This was her one and only chance for some fun without responsibility.

Dramatically, Frankie threw her arms around her neck and gave a sob. 'I'll miss you. You never leave me on my own. Can't I come with you?'

Seeing Frankie's expression, the excitement soon wore off and was replaced by concern for her sister. 'What's wrong, love? What are you frightened of? Mum and that drunk she's married to? She'll just get pissed and fall asleep somewhere. If you want anything, go and see Gertie, she'll look after you. Come on, this is my only chance of a holiday. I'll probably never get this chance again.'

'Sorry, I don't mean to spoil it for you. It's just Derek... he's been a bit weird lately. I don't like it.'

'What do you mean, weird? What's he done? Is he fiddling around with you, Frankie? That bastard, I'll kill him if he is.' A surge of anger filled her. That drunken bastard had been sniffing around her little sister.

'No! Nothing like that, he just makes weird comments. He said my tits are growing and they look nice. And that I never sit on his knee any more.'

'So that's his game, is it? He has hung on until you are sixteen, and now he thinks he can mess around with you. Has he touched you, Frankie? I want the fucking truth, now!'

'He hugs me a little sometimes but nothing like you're talking about. But I just don't want to be alone with him.' Frankie blushed and looked down at the floor.

The sullen look and the tears welling up in Frankie's eyes stabbed at Julie's heart. She had fallen in love with Frankie on the day she had seen her. It was the only good thing to come out of her mother's ridiculous marriage. 'It will be okay, Frankie, I promise. Go and stay with Gertie for the week. They'll not even notice;

they're so pissed half the time. Please, love. Do as I ask.' With a
heavy heart, she hugged Frankie close.

After packing the battered suitcase she had borrowed from
someone on the estate, Julie had gone into the living room. It was
basic, but home. A two-bar electric fire with an old, battered, mismatched armchair at either side of it. None of the furniture
matched and the house stank of booze. Her mum still worked at
the paint factory. Her stepfather made a point of getting up early
in the morning and had woken their mother from her drunken
stupor to make sure she got to work on time. Of course, he did
bugger all. There was no love lost between them. They tolerated
each other because of her mum.

'Lend us fifty pence for the electric meter, Julie. I don't seem
to have any change,' Derek had said to her. 'It's for your mum, for
when she gets home.'

'You never have any change, and we both know that Mum is at
the off-licence, so don't lie to me. Here, take your fifty pence.'

'Why don't you like me?' he had slurred.

'Simple. Because you're a lazy bastard. Look at you. That old
table at the side of you with a quarter bottle of whisky at your
side. For God's sake, you don't even use a cup any more. You're
disgusting! Sat near the fire with your racing newspaper, stinking
of booze and piss. That's why I don't like you. Get over it.'

'Frances likes me. She sits on my knee and we talk,' he had
said to her. The mention of Frankie made her blood boil and the
hairs on the back of her neck rise.

'What have you been up to with Frankie?'

He had laughed and turned his head. 'That's my business. But
she doesn't find me disgusting, like you do.'

Julie had seen red. It was like a film of red covering her eyes. Walking into the kitchen, she had picked up the large carving knife that they used to cut the bread with and walked back into the lounge where Derek was sitting with his back to her in his battered old armchair.

Bending over the back of the chair, she had whispered in his ear, 'Would you like me to sit on your knee, Derek? What do you do with Frankie? Tell me.'

'Frances is warm and loving. She's not like you. We spend a lot of time together when you and your mum are at the factory.' His slurring and his cocky manner disgusted Julie, and she moved her head aside from his whisky breath. His body odour and unshaven face sickened her. The very thought that he had been taking advantage of Frankie made her blood boil.

'Her tits are growing, don't you think?'

'She's growing up into a woman, alright. All the lads on this estate will be after her soon enough. Her tits aren't as big as yours are, though. Yours are lovely.' He had chuckled to himself, which enraged her even more.

Trying to control herself, she held tightly on to the knife in her hand, not actually knowing what she was going to do with it. He had been fiddling about with Frankie. The very thought of it made her feel sick. She had been Frankie's mother. She had changed her nappies from a young age and protected her. Now she knew why the girl was so scared about being left alone with him.

Without a second thought, she leant over the chair a little more. She was almost cheek to cheek with him. Disgust and hate filled her whole being; she raised the knife and slit his throat from left to right. It was one swift movement and the knife dug deep. He hadn't seen it coming. Shocked by the amount of blood that spurted out,

Julie had looked on in horror. The whole of the fireplace was red. The wall was red and Derek was slumped in his chair with his head at an angle, with blood dripping down onto his shirt and trousers. Everything seemed to be red. Dropping the knife, she had looked at the bloodbath before her. She had murdered him in cold blood. She would go to prison for life for this. What was she going to do now? The flat seemed eerily quiet and all she could hear was the clock ticking on the wall. She sat with her head in her hands, frightened. Her bloody temper... it always led her into trouble. However, no one was going to hurt her little sister.

Feeling herself shake with shock, tears brimmed on her lashes. She sat with her head in her hands for a moment trying to come to terms with what she had done. Suddenly a thought occurred to her. She brushed her tears away and stood up. Taking a huge sigh and looking around at the scene before her, she knew she had no option but to leave.

She was going to Spain tomorrow. Everyone knew it and they wouldn't think it was strange that she'd gone. She decided she was going to take Frankie with her after all. Leave this country and the mess behind her.

Gathering her thoughts, avoiding looking towards Derek and the blood, Julie walked into the kitchen where she washed away what little blood she had on her hands, and cleaned the handle of the knife. She dropped it beside Derek on the floor. It was strange. All the blood had spurted forward, so there was hardly any on her.

She ran into the bedroom and frantically searched around underneath her mum's old iron bed. At last, she found what she was looking for: the old rusty biscuit tin which her mum kept all her important documents in. She found Frankie's birth certificate. She could get one of those yearly passports from the Post Office in the morning. All you needed was a birth certificate and a photo.

Thinking quickly, she went to the large, pig-shaped pot on the mantelpiece. She realised she would need as much money as possible if she was taking Frankie with her, and this was where all the housekeeping money was kept. Ignoring the blood, which was now drying quickly with the warmth of the fire, she took what little there was inside the pot and put it in her pocket. She pulled some of Frankie's clothes from the old clothes airer and stuffed them in her suitcase. Then, picking up her case and handbag, she walked out and made her way to Gertie's as calmly as she could, to collect Frankie. Although her heart was pounding and her legs felt weak, on seeing one of the neighbours, she forced a smile.

'You're off then, Julie. Have a good time, don't get too drunk.' The man had laughed and waved at her.

'Yes. See you soon.' She waved back and continued making her way down the steps with her heavy suitcase.

She breathed in the night air, trying to compose herself before she got to Gertie's flat.

She wanted to distance herself as far from the estate as possible and was mentally trying to form a plan in her mind. Running away to Spain and escaping a life sentence in prison seemed to be the only way.

7

A NEW WAY OF LIFE

'This is the life, Ralph. A cool pub away from the sun and a cool glass of Irish Guinness, followed by a whisky. Who could ask for anything more?' Taking a large gulp of his pint, Paddy looked around at the people in the pub, doing just the same as himself. It wasn't much but it was their local pub and he enjoyed meeting up with their friends and bantering.

'I could. Look around you. It's a shithole. Is this all there is? Am I going to end my days like that old bloke in the corner, sitting here day in day out until I am ready to die? I want better memories than this to take with me.'

'You're always reaching for the stars; isn't the moon enough?' Paddy laughed. Ralph always wanted more; he was a dreamer who would not settle for his lot in life.

'Looks like trouble brewing over there. Those men arguing.' Paddy nodded his head in their direction. 'It looks like it's getting more heated. We'd better go.'

Turning around, Ralph saw three men arguing in the corner of the pub. Suddenly, out of nowhere, punches began to fly.

Tables were being knocked over and glasses smashed on the floor.

'Stop it. Stop, you lot. This is my pub and I'll not have you wrecking the joint,' shouted the publican.

Looking at the publican, Ralph noticed he was panic-stricken and scared. Turning again to see the fight at the other side of the room, he saw that others had joined in and it was getting louder and louder. People were leaving, not wanting to get dragged into it.

'Bollocks to this, Ralph, come on, let's get out of here before the shit hits the fan. I don't want to be in the firing line of one of those fists.' Although Paddy was brave, he was no fighter.

'You can shut the fuck up,' a man shouted at the publican, while picking up a bar towel to wipe his bloodied nose. 'Wrecking the place, are we? I'll show you what wrecking the place is. Come on, lads. This fat bastard says we're troublemakers!' Walking over to the wall where the newly installed jukebox was mounted, he pulled at it with all his might, knocking it off its hinges. Suddenly it crashed to the floor.

The publican looked around for help. There was none. People were leaving. 'For God's sake, mate. That jukebox is rented. Look, leave now and we'll say no more about it.' After going around the other side of the bar, the publican tried appeasing the men. He offered them a drink to calm down. However, now they were all fired up with anger. Picking up a wooden chair, they smashed it, breaking off the legs. They thought it was funny. Their fight now suddenly turned on the publican and their surroundings. They were like naughty schoolboys, vandalising this poor man's business and causing mayhem. They'd had far too much to drink and didn't care. Strutting around the other side of the bar, one of them picked up a bottle of whisky and took a huge gulp, totally oblivious to Ralph and Paddy. Jeered on by his friends, he reached over the bar and passed the bottle over. Their own argument was forgotten; this was a free-for-all and a lot more fun than their own feud.

'I'm calling the police; get out now,' shouted the publican.

'Do that, you fucking grass, and it won't only be this rathole that gets hurt. Now, let us see that till of yours. It must be full of money, with the prices you charge. You thieving bastard.'

Terrified, the publican opened his cash register and the notes and coins he had in it were scooped out and into the man's pocket. He was at breaking point and tears welled up in his eyes. The other two men were tipping up tables and stubbing their cigarettes out on the fabric that covered the corner seats. They were venting their anger and they were enjoying it.

Slowly and calmly, Ralph walked over to one of the men who was holding a wooden chair leg and smashing at the jukebox lying on the floor. He was going crazy, raining down blow after blow until the electrics blew completely.

'Do you like breaking things, matey?' Ralph asked, but the man wasn't listening. He was like a crazed animal. Ralph grabbed his arm with the wooden chair leg in it and held it aloft. 'I said, do you like breaking things? Because so do I.'

Annoyed at being interrupted, the man glared at Ralph and then at his friends. 'Hey, guys, this fucking joker thinks he's funny. Let's show him who's in charge here.'

Ralph squeezed the man's arm tighter and pulled it behind his back. The other men stopped what they were doing when they heard the loud crack of the bone being broken. Letting go, they all looked on as the man's arm hung awkwardly at his side. Now only shouts and howls of agony filled the room.

'What the hell did you do that for? You've broken his bloody arm! We're only messing.'

'So was I. Now fuck off and let me finish my pint in peace.'

Ralph walked calmly back over to the bar and stood beside Paddy, who seemed to be enjoying it all. He knew all about Ralph's temper, which was what made him a great bare-knuckle boxer.

The man who had stuffed his pockets ran around the bar. Picking up a chair leg, he ran towards Ralph. 'You bastard. I'll show you.' Swinging it above his head, he aimed it at Ralph, who dodged the blow and threw a punch into the man's stomach. The blow was so intense it knocked the man backwards, and he banged his head on the floor.

The third man wasn't so brave without his companions. Looking around, he could see one of his friends howling in pain with a broken arm and the other one lying on the floor with blood coming from the back of his head. He instantly dropped the chair leg he was holding.

'I'm off, mate. I want no hassle.'

Ralph and Paddy watched him run for the door.

Ralph crouched down by the man lying on the floor, who tried kicking him away, not knowing what Ralph was going to do next. The man could not get up yet. He was still dazed from the punch he had received and the bang to his head had made him dizzy.

Ralph sat on his legs, went through his pockets, and retrieved the stolen money. Coins fell onto the floor as the man lay helpless. Approaching them both, Paddy reached down and took the notes out of Ralph's hands.

Standing up, Ralph brushed down his trousers and held out his hand to the man on the floor to help him up. Unsteadily standing and swaying, the man wiped the back of his head and saw the blood on his hand. That was enough to make him walk unsteadily towards the door, holding on to the walls to keep him up as he went. He wanted no more fighting and Ralph had proved he was more than enough to take them all on.

'Give the publican his money, Paddy.' Ralph looked towards the publican and nodded.

Paddy's eyes widened. 'You sure, Ralph? You worked bloody hard for it. This place would have been in pieces if you hadn't stepped in, and you' – Paddy turned towards the publican cowering behind the bar – 'you would have been battered within an inch of your life. Get up, you weak bastard.'

'Give him the money,' shouted Ralph. 'And I mean all of it, you light-fingered bastard!'

Sighing and disappointed, Paddy reluctantly put the money on the bar.

'Is that all of it?'

'Virgin's honour. There are some more coins on the floor over there, but I'm not scrambling about on my hands and knees; he can do it himself.'

The publican scooped up the money quickly and started pushing it back into his cash register, thanking Ralph for his help and generosity.

'Drink each on the house, lads. And if you help me tidy this place up, I'll make it two.' The publican was all smiles again, now that his bravery had come back.

'I don't tidy up. That's women's work. I will take the drink, though, and of course, my wages.'

The publican stopped short in the middle of pulling Ralph's drink and looked at him, puzzled, from across the bar. 'Wages?'

'Yes, wages. I just saved you from a battering. Your money drawer is full of your profits and that's all down to me. Now I want my wages for risking my neck and helping you out.'

After weighing up the situation, the publican agreed. The situation could have cost him a whole lot more. Who knows?

Those bloody maniacs could have burnt the place down and he could be in hospital now.

'And what would you say was a fair wage, mister?'

'Five pounds. Don't forget I've seen the money and I know you have it. It's pretty obvious that you need someone to look after the place... and yourself.' Ralph took a sip of his drink and waited.

'That's extortion. You really want me to give you five pounds? What about I give you two pounds and we call it quits.'

'What about you call it five pounds. I'm not bartering. Those guys will be back, possibly with a few more friends for revenge, and I will just stand back with my two pounds and let them rob you.'

Nodding, the publican opened his cash drawer and laid the five pounds on the bar.

Ralph picked it up and put it in his pocket. He could not believe his luck. He had taken a chance asking for five pounds. It was a lot of money. However, it had paid off. 'My name is Ralph. Should you ever need any muscle again, just ask around. I work at the quarry. Nice doing business with you.' He reached out and shook the man's hand, then turned towards Paddy. 'Come on, let's go.' With that, and his five pounds in his pocket, he turned on his heel and headed for the door, leaving the publican to clear away the mess. Paddy was hot on his heels behind him.

'What the hell did you do that for? We could have had the lot.'

'Because, Paddy, to take the lot would be theft and I would be in a police cell by now.' Reaching in his pocket and waving the five-pound note in the air, Ralph smiled. 'This was given freely. He knows my name, where I work and, believe me, he will ask around about me. All above board. It is the best way. In addition, here, considering you did bugger all and I am in a generous mood. Here's two pounds, much more than you earnt.' The smile on Paddy's face satisfied Ralph. Now everyone was happy and he had just learnt a new way to make money.

Ralph now realised that people felt better if they had someone to fight their battles for them; it made them feel secure and it was worth the payments to keep their properties safe.

It didn't take long for word to spread about Ralph and what he'd done. A couple of nights later, there was a huge banging at Ralph's front door, nearly knocking if off the hinges. Young Irene smiled when she opened the door and saw Paddy there. Although she didn't particularly like him and his cocky ways, he was Ralph's friend and so she tolerated him.

'How nice to see you, Paddy. Come in.' No sooner had she said it than he pushed past her and walked to the table, where Ralph was eating his evening meal.

'A fight has broken out in the Pig and Whistle. The landlord has sent me to fetch you. It's bloody chaos in there, by all accounts. Come on, get your coat.'

'I'm eating, Paddy. Can't you see? I've done a full day at work, and now I'm hungry. Irene, love, bring another plate for Paddy. He is bound to be on the scrounge, he always is.'

Nonchalantly, Ralph carried on raising the spoon to his mouth, enjoying the warm Irish stew, while Paddy was all excited, pulling at his shirt sleeve to follow him.

'No thanks, Irene,' Paddy said. He eyed up the steaming pot of stew and licked his lips. 'Well, maybe later.'

'You're always trying to get my Ralph into bother. Now, why don't you wrap that filthy sheepskin coat around you and bugger off. God knows, you look ridiculous in it anyway,' snapped Ralph's mum.

'I think it makes me look distinguished, Ma.' He straightened his baggy, moth-eaten sheepskin coat and flashed Ralph's mother a smile which was more of a grimace, determined to let it go. He had bigger things on his mind.

'It makes you look a fool.'

Seeing that this argument was getting heated and wouldn't stop, Ralph pushed his plate away and stood up. 'Put that back in the pan for me, Irene, I'll have it later. Right, let's see what all the fuss is about, shall we? Lead on, Paddy.'

Paddy's eyes lit up and he couldn't get to the door quick enough. He filled Ralph in about the trouble in the pub as they walked and as they approached, Ralph could hear the shouting and arguments above the jukebox.

Ralph stood outside in the dark with only the lights from the pub lighting up the night and rolled up his sleeves. He knew that this was going to be real trouble. His bare-knuckle fighting experience would set him up well for occasions like this. It was all about survival. Prison was a battle, too, and this was going to be no different.

'Just before you go in, I want you to take this.' Paddy reached into the inside pocket of his sheepskin, took something out and handed it to Ralph.

Shocked, Ralph looked at the gun in his hand. 'Where the hell did you get that from? If the coppers come, I'm back inside prison for a very long stretch. For fuck's sake, put it away.' He held it out for Paddy to take back.

'Insurance.' Paddy didn't take it.

'Where the hell did you get it?'

'All the old soldiers came home from the war with their weapons. No one checked. God, there must be a million of them stuffed under mattresses around the world.'

It had never dawned on Ralph that some old soldiers still had their weapons. He had never really thought about it. He pushed the gun into Paddy's hands. 'No, Paddy, no way. You want to play cowboys and Indians with guns, then you take it in there. If you feel we need the security, then you use it. I'll use my fists and you can use whatever you want.'

Inside, all Ralph could see was chaos and mayhem. Men were holding their friends back from fighting. Everyone, it seemed, was arguing and fists were flying. Tables and chairs had been knocked over. *Christ*, Ralph thought to himself, *this is more like a prison riot!*

When he saw them, the barman ran over to Ralph and Paddy. 'Thank God you came, Ralph. It started with a few drunks shouting about those political meetings they go to and now the shit has hit the fan. The last thing I need is the police coming and them knowing I called them. That one there, he started it. Shooting his mouth off about the Irish.'

Weighing up the situation, unnoticed by everyone in the fight, Ralph decided that the man standing on a chair in the far corner stirring up everyone's blood should be the one he started with.

He walked over to the chair, pushing past everyone and dodging their fists, then reached up and grabbed the man by his shirt. He pulled him off the chair. With one meaty paw Ralph punched him in the face and then he followed it with the other one. There was a satisfying crunch when he squashed the man's nose. Realising this man was a coward and just liked to stir up trouble, Ralph left him rubbing his chin and wiping the blood away from his nose. He could see that he had broken it by the shape of it, and already his eye was swelling, too.

'I know who you are, Ralph Goldstein. You think you're a hard man? We will see, shall we, when you are begging for mercy. Don't think I'll forget this in a hurry. You'll pay for this when my friends hear about it.' Trying to save face in front of the others, he stood up. He was slightly unsteady, but he walked out of there, kicking over a table full of drinks as he went, just to make his point.

'That's just fine with me, you little shit,' Ralph shouted after him. 'Now go and tell them, like the cowardly bastard you are.'

There was no reply and so Ralph turned to the rest of the brawlers.

'Right, you lot,' he shouted. 'If any one of you wants a free-for-all fight, then come to me. Let's see how brave you are without big mouth goading you on. You.' He pointed to a man shouting and swearing. 'Shut up and sit down. Do you really want to spend the night in a cell once the police hear you? Believe me, once the police give you a good beating with their truncheons, you'll wish you had shut your mouth.'

Everyone seemed to stop what they were doing and turned. One drunk man ran towards Ralph, intending to throw a punch, and was greeted by a hard kick in the balls. It took the wind out of him and he bent over, holding them, crying out in pain. The tears in his eyes were more than enough to silence him.

What Ralph had said seemed to seep into their brains slowly. They all knew the stories about the police beatings and on top of that, the worst troublemakers got another hiding when they spent the night in the cells. It was time to stop. They had vented their anger and made their point. They could all hear the police whistles blowing outside and did not want to get involved. The best thing to do was get out of there as quickly as possible.

The doors were flung open and three police officers ran in. They stopped anyone left there from leaving, putting their arms behind their backs and shoving their faces into the walls, then handcuffing them.

'Well, well, well. If it's not our friend Ralph,' said the police sergeant, as he walked towards Ralph. 'I thought you might be at the back of all this. Life on the outside getting too much for you?'

The sneering sarcasm dripped from the copper's mouth. 'Need another spell inside to make you realise that you can't win?' The police sergeant stood in front of Ralph and grinned. It wasn't their first meeting. Ralph's face dropped. He gave a huge sigh and held his arms out in front of him for the handcuffs. There was no point in arguing; it only made things worse.

'No, wait, gentlemen. Ralph wasn't involved,' shouted the barman. 'It was just a couple of blokes arguing about some woman or other. You know what it's like, officers. They get their wages, have a few drinks, and all that Dutch courage starts a fight. It's no problem. As you can see, they were leaving anyway.' The barman was doing his best to appease the police. Ralph had helped him and now it was his turn. 'Come on, sir, have a drink on the house.' he said, beaming a smile and pouring a pint of Guinness. He was doing his best, but it didn't seem to matter.

'Search them. And you, Ralph, you can still pop down the station and tell me what you were doing here.'

A cold chill ran through Ralph when he remembered what Paddy had in his coat pocket. Turning towards Paddy, who was also being handcuffed, his heart sank. A bloody gun! God help them both. Paddy gave him a slight wink.

'Nothing, sir,' another officer said. 'They are both clean.'

'Put them in the van anyway. This lot think they can do as they like. Well, it's time they were taught that we won't put up with it. We are officers of the law and it's time this lot realised it and abided by the rules.' The police sergeant seemed to enjoy the fact that he had Ralph in his power again. 'I'll have that drink another time, barman,' he said, then walked out.

* * *

Early the next morning, limping out of the police station covered in cuts and bruises, Ralph looked at Paddy. 'That fucking gun of yours. What did you do with it?'

It was the first chance they'd had to speak since the night before. They had both been put in cells, questioned about their whereabouts and given a beating. They knew what was coming and accepted their fate. No one cared about them. They were ex-cons, the scum of the earth as far as the police were concerned. Who gave a shit if they took a beating to keep them in line? More to the point, who were they going to complain to? This was the police!

'I slid it along the floor behind the bar when I heard the whistles. Thank Christ it didn't go off. Can you imagine that?' Paddy did his best to talk but his mouth was swollen. His ribs hurt, too; he thought they were possibly broken.

'Then we need to get it back. I want that gun where I can see it. We don't need that shit coming back to us. I have had enough of all of this.'

'You want to go back there now?' Paddy was amazed. He was tired and weary and his whole body felt on fire from the beating he had taken.

'Yes, I do. I will not give them coppers another excuse to treat us like this, or worse. Do you hear me? The next time you have one of your bright ideas about playing cops and robbers with guns, I'll kill you myself. Come on.'

Although it was early morning, they banged on the door. There was hardly anyone around apart from a few men making their way to work. Babies were in their prams on the paths outside the doors while women cleaned the house.

Shocked at their appearance, the publican opened the door wider. 'Come in, Ralph, Paddy. Dear God, you look like shit. What did those bastards do to you? Come in. I'll get you both a stiff drink. You both look like you need one.' The publican led the way into the dimly lit pub and handed them each a large whisky, and Ralph gulped his down. Now it was time to get down to business. 'You know what I've come for, so hand it over.'

'Sure, sure, Ralph, mate. You know I would make good our arrangement.' Opening his cash register, the publican took out a five-pound note and put it on the bar. 'That's the going rate, isn't it? Thanks. I'm sorry you took that beating, though.'

Confused, Ralph scooped up the money and put it in his pocket. 'And the other thing?' he said.

'Safe.' The publican handed over a tea towel with the gun wrapped inside.

Ralph opened it slightly to check it, then nodded. His business was done here and now he needed to go home. There was no point telling the foreman of the quarry he wouldn't be in today. He was sure he'd have heard the gossip already. That was, if he had a job to go back to.

'Thanks for the drink.' Ralph handed over the gun to Paddy to hide in his torn, bloodstained coat, then stood up to leave.

'Ralph!' shouted the publican, 'I've told a few of my friends that you helped me save this place. They would like the same arrangement, if that's okay.'

'Arrangement?' Now Ralph was confused. He was too tired and weary to ask, but he felt he had to. 'What are you on about?'

'Looking after the place, if we need you. Keeping us all safe.'

Ralph's brain was working at full speed now. An idea was forming. All of this had fallen into his lap without him having to do anything. Well, nothing out of the normal, anyway. All he had done for most of his life was fight. Now it seemed fighting was going to pay off.

'Protection, you mean?' He looked first at the publican and

then turned towards Paddy; they both smiled as best as they could through their swollen faces.

'I'd want some kind of retainer. A weekly down payment to pop in now and again and make my presence known. Then, if anything were to happen, like last night, it would cost more. Let's say two pound a week for now and we'll see how it goes. That's every week, mind you.'

'That is fine with me, Ralph. You just do your job and I will do mine, knowing that I can call upon you anytime. What price peace of mind, eh? This is my living; I can't afford to close up.'

'I'll pop by next week to see if you still feel the same and collect my money, if that's okay.'

'Nice doing business with you.'

Once outside, Paddy and Ralph smiled. They wanted to laugh but their swollen faces would not allow it. This was more than they had hoped for and if their legs had not been so swollen from the truncheons hitting the backs of them, they would probably have jumped in the air.

'Bloody hell, Ralph. They want to pay us protection money. How cool is that? We're like gangsters. A pound a week each, and more if we stop the fights. That's brilliant.' Paddy felt like punching the air but his injuries prevented it.

'I know. Let's see how it goes, shall we? We don't want to get too excited yet. It's me that will be taking most of the flying punches, so let's just call the split sixty–forty. You drum up the work and I'll do what's necessary, and for God's sake keep that gun out of sight!'

8

JUDGEMENT DAY

After weeks of applying for visiting orders to see her mum, Julie finally got the answer she wanted: her mother had agreed to see her, but only her. Frankie had nagged constantly about seeing her, but if their mum didn't want to, there was nothing she could do about it.

When Julie walked into the prison, she didn't know what to expect. Inside, it was dark and dingy with a stench of disinfectant. She was shown into a room with wooden tables and chairs and knew that sitting at one of them was her mother. She was struggling to recognise her, and was pleased when a smiling, grey-haired woman beckoned her over and shouted her name.

'Julie, over here, love. Come sit down.'

Hardly believing her eyes, Julie walked to the table and sat down. She felt nervous seeing the prison warders standing at either side of the room. It made her shiver. It was a grim place.

'Hello, love. How are you?' Genuinely pleased to see her, her mother reached out to touch her hand.

'No touching,' the guard shouted.

Gently slipping it away, the sadness in her mum's eyes was apparent.

'You look so different, Mum, I hardly recognised you.' This was not the drunken woman Julie had left behind. To start with, she was sober and her words were coherent. She was washed and, although she wore prison uniform, it was clean and ironed.

'I know, love. I look different, don't I? Better, in fact. Wouldn't you say so? Apart from the grey hair, of course. I can't do anything about that. They don't have hairdressers here.' She laughed. Although years of alcohol had taken its toll on her face and made her look older than her years, Julie had to admit, her mum looked the best she had seen her in a long time.

'Everyone knows you and little Frances have been living in Spain. I have the two cards that Frances sent me in my cell. It looks like a lovely place. Did you enjoy yourself?'

'We both had a great time,' Julie lied. Now was not the time to pour her own bad news on this situation.

'How is Frances? Did she enjoy herself? You stayed there for a long time. Why did you come back?'

Julie did her best to make Spain sound more glamorous than the truth. She knew they were both skirting around the facts. This was all very polite preliminaries for the prison warders' ears. Looking across at them, Julie saw the one nearest to them walk towards the other one at the far side of the room. He had heard enough and was bored.

'Mum. That night when you were arrested,' Julie whispered, once he was out of earshot. 'What happened? I need to talk to you about it.'

'No, you don't. I know. Do you understand me? I know!' Looking furtively around at the guards, then back at her daughter, she nodded. It was as though her eyes looked into Julie's very soul.

'What do you know?'

'Everything. You have a long time to think in here. Put the pieces together like a jigsaw. I was drunk, of course. All I remember is the police coming and I was covered in blood. You were never there and Frances was at Gertie's place, wasn't she?' Her mum emphasised her words, trying to drill the story she had obviously told the police into Julie. 'Only myself and Derek were in the flat. It wouldn't be the first argument we'd ever had, would it?' Her mother shrugged nonchalantly again. 'You're my little girl, my first-born, and you have always had to look after me. I haven't been a very good mother to you. Now it's my turn to protect you. And it's much easier when you're sober.' She smiled and gave a little laugh.

There was a moment's silence as they both gathered their thoughts. Guilt wracked Julie's body. She wanted to shout out to her mother that she had killed Derek and why she had done it, but her mother didn't want to listen.

Smiling and doing her best to reassure her, her mum carried on. 'I'm okay, Julie, love. They've put me onto a rehabilitation course for alcoholics. I am clean. I get three meals a day. I have a good cellmate, Laura. She knows the ropes; she's been in and out of prison most of her life. Nobody bothers me. I'm okay. I feel at peace with myself. Although I am glad you have come to see me, it gives me the chance to say that I am sorry for all I have put you through. I have been a stupid woman. Don't make my mistakes. Enjoy life, have some fun. Look after Frances for me.'

The hint of emotion as her voice broke stabbed at Julie's heart.

So that was it. Her mother was prepared to take all the blame just so that her daughters could walk free and start a new life. This was her apology. This was what any parent would do for their child. Unconditional love.

Ignoring the guards, Julie reached across and squeezed her mum's hand. 'I will look after Frankie. You know that, don't you,' Julie said. It seemed they were both fighting back the tears. This was not the place. She would cry once she had left and, no doubt, her mother would do the same. In a strange way, they were very much alike. They were both fighters.

Rising, Julie went to get them a couple of drinks. It gave them both time to compose themselves. A few minutes later she handed her mum a hot cup of tea.

'Thank you for not bringing Frances with you. I would have hated you bringing her here. It's not for her eyes. I know you can handle it, but Frances is not like you. She's not strong like you. When the time comes, I don't want you to come to the court case. Leave the past behind you. Do it for me. Live your life for me, the life I never had. I see great things for you. Prove to me that I am doing the right thing, making this small sacrifice, eh? Make me proud.' The knowing look between them spoke the words they couldn't say.

'I'll try, although I think we might be staying at Gertie's for a while now. Do you know the council have given the flat away already? We have nothing.'

'Then...' Her mum let out a sigh and sat back in her chair. 'You have nothing to lose. You will find somewhere. I know you will. I have full confidence in you.'

'I will make you proud, Mum, and I will look after Frankie, too. I promise. Do you hear me? I promise from the bottom of my heart to make good of all this mess.'

A smile crossed her mother's face and she rubbed Julie's leg with her own under the table, while casting another furtive glance at the guards, who seemed disinterested by this female heart to heart.

Standing up, Julie's mum put out her hand and brushed away

Julie's tears. Looking up at the guard, she expected a reprimand, but none came. He turned his back as though not to notice.

'Do me a favour. Don't ever come back here. I've seen you and that is enough. You look fit and well and that means Frances does, too. This is goodbye, Julie, love. Never come and see me again. Go forward, never look back. Be lucky, darling.' With that, she walked towards the door, then turned one last time and blew a kiss.

Heartbroken, Julie pretended to catch it, like she had when she was a young girl. Slowly Julie mouthed the silent word, 'Sorry.'

That was the last time she would ever see her mum. She had made her promise and she would keep her word to reward her mother's sacrifice. She would go forward and she would look after Frankie. This was the price she was paying. These were the consequences of her actions that night.

Bloody hell, she thought as she walked out of the grim prison walls. *Haven't I paid enough for my sins over the last few months? Will it never end?*

9

FAMILY CONNECTIONS

Sitting with his son in the new Wimpy burger restaurant, watching Shaun eat his burger and fries, warmed Ralph's heart. He'd missed so much of his son's childhood while in prison. He liked to spend time with him alone. Being able to waste a few pounds on the boy was his way of trying to make it up to him. The last couple of years had been prosperous. Word had spread and Ralph was now in demand. Looking up at the windows, his heart sank. Paddy was knocking on the window to attract his attention.

'Ralph! Ralph, mate.' Paddy edged his way into the long bench seats the Wimpy bar had and put his elbows on the table, then reached out for one of the French fries on Shaun's plate.

'Leave it, Paddy. You want to eat, buy your own, and watch your words. Can't you give me a minute's peace? You're like my bloody shadow!'

'Yeh, okay, keep your hair on. It's just that there's a restaurant owner that wants a word with us.'

'You mean wants a word with me. Not now, mate. I'm spending some quality time with my son. It will have to wait.'

'It's your choice to still blow rocks up at that quarry. Why don't you give it up and do what you do best full time? It's been ages now and we're... I mean you are making good money.'

'Because it's a steady income. Everything else could be taken away in the blink of an eye. It's good for the family, too. It gives them something reputable to say about me for once. So, what does this restaurant owner want? And think on before you say too much. Shaun is very sharp-minded with big ears!'

'I don't have big hears, Daddy.' His red-haired son looked up at him. His face was covered in tomato sauce and his cheeks were full of his cheeseburger. He reminded Ralph of a gerbil storing his food.

'No, lad. It's just me messing. You carry on and eat that burger of yours. Is it nice?' Ruffling his hair and smiling at his young son, Ralph felt content. The last couple of years had been fruitful. He helped many of the local pubs out, offering a bit of muscle. They paid up and everyone was happy.

Ralph watched as the boy finished chewing and swallowed the food. 'You finished, son?' Shaun nodded, his face happy and smiling. 'Let's drop you off home. Come on, Paddy, let's go and see what all this is about. You won't rest until I do. And don't walk so close to me, you smelly bastard. Has your hair always been greasy?'

'Well, it's better than all that stuff you put on yours to oil it back. All that black wavy hair needs a lot of care.' Paddy couldn't help laughing. He always laughed.

* * *

Sitting opposite the restaurant owner, Ralph watched the middle-aged man nervously wringing his hands as he spoke. The restaurant was closed so they had the whole place to themselves.

'Mr Goldstein, I am losing a lot of money. All these burger places… and now a restaurant has opened up opposite me.' Following his eyes, Ralph looked out of the window across the road. 'He's undercutting me on price.'

'Why not just drop your own prices? Put something on offer or something.' This talk was going nowhere and Ralph was bored. This was restaurant competition; what did it have to do with him?

'I can't run at the prices he is charging; he has his whole family working free. They are all in it together. They work around the clock, night and day. And I get the feeling they know people, if you know what I mean. I have had a couple of threats to close down and move on, but I can't afford to. I have been here for twenty years. This is my living and my home.'

'Threats? What do you mean?'

'They have put cockroaches in the kitchen. That was enough to kill my custom for a while. Now it has got a bad name. They want to take my place over and they don't want to pay for any of it. They have offered me a pittance compared to what it is worth. I will be bankrupt. My whole family will be out on the streets.' The desperate restaurant owner sat before Ralph, hoping for answers.

'So what do you want me to do? I can go and have a word with them, but it sounds like it's pretty much sewn up. They want to take a going concern from you at a pittance. You are going to be skint anyway and so you will take anything they offer. They win and you get the clothes you stand up in. Am I right?'

'More or less. I knew you would see it my way, Mr Goldstein. Also, I am coming to you because we share the same star. I can trust you.'

'Star?' Ralph was puzzled. He liked being called 'Mr Goldstein' – he had never been called that unless he was in court – but he was at a loss. 'What are you on about, star?'

'I am Jewish, Ralph. Like you. We help each other, don't we?'

The pleading look in the man's eyes made Ralph almost feel sorry for him.

'I don't do religious crap, mate. Yes, I'm half-Jewish, but I don't do favours. They don't pay the bills.'

'I understand that. Here.' He slid an envelope across the table to Ralph and waited. 'Do what you have to. I'm a simple business-man. It's worth what is in that envelope to keep my livelihood, if you can help me.'

Opening the envelope, Ralph nearly choked, but did his best to hide it. It was full of twenty-pound notes. It was the most money he had seen in his life. There must have been a couple of hundred in there. Looking at Paddy, who was straining his neck to see inside the envelope and licking his lips, he knew he felt the same.

'Can you help me, Mr Goldstein? You can see I am serious now.'

'What do you want me to do? Specifically, I mean.'

'Just put them out of business for a while. Give me a chance to get back on my feet and get my old customers back. Let me hear the cash register ring again. I am a desperate man with a family to feed. This is all I know. I can't start again. I am too old to start again from scratch.'

'Let me think on it for a few days. I'll get back to you.' Ralph put the envelope down on the table and stood up, ready to leave. He could see Paddy was ready to take the money and run. He could also see the confused look on his face. Agreed, it was a lot of money, but it could also be a whole lot of trouble and a long prison sentence. How many years would that money keep his family for while he rotted in jail?

'Take the envelope. I trust you. You are my last hope. Shalom, Mr Goldstein.'

Hearing the old Jewish greeting his father used to say struck a chord with Ralph. He hadn't heard that word in years. 'No one has ever said they trusted me before and especially with an envelope like this. Okay. Let me think on it.' As he walked outside with Paddy bouncing at his side, Ralph was already thinking about the poor man's plight.

* * *

'You look tired, Ralph, darling,' said Irene. 'Come sit by the fire with your ma and I'll make some tea. I was thinking we could maybe buy one of those record players everyone is buying. The record shop has so many lovely songs. The radio is all well and good, but your ma likes that Cilla Black. We could buy some, couldn't we, Ma?'

Ralph waited until Irene had gone into the kitchen, then looked across at his mother. 'Well? Is that what you want?'

'Not really. It would be nice, but I just want you to be safe. Do not risk your neck on my behalf. You don't earn that kind of money at the quarry. Are you okay, son?'

'Yes, I'm fine. Actually, Ma, no. Would you say that just because I'm half-Jewish that makes the Jews my family?' The restaurant owner's words had struck a chord with Ralph.

'I suppose it does. They all stuck together during that awful war. They only had each other to depend on when things got rough. So yes, I suppose that is the way they see it, as family. Your dad and I dropped religion at the door of our house, both of us left it outside. It caused us a lot of pain and trouble. But there was a time when it must have seemed like it was them against the world, and your dad went to fight in the war when he didn't have to. Why do you ask?'

'Nothing. Just a thought.' Pondering and staring into the coal fire, Ralph realised he had never really thought about who or what he was. His ma was right; they had dropped religion at the door of the house. There was no escaping it outside, but he felt it was for other people, not for him. That was another reason why Irene's family had looked at him with suspicion.

Irene appeared from the kitchen with a tray of tea. 'Here is your tea. I'll put yours at the side here, Ma, and there's some biscuits. Bourbons, your favourite.'

Ralph reached into his pocket and took out some money. Irene's eyes lit up at the sight of it. 'You and Shaun go and buy your record player and some tunes for Ma, eh? There is extra in there for you and Shaun. Buy something nice, you deserve it, love.'

Irene threw her arms around his neck, and kissed and hugged him 'Thank you. You are the best husband a woman could have.' Irene was excited and elated, her flushed face nearly as red as her long hair. While holding the money in her hands, she planted a big kiss on his cheek and whispered in his ear, 'Maybe I will treat you to something later.' Then, blushing, she looked up at Ralph's mum, who tactfully turned to pick up her teacup.

Putting his hand in his pocket, Ralph felt the envelope. Maybe he should honour his birthright. This restaurant owner had turned to someone he felt was one of his own kind. Someone he could trust. Yes, he would help him; he just had to figure out how. It was going to take more than a few fists flying to close their restaurant down.

* * *

'So, have you had enough time to think about it, mate?' Paddy's impatience was beginning to annoy Ralph. He had come to work this morning in a good mood; Irene had seen to that. Life felt good at the moment. Then he spotted Paddy hanging around like a lost soul, and trotted over to him.

'Put these ear defenders on, Paddy, before you let your mouth run away with you. You shouldn't even be here.'

Paddy took them, did as he was told and shrugged. Then he looked at Ralph as everyone scattered and moved behind a rock or anything else they could find for shelter.

BOOM!!!

A huge explosion shook the ground they were standing on, the noise deafening. Another one soon followed. Paddy lay on the ground as the blast blew dust and stones into a thick cloud above him.

Someone shouted, 'All clear!' and Ralph walked over to Paddy and helped him up. 'For fuck's sake, my legs are shaking!' he shouted. He looked terrified; he'd been to the quarry many times but never early enough to experience the explosives. 'Why the hell would anyone want to work in a place like this? It's hell on earth!' He dusted himself down and shook the gravel and dirt off his jeans, then sat on the ground to compose himself. He lit a cigarette.

'You get used to it. Anyway, I enjoy it.' Inwardly, Ralph smiled. He could see Paddy was well and truly shaken up. Everyone felt like that in the beginning, but you got used to it.

'Well? I've nearly died waiting for an answer. What have you decided? What are we going to do? I know some guys that could help with a bit of rough stuff. They like a fight. So, what is it to be, Ralphy, boy?'

Wiping the sweat from his brow and looking around, then at Paddy, Ralph smiled. This had given him an idea. 'I wasn't sure, but I am now. We won't be needing your friends. Anyway, I didn't know you had any friends.'

'Well, I have. I go to some political meetings and that is how we met. Good blokes.'

'What political meetings? You mean those bloody hooligans you hang out with that think Ireland is for the Irish? They are not politically minded, they're thugs and you're no better. Leave me out of it.'

'Well, don't you feel like that? Ireland for the Irish? They're good blokes and we have to fight for what is ours.'

'Fuck off, Paddy. You sound like a parrot. My motto is simple: live and let live. I'm not interested in following the crowd. I am my own man. I have my own way of handling things.'

'So, what about the restaurant guy? Are we going to help him, or not?'

'If you're so interested, here! Take the money. You and your friends can sort it out.'

Realising he had pushed Ralph too far, Paddy accepted Ralph's word. 'Sorry. You know me, I just get a bit excited about things. This is business, and you're the boss.'

'Actually, I am going to do it, for lots of reasons. It will only take the two of us. All of this' – Ralph waved his arm at the quarry – 'has just given me an idea. Meet me later, around the back, after closing time.'

'Here you go, boss, everything's locked up for the night.' Ralph handed his supervisor the keys to the dynamite and explosives cupboard.

'Everything in order? I had better take stock and count what's in there. Come on. You can sign the docket with me. We have to have proof when dealing with explosives. You're a good guy,

Ralph. You've taken to this work like a duck to water and I have to admit you're a great explosives man.'

'Thanks, boss. Will that show in my wages?'

The foreman laughed. 'You're good, but I'm better.' He opened the cabin door and said, 'Isn't that your mate, Paddy? Bloody hell, hasn't he got a home to go to?'

'Yes, it is. He's come to pick up a present I bought for his mother's birthday. Hang on a minute.' Ralph shouted out of the cabin door, 'Oy, Paddy, I'm going straight home. Your ma's birthday present is in the office, over there, with my coat. I have stuff to do here. See you, mate. Say "happy birthday" to your ma from me and the family.'

Seeing the confused look on Paddy's face, Ralph stared at him. Then Ralph saw the penny had dropped. If nothing else, Paddy's mind was sharp.

'Thanks. See you later, mate.'

'Right, that's done, boss. Let's go and do the stock take, shall we?'

'We're a little down on explosives, to my reckoning. What do you think?' The foreman checked his list and counted again.

'Don't forget, I told you earlier that I had to double up on that last job. It didn't blow properly. You always get a few duds.'

'Ah, yes, so you did. It was over the west side, wasn't it? I remember, now, I wrote it down in the office. Well, taking that into account, it all looks present and correct here. Time to go home. See you in the morning.'

By the time Ralph got home Paddy was already waiting outside for him. 'What's in the package?' he said.

'Well, I wouldn't put it on your ma's birthday cake and light it. Tonight, at midnight, meet me at the restaurant.'

'Explosives? You're going to blow the place up?' Paddy's jaw dropped.

'Fists aren't going to close that restaurant down. It will just cause more fighting. Keep your hands out of the package; you don't know what you're doing. And don't light your fucking cigarettes near them. Tonight.'

After playing the dutiful husband and father, Ralph went to bed. He waited until Irene was fast asleep, then got up and quietly left the house.

The streets were dimly lit and so Ralph walked around the back alleys, which were even darker, doing his best not to trip over someone's dustbin.

'That you, Ralph?' he heard Paddy hiss, as he approached the restaurant.

'Yes. You okay?'

'No, I'm not okay. Here, take your package. That is the last thing I need on me if I get pulled by the law. What are you going to do? This is not a free-for-all at the quarry. They will know it was us.'

'No, they won't. Now shut up and follow me.'

'Do they all live there? What about the people upstairs? If you're going to blow the place up, you'll kill them. This is going too far.' Paddy was starting to panic. This was a whole new experience for him. He liked a brawl. He had a gun and he liked threatening people. But explosives... that was a whole step upwards.

'Will you shut the fuck up? Don't you think I haven't thought about that? If I didn't know better, I would say you're losing your bottle, Paddy. What happened to the hard man, eh? Not so brave without your new friends. I have thought it all through, trust me. Right, you're the king of breaking into places. Open that door without causing any damage.'

His whole life, Paddy had been in and out of prison for

burglary or theft. And this would be easy, especially for a cat burglar like Paddy!

'Careful how you open it – there's a brass bell above the door before you open it properly. Reach up and hold that bell so it doesn't make a noise.'

'We're in, Ralph, mate,' he whispered. 'Now what?'

'Now it's my turn. Let me do this and then go and turn the gas on in the kitchen. Turn it on full, now.' Ralph carefully unwrapped the putty explosive he had taken earlier that day. This was the easiest kind of explosive, but it could do so much damage. He had taken some dynamite with him, just in case he needed it, but had changed his mind. What with these and the gas, the place would be a bombsite in a few minutes. Now he had to get the innocent people out of the way.

'Paddy, when I say so, go and start a fire in the dustbins out the back and then shout "Fire!" That will raise the alarm and also distract everyone, so we can get out unnoticed.'

Paddy was pale and sweating. Looking at the explosive in Ralph's hand, he felt sick. He had thought it was just a few sticks of dynamite that had to be lit. God only knew what that stuff was and he had been carrying it around!

'Watch this.' Ralph moulded the putty substance in his hands and pressed it into the brickwork. It was like playdough. 'This stuff can't be ignited easily, so stop panicking. To be ignited there has to be extreme heat or shock waves. It needs a detonator to create a circuit. What I'm going to do is put it on a timer using that old clock.' He pointed at a clock in the restaurant, and Paddy went to get it for him.

Paddy watched intently as Ralph worked. It seemed like it took forever, but it was a couple of minutes at most. He'd taken the second hand off the clock, then put the wire with an old drawing pin through the back of the clock, and did the same from the front, then both wires were connected to the detonator and the plastic explosive.

'What is that going to do? A few bits of old wire with a drawing pin.' As frightened as he was, Paddy was intrigued.

'I've created a circuit and also given us a bit of time – a minute, to be exact. Once the hand starts to move it will hit the drawing pin and that will trigger the detonator. Simple, really. Now go and start that fire in the bins. Make sure you use a cigarette; that way the police will think that is what started it. The gas will cover the tracks of this explosive. It will just be traced back to someone not checking everything was turned off in the kitchen. You then shout "Fire!" Then piss off, fast as you like. I'll see you sometime tomorrow.'

'What about you? How are you going to get out?'

'Don't worry about me. I need to hang around to make sure this goes off properly. But we both have alibis: I'm in bed and you're in bed with someone's wife... probably.'

Luckily, Paddy was as quiet as a mouse as he went through to the kitchen, then out of the back door. Ralph could hear the dustbins crashing and then the shouts followed. 'FIRE! FIRE, EVERY-ONE!' That was Ralph's cue to leave. He could already hear the scrambling of feet above him, which meant people were alert and getting out of bed. When the door was closed far enough, he let go of the bell, dropped the latch and shut the door. He was glad of the night air because the gas was already making him a bit light-headed.

People were already coming out of their houses and lights were going on. Just as he got to the bottom of the street, he heard an explosion and turned to see. The building was ablaze. Black smoke filled the sky and he could hear shouts of panic. Standing in the shadows, he watched and he waited. *One... two... three*, he mentally counted to himself. Suddenly an almighty explosion shook the street, shortly followed by another one, where Ralph had strategically put the putty explosive into the brickwork. Leaving the burning chaos behind him, he pulled the hood on his coat over his head and walked home. He knew Paddy would already have done the same.

* * *

The next morning, as he was leaving for work, all he could hear was people talking about a restaurant a few streets away that had blown up. He spotted some of his workmates on the corner and offered them a lift in his car. They were full of stories about what had happened.

'Did anyone get hurt? Is anyone dead?' he asked. This was his main concern. He wanted to close the restaurant, not kill innocent people.

'No, there were a few injuries but thankfully, it seemed everyone got out in time. Just as well. It was probably some kids setting fire to the dustbins. It happens all the time. But for that stupid idiot who owns the restaurant to leave the gas on... well, if you ask me, he asked for it. Let's be honest, they could have all died in their sleep from the gas. The newspaper shop next door has a great big hole in it. They are out of business for a while and the street is just full of bricks and rubble. The police are hanging around because the bloody kids are stealing everything they can get their hands on, especially from the shop. However, it's all smoke-damaged and they should have insurance. It's going to take ages to clean it up. People have been moved from their houses for safety until the building is secured,' said Terry.

'Sounds bad, but at least no one was killed.' Ralph's conscience was salved. No deaths, only injuries. And nothing that couldn't be repaired.

A few days later, even he was surprised to see that everything seemed to have returned to normal. The only difference was the big gap in between shops, where the restaurant had once stood. The other shops were open and so was the restaurant across the road. Slowing down and looking out of his car window as he approached the restaurant, he saw the owner putting his menu in the window. Business as usual. Once they had both spotted each other, they acknowledged each other with a nod and Ralph drove on.

10

Julie was standing in the queue at the bus stop with the icy wind battering against her. She wrapped Gertie's old, tatty coat around her to keep warm. It was baggy, it was second-hand, and to make matters worse it smelt of fish.

She had managed to get a job in a local fish-packing factory. At least there were plenty of jobs to be had. Liverpool was full of factories and all of them were hiring. You could leave a job on Friday and start a new one on Monday.

It was leaving time for all the workers and so the buses were packed to the hilt. After struggling to find a seat, Julie sat next to a well-dressed young woman. Still smelling of fish from the factory and wearing her overall and wellingtons, Julie felt slightly embarrassed. Ignoring the woman beside her, Julie looked directly ahead of her and lit a cigarette. She could feel the woman staring at her and it was beginning to make her blood boil. Then suddenly the woman spoke.

'Hey, it's Julie, isn't it? I remember you from school. You were in the year below me. How are you doing?'

It was the first friendly welcome Julie had heard in a long time. It seemed warm and genuine. It took Julie off guard.

She inhaled on her cigarette and then stammered, 'I'm sorry, I don't remember you. Refresh me.'

'I'm Donna. Don't you remember me? Well, no matter. I remember you. You live on the old estate, don't you?'

'Yes.' Julie took in the woman as she chatted on as though they had been friends for years. The young woman was made up to the nines. Her makeup was perfect and her clothes looked new. Her tight-fitting, bell-bottomed trousers looked great with her pink poncho and matching bandana in her hair. Looking down at herself, Julie felt jealous.

Donna's appearance made Julie feel embarrassed about her clothes, which were all from a local second-hand shop and were worn and mismatched.

Julie had been doing odd jobs – cleaning offices and working days in the fish-packing factory when they needed a spare pair of hands. Now they had offered her a full-time job and Julie had taken it so that she could save enough money for a deposit for a place for her and Frankie.

Now Frankie was feeling a whole lot better, she would be able to get a job, too. That would make things easier. Two wage packets were better than one.

'So, what are you doing with yourself? Are you working?' Again, Julie looked at Donna. Of course she was working. Her clothes were all up-to-date and new. She looked and smelt amazing.

'I work for a model agency. I do some modelling.'

'Modelling? I didn't know there were model agencies around here.'

'Yes, there are if you know the right people. The money is good and the hours are to suit yourself.'

Julie felt that underneath all that makeup, Donna was blushing. However, she had captured Julie's interest and she wanted to know more.

'Well, you obviously know the right people. You look amazing. What is this model agency called, then? I don't suppose they are hiring. Yeah, I know I look like shit now, but I scrub up okay.' Julie laughed. She was intrigued and excited, and wanted to know more. This sounded more like it. Modelling! 'Oh, God, do they need one of those expensive portfolios?' Julie's heart sank. That kind of thing was going to cost a lot of money. Money she didn't have.

'No, you don't need anything like that. You just go and see Carrie. She owns the place and it's up to her if she hires you or not. It's not always modelling in front of a camera, like you see on the television.'

Modelling? Yeah, right. Since when did anyone do modelling without a camera? Julie felt suspicious as Donna skirted around the details of her modelling job, but she was definitely interested.

'You could come with me now, if you want to. It doesn't matter that you're still in your work clothes. That won't bother Carrie. She's a really nice woman. It doesn't matter what you look like, Julie. Isn't that what they invented makeup and perfume for?' Donna's laugh was infectious. 'I'm on my way there, now. But there are certain aspects of the job that might not suit you.' Donna gave a weak smile, then turned and looked out of the window.

Shifting closer in her seat towards Donna and linking her arm, Julie grinned. 'Now that sounds like a great idea. I'm sure we can iron out anything I am not sure about when I meet... er... what did you say her name was again?'

'Carrie. Carrie Smeltzer. She looks after us all. She's great fun, you'll like her.' They continued to chat like old friends about nothing in particular. Even though Julie had her own ideas about the modelling job and the woman who hired people, she kept them to herself for the time being.

At long last it was their turn to get off the bus. Julie followed Donna as she walked down the high street in the better part of town. She was looking for an office building and was slightly surprised when Donna stopped at a house. Three stone steps led up to the front door. Walking into the long hallway, Julie thought that at some point this house had been turned into flats. Maybe the office was one of the flats. Slightly puzzled, she carried on following Donna's lead and they entered the kitchen.

Six scantily clad women were sitting at the table in dressing gowns and curlers. A few were eating and the others had finished their food and were lighting up their cigarettes and drinking tea. All the teacups matched the saucers. At the head of the table, Julie saw a blonde woman with a large teapot, pouring the tea. She was obviously in charge and this was obviously Carrie.

'Carrie. This is Julie, an old friend of mine.' Donna blushed slightly. 'We used to be at the same school. She's looking for a modelling job.' She sat down and helped herself to a cup of tea, leaving Julie standing alone.

'Phew, lady! What trawler did you just get off?' One of the other girls made a point of holding her nose and spraying perfume in the air. Julie was just about to say something when she was interrupted.

'Julie, you say. That is a lovely name,' said Carrie. 'Move up, ladies, give Julie a seat, she must be tired. You look as though you have had a long day, love. Cup of tea?'

Julie sat down and looked around the kitchen, then back at the woman pouring her a cup of tea from a floral teapot. Carrie was a middle-aged Amazonian, immaculately dressed in a bright red suit with leopard-print lapels. Her huge cleavage threatened to burst from the jacket. Her platinum blonde hair was piled high in a beehive and backcombed into perfection. She sat at the head of the table, holding a long, gold-coloured cigarette holder, making her look almost classy. Her bright red lips beamed a warm, genuine smile at Julie. 'Help yourself to milk and sugar.' Carrie looked at the others at the table. 'Ladies, don't you have other things to be doing?' As the others started to move, she turned her attention back to Julie. 'Now, tell me about yourself,' she said.

Julie felt quite nervous. She stirred her tea more than was necessary while she waited until the others had left them alone.

'It seems you already have a job,' Carrie prompted. 'So why do you need another one? Is it the glamour of modelling that draws you, darling?'

This was now the time to be honest. Julie was no fool and although she felt Carrie was pussyfooting around, it was time to lay her cards on the table. This was no model agency. It was a knocking shop, and Carrie was the madam.

'Carrie, right? Well, I think I have seen all that I need to. We both know what this place is. Stop with the airs and graces; believe me, there is nothing I haven't seen and done. I'm just at a crossroads right now. I need more money than I can earn at a factory and I have a younger sister to look after. She's sixteen, but she's been ill lately.'

Carrie exhaled a cloud of cigarette smoke, then picked up her teacup and took a sip. 'Well, that's quite a résumé, young lady. And yes, this is a brothel. We sell sex. You work and I take a commission. You can leave whenever you wish. I don't allow politics or religious arguments and I won't have squabbling among the girls. Any shit and you're out.' Carrie's warm, friendly smile had now disappeared and the businesswoman took her place. 'The only men that stay here are paying guests. I don't allow boyfriends or pimps to hang around the place.' Carrie had quickly realised that Julie was no fool and there was no point in making this work sound glamorous. It was what it was and however you dressed it up it came down to the same thing.

Now the facts were laid bare and both women understood each other. Julie liked Carrie. She was candid. 'Do all those other women live here?' she asked.

'A couple of them do. Donna doesn't, she still lives at home and makes up all kinds of excuses to her family about where she works. That's not my business. Why?'

'I need somewhere to live... and possibly bring my sister with me. We're staying at an old aunt's house but there isn't a lot of room there. I'm trying to save for my own place, but it's taking time.'

'How old is your sister?'

'Sixteen. Why?'

Narrowing her eyes and looking at Julie from across the table, Carrie blew the smoke from her cigarette into the air. 'If your sister needs a job, Julie, there is work to be had.'

Julie opened her mouth to protest, and Carrie put her hand up to stop her.

'Only working girls live here. It's not a hotel.' Carrie stubbed out the remnants of her cigarette. 'You could make a lot of money here. A girl like you... you know the way of the world, I can see that. There are no special shifts. Work when you want. That is, unless we have a party night and I need all my girls working. Call it a trial. What do you say, love?'

'I don't have any decent clothes. Not like the others. Basically, I have what I'm standing in.'

'That's not a problem. I can advance you some cash and we

can all look through our wardrobes. What size shoe do you take?' Now that Carrie had drawn her in, her smile reappeared.

'Size six. If I take an advance, I have to pay it back. If you have any cast-offs, I would be happy to take them. After all, I'm not going to be wearing a lot of clothing.'

'That is where you are wrong, Julie. The men like you to mingle and pour drinks. That helps them make their choice. So you wear your stockings and suspenders right up to your ass and you wiggle those French knickers in their face. The naked body is nice, but it looks a whole lot better with something slinky and sexy on it.' Carrie gave her a knowing smile and winked.

Julie held out her hand and smiled. She had a good feeling about this place. And, although it was a brothel and the name of the game was prostitution, it was her choice and this was the first act of kindness she had known in a long time. 'Let's shake on it and have another one of those cups of tea to seal the deal.'

'You got it, girl, but I can do better than that. Let's have a drop of gin.' The handshake was solid. They could each see something in the other that they felt signalled this was the start of a great friendship.

Looking up at the clock on the wall, Julie finished her drink and stood up. 'I'll come back tomorrow night, if that's okay,' she said to Carrie.

'You come back whenever you're ready.' Carrie took her hand and patted it. 'No pressure, and I'll sort out some clothes for you. I'm not going anywhere.'

The long bus ride home gave Julie thinking time. For the first time in a long while, she felt happy and excited. She felt in control again. Okay, it wasn't the career she had always dreamt of. However, men had been using and screwing her for most of her life. She might as well make the most of it. What difference did it make? Boyfriends would buy you a bag of chips and a few drinks in the hope that at the end of the night they would get something for their efforts. This was just cutting out the middleman. It was a transaction. Each of them wanted something. Sex for money. No sweet-talking and no bullshit.

More money meant she would be able to find somewhere to live for her and Frankie and get her away from that old estate where the young guys thought they were gangsters, in their cheap clothing, sniffing around any new, young woman on the block. Her beautiful little Frankie was better than that. Julie wanted more for her sister, just like their mother wanted more for Julie. And this was an opportunity to earn some real money and get herself back on her feet.

At the thought of her mother, tears welled up and she brushed them away, turning to look out of the bus window.

The more Julie thought about Carrie and the other girls, the more she liked the idea of working for herself. She knew she had to pay commission, but there was no tax involved. It all helped towards Julie's dream: a place of their own.

Julie returned to Carrie's house the next night, as arranged. Carrie had kept her promise and found a whole array of different negligées, suspender belts and shoes.

Things were a little awkward the first night. The other girls seemed to think they were superior, but once they had been bitten by Julie's quick remarks, they soon realised they were no match for her. She was as hard as nails and fell into the routine like she had belonged there all her life.

* * *

Over the next few weeks, Julie and Carrie became the dream team. Carrie doted on Julie and her mad schemes and they were like two peas in a pod. There was jealousy and bitchiness between some of the other girls, but they all gritted their teeth and smiled once the red light went on in the window, indicating they were open for business.

During their usual morning coffee and toast, Julie and Carrie sorted out the rota. 'Your sales are going down a little, Julie; you're no longer the "new girl". I think we need to give you a new look. This afternoon, darling, you go blonde! It's all arranged and I have bought the products. A little bit of peroxide mixture in a bowl and an old toothbrush to touch up the roots and you will look a new woman.'

'It seems a bit drastic. I know you've been going on about it for a while but I'm not sure.' Frowning, Julie stood at the side of Carrie and looked in the dressing table mirror, running her hands through her own light brown hair. It was shoulder length and parted in the middle. She thought it made her look younger. 'Do you think it would suit me?'

'Why not, darling? Do you think I was born this colour?' Letting out a loud laugh, Carrie reached for her perfume and sprayed it around her. 'Go and do what you have to do but this afternoon, that dowdy, mousey hair of yours is gone.'

* * *

The powdered peroxide mixture stank to high heaven and made Julie's eyes water. 'God, is it supposed to be that strong? I'm nearly choking.'

'Don't worry, Jules, I know what I'm doing. I've been doing it for years. Here, put this towel around your shoulders then light a couple of fags.'

Donna and Rachel sat at the kitchen table with a gin and

tonic each. It was all good fun to them. 'Come on,' Donna said, 'if your hair falls out there are plenty of wigs upstairs!' Some of the other girls wandered in, poured a drink, lit a cigarette and looked on, while touching up their makeup.

'Yeah. If it looks okay, we'll all have our hair done blonde,' said Rachel. 'We could be famous. The blonde brothel!' Again, they started to laugh.

'Shut the fuck up, you two. It's not a sideshow.'

'No, Julie, love. We wouldn't miss this for anything.'

All the girls liked Julie, although there was a little resentment about the way she had pushed her way in and made her presence known, even stealing some of their best customers. But that was the name of the game. The regulars always wanted to try out the new girl; whether she kept them or not was up to her. It just happened that Julie did keep them, no matter what. If they gave a blow job, Julie would put jam on it!

Clapping her hands together, as was her habit, like some head teacher, Carrie ushered them out of the room. 'Come on, girls, time to get ready for this evening. You will see it all soon enough. Now, let me get on. Go on, scoot!'

'Come on, Donna, show's over,' said Rachel. She turned to Julie and added, 'See you soon, Blondie.'

It seemed like an age, waiting for the bleach to lighten her hair. Her scalp felt itchy and stung somewhat, but she had started so she had to finish.

Soon she was leaning over the sink while Carrie poured jug after jug of water over her hair to rinse it. 'You're drowning me!' she complained. 'I can hardly breathe!'

'Right, that's enough. Come on, sit here and let me towel it dry.'

'Let me see it first. I want to see it.'

'No, let me dry it first and give it a comb through. You'll see it soon enough.'

The girls crowded into the kitchen and stood waiting. Sitting in the dining chair, trying to dry her wet face, Julie could see nothing. She looked up at their faces, waiting for some reaction, but none came.

'Not a word, ladies, or you will be banished from the room.' Carrie's stern voice filled the kitchen.

Carrie smiled, very pleased with herself. 'Okay, I think that's enough; you can style it as you like. Here you go, honey. Go into the lounge and look in the big mirror over the mantelpiece.'

Julie went, and stood in front of the mantelpiece and looked up at the mirror. Facing her was a very different woman. She was blonde. Her scalp was still a little pink from all the bleach, but she was a beautiful peroxide blonde. It looked great. Turning from side to side to see her blonde, damp hair from all angles, she smiled. This was another woman entirely. A completely new Julie. A fresh start for a new woman.

'HOORAY!!' All the girls clapped their hands and smiled when she went back into the kitchen.

'You look great, Julie. You were meant to be blonde,' said Donna.

'Oh my God,' Rachel shouted, 'it's brilliant. Well done, Carrie.'

Carrie accepted their praises graciously, then turned to Julie. 'Well, darling. What do you think?'

Running her fingers through her newly blonde hair, Julie had to admit it suited her. Gone was the brown-haired Julie with the shit past. This woman was going forward. Tonight, she would knock their socks off. Julie turned to looked at Carrie. 'You've done a great job. Thanks, love.'

'You're welcome. Now, go and get changed, ladies, it's nearly time for business. Off you go, everyone!'

That evening was a great success. Julie's hair seemed to give her more confidence than usual. She flirted and sat beside the men in her black bra, panties, stockings and suspenders, rubbing their legs and lounging around while they drank and eyed her up. More punters meant more money. The men were making their choice for the evening and their choice was Julie.

11

'Fancy a drink? I've got a proposition for you. All cash in hand, the way you like it.'

'If you're buying, then I'm drinking. Why do I feel like I am going to need a large whisky? What have you got up that grotty sleeve of yours, Paddy?'

After getting served at the bar, Paddy led the way to a corner booth. Even though it was early evening, the pub was packed to the hilt. If there was one thing Paddy liked, it was a good old gossip and plenty of drinks to moisten his throat.

The booth stank of tobacco, the tin ashtray in the middle of the wooden table was overflowing and the wooden benches they sat on had seen better days. No one seemed to care about the surroundings. It was somewhere to go and have a drink away from work, the wives, and the trouble brewing in Ireland. There always seemed to be someone disputing what was going on these days. Always someone standing on a street corner surrounded by a crowd while they mouthed off about their rights, which usually ended up in a fight because someone disagreed with them. What was the world coming to?

Ralph waited while Paddy licked along the cigarette paper, making it stick to hold the tobacco in.

'Those things are disgusting and they make your teeth yellow. And they stink to high heaven. Buy some proper cigarettes, man.'

'Bloody hell, you're full of airs and graces these days. I am in my good trousers having a few drinks with my mate and you look like you're bored of me already.'

'You're only here because whatever it is you need, you can't do it alone.'

Paddy lit his roll-up and leant forward, almost touching Ralph's face, and spoke in a low whisper. 'Do you remember when I told you about the gun amnesty after the war? Wait! Wait!' He held his hands up. 'Let me finish, Ralph boy, then you can interrupt.' He took a drag on his roll-up. It had burnt almost down to his yellow nicotine-stained fingers, and the ash had fallen onto the table and his coat. 'Where do all the guns and weapons go? Once collected, what do you think happens to them?'

Ralph sat back on the bench seat, frowning and stroking his chin. Now Paddy had captured his interest. It was not something he had ever thought about before and it seemed everyone had something stuffed under their mattress. 'Well, I suppose they are crushed or something – destroyed. The last thing they want is for them to get into the wrong hands, otherwise it's been a waste of time. Like that one you have in your coat pocket.'

A huge smile appeared on Paddy's face. 'That is what everyone thinks, mate.' He tapped his nose to press his point, then gulped his whisky back and set the empty glass on the table.

'Okay, you have my interest,' Ralph said. 'Spill the beans, you know you're dying to.'

After looking around to see if anyone was listening, Paddy

filled Ralph in. 'I know for a fact that some of the police that collect them sell them on. Who is to know how many there are?'

'How the hell do you know that?' Astounded, Ralph's jaw dropped.

'Because I keep my ear to the ground.'

'Fair point. But the police selling weapons. Strong accusation, Paddy, and one that could put you behind bars or get you a good kicking with that big mouth of yours.'

'No, even I am not that stupid, but I wouldn't mind a piece of the action. There's mega money to be had. What with that, and every business in town paying us a protection fee, we could be millionaires. I have always fancied myself on a yacht somewhere in the sun.'

'No, you just fancy yourself. Why anyone else does is beyond me, but there you have it. There is nothing so fickle as women.'

'It's my charm. The girls like a good time and a laugh, not some serious misery guts like you, always overthinking things. Why have a glass that is half-empty when it could be half-full? You have become boring since you got married. Always trying to do the right thing for your family. Have some fun, Ralph boy. Be reckless. You know you want to.' Paddy gave him a sly wink. 'Anyway, talking of booze, I've met a bloke from Liverpool. He delivers barrels of beer to the pubs there and a few always slip off the back of his lorry. I thought we could go there and get some. We could sell them here. It would keep your publicans happy. Now and again all the profits would go into their own pockets and not the breweries'. That means their gratitude will make them pay more. We'll make a packet. To good old Liverpool, land of the Beatles.'

'Liverpool?' Ralph was astonished by Paddy's carefree manner. 'Do you know how far away that is from here? Just for a few barrels of beer. For God's sake, it wouldn't cover the petrol.'

'Yes, it would. And I do know where it is, I've seen the map.

We can go on the ferry, and pick up more than a few barrels That is, when we get some cash from the next job I'm just warming up to.'

'Surely you can pick cheap booze up from anywhere. Why Liverpool? And why do you need me?' Ralph still couldn't comprehend why they had to venture so far. It seemed ridiculous.

'Because, Ralph, my old mate. Firstly, you don't shit on your own doorstep. So take a few days off, tell that boss of yours a long lost aunty has died or something. Secondly, we're partners. I hate to say it, but I trust you. You have never tried cheating me out of anything yet. I have lots of mates but I wouldn't turn my fucking back on them. But you have always stood in my corner and watched my back.' Paddy turned back to Ralph. 'Thirdly, there could be trouble. I have a fair idea about the contacts, but I'm not a hundred per cent sure. It's a good idea, though.'

'No, it's not a good idea. You're half-pissed and rambling on about sailing on yachts and the easy money-making scheme. It's bollocks, Paddy. You're all wind and piss. Now, I am going home.'

'Wait! Just a bit longer. Sorry, I will carry on, five more minutes, eh?' Paddy grabbed on to Ralph's arm. 'Listen to me. Some friends of mine were a bit pissed the other night and boasting about their good fortune. Their loose tongues are our good fortune. What do you say?'

'I would need to know more. By "friends", I presume you mean those trouble-causers from your political meetings?'

'Yeah, yeah, I know. They would welcome you into their party; they know you're a real handy guy to have around. They have heard a lot about you. But I have told them you're not into politics. You're a simple man.' The grin and the laughter annoyed Ralph. He had to agree, Paddy's idea seemed a good one. But if it sounded too good to be true, then it usually was. If it was that easy, why hadn't anyone else done this gun-running?

'Find out more. I don't like half of a story. You don't just walk into the police station with a shopping bag and walk out with guns. Dig deeper. This could be a trap. Maybe your friends are testing your loyalty, have you ever thought about that?'

'Mm, you have a point there. I never thought about that.' He nodded. 'I will look into it further, but if it's good, are you in?'

Ralph didn't like the idea but he nodded along with Paddy if only to get him to be quiet.

'I knew I could count on you! Anyway, back to today's business. The taxi wars.' Paddy leant further across the table to get closer. 'As you know, there is another firm in town. Newer cabs, cheaper prices and they even have those flash radios in. That's what is putting the other taxi rank out of business. The taxi owner is desperate to get rid of this new lot. He is losing money hand over fist and is prepared to pay good money to get his business back.'

'How much?'

'Good money, couple of hundred. He can soon earn that back once his taxis are back on the road and in full charge again. If he carries on like this, he will be skint in no time. I think we should go and give this other taxi boss a good hiding and a good talking to. I have my faithful friend in my pocket. That will scare him to death, if I threaten to put a bullet in his brain.'

'You still carrying that gun? Wake up, Paddy, if you're found with it on you, you're going down for a very long time, especially with your record.'

Tapping the breast of his coat, he laughed. 'Believe me, this is the best way to threaten someone without getting your knuckles grazed.'

'Yes, unless you're too pissed to put the safety catch on and it blows your bollocks off. How big is the other cab firm? How many cabs exactly?'

Paddy's eyes widened and the grin disappeared from his face. He was following Ralph's train of thought and he didn't like it. Shaking his head until it almost fell off, he paled. 'No, Ralph. No more of your explosive shit. A good kicking and a few threats is what it will take. They know your reputation; it will be money for old rope.'

'Oh, shut up, you coward. Explosives are like women. Treat them lovingly, with respect, and they will do whatever you want. And it's a clean finish. All sorted in one, no arguments.'

Ralph put his glass down and stood up, then put his arm around Paddy's shoulders. They had both had enough to drink. 'Come on, let's walk and talk.'

Once outside the warmth of the pub, the cold wind hit them and made them feel even more light-headed. 'The walk will do us good, sober us up a little. You go and get your taxi owner's money up front, no messing. Also, bring your ma's stew pan to that bedsit of yours. I say stew pan, it's more like an enamel washing-up bowl. How many of you are there in your family?' Ralph slurred slightly, but he was trying to clear his head. This was business.

'There's loads of us, we're good Catholics. But you know my ma uses it for both washing and cooking. Why do you need her stew pan?'

'I can't keep using the stock from the quarry; they'll get suspicious. We need to make our own.'

They were walking along with their arms around each other's shoulders to stop them from swaying, and Paddy stopped short. 'What the fuck? What do you mean, make our own... are you crazy? Make our own bombs? Properly made ones, maybe, but you mixing shit up in my ma's stew pan... bollocks to that, Ralph.'

'Shut up, people will hear you,' Ralph slurred. 'Believe me, it will work. You said you trusted me. Anyway, if I didn't know what I was doing I wouldn't suggest it, would I?'

The mention of explosives seemed to sober Paddy up. 'I don't know. It's a hell of a chance. What if it doesn't work? You're nuts, sometimes. All that quiet and calm exterior and inside you're the very devil himself.'

'Get the money, Paddy. Oh, and steal an old Transit van while you're on. We'll sort it out tomorrow. Stealing and threatening, that's your department.'

'Thanks for that – is that what's going to be on my headstone? "Here's to Paddy, the man with the nicked van and a stew pan".' They had both had far too much to drink and let their hair down. Their laughter was infectious.

'I'm going to the chip shop on my way home, I promised Irene.'

'You cheap bastard! Now, go. Go to the chippy and impress that wife of yours. If you're lucky she might drop her knickers.'

They both started singing loudly until someone shouted from their bedroom window, 'Hey, you two, shut up. My kids are asleep!'

'You don't know good singing when you hear it,' shouted Paddy, full of Dutch courage.

'Maybe not, Paddy lad. But you will know a smack on the nose when I see you tomorrow. I know who you are. Let's see if you're brave when you're sober!' the woman shouted.

Paddy turned back to the window and cringed. 'Her husband's a big bastard. See you tomorrow.'

12

'I've had an idea; look at this.' Excited, Julie waved the newspaper under Carrie's nose.

'Sofa for sale? We don't need a sofa.' Carrie brushed it away.

'No, underneath that bit. Look at the personal columns.' Julie pressed her point further.

'Wife swappers? So what of it, darling? People have been doing it for years. Something to spice up their marriages without cheating on their spouses.' Sitting before the huge mirror in her black satin dressing gown, her long cigarette holder in her hand, Carrie exhaled smoke as Alice worked her magic with her platinum blonde hair. As always, her signature look was an elaborate beehive, backcombed, teased and lacquered to perfection. There was so much hairspray on it, it never moved.

'They are all PO box numbers. You have to write to them.'

'Julie, love, in case you hadn't noticed, to be a wife swapper you have to have a partner to swap. Do you have a partner?' Carrie laughed, brushing her away.

'No, but this has given me an idea. For God's sake, think about it. They are giving sex away free. They need somewhere to go and have a party. And I know the perfect place.' Beaming and taking a bow, Julie waited, extremely pleased with herself.

'They wouldn't come here, darling. Firstly, as you say, it's free sex; they do it for free. Secondly, they have these parties at each other's houses. I don't know, maybe they take turns or something. Come on, Jules. What is going on in that head of yours?' Bored with the conversation, Carrie turned back to look in the mirror while Alice sprayed a kiss curl in place alongside each ear.

'I'm going to write to them. Offer them a safe haven – at a price, of course – where they can be themselves. No strangers in their home eyeing up the silver. They want some porno fun? Well, they can have it. And everyone knows, in our profession, we're like priests. Everything that goes on here stays here.'

'You are wasting your time, Jules, love. They make their own arrangements. They would be offended if they were invited to a brothel; they don't see it that way.'

'It's got to be worth a try. We have to offer something different. There are loads of brothels around here and near the docks. We have to be unique!'

Reaching through the cloud of hairspray, Carrie took Julie's hand and patted it. 'Okay, give it a go. Just don't be too disappointed. There are some stamps in my bag. Pass it here, will you, love.'

Alice was now putting enormous, round, gold-coloured clip earrings on Carrie's ears. She wore lots of bulky gold necklaces and rings, none of them real. Julie looked at Carrie properly for the first time in the couple of years.

Time had gone so fast. Frankie was working now and seemed happy enough, but Julie wanted more. When she looked around the brothel, she imagined herself owning it so she would never have to turn another trick. She would be the one collecting money at the door and make a damn good job of it. *One day*, Julie thought to herself, *I will be draped in gold, and all of it will be real!*

'Why I am writing letters to improve your brothel is beyond me! But if you want, I'll leave – and take my bloody customers with me!'

'Whoa! Hold on there. Keep that temper of yours under control.' Carrie stood up and put her arms around Julie, who was now standing like a stone statue, hands on hips, an indignant look on her face. 'No more of this nonsense, eh?' Carrie's soothing, motherly voice filled Julie's ears and she relaxed a little. She couldn't remember the last time anyone had held her without any hidden motives. 'Anyway, go and write your letters and I'll see you soon. Oh, before you go, Raymond is coming tonight. Make sure the French maid outfit is laid out on the bed for him. He likes to wear it when he comes here – and don't forget his feather duster!'

Julie burst out laughing. 'Bloody hell, I won't. God only knows what he does with that. How on earth did you get a black French maid's outfit for a twenty stone, sixty-year-old man?'

'I know a good seamstress, darling.' Carrie's drawl had been perfected over the years. Everyone was 'daarrling'.

'You must know a bloody good wigmaker, too. He's as bald as a coot under that mop. It's bloody scary when he's on top of me puffing and panting away and his wig keeps slipping. He thinks I'm having an orgasm and I'm trying to hold in the laughter. But yes, Madam Carrie.' Julie curtsied. 'I will make sure everything is in place.' She burst out laughing.

Hearing a noise in the back yard, Carrie turned to leave. 'That must be my delivery. We'll speak later.'

* * *

Four men were wheeling barrels of beer and Guinness into the yard. 'I told you, Ralph. This is a real money-spinner, isn't it? We'll load our van up later and leave.'

Ralph had gone with Paddy to Liverpool; it was a change of scenery but it was raining.

'What is this place? Why are we leaving barrels in someone's back yard?'

'Oh, it's just some old knocking shop. They buy the booze that's nearly past its sell-by date. It saves throwing it down the drain, but I bet it gives the customers the shits!' He laughed.

Stopping in his wake, Ralph looked up and saw a young beautiful blonde woman standing there with her hands on her hips.

'What the fuck are you looking at? If you want to look, go around the front and pay like everyone else.'

Ralph smiled. He instantly liked the woman; she had spirit and she was beautiful. 'Morning, miss!'

'I'm not a fucking schoolteacher. Are you Scottish?' Sticking out her chin, she pouted, her hands still firmly on her hips for a fight.

As the man stood up from the barrel he was rolling, she could see him more clearly. He was handsome and muscly. A lock of his black, wavy hair had fallen down his face.

'Irish, miss,' said Ralph respectfully. 'And no, you're not like any schoolteacher I ever met.' He smiled.

'Oh well, it all sounds the same to me.' Swiftly turning in one of Carrie's old satin dressing gowns, she left, but not before giving him a full view of her naked legs. She looked over her shoulder for one last look at this handsome stranger. He was nice and respectful, unlike the others who looked down their noses at her.

* * *

'Bloody hell, Donna, why don't any of our customers ever look like him? Does he come on a regular basis? I've never seen him before.'

Laughing like a schoolgirl, Donna was surprised that Julie had even noticed the man delivering the beer; she never usually noticed anyone without their wallet in their hand. 'Ooh, has someone taken your fancy? I haven't seen him before either. Go on, make him spend some of his money – that will satisfy your curiosity.' The laughter stopped when Carrie walked through carrying her purse.

'Eyeing up the workforce, Julie? Well, let's hope he keeps his wallet close to his chest. We all know how light-fingered you can be. He'd better count those barrels first.'

Scolded and leaving the room like a spoilt teenager, Julie stood on the landing and looked around the house. It looked more like some old folks' home than a place to have sex. It needed more glamour. All the other brothels had the usual red lamp in the window showing they were open for business, but this place looked seedy.

Brothels like this were all over Liverpool, especially on the docksides and in the town. The bedrooms looked like somebody's guest room. The loft had been converted into another bedroom and was more self-contained. It was nice, but it was a hell of a walk when the other rooms were occupied.

Julie had mentally decided long ago that this was a lucrative profession and so where Carrie stashed all the money she earnt was a quandary. God alone knew, she certainly didn't spend it on the house.

* * *

'Come on, it's time to get our stash. Fuck me, is that all it took to make you blush, some old tart in a dressing gown?' Paddy laughed as Ralph blushed.

'She had a small black rose tattooed on her thigh; did you see it?'

'Nope, I was too busy looking at that cleavage. She was a right uppity cow. Miserable bitch.'

Loading the empty barrels on the truck, Ralph looked up at the windows, hoping for another glimpse of the blonde with her black rose tattoo.

'She had fighting spirit – I like that. And there has to be a story behind why she's here. No one picks that kind of work if they don't have to.'

'She's another old tart; here, if you want to screw her, I'll give you a couple of quid. Anything to get your mind back on the job in hand.' Paddy laughed and reached for his wallet.

'No thanks. We have stuff to do. I don't want her to think of me like all the other men.' Once they had finished, Ralph took one last look at the windows before they drove away. He had liked what he'd seen instantly. It was a shame they lived so far away from each other.

13

LOVE AND HATE

Although Julie hated smiling and letting smelly, balding men paw at her, she went out of her way to make them feel welcome and comfortable with their strange requests. Some just wanted to be slaves and would walk around serving drinks dressed only in a thong, like some Egyptian eunuch bowing to Cleopatra. She would make a point of barking orders at them and slapping their arses as they walked past. They wanted dominance and humiliation. Well, she bloody well gave it to them. It was a good way to vent her anger.

It also made the other men who sat in the large lounge, drinking and partying while waiting for a spare room, with the girl of their choice sitting on their lap, laugh out loud. 'Go on, Julie, show him who's boss,' they would shout, watching the performance. It added to the mood. It was seedy and sexy. That is what they came for. Everyone let their masks slip and all of their fantasies came rolling out – at a price, of course!

Money! Money was the only thing that meant anything. And Julie had decided to have plenty of it. She would do whatever it took to have security and not living hand-to-mouth any more.

Standing outside of the paint factory, Julie looked impatiently at her watch. She had heard the horn that indicated the shift was over blow nearly half an hour ago. Where was Frankie?

She'd watched as workers had come out, lighting up cigarettes and chatting, but there was still no sign of her sister.

'Have you seen Frankie? Is she still in there?' she shouted out to some girls she knew from the old estate. Their long white overalls and turbans splattered with paint made them easy to recognise.

'She's not been in today. We haven't seen her.'

Puzzled, Julie walked up to them. 'I'm her sister, Julie. I've come to meet her.' Suddenly not wanting to look foolish in front of them, she laughed and slapped her forehead. 'What am I like? Of course, she's not well. Sorry, girls.' Walking away, she decided to make her way back to the bedsit and see if she was there. She would take a bit of shopping with her so there was some fresh bread and milk.

Julie slammed the front door behind her then ran down the long hallway and up the stairs to their bedsit. 'Frankie, you here?'

'Yes, course I am.'

Relief washed over Julie when she heard Frankie's voice.

'Where else would I be? I've had a long day. I'm going to make some chips; do you want some?'

'A long day?' Remembering that Frankie hadn't been to work, she played along with this little scene. 'How was your day at the factory, love?'

'Oh, same old thing. We're out of bread, I'll go and get some. Nothing like a chip butty, eh?'

Holding up the carrier bag, Julie said, 'No need.' She opened it to take out the bread and milk. 'Got you some biscuits and tea, as well.'

'Oh, thanks. What would I do without you?' Frankie kissed

her on the cheek. She was eighteen now and so much had happened in her short life. As much as Julie tried keeping her in line, Frankie seemed to resent it. 'Right, the chip pan is hot. I'll just peel another couple of potatoes and we're ready to go. Will you butter the bread, please?'

Feeling her temper rise, Julie opened the loaf, took some slices out and started buttering them. She was angry. All of this was bloody lies! Why? Why was Frankie lying to her?

'Julie, do you think you could lend me some money until payday? I'm a bit skint.'

As much as she loved Frankie, she had learnt by now that Frankie never intended paying her back.

'Sure, love, what is it for? How much do you need?'

'Would ten pounds be okay?'

'Ten pounds! Are you bloody crazy? That is an awful lot of money. What do you need that amount of money for?'

'What does it matter? I'm just a bit short, that's all, and there are a few things I need. Come on, you can earn more. All you have to do is turn another trick. What's one more blow job, eh?'

The words stung Julie's heart. Is that what her sister thought of her? *Good old Julie, one more blow job and I can borrow more money that I never have to pay back.*

'Do some overtime, Frankie. Or turn up for the job you have. I work all the time so you can scrounge off me. Maybe it's time you learnt to do the same and then you wouldn't be skint all of the time.' The urge to slap her sister hard across the face was growing and she had to concentrate on buttering that damned bread!

'Have you been spying on me?'

'Do I need to, Fran?'

Frankie almost threw the plates of chips on the drop-leaf table, then pulled herself up to her full height; she was taller than Julie, now, with long legs and a slim waist. She turned quickly, her long dark hair flying out as she did so, and glared at Julie. 'How dare you spy on me! Don't you think I'm entitled to a little fun now and again?'

'I just discovered you hadn't been to work when I went to meet you. I wondered if you were ill.' Julie was trying hard to keep her composure, but inwardly she was fuming.

'So what of it? What does it have to do with you?' Frankie stood with her hands on her hips, indignant.

Julie sat down, shocked and surprised at Frankie's outburst. What had brought this on? Why was Frankie turning on her like this? All she had ever done was look after her. Looking into Frankie's eyes, it felt like the first time she'd looked at her properly in the last couple of months. Frankie had become stubborn and selfish.

'Don't be nasty, Frankie; I'm just looking after you. That's what I do.' Julie had hit rock bottom and she knew it. She had used sex as a bartering tactic in the past but now she was just another prostitute and she hated it. But it was a wage and she kidded herself it was only until they got some savings together, although between keeping Frankie and paying the rent, there never seemed to be anything left.

'If that's the case, why are you moaning about a few quid?' Frankie pouted sulkily. She always got her own way with Julie, and she knew Julie would hand over the money she needed. She was bored with going through this charade time and again when the end was always the same: Julie would open her purse and give her whatever she wanted.

'I'm sorry I haven't been around much lately. I suppose you miss Mum. We could go and see her if you like? I know she said not to, but we can if it will make you happy. It's not a problem.'

'I do miss Mum! And it's your fault she's in prison,' Frankie shouted, while pointing an accusing finger. Frankie's face was flushed with anger. It seemed like everything she had bottled up was now pouring out in a torrent of venom. 'You told Mum what I said about Dad, didn't you? You made her angry, that's why she killed him!'

Frankie was shouting so loudly the neighbours in the bedsit upstairs started banging on the floor and shouting for them to shut up. They had turned up their television to drown out Frankie's hysterical screaming.

'Calm down, the neighbours can hear you. No, I didn't tell Mum anything, I swear. Maybe she heard or saw something, I don't know.'

'Like I give a fuck about the neighbours. Who cares about the people in this shithole? And what was there to see or hear? Absolutely fucking nothing. I lied, Julie! Don't you get it? I lied! Dad never did anything like that to me. He was too pissed to do anything. I thought you would just take me on holiday with you, but no, you had to tell Mum and look what's happened now. This is all your fault. You and your big mouth!'

Julie sat back in the chair. Her head was spinning and she felt sick and dizzy. She couldn't believe how spiteful Frankie was being. It was as though she enjoyed hurting her.

The bile rose in her throat. She couldn't believe what she was hearing. Their mother was in prison, Derek was dead, and all because of a teenage girl lying her head off because she wanted to go on holiday. Without thinking, she stood up and slapped Frankie so hard across the face that she staggered backwards and fell on the floor. Instantly she felt guilty.

'You lied about an innocent man. Okay, I never liked Derek, but he didn't deserve that. Mum is in prison for ten years. Have you no conscience, Frankie?'

Frankie was lying on the floor in floods of tears. She turned around to look at Julie. 'You're just a cheap whore, Julie. Yes, Julie the cheap whore with airs and graces. Do you think I want to tell my friends my sister is nothing but a slut?'

Slapping her again, Julie saw red. 'Derek would have tried touching you up before long. God knows when he was pissed and it was dark he would have poked it anywhere. Everything I've ever done and still do is for you!'

Frankie's face was smarting from the slaps she had received. It felt as though her face was on fire. She wanted to lash out and hit Julie back, but she knew she didn't have to. Tears rolled down her face from anger and pain.

The argument carried on, the sisters screaming and shouting at each other like two hellcats. 'Everything is your fault! Stop trying to control me. I don't need you any more!' Frankie wiped the tears and the snot from her face, then grabbed her coat and ran out of the door before Julie could stop her. She slammed it behind her.

Tears rolled down Julie's face and she buried her head in her hands and sobbed. Yes, it was all her fault. She had acted far too hastily in killing Derek. Her temper had always been her downfall. After wiping her mascara-stained face, she looked around the bedsit in dismay. Frankie was right. It was a shithole. But at least they didn't have to share a bathroom with strangers, like some people she knew. She had been so busy lately she had taken her eye off the ball and neglected Frankie. She picked up her handbag, took out her compact and reapplied her makeup. After putting it back in her bag, she fished out her purse and opened it.

Taking out the ten pounds which had caused this argument, she put it on the table and walked out in despair. It was time to put a brave face on, as always. Why did Frankie hate her so much? Derek would have done something to her sooner or later, she convinced herself. He had said himself he had noticed her tits and she was growing. Why would he have his daughter of sixteen sitting on his drunken knee? She had done the right thing and kept her sister safe. Wasn't that what she was supposed to do?

* * *

Later that evening, back at Carrie's, Julie was still bothered by her argument with Frankie. Business was slow tonight, but there was a sudden flurry of excitement from one client that caught Julie's attention.

'What's that guy going on about a fire, Donna?'

'Apparently while he was driving into town, he saw the fire engines. One of those houses in bedsit city is on fire. Black smoke everywhere, sounds awful.'

'Where? What do you mean?' Panic rose in Julie. She had never told the others where she lived, it was none of their business, and the policy here was your private life was your own.

'Bedsit land. You know where that is.'

'Hey, you. Where was that fire you're talking about?' Julie shouted out. Her mind was working overtime.

'Walker Street. Great big fire from one of the bigger houses. Absolute chaos. The firefighters are going in and rescuing some of the tenants. All the traffic is diverted,' the punter said.

'Carrie, I have to go. I'll be back soon.' Julie grabbed her coat and headed for the door.

'What's wrong?' shouted Carrie. 'Do you want me to come with you? For God's sake, come back in and put some proper clothes on!'

'Oh, shit, yes.' She turned back and pushed her way past everyone, ran up the staircase, entered the small box room which they all used as a changing room, pulled on her trousers and jumper then ran back downstairs.

'Julie, what is it? What is wrong?'

'I'll be back later. Sorry, I have to go. I'll tell you later.'

For once, she was lucky. No sooner had she got to the bus stop than she saw a bus coming. She needed to get to her bedsit. Christ, what if Frankie was in there?

Crowds of people stood watching from afar. The stationary fire engines had their blue lights flashing. Standing there watching the flames, all Julie's fears came true. It *was* her house that was on fire. Firemen were pointing their hoses at the building while they gushed out water. Panic-stricken, she pushed her way past the crowd towards a fireman.

'Stand back, miss, please.' He held her arms to stop her from going any further, but she struggled.

'No, wait! I live here with my sister. Have you got everyone out?'

'We think so, miss. We're just checking the building now. There are some ambulances over there – some of the people we brought out are in the back of them. Now please, stand back.'

She ran over to the ambulances parked around the corner and looked around as best she could, then pushed past people who were sitting inside the ambulances with oxygen masks on. There was no sign of Frankie. Maybe she hadn't come back. Hopefully she had gone to Gertie's house. *Dear God*, she prayed inwardly, *please let her be safe*. Tears of despair rolled down her face and she sat on the pavement watching the blazing mayhem before her.

Whatever worldly goods she had were in that bedsit. They were all gone. Everything was bloody gone. She was sick of forever starting over again!

A couple of hours later the fire was out and only black, smoking embers remained. The building was still intact but everything would either be burnt, smoke damaged or wet through from the firefighters' hoses.

Julie was tired and freezing cold, and still sitting on the pavement. Most of the crowd had seen enough and decided to go home. Lucky them! They had homes to go to.

Ralph and Paddy came out of the pub they were staying at for the night, to see what all the fire engines were doing. People were gathered around as the firemen held their hoses up, spraying water onto the building opposite. 'Let's go and see if anyone needs help, Paddy.'

'Bollocks, it's their town and their burning building. I'll just stay here and watch. You do the heroic thing, Ralph.' Walking across the road, Ralph looked amongst the crowd. Everyone seemed okay. Looking past them, he noticed a woman sitting on the pavement. It looked like the woman he had met earlier at the brothel. Walking up to her, he didn't know what he was going to say, but felt he should say something. 'Are you okay miss? We meet again, eh. It must be fate.' He smiled. He felt like a stupid teenager trying to muster up a conversation. He could have kicked himself, he sounded so stupid.

Forlornly, Julie looked up. 'Who are you?' She was in no mood for small talk from customers.

'I delivered the beer barrels. To your place. Do you remember?' Again, he was hopeful, but there was no sign of recognition in her eyes.

Bored and saddened, Julie looked up again. 'So my house has burnt down and now I have an Irish stalker. Just fuck off, will you? I am not in the mood.'

Ralph couldn't help but laugh, even though the occasion didn't call for it. 'Is "fuck off" the only words you know, miss?'

Julie had to stop herself from smiling. She remembered him

now. She couldn't see him properly what with all the people and the blue lights flashing in the dimness of the street. 'No. I know another one. "Bollocks".'

Ralph took out his wallet and handed her ten pounds. 'Get yourself a taxi. Go to a friend's or something.' She looked as miserable as sin. He didn't know what else to do.

Coming to her senses and out of her misery for a moment, Julie looked at him properly and brushed her tears away. For a brief moment in time their eyes met. 'Why would you do that? Are you hoping for a quickie or something here in the street, you sad bastard?'

Another man stepped forward. 'Not working tonight, Julie? Never expected you to be a street walker, but then nothing surprises me when it comes to you,' he sneered.

Julie looked up and recognized him as a client from the brothel. Standing up, she swung her heavy-ladened handbag at him. He ducked and Ralph took the full force of it as it hit him on the head! 'Fuck off, you creeps. Leave me alone!' Snatching the money out of Ralph's hand, she walked away.

* * *

'Hey, mister! Do they know what started it?' Julie shouted out to one of the firefighters, as they were packing their things away.

'Not sure. There will be an investigation but from what we can tell, it looks like a chip pan fire.'

'Chip pan?' Oh, God, no. Julie's heart sank as realisation dawned on her. Frankie had been making chips earlier. Julie didn't know if she had turned the gas off on the little Belling cooker they had or had forgotten about it.

'You had better find somewhere to stay tonight, miss. You won't be staying here, that's for sure.'

Nodding, Julie stood up. Her legs ached and her bum was numb, she had sat for so long on the pavement. She trudged slowly through the streets to Gertie's flat. It was the early hours of the morning, but she had to check if Frankie was there.

After shouting her name through the letter box, because she knew there was no way that Gertie would open the door at this time of night unless she knew who was there, she waited for the bolts to be withdrawn. At last, the door opened.

'Julie, whatever is the matter?' Pulling her dressing gown around her, Gertie stepped forward and pulled Julie into her flat. She could see that she was shaking, whether from the cold or fear, she wasn't sure.

'Is Frankie here? There's been a fire at the bedsit,' Julie blurted out. 'She isn't there. Well, I don't think so, but they seem to have checked. I needed to know if she's here, Gertie. I need to know if she is safe.'

'No, she isn't here. Sit down, love, and tell me all about it. You look frozen to death. I'll put the kettle on.'

Worn out and not listening, Julie went and sat in the living room. A thought crossed her mind: *'Here lies Gertie, I'll put the kettle on' will be put on her headstone.* It was her answer to everything.

'You will be staying here tonight, won't you? I'll get some spare blankets out. I haven't seen Frances, but I do know that she has a boyfriend. I'm not sure who he is but he doesn't live far from here. I think that's why she's around the estate a lot. It's not to see me, but to meet him.'

'A boyfriend? I didn't know about that.' She was rubbing her hands together to get warm as the fire started to glow. It seemed to Julie there was a lot she did not know about Frankie's secret life. She was tired and yawning. The electric fire Gertie had switched on warmed her bones. She could feel her eyes drooping. She never did drink that tea.

There was still no sign of Frankie when Julie woke, mid-morning.

Stretching and yawning, she looked up at the ceiling and tried to get her bearings. Then she realised she was in the safe haven of Gertie's flat. 'What time is it, Gertie?' Although the curtains were still closed for her benefit, Julie could see daylight peeking through.

'Nearly lunchtime. I left you to sleep. You looked like you needed it. Anyway, I have been down the police station to see if they knew anything about Frances. No, don't interrupt. She needs to know where to find you, and we both know it won't be at some posh office, don't we?'

'Sorry. How long have you known that I work at the brothel in town?'

'Long enough. That's not the point, now. Anyway, there were no serious casualties last night. Just some smoke inhalation. People were taken to hospital for observation and will be out today. Unfortunately, Frances is not amongst them.'

'We argued last night at the bedsit. She was making chips and I'm not sure she turned the pan off. I know I never checked it. I've made all those people homeless. All their stuff, including mine, has gone up in smoke. We're in shit, Gertie. Or rather, I am.'

'Oh, I wouldn't worry about that now,' Gertie said with concern. Even she knew the police would see it as some sort of arson. 'But you had better make yourself scarce. As for Frances, she will turn up eventually looking for you. I doubt she knows yet or else she would have already come. By the way, I like the new look: it suits you. Very glamorous.' Gertie smiled as she admired the new blonde Julie.

Running her hands through her hair again, Julie smiled back.

'Thanks, Gertie. I thought I would have a change. Do you approve?'

'Yes, I do. Very nice, indeed. You look as though you were meant to be blonde. Now, let's get you some breakfast.'

'No, thanks. I'll just go and have a wash. I have things to do.'

'You know best, love. If you need somewhere to stay until you sort yourself out, you know where I am. When Frances turns up, and she will, I will let her know you're very worried about her.' Gertie looked at Julie's posture as she left the room; she seemed to have the weight of the world on her shoulders.

14

THE RECIPE FOR SUCCESS

'Keep stirring, Paddy, and don't even think of lighting that roll-up in your mouth.'

'What the hell is this stuff? It smells like almonds; it's disgusting. And why can't I light my roll-up?'

'Light it and find out. Now, just keep stirring while I clean this stuff away. Although your place is such a shithole, if it was searched they wouldn't find anything anyway. Still, I'll clean everything away and then I know it's done properly.'

'So, what is it?' Paddy stirred the mixture in the bowl. 'It looks disgusting and it stinks to high heaven.'

'Basically, it's a mixture of diesel and fertiliser. The other ingredients I will keep to myself, thank you very much. You're mixing the bomb mixture we're going to use.'

'Holy Jesus! No fucking way. You have me stirring up explosives? Are you fucking crazy?'

'Oh, stop being so dramatic. I know what I'm doing. Stir it into a paste, nice and firm. Believe me, that smell is going to cover our tracks. The simplest things are the deadliest – a bit like your farts!'

'My ma is going to go bonkers when she sees this bowl. Why didn't you just go out and buy a new one?'

'Because we couldn't let anyone know we have bought a new stew pan. That really would cause suspicion. You give your mum the money to buy a new one when we're done, you cheap bastard. Just give her the money and let her get on with it. We don't need to bring suspicion on ourselves. This way is the best. Now, keep stirring.'

Ralph peered over Paddy's shoulder, then reached over and took a small piece of the dough-like mixture from the bowl. Carefully moulding it in his hands, he smiled. It was ready. 'Perfect, Paddy, we'll make a chef out of you yet. Where is the van?'

'Parked in the car lot behind the taxi office.'

'Come on, we have to go. It's the early hours so hopefully the streets will be deserted by now.'

'What about the rest of the mixture? There's quite a bit left.'

'Back-up.'

Paddy cringed as Ralph stuffed the mixture in his pocket. Explosives were out of his league.

When Ralph saw the van, he was impressed. If nothing else, Paddy was a good thief. 'Nice van,' he said, 'where did you get it from?'

'Stole it from that new builders' outside of town. You see, Ralph, I think sometimes. We don't want a local stolen van reported, do we?' He stuck his tongue out.

Nodding, Ralph gave him the thumbs up and got in the van. 'It's a shame, it's a nice van.'

'What do you mean, it's a shame?' Paddy fired the engine.

'Never mind. Park in the middle of the car lot, in between the other taxis, if you can.'

When they got to the taxi firm, Paddy parked in between two of the taxis on the lot. Each space had a number. Each of the taxis had its own car parking space, so the owner could keep track of which ones were being used. 'Keep a look out, Paddy, my old mate, and when I say run, bloody run for your life!'

Whether from the cold or fear, Paddy was shaking, but he nodded. 'Whatever you say.' He could feel his palms sweating as Ralph nonchalantly got out and opened the back of the van. Taking the almond-scented, dough-like mixture out of his pocket, Ralph moulded it into a square then pushed a box of matches into the middle of it and opened the box, showing all the matches within.

'A box of matches and a cake mixture. What the hell is that going to do?' Paddy stared at Ralph, confused.

'Watch and wait. Why do you think you're not allowed to smoke at a flour mill? All that dusty mixture floating in the air can be quite toxic.' He opened the drawer of the matchbox a little further and checked the contents again. Then he lit two matches and waited for them to burn. 'Time for you to go. We're going to need something to get us home. I need to wait a few seconds to make sure this works.'

'Are you sure about this? For fuck's sake, man... oh, never mind.' Paddy could see Ralph was ignoring him and concentrating on the business in hand. 'Whatever you say. I'll meet you around the back.' Not needing to be told twice, Paddy wrapped his coat around himself and fled.

Ralph smiled to himself as he watched Paddy quicken his pace and run around the corner. Then he placed the lit matches in the box and waited for them to spark a reaction and light the others. The spark from the matches would ignite the explosive like a firework. When he was happy with it, Ralph turned and ran away as fast as his legs would carry him. The blast from the van was deafening. The explosion knocked him to the ground. He knew he had waited far too long to make sure the matches ignited each other. He'd also gently rubbed some of the wooden sticks with petrol, which had triggered it all quicker than he'd expected. Well, you learn from experience. Rubbing his head and scrambling to his feet, he looked over at the burning van. He needed to get away before the petrol tank blew and ignited the taxis beside it. This whole place was going to be an inferno.

His head was bleeding, but adrenalin forced him to run even faster. As he tore through the alleyways, he could hear explosion after explosion in the background. Where was Paddy? He was nowhere to be seen, the bastard!

Wiping the sweat from his brow, he was thinking about what he was going to do to Paddy when he caught up with him, when suddenly a car screeched to a halt beside him, nearly hitting him. 'Get the fuck in. Shit, you have gone too far this time,' Paddy shouted at the top of his voice.

Puffing and panting, Ralph got into the stolen car. 'I thought you'd pissed off and left me here,' Ralph gasped.

'Don't be fucking stupid. I had to steal this old banger then find you. There was no way I was going to park up around the corner like a sitting duck. The whole place is going up in smoke.'

Panic and adrenalin filled the car as Paddy put his foot down on the accelerator and sped through the streets.

Ralph lit two cigarettes and handed Paddy one. 'God, I need a smoke.'

Paddy grinned and then suddenly they both burst out laughing. Either the madness of the moment or relief that they had got out of there in one piece seemed to make them laugh louder than usual, almost hysterically. They quickly turned and saw the inferno a couple of streets away, flames almost reaching the sky.

Their breathing had started to return to normal. 'Apart from the odd gossip, there is no real concern for the taxi firm. The cars were all parked in an open parking lot and no one was hurt, apart from me of course.'

'I see you have cut your head. You okay? What is Irene going to say?'

'Yes, I'm fine; I just fell from the blast, that's all. Don't worry about Irene; she'll just think I've been fighting again. Anyway, that taxi owner will be insured for all of his cars, though I doubt he will want to start up again around here.'

Over the next few days, the owner of the burnt-out taxi firm tried blaming everyone for the fire and the end of his business. The drivers soon switched their loyalty and begged the other taxi firm to give them a job.

Thankfully, only one person suspected Ralph. Back at work, he was surprised when the foreman at the quarry sought him out and shouted for him to go into the portacabin which served as an office-cum-canteen. The only other building around the quarry was a metal shed which held all of the explosives.

Ben, the foreman, poured two cups of tea and sat down. 'Shut the door. That limestone can blind you when you stare at it for too long. But sometimes the blind can see more clearly. You are a good explosives man. Some would say you have a gift for it.'

Ralph looked out of the small window, sipped his tea and waited.

'How's the family, Ralph? Everything okay?'

'Everything is just fine, thanks, Ben. And yours?'

'Yes, they are all good.' Ben let out a huge sigh and rubbed his face, almost rubbing the skin off it. 'I don't know what you're up to, but leave me out of it.'

'Meaning?' Ralph wore an innocent poker face that showed no emotion, although he knew what Ben meant.

'I don't want this coming back on me and my family.' Ben stood up and walked around the portacabin. Everyone knew the taxi owner wanted revenge and wasn't prepared to accept his fate. The police and fire investigations unit were all over it.

Ralph drew on his cigarette and blew the smoke into the air. He looked Ben directly in the eyes. 'I don't know what you're talking about.' Stubbing his cigarette out, Ralph stood up and opened the cabin door. 'Thanks for the tea.'

Ben was a good man. He'd given Ralph a job, knowing he was just out of prison. He didn't want Ben to face any consequences for his actions. If need be, he would confess.

Over the next couple of weeks, things seemed to get worse. Gossip was rife and, as presumed, the taxi owner was pointing the finger at Ben. Apparently, they had already had an argument a few weeks back over the price of the cab fare. And he was an explosives expert. The fire investigation had said it was some form of handmade bomb. Ralph was in turmoil. This was not how he had planned for things to turn out. Stupidly, he had presumed it would all go away, but that wasn't the case. This indeed was a lesson and he would make damn sure it would never be repeated. First things first, he needed to clear Ben's name. He owed him that.

'Hey, it seems we are in the clear, mate. We're under no suspicion. That boss of yours is going to take the rap. I call that game, set and match.' Paddy was laughing like a naughty child who'd had his hand in the cookie jar and got away with it. This was all a big joke to him and he was more than happy for Ben to take all the blame.

'Shut the fuck up, you prick. Ben is an innocent man and we both know it.' Ralph was angry at Paddy's flippancy. 'Why are you running after me in the street, anyway?'

Picking up his pace, Ralph carried on walking. 'This is my mess, Paddy, and I am more than determined to clear it up. I'm sick of that taxi owner. He can claim his insurance. I need it sorting and I need to sort it now. Are you coming?'

'Where? Where are you going in the middle of the day? What is your problem? Slow down, for God's sake. We're in the clear. Who cares who takes the blame as long as it's not us?'

'I care; I've been stupid, thinking I could get away with it. I didn't plan ahead.' Although Paddy was there, Ralph was muttering to himself; he was a troubled man and he didn't need Paddy's stupid jokes.

The smile dropped from Paddy's face. He knew Ralph when he was angry; he was not a man to be trifled with. 'Of course I'm coming with you, Ralph, wherever it is.' Still doing his best to catch up, Paddy was out of breath. 'For God's sake, slow down, will you, mate?'

Slowing his pace, Ralph turned to face him. 'I'm going to see that two-bit taxi owner and silence him for good.'

Paddy's eyes widened in horror. 'You're going to kill him? Shit, you can't do that, it will look like that Ben has done it. He'll still get the blame. What is the point of that?'

'No, I'm not going to do that. But what I am going to do is make sure that taxi owner knows it was me and finds out what happens when you open your mouth too wide.'

Seeing the holdall on Ralph's shoulder, Paddy became suspicious. 'What's in the bag?'

'Everything I need to put a driver out of work and keep his gob shut. Maybe we should have done away with him in the beginning.'

Panicking, Paddy grabbed Ralph's arm. Ralph scared him when he was in this mood. He was single-minded.

Angrily, Ralph grabbed Paddy by his shirt and pulled him forward so they were face to face, almost nose to nose. 'Go fucking home or go and play with your friends. I really don't care which, just get off my back, you cowardly fucker. You had your share of the money but you're not prepared to finish the job.' Ralph's angry tone was more than enough to stop Paddy rambling on about the whys and wherefores. 'Now, leave me alone,' he rasped into Paddy's face, then threw him backwards into the wall.

Paddy paled. 'Okay, Ralph, I get it. I'm coming with you.' He was afraid, but was doing his best not to show it. He knew better than to cross Ralph, especially when he had a bee in his bonnet. He walked alongside Ralph, and neither of them spoke.

It seemed like they had walked forever when finally, Ralph stopped. More confused than ever, Paddy cast Ralph a sideways glance. They were standing in front of a house on the better side of town.

'He should be on his own this time of day. I've driven past the house a couple of times; his wife works. That's why I didn't bring the car, I don't want people spotting it parked outside the house. These posh suburbs have nosey neighbours.'

Standing outside and looking at the house, Ralph thought about his own home. In comparison, it looked like a shed. This was a better life, upmarket and not so working class. He took in the small garden at the front of the house with its neatly cut hedges, and the fresh paint on the door and windows. His own home was cosy and clean, but nothing like this. He had decent money coming in on a regular basis from his protection racket, so why didn't he live here, in a place like this? It wasn't jealousy, it was envy.

'Why are we standing here? I thought you didn't want anyone to know we've been here. You're attracting attention to yourself by just standing and staring at four brick walls.' Paddy was anxious to leave already.

That woke Ralph from his thoughts and he nodded. 'Don't you ever wish you lived in a place like this? The road is clean and tidy. There is a better class of people here. Look at the houses, Paddy. This is where I would like Shaun to grow up, in an area with gardens and people who cut their hedges on Sundays.' His voice was barely above a whisper.

Paddy's disinterest said it all. He had never known any better than he had and had no ambition to better himself. 'I love the streets, with the pubs and our own kind of people. These are stuck-up snobs who think they are better than us. They wouldn't let jailbirds like us live around here.'

'Our kind of people?' The words stung Ralph. He knew Paddy was right; he was an ex-con, but the truth hurt. 'Come on, we have work to do. Let's go around the back way.' Pulling his bag over his shoulder, Ralph walked ahead. He took a moment to look around at the small but impressive back garden, then tried the door handle. The door opened. This was going to be easier than he thought. Stepping into the kitchen, he saw the taxi owner sitting at the table drinking a cup of something.

'Who the hell are you? Get out my fucking house, now!' The taxi owner threw his mug at them then ran towards Ralph and threw a punch.

Ralph dodged it and grabbed the man's arm before he could throw another. 'You've had your turn, mister taxi man. Now it's my turn.'

'I'll call the police. Get out, you skanky bastards. You don't frighten me.' He kicked out at Ralph, who dodged him. Unfortunately, Paddy, who was standing at the side of him, wasn't so lucky. He howled with pain as he bent over, holding his balls.

Ralph put the taxi owner's arms behind his back and shoved him hard against the wall. 'Listen to me, you bastard. Calm down and behave. I just want a little talk. Keep calm, now. I am going to let go and give you a chance, but make one false move, and I won't be so patient a second time.'

The man nodded his head and Ralph eased his grip on him.

Ralph pulled up a chair and sat down. He looked across at Paddy, who was still rubbing his crotch. 'You okay?'

'No, I'm fucking not okay.' He jabbed his finger hard into the man's arm to make his point, then spat in his face. 'I'm going to make sure your balls are ballooned before we leave.'

Ignoring him, Ralph carried on. 'My name is Ralph. I blew up your taxis because you were stealing custom from a fellow cab driver.'

'You blew my taxis up? I don't know you. But I do now, and I will make damned sure the police do, as well. Now, get the hell out of my house,' the taxi owner shouted.

'Paddy. Do you have your friend with you? What's your name, mate?'

As their eyes met, Paddy smiled, and he reached into his inside coat pocket, took out his gun, and pointed it at the man's head. 'He asked what your fucking name is.'

Holding his hands up in submission, the man turned towards Ralph. 'Geoff. My name is Geoff. Are you going to kill me?'

'No, Geoff, but you are going to do me a favour. You are going to change your statement about Ben Miller. He's a good man, a decent one, and you are going to tell the police that. So, that brings us to the point of me telling you that I am to blame. I realise the minute I leave here you will be on to the police and giving them my name.'

'No! I promise I won't. You can just leave; I won't say a word. I promise you.' Holding his hands together as though in prayer, Geoff fell to his knees.

'Now, we both know that's not true. You are just saying that because Paddy here, is holding a gun to your head. But I am going to leave you with a little reminder. You change your statement, drop your accusations and forget my face. Now, stay on your knees and hold your hand up.'

Visibly shaking, Geoff turned towards Paddy then back to Ralph. 'What are you going to do? You don't need to do anything. I promise, really, I do. I will do everything you say. Promise.' Spit dribbled from his mouth as he spoke.

Ralph unzipped his bag and took out a portable electric drill. 'Did you know, Geoff, there are more accidents caused in the home by DIY than anything else?' he said.

'What do you mean? What are you going to do?' Panicking and pleading, Geoff crawled towards Ralph. 'Please, just go. I have not seen anything. I don't know anything.' Tears rolled down his face and he was on his knees, begging.

Ralph was totally focused on the job in hand. He plugged the drill in and tested it to make sure it was working, then handed it to Geoff. The puzzled looks on Paddy and Geoff's faces spoke volumes. 'My friend here is going to hold that loaded gun to your head and you, Geoff, are going to drill through the palm of your hand.'

'No! I can't, I can't. Please don't make me. You have made your point. Go! Leave me alone. Just bloody leave. I can't do that.'

'You can't, but I can.' Ralph looked at Paddy. 'Hold his arm, mate.' Ralph spoke slowly and calmly as he ignored Geoff's pleadings. Geoff's voice was becoming higher in pitch as he did his best to resist and fight Ralph off.

Standing up, Ralph dragged Geoff to the wall and grabbed his hand, holding it against the plaster. 'When you pick up a drill, Geoff, it is usually because you're going to drill a hole into some-thing.' Without a second thought, Ralph started the drill and pressed it against the palm of Geoff's hand. As the drill bit pierced the flesh, blood spurted out onto Ralph's face and clothes. Geoff screamed and yelled, kicking out and trying to free himself. Tears rolled down his face.

Leaning forward, Paddy shoved a dishcloth into Geoff's open mouth. 'Shut the fuck up, the neighbours will hear you!'

Satisfied, Ralph stopped the drill and let go of Geoff's hand. He dropped the weeping and wailing Geoff into a crumpled heap on the floor. The spasms in his body were visible.

'What a stupid accident to have. Still, I suppose the hospital staff will have seen worse. Now, Geoff, are you going to retract everything you have said about Ben Miller?'

Geoff pulled out the dishcloth with his good hand and, with all the strength he had left, he shouted, 'Fuck off, you animal! Look what you have done to me!' He held his arm up and blood poured down it, trickling to his elbow then dripping to the floor.

'Okay, well, I see that hasn't taught you a lesson, so maybe this will.'

The sight of the torn flesh and blood made Paddy feel sick. He was horrified at Ralph's nonchalant manner. 'You're going to do it again?'

'No, Paddy, we all need a good hand. It might have touched the odd nerve, but it will heal, and when Geoff here is feeling brave again he will sing like a bird. So, what is it to be, Geoff? Do we go for your tongue or your legs? You being a taxi driver, I think I might go for the legs. That will put you out of action for some time. Get your money from the insurance and start your business elsewhere.'

Geoff shook his head. Sobbing as he spoke, he said, 'No more, please. No!' His eyes widened with horror. He could see Ralph was enjoying it and that made it worse.

Looking around the kitchen, Paddy started to panic. 'Ralph, we should go, someone might come in. We've been here too long.' Paddy wanted out of there; the gory sight of the bloodstains smeared on the wall and on the floor, and Geoff curled up in a ball on the floor, silently muttering to himself and praying to God to help him, while holding his hand, turned his stomach. This was a side to Ralph he hadn't seen before. He was callous, and what was more, that evil, cold look in his eyes made Paddy squirm.

'Hold him down and then we'll leave,' Ralph commanded.

Paddy did as he was told, more out of fear than friendship, and wrestled Geoff into submission, straddling him, even though the fight had left Geoff's body. 'He's pissed himself, Ralph. Come on, let's go.'

Ralph pushed the dishcloth back into Geoff's mouth and grabbed his leg, pulling up his trousers so that his lower leg was laid bare. He started up the drill again. Holding the leg tightly, Ralph pushed the drill into the back of Geoff's knee. The muffled, strangled howl that left Geoff as the drill bit pushed its way past the bone, almost piercing the front of the kneecap, satisfied Ralph. He stopped the drill and he nodded to himself. 'There, that should do it. You can get off him now, Paddy; he's not going anywhere and he can't run to the neighbours. Just remember what I've said, Geoff, or next time it will be that loose tongue of yours.' Ralph set the drill on the floor then stood up. He rinsed his hands and blood-splattered face under the tap. He looked down at his bloodstained shirt, then took off it and his trousers.

Ralph reached into his bag, took out a fresh set of clothes, then started to get dressed. He picked up his bloodstained clothes and pushed them into his bag. 'Time to go, Paddy. Sorry I didn't bring anything for you.' After unplugging the drill and stuffing everything into his bag, Ralph looked around the room, making sure he hadn't forgotten anything, then he calmly walked out of the back door with Paddy hot on his heels.

'I don't know about you, Ralph, but I need a drink. Was it necessary to do that to his leg?!'

Ralph didn't want to admit it, but he had enjoyed what he'd just done. Watching that man pray for mercy had made him feel powerful.

15

A PLEASANT SURPRISE

'Oh, wow! This is like Christmas. Look at all these letters, Julie.' Donna stood in the lounge and threw a huge bundle of letters in the air, letting them cascade onto the floor. 'Come on, let's open them.'

Shocked and surprised, the women all looked around at each other. This was unbelievable. All the letters had Julie's name on the front, which meant only one thing: they had come from the wife swappers – or swingers, as they liked to be known – she had written to.

Smiling, shaking her head in disbelief, Carrie looked at all the different postmarks. 'Well, I always admit when I am wrong. I never thought you would get one letter in return, never mind all these.'

'I knew they would answer. I told you all they would and you didn't believe me. It doesn't surprise me at all.' Inwardly, Julie was just as surprised as everyone else was, but didn't want to admit it. She tried to show no enthusiasm, as if she was taking it all in her stride. Secretly, she was dying to open them.

Everyone was laughing and joking as they tore open an envelope each. Carrie took in the excitement of the women lounging around in their underwear and robes and clapped her hands together to gain everyone's attention. 'Let's see what strange requests are in those pages before you all get excited, ladies. And you, Marlene, don't you have an appointment in a few minutes?' Carrie was never one to let anything interfere with business although she, too, was intrigued by it all.

Looking across at Julie, she smiled at her. 'So, Julie, you have won this battle, but you haven't won the war.' Although Carrie liked Julie, she felt this was one time to put her firmly back in her place and remind her who was running things around here.

'What's that supposed to mean? I thought you would be pleased. After all, business is business.' Julie took a drag on her cigarette, slightly peeved at Carrie's offhand manner.

'I say who parties here. This is my house, remember that.'

'Why do I get the impression that you hate the fact that they have answered me? You would have loved to say, "I told you so". Well, you were wrong. You were all bloody wrong!'

'Listen,' Angela said, 'this lot has a party of friends that meet up on a monthly basis and would like to talk to us to discuss matters. Matters? What does that mean? Sounds like a bloody solicitor.'

'Amongst your letters you will also get the weird and the curious. They'll want to know what goes on in a brothel. It's all a bit mysterious. Some of those answers will be from weirdos just wanting to come here for a snoop around.' Again, Carrie had her say, putting Julie's back up. The icy glare between them said it all.

'Well, I don't care if you want them or not. I have proved my point. There is a market out there for people who need somewhere to hold their sex parties – even if it's a shithole like this. When was the last time you had this place decorated?'

Julie's criticism annoyed Carrie. 'Rein it in, Julie! If you don't like it here, then leave. That door opens both ways. And now that you're living here, show some respect.'

Standing up, her face flushed, Julie stomped out of the room. She had heard enough. This place *was* a shithole, and with new customers on the horizon it needed freshening up, but Carrie was too tight-fisted for that.

The cracks had begun to show between the two women over the last few weeks, if not before. Although they liked each other very much, they were both hard-headed businesswomen, and Carrie liked to bring Julie back into line when she felt it was needed. Lately, she had felt that Julie was becoming too big for her boots and needed taking down a peg or two. On the other hand, she was good to have onside.

Still standing in the doorway, Carrie clapped her hands together to gain their attention again. She looked at the letters on the floor, then back at the women. 'Those are for me, I believe. Hand them over. All of them.' Reluctantly, the women picked up the letters from the floor and handed them to Carrie. Silently, they left the room. The laughter had gone; it was back to work.

Looking down at the bunch of envelopes with Julie's name on the front, Carrie felt there was only one thing for it. She walked up the stairs, opened Julie's bedroom door, and walked in. 'These are yours, I believe.'

Lying on her bed dressed in a black, see-through, baby doll nightie and stockings, Julie exhaled smoke and looked up at the cracks in the ceiling. 'They're not mine, I just wrote the letters. This is your place, you sort them out.'

'Don't be like that. It could be a good idea, but I can't have you trashing me in front of the others. I am still in charge here. Don't get ahead of yourself. There are some very strange people out there. Let's be honest, we meet them all of the time.' Carrie sat on the bed beside Julie and took her hand. She knew it was time to bring up the taboo subject. Nothing had been said of late. 'I take it you still haven't heard anything from Frankie. It's been two months since the fire.'

Sitting up and stubbing her cigarette out in the ashtray at the side of the bed, Julie's body tensed. 'I know how long it has been, I don't need reminding. I am grateful you let me stay here. And I know Frankie is alive and kicking. Apparently, she has a boyfriend and she's staying with him. That is all the information I have.' Julie picked up her cigarettes and lit another one.

'Who is this boyfriend? Someone you know?'

'I have no idea. I'm the last person to know her plans. I'm only her sister!' sighed Julie. 'I've left messages and given money for Gertie to pass on to her, in case she needs it.' She swung her legs over the side of the bed to stand up.

'All will be well, you'll see.' Carrie smiled, trying to make light of it. 'They'll have a tiff or something and she'll come and tell you about it.' Carrie realised Julie was making herself busy, touching up her lipstick and brushing her hair, more for something to do than because it needed doing. It also meant this conversation was over. 'Your roots need touching up. We'll sort it out soon.' Carrie walked to the door and opened it. 'Don't forget your letters.'

Julie looked at the envelopes on her bed and picked one up. They all seemed to have the same set-up. Swinger parties that had started small but were now growing in numbers. They couldn't exactly hire the local community centre and so the brothel seemed like the next best thing. It was better than having a whole load of people turning up at your house. Less conspicuous.

Julie liked the sound of one letter very much, from a woman called Sue. She was a hairdresser and had her own salon. Her husband was in the insurance business – very respectable. They had been married fifteen years and had felt they needed something to spice up their life without cheating on each other. Sue had given a lot of information about herself and seemed friendly and warm. Julie decided she would meet Sue. It was obvious they had money to spend and that was the name of the game.

'Julie! Julie! Norman's here,' Angie shouted up the stairs, interrupting Julie's thoughts.

Julie's heart sank. Bloody hell, Norman. She had forgotten all about him. He could only shag her lying on his side once he had taken off his tin leg or with Julie sitting on top of him. She didn't think he had ever had his fake leg updated since the day he'd had it made. He was a regular, and must have been sixty years old, and he always took ages.

After planting a bright red lipstick imprint on his lips, Julie guided him upstairs to her room. She could see he was eager to get started. 'Why don't we lie on the bed together and do it from behind, with you on your side, my darling Norman? I have missed you.'

After taking out his teeth and putting them on the bedside table, he sat on the bed and slipped his good leg out of his trousers, then lay down. As was the routine now, Julie moved his trousers, still with the tin leg inside, to the other side of the room.

Julie wanted to read some of her other letters and this was the best way to do it. Norman was quite happy helping himself while Julie lay on her side, facing away from him, making all of the right noises in all of the right places... while reading her letters.

Once Julie had made up her mind, there were only three letters out of the bunch that interested her. These ones seemed genuine. The others were just as Carrie had said: people curious to see what went on behind brothel doors and possibly thinking the women that worked there were up for a free party... not on your life!

'I've telephoned one woman called Sue,' Julie announced to the others around the table the next day. She liked being in charge. 'She seems to be quite well off and obviously doesn't want the scandal.'

'What about the others? You know I'm not sure about this. What about our other customers? We have money to make and we can't hold wife-swapping parties. This is our bread and butter.' Carrie sighed; she wasn't sure about Julie's scheme at all. It all seemed a little crazy and bizarre. But she had come to learn that Julie was impulsive and impatient, sometimes for the good and sometimes for the bad.

Julie fought her argument. 'What have we got to lose? It's one night. Let's see how it goes and if it's no good, we'll never invite them back.'

Donna yawned and scratched her head. The hair lacquer from last night was still making her hair stiff and it stood up on end. Remnants of makeup showed on each of them. 'I'm game, I suppose. I'm as curious about them as they are about us. What about you, Angie?'

'I don't like it. We don't know anything about these people. What are they going to do when they get here?'

Glaring at her, Julie snapped, 'Since when did you become a prude? You know this is a brothel, right? Well, I didn't realise you asked your customers for a life story before you went upstairs with them. What else do you think they are coming for? Titillation, Angie. It sets the seedy scene for them. Gets them all excited. They are going to buy drinks.' She looked across at Carrie, who liked selling her cheap booze at a higher rate than the norm. That was her extra income without having to do anything. 'And if they want to try a professional, like us, they can. Our regular customers will find it intriguing. The swingers will probably give us women a grope, but I will meet with this Sue woman and point out that we are only for *rent!*' Julie shouted, waking them all up.

'Well, you seem dead set on her, Julie, so have your meeting and get back to us.' Carrie tried dismissing it, secretly hoping it would come to nothing. There was no point in opposing Julie; she had to find out for herself what a waste of time it was. 'Make it on one of the quiet evenings and then we won't lose money if it all goes pear-shaped.'

Standing up and purposely knocking the table with her leg, making the teacups wobble and their tea spill, Julie stormed off to arrange her meeting for later that day. She was determined to make this work, if only to save face in front of the others. 'Fuck them all,' she muttered, 'they will soon be smiling when the money rolls in.'

Later that morning she met up with Sue and Julie liked her instantly; she was, as she'd predicted, very well-to-do. She lived in the suburbs away from Liverpool, was in her late forties and had long, bottle-coloured, auburn hair. Her makeup was well done and her clothes were expensive. She was warm and funny and liked the idea that Julie did not judge her extra-marital parties.

Julie had set out the rules firmly. None of the women that worked at the brothel were there for free. They could hold their parties there for a fee and the customers that came didn't get a free fuck from any of the wives. Nothing was for free. What they did between themselves was their business. Then they would improvise. This was a business transaction only.

Sue agreed to all terms and was already taking out her purse with a wad of notes in it to put down a deposit.

Eyeing up the purse full of money, Julie smiled to herself. She had been right. They had money to burn. Julie and Sue arranged the time and date and they shook on the deal.

16

GUN-RUNNING

The plan seemed easy. The warehouse at the old army barracks on the edge of town was full of wooden trunks. Each trunk was full of guns, grenades and whatever else. One wooden trunk with guns was exchanged for one with scrap metal that weighed and looked exactly the same. If, by chance, a trunk was opened during the yearly inspection – which was rare, because the two greedy security guards, who looked after them, always took them from the back – it was full of scrap metal that weighed the same. How were they to know what was inside? The old wooden trunks were securely locked. They had been there for years, possibly since the war. Of course, the security men wanted their money and then there was the cost of transporting it. Some of the weaponry would probably go missing en route. So Mr Smith and Mr Jones, aka Ralph and Paddy, took all the risks and would only end up with a third of the money at best.

Ralph was standing on the street corner on the dark winter morning and he couldn't believe his eyes when Paddy turned up.

'You've nicked an old bread delivery van?'

'Yes, no one will take any notice of a bread van at this time of the morning, will they? Anyway, it was the best I could get at short notice.' Paddy laughed.

'Fair point, I suppose. All the scrap metal we need is at the quarry yard. I dumped it there last night. No one will be around yet. Let's go before they all get to work.' Ralph laughed as he got inside beside Paddy. 'You do realise, no one is going to get a bread delivery today!'

At the army barracks, the security guards were in their little hut outside of the warehouse, drinking tea. They did not seem to do much, but to be fair there was not much to do. Paddy turned the van headlights off as they approached.

Ralph watched them as they took the huge key ring holder and led the way to the warehouse. There were three large keys in all. Nothing elaborate, like Paddy had pointed out yesterday. Who would think of coming here for guns? Only people who had the knowledge, like themselves. The visitors were friends of friends, and so on.

'Do you have the money, Mr Smith?' The security guard in charge looked at Ralph, with his hand out.

Ralph handed over a hundred pounds, as agreed. It was a lot of bloody money to lose if they didn't get anything in return.

Eagerly grabbing the money out of Ralph's hands, the security guard stuffed it in his pocket. 'You can have five. Do you have the scrap metal?'

Frowning and turning towards Paddy, Ralph shook his head. 'I thought you said six trunks. That's what I've counted on and that's the amount of scrap I've brought. All carefully weighed out.'

'Five, six, who cares? Let's just get on with it.' Paddy was nervous. This was big stuff and he wanted out of there. Although he liked the thrill of the chase, his nerve left him when the plans were in place.

'A hundred pounds was for six trunks. That's the difference. Now, lads, do you want to give some of that money back?'

'Oh, bloody hell, who you going to complain to, mister?'

'No one, but I will make damned sure you won't be spreading the word, either.' Ralph grabbed tight hold of the guard by the front of his jacket, then slammed him against the wall. 'Don't fuck with me, old man. A deal is a deal and I won't be complaining, but I may break your bones and then let slip to the authorities that you're selling their goods. Now, play fair, keep up your side of the bargain and we could have a good working relationship. Try and cheat me and you will regret it.' Ralph had expected some trouble. This was all underhand and everyone was out to swindle everybody else. He had to make his point early on, so that they wouldn't think they could swindle him again.

The security guard paled and held up his hands in submission. 'Yes, yes, six. I had forgotten how many we agreed on,' he lied. He knew Paddy but had never met Ralph. He had expected this to be easy money and was sadly mistaken.

'Go with them and get the other trunks while I empty the scrap out of the van.' Ralph spoke with authority, then looked at the other security guard, who was just standing there. 'That means you, too.' He glared.

It was hard work and the guns and scrap were heavy. The dust from the trunks, which looked like old wooden coffins, nearly choked them as they pulled them off the shelves. They shared out the scrap metal to replace the guns as best as they could. Thankfully, Ralph had had the foresight to weigh it beforehand and label it with the weight. He knew this had to be a quick operation, no hanging around. Just get the guns and get out of there, no questions asked.

The drive back was slow. The weight was so heavy the bread

van could hardly cope, but no one paid any attention to it as it rode along at twenty miles an hour.

'We need something sturdier if we're ever going to do this again. I hadn't realised how heavy this lot would be, Paddy.'

'Yes, thankfully we're not going uphill or we would never make it. What are we going to do with them now?'

'Jeez, do you never think ahead? We have a vanload of guns and you are driving along a country road in a bread van wondering what you are going to do. Park it outside your bloody house?'

'Come on, Ralph, that is your side of things. I am the salesman. You are the thinker.'

Begrudgingly, Ralph nodded. 'Well, it just so happens I thought of that, *too*!' he barked. 'When you first mentioned this, I looked around at some old derelict garages and put some locks on one. We'll store them there for now and arrange for transportation tomorrow. You do have all the contact details, don't you? And the money will be upfront?'

'Sure do. These guns are going to Spain. I wanted the money in our cash, not their potatoes. That comes today when I confirm the delivery.'

Ralph laughed aloud. 'Potatoes! You bloody idiot! You mean pesetas. Oh, for God's sake, Paddy, I don't know why I bother.' Ralph shook his head disbelievingly. 'Well, you can confirm it now and nothing leaves here without payment in Irish punts.'

There was silence and Ralph waited for another one of Paddy's revelations. He knew he had not thought this through one little bit. Just the excitement of disappearing into the night collecting guns had been on his mind.

'Er, Ralph, I know I should have said this earlier, but how are we going to get them to Spain? Do you have any ideas?'

'I knew it! I bloody knew it. You fucking idiot!' Ralph slapped the dashboard. 'Well, I didn't know they were going to Spain so I won't be driving there today. But yes, wherever they were going I figured we'd have to sort it, so I had a word with that big furniture removal company. They take stuff all over the place. You give them the address, sign the paperwork and they deliver. No one stops them. If they did, they would be stopping every removal van in town. I will ask if they do overseas.' Ralph shook his head in dismay.

After they had dumped the trunks into the garage without being seen, Ralph looked at his watch. It was nearly 8 a.m. His first port of call would be the removal firm.

* * *

Over the next forty-eight hours, Ralph put his plan in place. The money came through and all was good. The removal men went overseas all the time. It seemed too good to be true.

Unlike Paddy, Ralph did not want to be greedy. He only wanted to do it once every couple of months. But Paddy being Paddy, he wanted to do it on a more regular basis.

'Come on, you want to move house and keep young Irene happy. Your ma would like a nicer view from the window, and think of your little sprog. He wouldn't be growing up on the streets, as we have. Just a few more jobs, that's all it will take.'

As enticing as it sounded, it was a risk. However, Ralph had ambition. He didn't want to just settle for his lot in life. There had to be more, surely. Other people seemed to have the luck of the Irish; why not him?

'Personally, I think you're pushing your luck. If we carry on like this, that warehouse won't have anything left. Don't get greedy. And remember, we're not the only ones using that place.'

'No, Ralph, mate. This is just the beginning and now the security guards know better than to cheat us. Have another drink; we both deserve one. We pulled it off. We're bloody geniuses!'

'One more and then I'm off, okay? I have to be at work tomorrow.'

'Why do you keep that old job? You don't need it. The money is rolling in. Give it up.'

'I have my reasons. Reasons you wouldn't understand. And I have told you a million times, it looks better that I have a job. It's a nice cover. It sounds respectable and that is what I want for my family. For them to be able to hold their heads up and have a working man in the family.'

'It sounds like a lot of effort to please everyone else, to me. But if you're happy, then so be it.'

As he walked home from the pub, Ralph looked at his house. It was certainly nothing to be proud of. Maybe a couple more gun-running trips would provide somewhere more decent. The income from the pubs was decent, plus the odd jobs he got on the side. All in all, it seemed watertight and profitable. The only way to move on was to take a gamble. Maybe Paddy was right.

After another hard day at the quarry, Ralph had made his mind up. He would do some more of the gun-running. Irene would enjoy looking at better houses to rent. His ma and Shaun would have the very best he could provide.

He'd missed so much of Shaun's childhood and he didn't want to miss any more. Irene and his mum stood by him and never asked any questions. Although he had hated to see the disappointed look on his mother's face when he had been constantly arrested, she had stood by him and ignored the gossips.

He felt he owed it to them to keep the job at the quarry as it was something Irene had going for her in the community. They had a wage coming in. That gave her status and respectability.

Besides, he still feared the protection money might dry up, and then where would he be? He had a family to provide for.

Ralph opened the door of the Golden Lion pub and was engulfed by a cloud of nicotine as he walked towards the bar. Everyone was in high spirits; they'd just had their wage packets and it was time for some serious drinking after a hard week at work.

'Ralph.' The landlord spotted him and instantly picked up a glass and turned to pour him a whisky. 'Nice to see you. Hope there isn't going to be any trouble in here tonight. You know what it's like, they have a few beers and all turn into fighters. What is it they say about Friday nights?' The fat, balding landlord laughed aloud as he put the drink on the bar. 'Here's your change.' The landlord discreetly handed over the money Ralph had come for.

'Is everything okay? No hassle or troublemakers?' Ralph asked, putting the money in his pocket.

'No, mate. Everyone knows you're not one to be trifled with. And they know you drink here,' he said, giving him a wink; they both knew what he meant.

'If you need anything, let me know.' Ralph shook the man's hand, then gulped back his drink. He spoke to a few of the other men in there, then left. He did the same with a couple of the other pubs. He liked to make his presence known. After all, that was what he was paid for: protecting the pubs and the people that ran them.

In the last pub, and the one he knew Paddy frequented more than most, Ralph looked over to his usual corner booth, which Paddy used like an office. Ralph could see Paddy was busy with some scheme or other. He was handing over a wad of cash and laughing. He didn't know the two men Paddy was sitting with and so presumed that, as usual, it would be his bookies. Who else would he be handing money over to?

'Ralph! Over here, mate. Come and meet my mates.' When Paddy spotted him, he shouted and beckoned him over. 'Boys, this is Ralph, the person I was telling you about.'

Frowning and eyeing the two men suspiciously, Ralph stood waiting for a better introduction. He didn't know these men. And what had a drunken show-off like Paddy been boasting to them about?

'Evening. And just what have you been telling them about, Paddy? Your mouth been running away like a steam train again?' Ralph waited, stony-faced, for some kind of explanation.

'I was just telling them how you ran things in this part of town. Everyone knows you and fears you, my man.' Paddy was slurring his words and grinning, spilling his drink on the table as he waved it in the air to raise a toast to Ralph.

'I'm not impressed. As usual, you're making a fool of yourself. I suggest you go home. In fact, come on, I will take you myself. Show's over, boys.'

'Leave him be. He's just having a little fun. You know what he's like. But we like what we've been hearing about you. You're a hard man, and don't suffer fools gladly. We like that kind of man in our group.' The man who spoke had an especially strong Irish accent.

'Group? What kind of group is that, then? I'm no singer.' Sarcasm dripped from Ralph when he realised that this was one of Paddy's political friends. Paddy was up to his neck in it and now he was handing over money to them.

'We could always do with a man like you on our side. We were just leaving.' The two middle-aged men stood up and one pushed Paddy's drink towards him, spilling it all over the table and his trousers.

'Hey! Watch out.' Paddy stood up and attempted to brush his trousers down, but they were soaking wet.

'I thought you said he wanted to join us? Full of shit, as always.' The two men snapped at Paddy in disgust as they walked away.

Ralph looked around to see that they were leaving, then turned back towards a drunken Paddy. 'Just what have you been saying, you bloody fool? What are you paying them for?'

'I haven't said anything. I just pay my club membership dues. It helps keep them onside. You know I have political friends. They're interested in a guy like you, handy with his fists and stuff.'

'Come on, we're leaving!' Ralph grabbed Paddy by his arm, almost yanking it out of the socket, and pulled him towards the door. Paddy's legs almost buckled beneath him when the cold night air hit him. Holding his mouth with his hand, he turned his head, then vomited by the kerb.

'Bloody hell, Paddy, you're a disgrace! Wipe your mouth – let's get you home to sleep it off.'

'Sorry.' He wiped his mouth with the back of his hand, and Ralph put his arm around Paddy's shoulders, making it easier to walk him home.

'Why didn't you bring the car? You're always bloody walking. Why?'

'Because unlike you, I don't like to be tracked. I also like the alibi that my car is parked outside my house.'

Tapping his finger with his nose, a drunken, sick-stained Paddy tried smiling. 'You know, you're a clever old bastard.'

Smiling to himself and turning his head away from Paddy's bad breath, Ralph had an idea. He didn't like Paddy's bravado, acting like he ruled the world. He liked secrecy, which is why the next gun run he did would be on his own. Paddy's drunken ways and the friends he liked to boast to were more than enough for Ralph. It was only a matter of time before they got their collars felt by the police. He didn't need Paddy to speed that up with his loose tongue. To be fair, he had done most of the work organising the guns' transportation. Paddy had mentioned another contact in Italy. He had all the details. If it was anything like the last time, it would be smooth running. Yes, he decided, as he staggered along holding up Paddy, this one he would do on his own.

'Shit, they've come on a minibus! My God, Donna, it's not very discreet, is it?' Donna and Angie peered through the net curtains from the lounge. Everyone was on tenterhooks because tonight was Julie's make or break night. Tonight, her wife-swapping party was happening.

Everything had been organised and Julie had even spread the word amongst the regular clients that there was a special evening planned, with some unusual guests. This had heightened curiosity and whetted their appetites. What other kind of event would be planned in a brothel but sex?

In charge of the situation, Julie stayed away from the window. She didn't want to look too excited. 'Well, they don't live around the corner and they'll have a few drinks first to get them in the mood. They're looking forward to it. I've been in contact with that Sue woman a few times and she and her friends seem very excited at the idea. And this way they all come together, not in separate cars. It's easier and cheaper.' Julie's nonchalant attitude annoyed them all.

The swingers had asked if they could come earlier than

planned so they could set things up. What that meant was anyone's guess. What was there to set up? But Julie and Carrie had agreed. This way, they could all get to know each other before Carrie officially opened the doors for business. When the knock at the door came, although nervous herself, Julie went to the door with Carrie. Giving her best smile and warmest welcome, she hugged Sue like an old friend. They had booked two of the bedrooms for their own entertainment, as they didn't want to wait until one was available.

Everyone was slightly nervous, not knowing what the night would hold, as the well-dressed couples walked through the door – all except for Carrie, who was pleased at the prospect of making money. It was a midweek quiet night when most of the girls spent their time hanging around waiting for a customer. Tonight, this would boost trade, and if all went well it could be a regular occurrence.

'Evening, darlings. Come in, get yourselves a drink.' Carrie had already decided what to charge, and as soon as Sue produced the money, Carrie's hand grabbed it and stuffed it into her bra, away from the prying eyes of the others.

All of the girls were wearing their usual satin camisoles, stockings and suspenders. Each and every one of them had made a special effort, having been warned by Carrie to look their very best. All of the couples Sue had brought with her seemed very friendly and very well-to-do. They were relaxed and chatting as they made their way into the large lounge for a drink.

Sue took off her long coat and to Julie's amazement she was only wearing black underwear.

Lost for words, Julie smiled, then stammered, 'I see you've come ready for action, then.' She knew these people held sex parties but she hadn't really thought about it properly.

'Oh, definitely. This is our chance to let our hair down. We're really looking forward to it. A brothel full of sex is more than we could have hoped for.'

Sue stripped the bed, then took out a rubber sheet and covered the mattress with it. 'This is for your benefit,' she said as she opened her handbag, took out a handful of condoms and threw them on the bedside table, then followed them with handcuffs and vibrators. She was bubbling with excitement and smiles.

Watching Sue get organised, even Julie was shocked. *My God*, she thought to herself, *these people really are serious.* Sue then proceeded to the next bedroom and did the same thing there. Now Julie felt nervous. This was more than she had bargained for. She had expected them to mingle and go upstairs for a quickie. It seemed that wasn't going to be the case.

As they walked downstairs to join the others, Julie was pleased to see that some of the regular customers had come. It might have only been due to curiosity but it meant money was to be earnt and that was the whole reason for this.

Everyone was laughing and joking in the lounge. The drinks flowed and the wives were lounging on the sofa provocatively in their underwear, enjoying the admiring glances of the strangers. Some wore leather, some wore short skirts and low tops with nothing underneath. Everything was already on display. The regular customers were in their element at seeing so much bare flesh so soon, but the ground rules had been set by Carrie: if they wanted sex, they had to pay for it.

Julie walked into the kitchen where Carrie was. 'Well, what do you think?' she said.

'I think it could go better than expected. What did she want, upstairs?'

'Oh, they've just brought a few sex toys and condoms. Believe me, Carrie, these are professionals. Even I am learning.' They both burst out laughing. This was going to be one hell of a night. Suddenly they heard clapping and cheering. They looked at each other and then proceeded to walk into the lounge. One couple, who Julie found out later enjoyed exhibiting their sexual exploits, were having sex in the middle of the floor, much to everyone's enjoyment. This was arousing the usual customers and in no time at all they were each leading one of Carrie's women upstairs for their own satisfaction.

The wives sat on some of the customers' knees and let them squeeze and touch them. It all added to the naughtiness of it all. Everyone was having a great time. It was turning out to be one big orgy. The staircase was lined with customers waiting for their turn in the bedroom with Carrie's girls. Some couldn't be bothered to wait and were performing on the landing. It all added to the atmosphere. Even some of the husbands paid for sex with the prostitutes, while their friends watched and cheered them on. They were different, unknown women, not the regular crowd, and it seemed there were no holds barred. All in all, it was a money-spinner for Carrie. They drank her bar dry, mingled with the customers and performed every sex act possible. Then the minibus hooted its horn outside and it was time for them to leave.

Sue pulled Julie aside. She didn't look her usual perfectly made-up self, as Julie had come to know her; she looked rather dishevelled. Julie hadn't seen much of her during the evening. 'I know you get paid on commission,' she whispered, 'but this is for you and you alone. Thanks, Julie. We had a great time.' Sue kissed her on the cheek then went and joined the others, as they all donned their long coats and went out to the minibus.

Looking down at the wad of notes in her hand, Julie realised there must have been about fifty pounds. She did the same as Carrie had done and stashed it in the top of her basque. This was for all the trouble she had gone to, making this evening possible.

She had earnt this. She had been right: sex sells. It is the only thing that never goes out of fashion. A smile crossed her face.

By the time they shut the doors and everyone had gone, they were all shattered. The house was a mess. Empty glasses were everywhere, the ashtrays were overflowing and there was even the odd discarded piece of underwear stuffed at the side of the sofas.

'I'm bloody knackered and saddle-sore.' Angie laughed, then yawned, then lit a cigarette. 'I've never seen anything like it. However, bloody hell, we must have made some money.'

'We'll have a count-up in the morning, ladies. Firstly, we need to get this place in some sort of order. Donna, Jackie, go and check the bedrooms they used, see how they've left them.' Carrie was still in business mode. Even though she felt like skipping at the amount of money that had exchanged hands, she wanted to remain calm in front of them all, as though this was a regular thing to her.

Julie waited for praise, but none came. She felt cheated. Not one of them had the decency to thank her or tell her it had been a good idea. They had all made their money and God knows what tips they had made in the sanctuary of the bedroom. Sue's friends had been a generous lot.

'I've brought down this old carrier bag of their used condoms... yuck. But at least they didn't put them down the loo and block it from flushing. They've left some handcuffs on the headboard. I don't know what we're supposed to do, we don't have the key. Better get the hacksaw out!'

They all burst out laughing. Everyone was in high spirits, even though they were tired. Over the coffee and sandwiches Carrie had made them before the big clean-up, they all exchanged their stories about the evening's events.

'I admire them,' said Donna. 'They aren't cheating on their

partners; they enjoy sex and they are consenting adults. Good for them. I thought they were really nice people.'

'Me too,' everyone chimed in.

'It must have been nice for them to be able to talk openly and be themselves without having to hide anything. We all know how that feels,' Donna added.

Again, they all agreed. They were all living a lie, telling their family and friends different things about where they worked. It was a living...

'Don't you have another group you were interested in, Julie?' Carrie asked. She had enjoyed the evening, and enjoyed the money even more.

'I didn't like the sound of them. They were all into that kinky stuff,' said Jackie.

'For God's sake! What do you class as kinky stuff?' Julie couldn't believe her ears. Considering what they did for a living, they were a bunch of prudes! 'As long as they keep their "kinky stuff", as you call it, to themselves, that's fine with me!'

'Yes, but I read that letter. They are called the Sado Club. What does that tell you?'

'Not much. Their business, up to them what they do to *each other*!' shouted Julie, as she cleared away the glasses and put them in the sink to wash.

'Okay, keep your wig on. I was just saying.' Jackie walked sulkily out of the room.

'When are they coming?' Donna had enjoyed the evening and welcomed the next.

'Tomorrow. Let's see how they get on... oh, sod this cleaning, let's do the rest in the morning.' Julie yawned and threw the cushion back on the sofa, then went upstairs.

The night had been a great success. She lay on top of her bed, looking up at the ceiling, and smiled to herself. She was pleased at how smoothly it had all gone. She felt a little cheated that Carrie had never mentioned giving her some kind of commission for all her hard work, but there was another group coming tomorrow and if that was a success, then Julie felt sure that Carrie would finally tell her she had done a good job.

* * *

The next evening, another gang of swappers turned up. This was a very different crowd from last night. They were not as organised and they didn't seem as friendly. On the contrary, they looked down on the women who worked there.

Carrie took it in her stride; as long as the money for the use of the rooms was paid at the door, she did not care. The drinks flowed, as they had the previous night, but the atmosphere was different. The ground rules had been set by Julie, but that didn't stop the husbands trying to grope the women that worked there. Carrie had quickly reminded them that if that was what they wanted then they would have to pay the going rate.

One man wore a bright red rubber mask, a thong, and was otherwise naked. You could see the sweat rolling down his back. Another one wanted hitting on the bum with a carpet beater. Julie shrugged; each to their own. But there was no way she was going to be like these subservient wives who seemed to enjoy having orders barked at them. Still, it was their fetish and they enjoyed it. It was their business.

Some of the regulars had turned up again. They enjoyed this strange parade of folk, but tonight was a real eye-opener for them. Suddenly they heard a man screaming from upstairs. The noise was deafening. Julie ran up the stairs, with Carrie hot on her heels. Throwing the bedroom door wide open, they saw one of the husbands sitting in the corner of the room. He was sobbing and shaking his head. Then they turned towards the bed. They both stood there in silence, not quite taking in what was before them.

Lying face down on the double bed, naked, her wrists handcuffed to each top corner of the bedframe, was Donna. She was not moving. Julie ignored the man in the corner and rushed over to the prone woman. She touched her shoulder and shook her. 'Donna, are you okay?' she said, but she knew she wasn't, because she wasn't moving. More to the point, she wasn't breathing.

Carrie stood in the doorway taking in the scene before her. She could hear the stampede of people running up the staircase. She saw Julie shake Donna, and she closed the door behind her and put her back to it.

'What the fuck has gone on here!' Julie shouted at the naked man. He was curled up in a ball, sobbing, in the corner of the room. He didn't answer and was obviously in some form of shock, so Julie kicked him hard in the leg and slapped his face. 'Listen to me, you prick. Tell me what you have done to her. She's fucking dead!' She turned towards Carrie. 'You go downstairs and tell them all the party is over. We're closed.' Carrie was still numb with shock as she stood staring at Donna on the bed. She was glad to have someone as strong as Julie to take over the situation.

Julie walked over and slapped Carrie's face. 'Listen to me, Carrie. Whatever has happened, we need the police and we need an ambulance. Now, get that painted face of yours downstairs, smile, tell them it's nothing, and get rid of them.' Julie walked over to the man; she had taken charge of things. 'And you, you fucking weirdo. You're going to prison for a bloody long time!'

He eventually spoke, saying between sobs, 'Is she dead?' He pointed towards Donna on the bed and wiped his dripping nose with the back of his hand.

'Of course she's fucking dead, you idiot. She's not that good an actress. What the hell have you done to her?' Shouting at the top of her voice and giving him another well-earnt kick, Julie waited impatiently for him to speak.

'We were having sex,' he stammered. 'She said she didn't mind it a little rough.' Looking up at Julie's face, tears streaming down his own, he raised his voice and said, 'I paid her extra for that,' as though that made everything okay and all his sins were washed away.

'Well, it's not going to do her much good now, is it, you bastard?' Again, Julie raised her leg and kicked him. 'You like it rough, do you, boy? How about this.' Bending down, she slapped him across the face. 'The police will be here soon. Let's see what they think of your extra few pounds.'

'No, please, don't call the police. You invited us here. You can't call the police,' he shouted, accusingly. 'Please don't,' he begged, while even more tears streamed down his face. It seemed as though he didn't feel Julie's blows.

'Give me one good reason why not?' Julie was suspicious. They had a dead body in the house; of course they had to call the police.

'Because... because,' he stammered, 'I am the police!'

Stunned, Julie stood and stared at him. 'What? You're a fucking copper and you've done this?' Julie was amazed at what she was hearing.

Julie walked over to the wooden chair and picked up his discarded jacket. She went through his pockets and found his wallet. Her heart sank when she opened it up. He was a copper and, more to the point, he was a chief inspector. Her throat went dry. She was stuck for words.

'You see, I'm not lying.' He mopped away his tears with the back of his hand and stood up. 'I could just leave here, now. This could have happened with any of your punters downstairs. I'll make it worth your while.'

'Don't fuck with me, mister. Believe me, I have been around the block too many times. You just want to save your own skin. They are going to love a copper in prison. Your life won't be worth living. What happened?' Sarcasm and venom spewed from Julie's mouth as she looked at the pathetic figure before her, quivering and shaking.

'I told you, we were having sex. I was behind her. It got a little rough and I held her down. I didn't realise she was suffocating in the pillow. It was an accident. She didn't cry out or anything. There was nothing to indicate she was in pain.'

The nervous tension in the air was broken by Carrie opening the door. 'They have all gone. Everyone, even the girls. They know something is wrong, but I've said nothing. You do realise, Julie, I'm ruined.' It was only just dawning on Carrie that this was the end of the road. The scandal alone would ruin her. Each in turn looked around at the others.

'Well, what are you going to do?' asked the man. He had now stood up and composed himself somewhat.

'Well, to start with you can put your trousers on!' Julie barked, throwing them towards him. 'What a mess. Do you know he's a fucking copper? Yes, a copper who likes suffocating women. Well, you can tell that to your colleagues when they get here, can't you. What did they say when you called them, Carrie?'

'I haven't yet.' Carrie's voice was subdued and she looked down at the worn carpet. 'I told your wife to leave and drive around the block until everyone had gone, and to come back in an hour or so.'

'What else have you told her? Does she know about this?' He started to shake and tears rolled down his red, blotchy face again.

Sitting on the edge of the bed near Donna's legs, he put his hands to his face.

'Who gives a damn about his wife? What do you mean, you haven't telephoned the police?' Angry and frustrated, Julie turned on Carrie. She couldn't believe her ears. What was she playing at?

Carrie walked over to Donna's limp body on the bed. 'Where are the keys for these handcuffs? We need to get them off her.'

'Are you crazy? This is a crime scene. We can't touch anything.' She pointed at the man. 'He knows that. Rather, he should. I am right, aren't I?' Julie turned towards him and waited for him to agree with her.

Turning to Carrie as the voice of reason and ignoring Julie, he pleaded, 'Help me! I can't go to prison. Do you know what happens to coppers in prison?'

Calmly, Carrie continued to look down at the floor, avoiding Julie's stare. 'So, what would you suggest, officer?'

Julie's jaw dropped. She couldn't believe what she was hearing. He had killed one of her employees, a friend she had shared jokes with, and Carrie was talking to her murderer with respect.

'We could get rid of the body.' Taking his hands away from his face, he looked hopefully up at Carrie. Now he was in police mode. He was calming down and instantly knew what Carrie was thinking: she didn't want the trouble or the scandal of the police at her door. She obviously had a lot to lose.

Her voice was almost a whisper. 'No one can find her here. I won't allow you to leave until you have cleaned your mess up. And you will owe me a lot of favours in the future. Whatever you decide to do, I don't want to know about it.' Having said her piece, Carrie walked out of the room and shut the door, leaving Julie alone with him.

Julie stood rooted to the floor. She couldn't believe what she had heard. It all seemed surreal, a horrible nightmare. She looked again at Donna's lifeless body and then back at the copper. Carrie was going to let this man off a murder charge just because he was a copper and she didn't want the scandal. Unbelievable!

'Well, Chief Inspector Connors, it seems you have been given a lifeline.' Julie spat the words out. She couldn't hide her revulsion and hate towards the man the way Carrie had. She didn't know what to do. She knew what she should do, but the odds were stacked against her. Who would believe her? Who would care? Donna was only a prostitute, after all. By the time he had perfected his sorrowful story of woe and what a tragic accident it was, he would probably get off anyway. Tears brimmed in her eyes and rolled down her face. She could not understand why, as she wiped them away. Possibly shock. Probably anger. 'You stay here,' she said. Turning, she left the room. She needed to get Carrie to see reason.

'Have a brandy, Julie, it will calm your nerves before we talk.' Carrie proffered the glass to Julie. She was sitting on the sofa in her living room and her stony face showed no expression.

Julie took the glass automatically and gulped it down in one. 'How do you think he's going to clean this mess up? Bodies don't just disappear, and everyone knows she was here tonight. Questions will be asked, you know. The other girls will want to know where she is. Have you thought about that? They heard him screaming. They know something is wrong. How are you going to explain it all?' Julie spoke calmly. There had been enough shouting and the brandy had soothed her throat, taking the hoarseness from it. She was afraid. There was no easy answer to a situation like this.

'I know what you're thinking about me and I don't blame you.' Carrie refilled their glasses. 'You're up to your neck in this, too. You haven't called the police, either. But wait!' Carrie held up her hand to stop Julie's outburst. 'Donna took his money, even though he had enough women to play around with. She also knew they were a weird bunch, but she didn't refuse. There is nothing we can do. She is dead and we are alive. We have to think of ourselves. That man up there may be begging for our help now, but if this went to court, he would make sure we were arrested and our completely sordid backgrounds would come out. Don't you think he would make damn sure some of his mud would stick to us?'

Carrie's words seeped through her brain and she sat down beside her. Carrie had a point. That slimy bastard up there didn't give a damn about anything but saving his own skin! Who would look after Frankie, wherever she was, if Julie went to prison? 'Who is to say he won't point the finger at us anyway?' Julie looked Carrie squarely in the face.

They were interrupted by a knock at the door. They both sat there, afraid to answer it. They held their breath, not daring to make a noise. What if someone had said there had been trouble and already called the police? Julie felt sick; this completely horrible situation was a nightmare. All they could hear through the deathly silence as they looked at each other was the sound of the clock ticking. Again, there was a knock at the door, this time more insistent.

Carrie stood up, went to the window and peered through the side of the net curtains. 'Oh, my God. It's his wife!' Panic filled Carrie as she turned to Julie.

Julie looked though the curtain and recognised the woman knocking at the door. 'Well, we had better let her in and that bastard upstairs can explain it to her. This is the deal breaker, Carrie. She will make the decision for us.'

Brushing her hair back with her hands and trying to compose herself, Julie went to the door. 'He's upstairs,' was all she said, and she pointed her thumb to the staircase. Curious, the woman looked at her but said nothing. As they both looked up, they could see Chief Inspector Connor standing on the landing, half-dressed. The knocking at the door had obviously worried him, too. He had probably thought it was the police and so came to look.

'What's going on, Pete? What's this all about? What have you done?' The woman ran up the stairs and looked at him, and when he pointed towards the bedroom, she walked in.

Julie walked back into the lounge and sat on the sofa beside Carrie, nervously wringing her sweaty hands together. Neither of them spoke. They could hear a muffled argument coming from the bedroom and they both raised their eyes to the ceiling and then looked back at each other. This circle was getting bigger. Like throwing a pebble in the sea. The more people that knew about it, the harder it would be to keep quiet and hide it.

The footsteps on the stairs made them both sit up straight. Either way they were in trouble. Donna had been dead a few hours now. Even if the police came, they would want to know why they weren't called earlier. Carrie was right. They were up to their necks in it and even though they were innocent, innocent people went to prison all of the time.

The angry, red-faced woman stood in the doorway looking at them both. 'He says you're prepared to let things go and not make it an official investigation if he clears this mess up. Is that right?'

Neither Julie nor Carrie spoke. Whatever they said would be incriminating. This was evidence against them.

Standing behind her, now fully dressed, Chief Inspector Connor nodded towards them. 'That's right, isn't it? You're prepared to forget about tonight if we sort it out. This is my wife, Janet. She's also in the force.'

'My God, it's true what they say, isn't it? You lot really do stick together,' Julie spat out. 'Personally, I think your husband should be hung, drawn and quartered. That is someone's daughter up there. What do you say?'

'I say, lady,' Janet folded her arms and looked directly at Julie, 'you can get off your high horse and stop being a victim. You invited us here. This was all your idea. We paid our money,' she said smugly. 'These brothels are two a penny; is there not a code of silence? Do you lot grass up all of your punters?' She sneered.

Taken aback, Julie looked at her. It seemed they had already made their story up. Now it was all Julie's fault because she had invited them here.

'Now, are you prepared to forget about this if we sort it out? My career is on the line and I've worked too bloody hard to lose it over something like this. It will come out about the parties and our private lives. I don't want that and I am damned sure you two don't, either.' Janet was cold and calculating. She didn't give a damn about any of them, just herself. 'I've got two kids and the last thing they need is this shit on their doorstep. That girl up there has no bruises on her, apart from her wrists where the handcuffs are. It could very easily be called a tragic accident and thrown out of court. Do you two want to take that chance?'

Both Julie and Carrie knew she was putting on a hard front to frighten them, but it was working.

Carrie nodded, not saying anything. She still didn't want to incriminate herself, although it was obvious whose side this over-weight, hard-faced, dark-headed woman was on: her own.

'We want insurance.' Julie decided to listen to what they had to say. Carrie and she had their backs against the wall. Two coppers against two prostitutes. 'We want none of this coming back on us. How do we know you're not going to report it and blame us? I am not taking your word for it. It's easy to say when things are heated, but what happens in the cold light of day?

More to the point, what are you going to do with Donna? You talk about her like she's a piece of meat.'

'Insurance?' Both man and wife looked at each other, frowning. They didn't understand what Julie wanted. They had presumed she would take a bribe. But insurance?

'What, you want us to sign some affidavit or something to say it was his stupid fault? What are you going on about, you stupid bitch?' Janet was in no mood for bargaining.

'Not to use, but just in case. If this is a pact of trust, then we all have to trust each other. You both have a lot to lose if your sordid little games come out.' Julie felt she was on stronger ground. She wasn't going to let them get away with this so easily and walk out of the door as if nothing had happened.

'So, what exactly are you talking about?' said Chief Inspector Connor, his eyes narrowed.

Thinking quickly, Julie realised she had blurted her thoughts out, but he didn't know what she wanted. Then an idea came to her. 'The handcuffs, with your fingerprints all over them.'

'That would prove nothing. I am sure Chief Inspector Connor has used handcuffs before,' said Carrie, now following Julie's train of thought.

'It would. Because not only do they have his fingerprints on them; Donna's will be there too. I am sure, if checked carefully, both sets of prints, sweat, body fluids, whatever you lot look for when investigating cases like this, will be all over them. It would put you together with the same dead body. Especially when her family report her as a missing person.' Julie had made her point and she could see that. Both Janet and her husband turned to each other.

Janet and Chief Inspector Connor shook their heads. This was the last thing they wanted. They both knew Julie was right. This was proof. It was not much, but it was something to start an investigation they were all trying to avoid. 'Bollocks!' shouted Janet. 'How do we know you're not going to run out of that door the minute our backs are turned?'

'Okay.' For the first time since the conversation started, Chief Inspector Connor nodded. 'Fair enough. We all have to trust each other, I suppose. However, I warn you. If you ever try using them against me, I will make damned sure you both go to prison for a very long time. Yes, you can have your insurance. Just remember what I've said.'

'Aren't we all forgetting something?' Carrie interrupted them all and waited until she had their attention. 'There is a body upstairs, in my house, and something needs to be done about it. Never mind your reputations, and your insurance, Julie. What about me?'

Gathering their thoughts and realising Carrie spoke sense, they focused on the issue of Donna's body. Time was getting on. It was the early hours of the morning.

'Right, okay then. So we're all agreed that we went home when you threw everyone out. And you threw us all out because...?'

'Because there was a drunken brawl. An argument between a couple of drunks over their favourite girl. It wouldn't be the first time I've had to throw someone out. It happens,' said Carrie, nodding in agreement.

'I want you two to disappear for a few hours. The café by the docks is always open – go there. We'll sort things out from here.' Chief Inspector Connor opened his wallet and took out some money. 'Off you go now, that will pay your taxi fare.'

'And my insurance?' Julie pressed the matter further.

'Come with me.' The snivelling, pleading chief inspector was now all business and in charge of the situation. Julie followed him up the stairs and went back into the bedroom. 'Here's the key to the handcuffs. You unlock them.'

Smiling at him, Julie walked over to the dresser and picked up a handkerchief. 'What? You mean put my fingerprints on them, as well, officer? I don't think so.' Holding the handkerchief, she took the key and moved Donna's cold hand so that she could see the lock, put the key in and turn it.

'You've been watching too many cop shows, Julie... using your handkerchief.' He laughed at her.

Ignoring his cocky manner, Julie looked around the room. She spotted a discarded carrier bag in the corner. Walking over to it and picking it up, she saw that it was empty. 'This will do nicely, officer,' she said, her voice dripping with sarcasm. Doing her best not to look at Donna, who thankfully was lying on her front so she couldn't see her face, she dropped the handcuffs in it. 'I'll go for that coffee, now.' She smiled, although inside she felt sick and was shaking. Her legs felt so weak, it took all her strength to walk back down the stairs.

'Let's go, Carrie, our work is done.' Julie turned to Janet, who was standing in the doorway, and looked her up and down with disgust. 'He's got away with it this time, love, but next time it could be you he suffocates.' Carrie stood up and followed her lead as they walked out of the house.

A few hours later, when the sun was rising, they went back to the house. Although they had both sat in an all-night café drinking coffee, talk between them had been limited, both women lost in their own worlds, with their own thoughts. The first thing they did when they got in was go upstairs. As predicted, there was no sign of Donna. The room was spotless, and even the bed had been remade. Unless you had been there, you would never know what had happened.

Even though exhausted, neither of them felt they could sleep and so they began tidying up the rest of the house from the night before. Abandoned half-glasses of alcohol were on the makeshift bar and they cleared them away in silence. Guilt and tension hung in the air. There were a million questions they wanted to ask each other, but neither of them spoke as they cleaned up.

'The girls will probably be coming back later.' Carrie broke the silence at last. 'We have to appear normal.'

'What do you think they have done with her?' Julie asked at last.

'I don't want to think about it. This place is giving me nightmares already. That's why I've been thinking. I've been in this game a long time; maybe now is the time to retire. I think I'll sell up and find a house by the seaside or something. Far away from here. I cannot carry on here; my conscience won't allow it.'

Incredulous, Julie looked up at her. 'My God, you have been doing a lot of thinking! What about me? You agreed to them walking away from a murder charge. Donna was my friend. Lovely, funny Donna who helped me so many times. I feel like I've betrayed her. I hate myself for it. And do you know something? That could have been me up there and you would have let him walk away. You don't give a shit about any of us. You act like a friend but you're not.' Julie was shouting now on the point of hysteria.

The smell of death seemed to linger in the air. Julie knew it would never be the same again with this hanging over them. As much as she hated to admit it, she knew Carrie was right. Guilt alone would eat them up and possibly send them crazy.

'I'm not opening up again and I want out of here, ASAP. End of story. They'll find something else. You go and find Frankie and sort things out. It's time you did.'

The other girls had come back, all curious as to why they had been asked to leave on the night of the party. Carrie told them there had been an argument that got out of hand and it was better that they left in case the police had been called. Carrie made excuse after excuse and she was emotionally drained. Julie could see that. Once Carrie had told them all she was retiring, the girls gradually started to drift off and find employment elsewhere.

A few days later, Julie showed Carrie a newspaper item. It told of a young woman found in the sea. Poor Donna, just thrown into the sea like rubbish and without a second thought. Julie would never forget Donna or that night. It would stay with her forever.

18

A NEW HOME

'Oh, Ralph, love, the new house is beautiful. Is it really ours? I never dreamt we would live in such a place, with all these fineries.' Irene and Shaun ran from room to room looking at their new house. It had three bedrooms, which meant Shaun would have his own room and they wouldn't have a curtain separating them for privacy, which also meant Ralph and Irene didn't have to wait until he was fast asleep to conduct their marital duties. Money had been tight before, but now it was a new era and a new beginning.

The house was rented, but it was better than the place they had left. Ralph looked out of the window as he drank his tea in the sparsely furnished kitchen. It just had a small garden, but it was enough for Shaun to breathe in some fresh air and kick a ball around. He felt satisfied.

'Ralph, it's not my business and I have never interfered in your life.' His mother looked concerned. 'How can you afford to rent a place like this? It's away from the streets and Irene's friends and family. What are you doing to provide all of this? Are you safe? That is all I care about. All of this' – Ralph's mother waved her arm around the spacious living room – 'doesn't mean anything to me. You are my son and I love you. Are you in trouble?'

'No, Ma. I've just had a stroke of luck. You know me, I'm not a millionaire but I always have some cash on the hip. Don't worry, just enjoy it. You deserve it. Come on, have a look around. Leave Irene planning what she is going to do with the place.'

His gun-running mission to some Italians he had contacted had gone well and been much easier than he had thought. They seemed to know what they were doing, and it was clear to Ralph they had done it before. They had provided the transportation. All he'd had to do was follow the instructions given and drive the van he'd stolen near to the airport and leave it parked up. They sorted out everything from there.

It all seemed very professional to Ralph. They had paid the money he asked for without a quibble, direct into his Post Office account. He realised that was his biggest mistake. Eyebrows would be raised and questions might be asked. People like him did not have that kind of money in their accounts. Next time he would ask for cash. He was not sure where he could have it sent or if he could meet one of the contacts so it could be handed over. He would have to think about that, should the need ever arise again. Now Ralph was working blind. He didn't know these people; all he had was a contact telephone number, which had cost him a fortune to call.

He hadn't liked keeping Paddy in the dark about his arrangement, but he wanted to test the water first, in case it all went wrong. Paddy was becoming too loud and too cocky in his approach to life. Ralph did not like the way he splashed the cash, buying a new suit and standing at the bar buying drinks for everyone. He was always known for borrowing money from somebody or selling something. But suddenly, he would have a wallet full of money and pay them all off. They all knew he didn't have a job and that he was a gambler. Hopefully they presumed he'd had a win on the horses, but the bookies would know different.

Maybe to ease his conscience he would give him a few pounds, though not enough to cause suspicion. Paddy had already been suspicious and a little jealous when he'd said he was renting a bigger house, but Ralph had told him a pack of lies about some savings his ma had and what he'd saved from the pub collections. Paddy didn't delve too deep; he wasn't interested as long as he got his share of the partnership.

* * *

Once back on Paddy's side of town, it didn't take long for Paddy to be hot on his heels. 'I've got another contact. My mates don't want to touch it, but they were talking about it and I've got the bloke's number if you want it. You're gonna need the cash with that posh new house of yours!'

'Why don't your mates want to touch it? I thought they were into anything as long as they could contribute to the Cause.' Ralph felt uneasy. He sipped his pint in the usual booth Paddy used as an office and listened.

'I don't know, maybe they're losing their bottle. Guns are guns and if someone wants to buy them, what do we care?'

'It all seems very odd to me. Is there something you're not telling me? I will find out, you know.' Scowling at Paddy across the table, he waited for the rest of the story.

'Nothing, that's all I know. Shall I make contact and you sort things out from your end? This is a big money-spinner.' Paddy's wide grin and smugness unnerved Ralph. His gut instinct told him this was trouble. Why didn't Paddy's friends want to be in on this deal? Still, if Paddy had the contact there was no harm in looking into it.

'Okay, but if I don't like the sound of it, the deal is off.'

'No problem, I'll look into it. Here.' Paddy took out a scrap of paper with a telephone number scribbled on it. 'This is the telephone number. Shall I give them a call?'

Ralph noticed the number was local, and again this made him feel uneasy.

Sighing and going against all of his gut instincts, Ralph nodded. 'Okay, but be warned, Paddy. Something is telling me not to touch this job.' After counting out the money they had earnt from the protection racket and sharing it, Ralph got back into his car and headed home.

'There's a telegram for you, Ralph,' Irene said, the moment he got in. She took it from the top of the mantelpiece and waved it in the air. 'Oh, mother of Jesus.' She crossed herself. 'I do hope no one is dead. Read it. It came just after you left.' Irene was wringing her hands. People hardly ever got telegrams unless it was something important or someone had died. She looked worried and sat at the table, exhausted, waiting for the bad news. He knew his mother was just as curious, but she showed no emotion as she looked up from her knitting to look at him. She said nothing. She knew there were no members of family to hear about. They did not have anyone else. Therefore, this had to be something different.

Tearing it open while Irene waited, he was curious himself. No one had ever sent him a telegram.

'Greetings from Italy, my newly found cousin,' he read. 'Call me so we can get to know each other and discuss family ties. I plan to visit England soon.'

That was all it said, apart from a telephone number underneath the message.

Puzzled, Ralph looked up at his mother and Irene and shrugged. Handing over the telegram for Irene to read for herself, he was bewildered. Ralph didn't have any Italian connections, except for the people he had done the gun-running for. But he had never said where he lived, and more to the point he had just moved house. It couldn't be them; they knew nothing about him. 'They must have the wrong person.' He exchanged glances with his mother and shrugged again. He was lost for words.

'Oh, yes, I remember your father saying something once about a member of his family emigrating to Italy. That was years ago.' His mother stopped knitting. 'Maybe they are looking up old family. You do, as you get older.'

Ralph knew his mother was covering to protect him. Whoever he had done the gun-running for had found him. He was sure of that. How, he didn't know. But maybe this was their discreet way of making contact again.

'Oh, goodness me. You never listen; I have mentioned them. Your father didn't like them. Always on the scrounge. They want to visit England; well, in my opinion that means free bed and lodgings. No, let them find another mug to let them stay at their house. Here, throw it in the fire where it belongs.' With that, Ralph's mother tore at the telegram and threw it into the burning fire. Ralph's jaw dropped and his face flushed red with anger. He wanted to shout at her to stop, but this was his mother and he could not.

Relief washed over Irene as she watched the telegram burn and Ralph could see her body relaxing. The torment was over for her. However, not for him.

'Go and make us some tea, Irene, love. I think we could all do with a cup,' said his mother, in a nonchalant manner.

Ralph was still standing near the table watching the embers glow. He was rooted to the spot. The telephone number was gone.

'Here, Ralph, love, you haven't given your old ma a kiss. Come closer.'

Dragging his heavy feet towards her, he bent down to her chair and kissed her cheek. Pulling him closer, his mother put her hand in his open-necked shirt, stuffed a piece of paper in it, and put her finger to his lips to stop him speaking. Their exchanged looks were enough. When she had ripped the telegram up, she had torn off the telephone number and crumpled it up in the palm of her hand to stop Irene from seeing it, before she had thrown the rest of it in the fire.

A smile crossed his face as he rose and patted his shirt. He could always depend on his ma to ease the situation.

Irene felt better now that her curiosity was satisfied and his ma had made a good excuse about long lost family on the scrounge. It all seemed feasible.

Going to the toilet and taking out the piece of torn paper, he saw the telephone number and kissed it. What would he do without her!

* * *

Later that day, he rushed to the telephone box on the corner and placed the call; he even went so far as to reverse the charges. Lighting a cigarette, he watched people eyeing him up as they passed by, but ignored them. Thankfully, the operator told him the charges were accepted. Ralph was so nervous he almost dropped the phone.

'You're a very honest man, Mr Goldstein. We would like to use you again. Same place, same price. Operators often listen in, so shall we say on the same day of the week? By the way, say happy birthday to your son from us all. Time to go now, goodnight.'

Ralph was about to interrupt when the line went dead. He

appreciated they had to be cautious but they had not given a date. Puzzled by the conversation, he went over it in his mind again and then dismissed it. He was no better off. Shoving his hands in his pockets, he walked home. What a waste of time that had been. *Maybe I should call back?* he argued with himself. Then he decided to leave it. There was no point.

'You look tired. Things not go as expected?' asked his mother when he walked in. She knew something was wrong by the worn expression on his face.

Shaking his head, he sat down beside her. She was watching some programme on the new television Irene had rented. 'On a lighter note, have you decided what to buy young Shaun for his birthday? I heard him say he would like a bike.'

Ralph looked at her. 'When is it?'

'On the twelfth, Ralph, in four days' time. Remember? He is your son, after all.' She laughed and turned back to the television.

Something struck a chord in Ralph's brain. Bloody hell, he had been given a date. They had mentioned Shaun's birthday! In four days' time those Italians wanted their guns. He liked their style. They had said everything but they had said nothing. Absolutely nothing to incriminate themselves. His son's birthday, indeed!

Excitedly kissing his ma on the cheek, he laughed. 'Then we'll get him his bloody bike, and you too, if you want one. Here.' He took out his wallet and handed her some money. 'Get the bike and the rest is for you to treat yourself. Where's Irene?' He looked around the room and towards the kitchen.

'Checking on young Shaun. He's watched his programme and gone to bed. I'm not sure he likes it in there on his own, though, that's why Irene keeps popping in to see him. It's all very strange to him and he's only a young lad.'

'He'll get used to it. Does he like his new school?'

'Not really, love. Not yet. He will when he makes new friends. I think even Irene finds it a little lonely now. We all have to adjust.'

'What about you, Ma? How do you like it here?'

'One armchair in front of the fire is the same as any other. The buses are nearby if I wish to visit or you can drop me off in your car. Don't worry about me.' She patted his hand and carried on watching her programme.

Ralph walked towards the bedroom to say goodnight to Shaun. Irene was sitting on the bed reading him a story and Ralph walked over and ruffled the boy's hair. Maybe he had been too hasty in wanting to move house. He had wanted better for them all, but it seemed they were not as happy about it as he'd thought they would be. To be honest, it seemed they were all homesick.

When he opened the door the next morning, he nearly tripped over Paddy, who was sitting on the doorstep smoking his usual roll-up.

'Bloody hell, what are you doing here at this time? Don't you ever sleep? And what are you doing sat on the doorstep?'

'Didn't want to knock this early but knew you would be coming out soon.'

'For God's sake, just knock in future, will you?'

'Yes, okay. However, it's not the same around here as it is back home. You can't just turn up and walk in as normal. All those bloody net curtains twitching. Nosey bloody neighbours.'

'Nosey neighbours live everywhere.' Angry at the disturbance and another stab at his change of house, Ralph walked to his car and threw his lunch box in. 'So? Get in and get on with whatever it is that has dragged you out of bed so early.'

'That job. It's on for tonight. I've sorted everything out. Is tonight good for you?'

Just about to turn the key in the ignition, Ralph turned to Paddy, shocked. 'Tonight? What the hell are you talking about? That doesn't give us any time at all. When are we supposed to collect the scrap, weigh it, get the stuff and send it... where? We need more time.'

'We don't have more time. The pressure is on, it's tonight or not at all.' Paddy took out his tobacco pouch and started to roll another cigarette. He looked uneasy.

'What's wrong, Paddy?' Ralph eyed him curiously. Normally, when a job was in the offing he was all guns blazing. Today he seemed quiet and distracted.

'Nothing. Maybe I wish we hadn't got involved in all of this, but we have and now we have to see it through.'

'Do you have the money?'

'Not yet. Not until I have given them the nod about tonight. It's not going far.'

'And just where is "not far"?' Ralph wasn't sure about this. It all seemed so rushed. But he would go anyway; if nothing else, he wanted the guns for the Italians. He could sort that out at the same time. This time he would include Paddy.

'I'm not sure. They're not saying much. Details on payment, I suppose.'

'Okay, we'll go to the warehouse after I finish work. I'll get some scrap together and you can meet me there. This had better be kosher, Paddy!' Ralph warned, pointing his finger in Paddy's face.

'Aah, Ralph.' Paddy smiled at last. 'I love it when the Jewish side of you comes out. Kosher, indeed!'

* * *

During a long day amongst his beloved explosives, Ralph gathered as much scrap as he could and stashed it away. He hoped that Paddy would not be too long, so as soon as the whistle blew telling the workers it was the end of the day, he could fill up the van and go to the gun warehouse. Ralph felt disturbed. Paddy had lost his usual exuberance; maybe he expected trouble. Or maybe it was himself being too cautious.

'Ralph! Over here.' Paddy sat in the stolen van and beckoned him from the window.

Wiping his brow and brushing down his denim dungarees, Ralph walked towards the van, looked at his friend and laughed. 'You know, it doesn't matter how expensive your clothes are, you still look like a scruffy bugger.' Paddy never seemed to brush his shoulder-length hair and, whatever he wore, he looked like a hippy.

'It's my style. Full of fashion, me. I make my own statements. Have you weighed out the scrap?'

'Most of it. I've been sneaking around all day. Come on, give me a hand to load it.'

When they arrived at the warehouse, the security guards were nowhere to be seen. That was unusual; they were normally ready and waiting for their pay. Looking inside their security hut, Ralph saw it was empty.

Then Paddy turned and looked at him apologetically. 'I'm sorry. They've got my ma.' He looked down at the ground and kicked some imaginary dust with his boot.

'What the hell are you talking about? Who has your ma?' Anger started to rise in Ralph. Somehow, he knew Paddy had betrayed him, but he did not know how. Then the warehouse door opened and four of Paddy's new political friends walked out. Two of them were the men he remembered seeing with Paddy in the pub. Ralph's heart sank. They were in the middle of nowhere and there were four of them. It seemed Paddy was up to his neck in it.

'You can leave now, Paddy, you've done your job. We have business to deal with. Your ma is safe,' one of them spat out.

Turning on his heel, Paddy ran to the van and got in. Ralph watched it drive away. He knew whatever this was about, he wasn't going to come out alive. These people were known terrorists. They used politics to cause chaos.

'Well, it's just us boys. Let's have it.' Ralph looked at the four men, prepared for the worst. He could see they were serious. He turned and looked into the distance. Paddy was long gone. The bastard. He had sold him down the river!

'We need a job doing. We've asked you nicely to join us, but you think you're some kind of hard man, don't you? Just do what we ask and we will leave you alone. Be a nice boy, now,' the spokesman of the four said without feeling.

'And what job is that, then?' For the first time in a long time, Ralph felt afraid. He had an idea of what was coming and he wished they would just get on with it. He'd been beaten up before, but this time he felt it would be more than a beating.

'Explosives. It seems you know your stuff. Paddy has told us all about it. He has also told us how you have been doing a little gun-running. Not one penny of that has passed its way to our cause. Well, let's see how many years you get when the police hear about it. Here you are with a vanload of trash, outside a gun warehouse. Doesn't look good, does it?' The man spat on the ground.

'Where is Paddy's ma?' Changing the subject, Ralph looked them squarely in the eyes.

'She's safe enough, but she's an old woman. Who knows what could happen to her? More to the point, who knows what could happen to yours, and that pretty wife of yours?'

'You want my help and yet you start by making threats. Not exactly the nicest way to start a conversation.' He knew they had him in an awkward position and these men were ruthless. They didn't give a damn who they hurt as long as they made their point. Now they were threatening his family.

Ralph felt angry Paddy had not warned him, but then this lot had put the fear of God in him and they had kidnapped his mother to boot. On top of that, it seemed they were going to stitch them up good and proper and a jail sentence was looming. Damn it! He had just got his life sorted out and he was back to square one. Letting out a sigh and tensing his body, he prepared himself for the worst.

'Our friends in the police force will be here in one hour. You can make up your mind and do as we ask or else you're going to wish you had. Either way, I know sooner or later you will do our bidding. Stop fucking about. We have business to do.'

'If you know the police and have all these influential friends, why do you need me?' Ralph's palms were sweaty. In fact, his whole body was, but he didn't want to show it. He wanted to wring Paddy's neck and run like hell.

'We need someone who can make explosives; we could do with a man like you working for us. I don't know why the boss recommends you. Personally, I think you're a piece of shit.'

'And where is this boss of yours? Why isn't he here asking me himself?' Ralph's blood boiled but he knew better than to make this situation worse.

'Doing a stint in prison, but he still runs things. He knows many important people who agree with his ideas. All you have to do is make the explosives and blow up a paint factory. The owner owes us money, a lot of money, and it seems he doesn't want to pay. You know how it is: you collect from the pubs. What you get is pennies. We like big money and we're going to blow that place to pieces... or rather, you are.' Turning to his friends, he laughed.

'What about the workers? You're going to blow up that factory full of innocent people going about their daily work? That place never closes. They have night shifts and day shifts.' Shocked, Ralph stared at them while trying to gather his thoughts.

'Not our problem; we have our orders. That sneaky, two-faced bastard has money and we want it.'

'And this is a one-off, you say?' Ralph thought about it. He could tell them he would make the bombs they wanted but make them duds.

'It may be once. It may be more. You're going to be our fall guy, big man. Everyone knows you're the explosives expert.' He looked at his companions. 'Let's show him we mean business.'

The three other men walked towards Ralph. He thought he should make a run for it, but where was there to run to? They grabbed him; he struggled and threw a few wild punches at them, knocking one backwards, but that seemed to ignite the situation more. A couple dragged him down to his knees and kicked him in the face and body, while another one held his hands behind his back. Taking out a gun, they aimed it at him, but instead of shooting him, they hit him hard across the head with it, almost knocking him senseless. He was dazed. His head was spinning and he'd heard his ribs crack. He knew they were going to kill him and waited for the one with the gun to shoot. The pain from his broken ribs was making it hard to breathe.

'You don't look so hard now,' the gunman barked.

Ralph had tried putting up a fight, but they had a gun and there were four of them. His nose was bloody from the kick in the face, and he could feel his eyes swelling up. He was lying helpless on the ground in pain. He did not want to give them the satisfaction of hearing him cry out, but his body hurt all over, and he could not help it.

'Enough!' their spokesman shouted. Walking up to Ralph, he grabbed his hair and yanked at it so that he was looking him in the face. 'So, what is it to be?'

Panting and breathless, Ralph was just about to give in when he heard car wheels speeding up the road. Looking through the slits of his eyes, he could see a vehicle and presumed it was the police. The door of the van flew open, still with the engine running. All of the men turned towards the van, puzzled. It was Paddy!

'Right, you bastards, who's first?' Paddy fired his gun at the man who was holding the gun at Ralph's head. The man fell to the ground beside Ralph, grabbing at his chest as his shirt went crimson with blood.

'You slimy bastard, Paddy! You're never going to see your ma again,' shouted the man in charge.

'Where is she? Tell me or I'll shoot.' It was too late. Be it out of fear or nervousness, Paddy fired his gun again at one of the other men, who collapsed beside Ralph. 'Pick that fucking gun up, Ralph, before that bastard gets it,' Paddy shouted. The gun lay on the ground beside the dead man. Ralph crawled and reached out to pick it up, when one of the other men stood on his hand. Pain seared through him but with all of his might, he crawled forward and sank his teeth into the man's ankle, making him scream out in pain. Grabbing the gun quickly, ignoring his own pain, Ralph fired, shooting the man in the balls. From his position on the ground, it was the highest he could aim at.

'Don't shoot, Paddy,' Ralph panted. 'Wait! Help me up.'

'No!' Paddy fired again, and this time it was at the spokesman of the four, who had run into the warehouse and was pulling the sliding metal door shut.

Walking up to the man Ralph had shot, Paddy watched him writhing on the ground, holding his crotch as the blood poured from him, howling in pain.

'Where is my ma, you bastard?' Paddy was sweating and red-faced; he pointed the gun at the man's head. Tears rolled down Paddy's face. 'Where is she!' he shouted.

The man pointed towards the warehouse. 'Thank you,' said Paddy, and shot him in the head. The dirt road was now covered in blood. 'Can you stand?'

'Yes,' Ralph panted. Paddy helped him up while he held his ribs. Pain burned through him and he could hardly breathe, but they had one last battle to fight. Who knew what that man in the warehouse had already done to Paddy's ma?

Running forward and jumping over the three dead men on the ground, Paddy opened the warehouse door. It had a dim light hanging from the ceiling. Everywhere else was pitch dark. Rows and rows of wooden containers were lined up on the huge shelves. It was a ghastly, cold place to take an old woman. They could hear muffled crying from a far corner, then a loud slap resounded and Paddy heard his ma cry out. 'Where are you, you bastard?' he shouted. 'Let her go. I am going to kill you anyway.'

Trying to control his breathing, Ralph held his finger to his lips. They did not know if this man had a weapon, but they knew what he was capable of. He hadn't lifted a finger to help his friends. Only himself.

Pointing to himself, Ralph ran his finger across his throat. Instinctively Paddy knew exactly what he meant. 'It's just you and me now; Ralph's dead,' Paddy shouted out.

Ralph stepped forward gingerly from behind one of the containers they were hiding behind, then turned towards Paddy and pointed his thumb in the direction of an old oil drum. 'Shadow,' he mouthed towards Paddy.

Looking in the direction of the oil drum, Paddy could see the shadow Ralph was pointing at. Without thinking, he just ran in the direction of it and fired his gun. Then Ralph heard another gunshot and saw Paddy fall to the floor.

Gathering every ounce of strength in his body, Ralph looked around for something to use as a weapon and saw a crowbar. He ran towards the shadow, where the gunshot had come from, raising his arm, the crowbar firmly in his hand. With one striking blow, he hit the man on the head. He knew he had taken him off his guard and heard the metal crack against his skull. Repeatedly, he rained blows with the crowbar down on him. Hate and anger consumed him as he threw blow after blow. Ralph realised this coward of a man had thought he was dead, and Paddy was lying on the floor bleeding to death. Thinking it was all over, this man was leaving Paddy's ma there to freeze and starve to death... the bastard!

'Stop! Stop, Ralph!' Paddy's mother was screaming through the rag that was wrapped around her mouth, bringing Ralph back to reality. As he looked down, he saw the dead man covered in blood. His head was crushed and there was hardly anything left of his face as he lay there. He took the cover off her mouth and then the frightened old woman took a gulp of air and shouted, 'Go and see if Paddy is alive.' She looked at her son.

Dropping the crowbar, his hand dripping with blood, Ralph walked towards Paddy. He could see that he was alive and was clutching at his arm, where he'd been hit. 'Are you okay, Paddy?' Breathless, Ralph knelt down and shook him.

Paddy whispered, 'Yes.'

He was semi-conscious. Ralph kicked him. 'Stay with me; I need to stop the blood.' He took off his huge leather belt and wrapped it around Paddy's arm as a tourniquet. It wasn't easy, as his hands were wet and slippery with blood, but he managed to fasten it around Paddy's arm as tight as he could.

'Is my ma alive?'

'She's fine,' Ralph panted. For the time being his own pain had left him and he needed to concentrate on getting them out of there. Who knew who else would come? 'Come on, try and get up.'

Weakly, Paddy held on to Ralph as he tried to stand up. His head was swimming and he vomited. Resting on one of the long shelves, Paddy looked on as Ralph staggered away and returned with his mother. Her hands were tied behind her back and she was shivering. Her face was tear-stained and she cried out hysterically when she saw Paddy and the blood.

'He's okay. He's going to be okay when we patch him up.'

'We've got to get him to the hospital,' she cried, as Ralph undid the ropes around her wrists. She rubbed them to get the circulation going.

'We can't do that. There will be too many questions. We need to sort this ourselves. Paddy, wake up, I can't do this on my own. For God's sake, wake up!'

Sweating and shaking, Paddy roused and nodded. They were all weak, but they couldn't leave that mess behind them. 'You too, Millie, I need you to be strong.' Ralph rubbed his hands on his jeans then held his ribs. He was finding it hard to breathe and he knew only adrenalin was urging them on. 'We need to get those bodies in the back of the van. We're going to take them to the quarry and bury them. There are lots of holes there. Right, everyone, take a breath. Let's drag him out first.' Ralph turned towards the oil drum where the man he'd beaten to death with the crowbar was. The whole floor was covered in blood and brains. Paddy's ma made the sign of the cross and then flung her apron over his head so she didn't have to see him. She grabbed one of his legs and Ralph grabbed the other. Puffing and panting, they dragged him as best as they could, leaving a trail of blood behind them. It looked like a massacre. They struggled with each body in turn and threw them in the back of the van. God only knew what was giving them strength.

'The quarry first, then we will go to yours, Millie.' As Ralph started the engine, none of them spoke. Paddy's eyes kept opening and closing, he was almost ready to pass out, but Ralph kept pushing him to keep him awake. The tightness of the belt had nearly stopped the blood flow.

Parking at the far end of the dusty quarry, Ralph pointed to a far desolate corner. 'This will do. People hardly ever come to this side. There is what used to be an old well, let's put them down there, if we can manage it. It's miles down to the bottom.' Once Ralph had parked as close as he dared to the open stone well that was covered by just a few planks of wood for safety, he got out of the van and opened the doors. He knew the area like the back of his hand, even in the darkness. He was sweating as he and Millie pulled at the bodies, and he sighed as he watched them slide down into the darkness of the well. 'Good riddance,' he said, as he got back into the van.

Pain wracked his body and he just wanted to lie down and sleep. He felt battered and bruised all over. Paddy was drifting in and out of consciousness by now and so Ralph only had Millie to help him. She was a short, stocky woman made of stern stuff who had had the life frightened out of her, but even she realised the importance of getting rid of those bodies. Murder was a serious charge and she knew her beloved rogue of a son would go to prison forever.

Once back at Millie's house, they all stumbled through the door. 'Boil some water, Millie, and undress Paddy. Let's see where that bullet is.'

'What are we going to do, Ralph, love? Is he going to die?' Worry was etched into her face. Paddy needed a doctor, but who could they call? Who would believe that she had been kidnapped and their lives had been threatened? Ralph didn't know who he could trust. Those men had told him they had friends in the police force, and they hated him and Paddy anyway. This would give them the ammunition they needed to lock them away for good.

'I'm going to try and take the bullet out. Get hot water and any clean bandages you have, now!' Ralph shouted. He was not sure what to do, but he knew he had to get the bullet out.

Paddy's clothes were stuck to him where the blood had dried, but Ralph eventually saw the extent of the damage. The bullet hadn't gone through the bone. It was in his shoulder and the black, blood-encrusted hole looked deep. Kneeling on the floor beside Paddy, Ralph took out his penknife. 'Do you have any whisky?' he shouted towards the kitchen.

Without a word, she walked into the living room and handed Ralph a bottle, then stood over him, wringing her hands. She was covered in blood and shaking but concentrated on Paddy. Ralph poured some whisky down Paddy's throat, nearly making him choke in the process. He took a large gulp himself, then he poured some on the bullet hole. 'You take a drink, too, to settle your nerves, and then go and get the bandages,' he ordered.

Poking his penknife into the hole, Ralph could not feel anything and thought he was making things worse. Then he felt the hard, embedded bullet. Poking around as best he could, he released it and out it popped. It was almost like taking a splinter out of your finger.

Pouring more whisky on the wound and taking another large gulp himself, he rested back on his haunches. He was tired and there was still a lot to do. 'I have some lint, Ralph; that hole will need packing. I know what to do. I've sterilised my old darning needle I use for socks. You take a break, then go and get washed in the kitchen. There's plenty of hot water. Thank you; you have done more than your bit for me and Paddy.'

Not having the strength to argue, Ralph got up, holding his ribs tightly. 'Are you sure you can manage?'

'I've suffered childbirth; I can do this.' She was starting to be in charge of the situation now the worst was over. 'Believe me, it's worse than the pain your ribs are giving you. Now, go and get cleaned up and then I will bandage those ribs when I've finished here. My God, you look a state. It's a wonder you can see through those eyes, all puffed up.' Her thick Irish accent and her bossy manner were a welcome relief to Ralph. She was in mother mode now and taking charge. He needed that.

Stripping down to nothing, Ralph could already see the bruises around his ribs forming. His whole body looked black and blue. He welcomed the warm water as he splashed it on his face and did his best to wash himself while watching the water turn red with the blood.

'He's all sewn up now, and I've put my quilt over him. He'll sleep now and hopefully he will be okay.'

'Bloody hell, can't you see I'm naked!' Shocked, Ralph tried covering his manhood as she waltzed up to him, heedless of his nakedness.

'Oh, shut up, Ralph Goldstein. It is not the first time I've seen your bare arse, and bloody hell, it's not changed much! I've changed your nappies, lad, and this is no time for modesty. Lean over the sink and let me rinse your hair – it's all matted with blood. Holy Mother of God, as if an old woman like myself would be impressed by your naked body!'

Blushing, Ralph leant over the sink, thankful it was only his arse she could see now. She nearly drowned him, pouring jug after jug of water over his head and scrubbing it with carbolic soap.

'Enough!' Ralph held up his hand to stop her. He was dripping wet and standing in a puddle where she had been overly generous with the water. He nearly slipped on her lino as he stood upright.

'Now, that looks better. I'll put the kettle on while you dry yourself off and then we'll bandage those ribs.'

Ralph realised she was glad of something to do. Her bossy manner was in place of the fear she had experienced. She was still in shock but needed to put it to the back of her mind. Ralph wasn't sure he'd be able to do the same.

19

THE MORNING AFTER

The next day, Ralph went home to face the music. Irene was distraught, as he had expected, especially when she saw his battered face. She was used to him staying out sometimes, so he didn't have to explain that.

'Let me get some hot water and clean you up, Ralph. Where on earth did you get those clothes?' Irene was beside herself.

'It was just a fight, nothing to worry about.' Leaning forward as best he could, he pecked her on the lips. Glancing towards his silent mother, he smiled. She was holding a mug of tea and her hands were shaking; she was nearly spilling it. He'd noticed her hands shaking before but thought nothing of it. 'Are you okay, Ma?'

'I am, lad. The question is, are you?' Her hands trembled as she spoke and she nearly spilt her tea again.

'I'm going to bed for a while, give me a shout in a couple of hours, I have things to do.'

Irene followed Ralph into the bedroom, helping him undress and pulling back the bed sheets. 'You won't be disturbed, Ralph. Shaun is at school and I have some shopping to do. It takes a long time getting back and forth to the shops from here. It was easier when the shops were just around the corner.'

Lying on the bed, Ralph let out a sigh. 'So you don't like living at this side of town? Well, you chose it.' He was tired and in pain. It had been a long hard night and now his wife was moaning about this bloody house!' You are the one who picked this house, no matter how far away the shops are. Anyway, changing the subject, have you noticed how Ma's hands shake lately?'

'Oh, yes, she does it all the time – that's why I don't give her any of my best china any more. She always drops it and breaks it. I don't mean to complain, Ralph. It's a beautiful house. I just wish I had a beautiful husband at the moment to share it with,' she said, stroking his battered face.

'If she wants a china cup and saucer, give it to her. I don't care if she breaks a million of them!' he barked at her. 'Since when did you decide what she can drink out of? And you're bloody ungrateful. You wanted this place, you chose it. Now go to the fucking shops and leave me alone. Also, go and call on the doctor and ask him to look in on Ma when he has the time.'

'The doctor has been to see her. They spoke together and she wouldn't discuss it with me.'

'And you never thought to tell me all of this while you were buying curtains? For God's sake, woman, are you so engrossed in yourself that you cannot think about others?' Tears brimmed in Irene's eyes but Ralph was too tired to argue any more. He closed his eyes and immediately fell asleep.

* * *

Ralph woke up in darkness. He yawned and tried his best to sit up. He could hear Shaun talking and the sound of the television coming from the living room. What time was it?

Rubbing his face, he got up and walked into the living room. He could see that it was dark outside. He must have been asleep for hours.

'There you are, Ralph, love. I'll go and make you a nice cup of tea.' Irene got up and went to the kitchen. Shaun was sitting cross-legged in front of the television. Ralph rubbed his face as much as he could bear and sat on the new sofa Irene had ordered on credit.

'How are you, Ma?' Remembering how he had seen her shaking earlier, he planned to broach the subject tentatively.

'A lot better than you, by the looks of it. You look like you have been run over by a steam train. I hope it was worth it.' Tearing her eyes away from the television, she looked his broken, battered body up and down.

'What about you? I saw you shaking earlier. Come on, Ma, this is me. Tell me what's wrong.' He tried smiling through his swollen lips.

'Very well, lad. I can see you're not going to let it rest. It's the shakes. Some form of disease, they say. They call it the palsy shakes, or something. It doesn't happen often, but my hands cramp a little, too, and I can't help Irene as much as I'd like. Don't worry, son, really, I'm fine.'

'What about the doctors? Can't they do anything?' Concern washed over Ralph. His mother had always been a strong woman who took care of everything. The very idea of her being ill made him feel sick.

'I've seen the doctor, there's nothing they can do. For now, I'm okay, and there isn't any immediate worry.' She patted his knee comfortingly. 'That is the end of it.' With that, she turned and carried on watching the programme Shaun was laughing at.

Ralph knew not to push her any further. However, he would find out more about this disease. 'I have to go out, Irene,' he said, as she came in with the tea. Seeing her face drop, he smiled. 'I'll not be long; I just have to pick something up for Paddy. Couple of hours, maximum, I promise.'

'But you're not well,' she whined.

'Leave him to go about his business, Irene!' his mother snapped. 'This stuff from the catalogue you ordered needs paying for, does it not! It does not appear by magic.' His mother watched her face go crimson with embarrassment.

First things first; Ralph needed to go and see Paddy. Then he had unfinished business of his own. He had suffered enough and was not going to let that Italian gun deal go without a fight. If nothing else, he needed the money. Irene seemed to be spending it quicker than he could make it.

'How is he, Millie? How's the invalid?' Ralph said as he walked into the house. He looked around the living room. He could see no sign of Paddy.

'Don't you worry, Ralph, boy. He's tucked up in his own bed. He seems to be on the mend. All is well here. I've given him something to ease the pain and help him sleep. Incidentally' – she nudged him in the ribs, making him wince – 'I've burnt your clothes, and Paddy's, as well. I think you should keep a low profile, too. You've had a close shave.'

'What about you? I never got to ask. Did they hurt you?'

She put a cup of tea before him, then took out the half-empty whisky bottle and put a drop in each cup. 'Don't worry about me, lad. I'm made of stern stuff. Just you two get back on your feet but keep your head down. That lot meant business and there are plenty more where they came from.'

Ralph knew she was right. Somewhere, sometime, there were bound to be repercussions, but he would cross that bridge when he came to it.

'Go up and see him, before you go.'

Paddy was snoring his head off. When he walked into the bedroom, Ralph knew he was going to be all right. By the look of it, Millie had been up all night mopping his brow with cool cloths to keep the fever down. Pulling back the sheet, Ralph could see she had put a clean dressing over his wound. He was safe.

* * *

After leaving Paddy's, Ralph walked around the street corner to where they had parked the van. He wasn't sure it would even be there, now. However, it was. Damn it! The keys had been in his pockets and he doubted Millie had checked before she'd burnt the lot. Ralph opened the door, then got in and hotwired it.

His first port of call would be the warehouse. He was curious to see what mayhem they had left behind and if the police had been. The inside of the warehouse would be covered in blood, of that he was sure. When he drove up, he saw the security guards in their cabin, unlike the previous night when they had done a disappearing act.

Ralph got out and opened the cabin door. He'd left the headlights on. Tonight he didn't care. 'You know what I've come for and the scrap is still in the back of the van.'

Their faces paled when they saw him. 'We thought you were dead.'

'Well, I'm very much alive, as you can see.' Ralph watched them exchange glances and shrug. They were obviously well informed. 'I want some good stuff, now, and you two can help me put it in the van.'

They nodded and led the way to the warehouse. It was clean! There was no sign of anyone having been there, let alone someone having had his brains bashed in. 'Who's been here?' he said.

'No one,' they stammered, then one of them added, 'You're a dead man walking, Goldstein. You killed the boss's brother. He may be inside, but he has many friends on the outside. Just take your stuff and leave. Don't ever come back!'

'So, you won't be wanting this then?' He was holding out a handful of money.

They looked at each other, then back at Ralph. 'No, just go. We don't want anything to do with you.'

'Wait,' said the other security guard. 'I'll take your money, but we've never seen you, okay? God knows who's watching this place. Go to the big one in London. A lot of this stuff is moved on there when we're running short of room.'

'London?' Ralph's curiosity was roused. He'd never thought about the prospect of other places doing the same thing. Trying to make a joke of it, Ralph smiled. 'Where would I go in London? I can't just go knocking on a door and ask if they have any guns for sale.' He laughed, trying to ease the tension. It was pretty obvious the guards didn't want him there.

'Wherever you go, just make sure it's not here. Our business deal is over.' Impulsively, the guard took out his pen from his jacket, scribbled a number on a scrap of paper and stuffed it into the pocket of Ralph's shirt. 'That's the guy that usually comes here. He's as crooked as they come, always takes more than he should. Just take your stuff and let that be the end of it.'

Glancing at the piece of paper stuffed in his pocket, Ralph nodded. These men looked nervous and agitated, as though they couldn't wait to see the back of him.

They all started loading the van in silence. It was a strange, eerie feeling with only the moonlight guiding their way as they loaded the containers. Ralph got in the van and drove away. He kept checking the side mirrors and out of the windows. He had a strange feeling someone was watching him, but he drove on, keeping a sharp eye out.

Two men stepped out of the darkness of the warehouse. 'Nice work, boys. It's good to know that Mr Goldstein is alive and well. I shall enjoy killing him. I thought he would come back to clean up his mess if he was alive. His mate must be dead or he wouldn't be alone. What number did you give him?' The man's face was full of hate and loathing as he looked at the guard who had given Ralph the note.

Shocked, the guard looked up. He now realised how stupid he had been. Even though he had lowered his voice, they had seen him give Ralph the scrap of paper with the telephone number on. Looking down at the floor, he shrugged.

'I just made something up to get rid of him.' He was lying through his teeth and he didn't want these two men to see right through him. He realised he was now on dodgy ground. He had given a genuine telephone contact number in London to Ralph. Billy the Dodger was always good for a laugh and he didn't care who he sold guns to. He always boasted about his job at the army barracks and the money he made.

'We don't need his kind hanging around here. Who is he going to complain to when he finds out the number is phoney?' One of the men said.

'I just said all that to get rid of him. He won't be back.' Doing his best to appease the two men before him, he gave a weak smile.

'You're dead right, he won't. That is the only true thing you have said all day.' Calmly, the man took out his gun and pointed it at the security guards. He fired two bullets. Each one of them was a direct hit in the head. Reaching down towards their dead bodies, he went through their pockets and took the money Ralph had given them. 'They won't be tipping anyone off about us, the two-faced greedy bastards. Come on, let's go. Let someone else find what Ralph Goldstein left behind him on his last visit to this shithole.'

* * *

Heading straight for the airport, Ralph knew he was earlier than the date given, but he didn't have anywhere to put the guns and he needed to get rid of them. He'd seen the deal through and if these Italians wanted the guns badly enough, they would sort it out. He left the van at the same place as before, and no doubt they would watch it for a couple of hours first. Ralph put up the collar on his coat, shoved his hands in his pockets and started to walk around the airport car park. He needed a ride home. There were many cars to choose from, but he wanted an old one. One that wouldn't cause suspicion when he dumped it later on. After picking the lock of a Morris Minor, Ralph got in and hotwired it. He would come back in a couple of days to see if his money was there. He doubted it would be, and he just wanted to see the back of the van, but he had kept his word, and his word was all he had.

20

'Hello, is that you, Sue?' Julie thought she had better put Swinger Sue in the picture so she knew they would be holding no more nights at the brothel. It was for the best and something she dearly wanted to forget. But the party with Sue and her posh friends had shown promise, and she had been decent to her.

'Julie! Is that you? How lovely to hear from you!' Sue's warm voice cheered Julie up no end. It was nice to hear a friendly voice, although she felt what she had to say would not be welcome.

'I know you can't speak properly, but the business is closing. Carrie is retiring and I'm sorry, I didn't know it at the time… personal problems or something,' Julie lied. Well, what could she say? 'Sorry for interrupting you at work. I just wanted to let you know before you arranged anything.'

'Well, I'm sorry, too.'

As Julie had predicted, Sue wasn't happy, but that was the end of it. At least she'd had the decency to let her know.

'What about you, Julie? What are you going to do now?'

Julie was taken off her guard; it had been a long time since anyone had shown concern over her welfare. 'I'll be okay, but thanks for asking. There'll be a street corner with my name on it.' She laughed, trying to make light of the situation.

'Well, if you're at a loose end maybe I could do you a favour.'

Julie couldn't believe her ears. What would Sue be able to do for her?

'It's just that I know someone who knows someone that runs an escort agency. The girls work the hotels and the deputy manager turns a blind eye for a commission. I know, you're probably not interested, I just thought it might get you back on your feet. You have been very kind to me. To us all. I would like to help you, if possible.'

'Hotels? What kind of hotels?' Julie listened intently as Sue told her that the girls were booked through an agency. They went to the hotel and what happened there was their own business, although it was pretty certain they were not there to escort someone to the theatre or dinner. That was a nice easy way of dressing it up.

'Let me get the number for you. As I say, once you give the deputy manager a few quid for his trouble, all is good.' The line went quiet for a few minutes and then Julie heard Sue's voice again. 'Here it is, love.' She read it out and Julie quickly jotted it down. 'Good luck and keep in touch.'

As soon as Julie hung up, she dialled the number of the agency, who didn't ask too many questions. They took their commission as a deposit when the escorts were booked. You got your money on arrival. It all seemed straightforward. They offered her a job as a trial the following night. This was a completely new ball game for Julie, but men were men and sex was sex.

Her next stop was to find another dump to live in. Cheap, clean and cheerful, that was what she needed right now. Something away from it all.

As she trawled the streets looking at decrepit houses, all with damp on the ceilings and mould in the bathrooms, Julie felt depressed. Was this it? Was this all she was ever going to amount to? Another bedsit and more men. She was sick of it. Her whole life summed up to nothing! The best of the bunch was an Indian woman's house. Sumatra. Apparently, her husband had been a landlord of a few properties and then died. It seemed poor, aging Sumatra found it all beyond her, but carried on anyway. She was a sweet little old woman who owned property and, if she carried on in business, it meant her son couldn't sell everything up and put her in a residential home. She took pity on Julie and reduced the rent. Well, that was that part of her life sorted out.

The next evening was her supposed 'date' at the hotel. She needed it. With no money coming in, what she had stashed away was beginning to disappear. Carrie had kept her word and given her some money towards her deposit, but there was still day-to-day living to pay for. She also still gave money to Gertie to send to her mum, although she still hadn't heard a word about Frankie.

It was an unusual set-up at the hotel. You were given a room number and just turned up at a designated time. Whoever you were going to meet had obviously already been out on the town and wanted a little fun to round off the evening. Most of the men were businessmen or travelling salesmen, all married, of course, but that was not her problem. She did worry that she never knew what she was facing until they opened the door, but by then it was too late. Donna's fate crossed her mind, but it was a gamble she had to take.

Julie's first client had been nothing special; when she had arrived, the old man was in his bathrobe, saving time by not having to get undressed! Not only were you watching the clock, but so were the men. They wanted their money's worth, and quickly. Then it was over and they couldn't wait to get rid of you and go to sleep.

When she walked into the bar area afterwards, the hotel manager was sitting on a stool, waiting for her. He handed her an orange juice and she handed him his money. It all seemed like a well-oiled plan.

When she had called the agency the next day, and the day after that, she got more work from them. They seemed to have a regular supply of customers wanting company, and so she was working again. You couldn't go to the same hotel too often as it would cause suspicion amongst the staff. So Julie's time was spread across various hotels who all did the same thing. It was not much, but it was a living.

For the time being, everything seemed to be going okay, though Julie was only working evenings. She wondered if maybe there was an extra income to be made on the streets during the day.

She tried it a few times but she didn't really like it, especially in the cold weather. It was grim waiting in the red-light district for a car to pull up, the punters taking their choice of the many women that worked the same corner. Some had complained that Julie was on their 'patch' and their pimp would have something to say about it. There always seemed to be an argument or a fight breaking out. She decided to leave them to it and try to get more work from the agency. The streets were too much like hard work and it was bloody freezing. God knows what chances you took when you got in men's cars. Hopefully, they weren't weird or going to kidnap you. No, Julie had decided, after another chancy encounter, it wasn't worth the risk. This punter would be her last.

When the man dropped her off back in the red-light district, she looked at a group of bedraggled women across the road and was shocked when she thought she recognised one of them. The woman's hair was dirty and uncombed, and her clothes were skimpy, leaving nothing to the imagination. Julie looked over again. My God, it was Frankie! She had hardly recognised her own sister.

'Frankie,' she shouted, and she started to wave her arms at the woman across the road, but it was too late, she was already getting into a car. She shouted again but there was no acknowledgement from the woman as she sped away with the stranger.

Distraught at the very idea of her beloved sister looking the way she did, Julie stopped one of the other women. 'Do you know that woman who just got into that car?' she half-shouted at them. She was panicking and trying to get their attention.

'Maybe, what's it got to do with you?' One woman dropped her cigarette and crushed it out with her shoe. She looked Julie up and down with distaste and turned her back on her.

'She's my sister. I've been trying to find her!'

Turning around again, a bored expression on her face, the woman looked Julie squarely in the face. 'We're all somebody's sister, love. Now piss off before you get into trouble.'

'Hey, you,' a greasy-haired, scruffy young man shouted as he approached Julie. 'Don't you stop my girls from working. If you want to talk to them, you pay. Time is money. Got it?' Then he smiled. 'Of course, that is, unless you're looking for work.' His smug grin sent shivers down her spine.

'Who the fuck are you, mate? I'm just asking a question.'

'This is my corner and these are my girls. Now, either start working or fuck off.'

'Who the hell do you think you're speaking to, you bloody pimp? No, I'm not looking for work, and I wouldn't work for a lowlife like you.'

A hard slap knocked her off balance, then the man grabbed her face. 'I won't tell you again, girlie... now, either pay up or leave.' Letting go of her jaw, he turned to the other girls and instantly they were handing money over to him.

Embarrassed and in pain, her cheeks stinging and burning, Julie had no choice but to leave. She vowed to herself she would go back tomorrow and try again. Her mind was troubled. How long had Frankie been on the streets? She looked awful, unrecognisable. Now it was time to do some investigating.

Julie went to see Gertie, who said she hadn't seen anything of Frankie in a while; she seemed to have disappeared. Doubt crossed Julie's mind a few times that it was Frankie she had seen. Maybe it was a trick of the light and someone who just looked a bit like her. The woman she had seen had looked older. She would definitely go back tomorrow, but this time she would be prepared to face that pimp. The next day could not come quickly enough.

The next evening, just before Julie's next appointment at the hotel, she went back to try and see Frankie again. Looking around the street corner, her heart sank. Frankie was nowhere to be seen, and Julie thought she must have imagined seeing her sister after all. But then, after waiting in a side alley for a while, she saw a car pull up and Frankie got out. *Thank God*, she breathed to herself and ran towards her.

'Frankie, is that you?' Reaching out to touch the woman's arm, Julie felt sick. She had been right. It was her sister.

'Julie!' The horrified, wild look in Frankie's eyes said all Julie needed to know.

'You're coming home with me. Now!' Julie started pulling her away when she was blinded by car headlights and a man got out of a vehicle. Putting her hand to her eyes to shield them, Julie waited.

'I thought I told you yesterday to fuck off,' he barked at her. 'You.' He turned to Frankie. 'You've only seen three punters tonight. Now, get your arse into gear and get to work.'

'Fuck you, mate, she is coming home with me.' Julie grabbed at Frankie's arm and started yanking her away, when suddenly she felt a crippling pain. The man had punched her in the stomach. She was doubled over and fell to her knees, the wind completely knocked out of her.

'I told you yesterday,' he spat at her, 'if you want to talk to my girls, you pay up.'

Realising she had no choice, Julie scrambled for her purse. Tears rolled down her face. 'How much?' she asked breathlessly.

'Five pounds for fifteen minutes. Now, pay up or you will get more of the same.'

Throwing the money at his feet, Julie stood up and pulled Frankie away.

'Hey, no funny business now, I'm watching,' the man warned her.

Looking across the road, Julie saw a greasy spoon. 'We're going in there, so fuck off yourself. In addition, don't ever go to sleep at night, mister; God knows I will be there with the carving knife to slit your throat.'

His surly manner annoyed her, but the clock was running and she didn't have time to argue with him.

Frankie followed Julie across the road, saying nothing, and when they got to the café, Julie knew why. Frankie's eyes were unfocused and she looked spaced out. The thin, sleeveless top she was wearing showed her arms were covered in bruises and needle marks and she was as thin as could be.

Julie sat her at a table and went and got two coffees and a sandwich. Through the windows she could see that slimy bastard across the road, watching them.

'Frankie, love, what happened? Why didn't you go to Gertie's? More to the point, why haven't you come and found me? And who is he?'

'He's my boyfriend. He loves me. We just need some extra cash so we can get married. He's good to me.'

Julie couldn't believe her ears. Frankie was defending that son of a bitch. Boyfriend, indeed! He was a pimp.

'You're on heroin, aren't you? Did he do this to you?' Julie was angry and she could feel her temper rising, but there was nothing she could do.

'It helps me sleep when I'm in pain. He looks after me.' Frankie picked up the sandwich and almost ate it in one. Julie was devastated. How could this have happened?

'Well, you're coming home with me. I don't care what he says. Come on.'

'I can't, Julie. He gets angry. You've seen what he's like. I can't just leave him. He's good to me,' Frankie whined.

'You mean he's your dealer, who has got you so hooked on that shit that you daren't leave. Don't you understand? That is what they do.' Julie was pleading with her, trying to get through to her heroin-addled brain, but it was useless.

Frankie shook her head. 'He's my boyfriend,' she kept repeating.

'How did you meet him?' Julie wanted to know how she had ended up here.

'I went to stay with him after we argued that time, but he was having trouble paying the rent and so he suggested if I turned a trick for the landlord it would help. I didn't want to, but you have to support each other, don't you? I told you,' Frankie stressed the point again, 'he looks after me. When I told him about you he said you'd be jealous and want to take me away from him.' Frankie looked at Julie sullenly.

'Jealous? Don't you see, he is just using you. What about all those others – are they his girlfriends as well? Don't you realise you mean nothing to him?' She felt like shouting at her and shaking her into waking up and seeing this man for what he was, but she didn't want to cause a scene in the café. Already people were looking over disapprovingly at Frankie sitting there.

'They just work for him. He treats me better than them.' Frankie's voice was low and sheepish as she looked at Julie. It was obvious to Julie she felt uncomfortable just seeing her. 'I have to go, he'll be waiting.' Looking out of the window, both of them saw him standing outside on the pavement, looking at his watch and pointing to it. Julie didn't know what to do. She had no real defence against someone like this. Frankie was hooked on heroin and brainwashed into thinking this pimp loved her. What was she going to do?

Frankie stood up in haste, almost knocking the mugs flying. She was panicking and afraid. She knew the consequences if she didn't do as she was told and Julie was only going to get her into trouble.

'Meet me again, Frankie.' Julie scribbled down her address. 'Come to my place and stay with me, let me look after you.' Again she pleaded, wiping away the tears from her face. Suddenly there was a tap on the window and, looking up, she saw it was Frankie's pimp pointing to his watch again. He looked angry and Julie didn't want to give him another excuse to hit her – or worse, take it out on Frankie.

'You've had more than your time to catch up on family values, now piss off and let me get on with my business. Frankie, get over there and stand under the streetlamp where they can see you better. You've wasted enough of my time.'

'Don't speak to her like that. I'm going to call the police! You're holding my sister against her will and you're a drug dealer!' Julie shouted at the top of her voice for everyone to hear. She was desperate and didn't know what to do.

'Holding her against her will?' His smug grin made Julie feel sick. 'Here, Frankie, I've got you a present. Something to help you sleep.' He was waving a small piece of foil and Julie saw her sister's eyes light up. Frankie was almost drooling. She snatched it out of his hand and ran across the road to stand under the streetlamp, like she'd been told. She didn't even say goodbye to Julie.

'Come here,' he said, and beckoned to Julie. Stupidly, she leant forward and was met by a head butt. She fell backwards against the window of the café. Her eyes watering, holding her bloodied nose, she vowed vengeance on him as he smugly walked away.

Tears rolled down Julie's face from both despair and pain. Her head was throbbing. She reached into her bag for a handkerchief, wanting something to hold to her nose to stop the blood. She had to be at work in a few hours. She needed to get cleaned up and plaster some makeup on before her eyes turned black.

The next day, she went to the police and poured out her story, telling them about the pimp that was holding her sister and that he'd assaulted her. They didn't seem interested and told her they would look into it, but they weren't taking her seriously and she knew it. Walking out of there, she wanted to cry. She sat on the steps of the police station and sobbed. No one could help her. She didn't know what to do. The odds were stacked against her and she couldn't work tonight. Her face was a mess. She had just about gotten away with it last night, but when she had woken that morning her eyes were black and puffy. She pulled herself together and headed home.

A couple of days later, there was a rap at the door. She opened it to see her sister standing there. 'Frankie!' she exclaimed. It was like a dream come true. For the last couple of days she had wracked her brain about how she could get her away from that man, and now she was here.

'You bitch, Julie. How could you,' Frankie screamed. She stepped into the room and turned on Julie, like a wildcat. 'You went to the police and they arrested him for assault. He spent last night in the cells! For God's sake, why do you always interfere? I'll have to work twice as hard now to pay his fine.'

Julie ignored her outburst. 'You're here. How did you get away? You can stay here with me. I'll look after you.' She sat her down on the worn-out bed settee.

Wringing her hands nervously, Frankie shook her head. 'He's waiting for me outside. He's only let me come in to tell you to leave us alone. I have to go.' Frankie stood up and walked to the door, then turned. 'Just leave us alone, Julie. He loves me but he has a vile temper. You're only going to make things worse.'

The police had tried, but without Frankie's statement, it would all come to nothing. Julie had only made things worse for her sister. No doubt Frankie would take a beating for all the trouble she had caused. For now, it was best left. They both knew where to find each other, whatever good that might do.

21

HARSH REALITY

Irene had enjoyed showing off her new house and all the new gadgets she'd filled it with to her family and friends. It had all been beyond her wildest dreams. Now... well, she missed home. This new house was miles away from the old neighbourhood and her family. In the old house, the kettle was always boiling for when family and friends popped in for a quick cuppa and there was always someone walking in the door with a fresh piece of gossip. Around here, everyone kept themselves to themselves and she felt homesick. Irene knew it was time to speak up and admit her feelings.

'Hey, where's my boy?' Ralph ruffled Shaun's hair fondly. 'You're getting bigger every day, son.' The little boy laughed and pulled his head away. 'I'll just go and say hello to my ma, Irene. What's for dinner?'

'I need to speak to you, while it's still in my head.'

Frowning, Ralph put Shaun down and told him to go and watch the television. 'What's wrong?'

'I want to go home, Ralph. Back to our own people. I hate it here.' She sniffed to emphasise her unhappiness.

Stunned and bewildered, Ralph looked at her strangely. He could feel his anger rising. 'Irene, you picked this bloody place! No, we're not leaving. You chose it. Now you live with it.'

'But I hate it here! My life is one big mistake; after all, I married you, didn't I?' Flinging her long hair over her shoulders, Irene stood there defiantly.

Calmly, Ralph looked up from the dining chair he was sitting at. He couldn't believe his ears. 'You mean I married you out of respect. Maybe Paddy was right. You dropped your knickers quickly enough for me. Who's to know if Shaun is mine? He doesn't look like me with all of that red hair.' His throat felt dry and he barely spoke above a whisper. At last the truth was coming out. Maybe after all of this time it needed to.

'How dare you! You took advantage of me. You said I wouldn't get pregnant the first time. It was all your fault. I deserve to be happy. All of these years with you in and out of prison. I have put up with all of that and I have looked after your crippled mother. Every day she shakes more and more and who do you think washes all the bedding when she wets herself, eh? All I want is to move house again and everything will be okay.' Lashing out at Ralph with all the misery she had bottled up, Irene couldn't stop.

At the mention of his mother, Ralph stood up and was about to slap her when he stopped himself. He wouldn't hit a woman, but he had grown to hate Irene now. 'If you want to go back, then you can go back alone. You're a millstone around my neck and always have been.'

'Please, Ralph, you're always reaching for something else. You're a bloody dreamer. Why can't you just be a good husband and do what I ask? God, sometimes when I was visiting you in prison, I was ashamed. It would have been better if you were dead; at least I wouldn't have people laughing and gossiping about me. Look at you. Covered in bruises. Your face is a mess.

How am I supposed to admit to people that punchbag is my husband!'

Trying to keep calm, Ralph listened as Irene carried on about being ashamed of him. But he could control himself no longer. 'You know what? I wish you were dead too. You hold me back; you never have any ambition other than that shitty family of yours and those backstreet houses. Your family may not like me but they are always glad to take money off me, aren't they? Well, you can go to hell for all I care. You're no fucking innocent in all of this. You've spent every penny filling this house up with rubbish. It's not the house that's not good enough, Irene. It's you!'

'I'm pregnant!' she shouted. 'Yes, that's right, I'm pregnant and I'm going to need my family around me to help me.' She banged her fist on the table so hard the milk bottle fell over, dripping onto their new lino flooring.

Glaring at her, Ralph couldn't bear it any longer. Picking up the bottle, he stood it upright, though God knows, he wanted to hit her with it. He was struggling to feed the mouths he had and now there was a new one on the way. 'Is this one mine?'

'How dare you. Of course it's your baby. I do my duty, don't I? Now, why don't you do yours and be a good husband for once in your life?'

'Duty? Is that all I am to you? I'm going out!' Ralph had had enough of listening to his wife's complaining. He had work to do, especially if there was another baby coming. He slammed the door and left, Irene's screams echoing behind him.

* * *

Ralph drove up to the airport and saw the van he had left there a few days earlier. Getting out of his car, he looked around. There were some people milling around with their suitcases, but nothing out of the ordinary. He tried the handle of the van and it opened. He was surprised it wasn't locked.

He got in and looked in the back. It was spotless! The once bloodstained van had been cleaned from top to bottom. He spied an envelope tucked under the passenger seat. He was even more surprised when he opened it and saw that his money was inside. He wanted to get out of there, quick. It was all very suspicious. Someone had cleaned up the van and left his money there. Maybe it was a trap.

He got out and nervously lit a cigarette, then walked back to his car and drove off. As he approached the airport gates, a car swerved and parked in front of him. Ralph rolled down the window and was about to shout at the occupants when a dark-haired, well-dressed man got out of the car, leaving another man sitting behind the wheel. The man opened his passenger-side door. Before Ralph could speak, the man pointed his finger to the side of the road. 'Park over there, Ralph.'

Frowning, but curious, Ralph did as he was told. This was not the usual kind of man he dealt with. The suit this man was wearing was very well-fitting and expensive. Ralph manoeuvred the van to the side of the road. He presumed this was going to turn out to be another fight and his body tensed in anticipation.

'Well, what do you want? You seem to know who I am but I've no bloody idea who you are.' Ralph took a last drag on his cigarette and threw it out of the car window.

'Quite a bloodbath in the back of the van you left for us.'

Stunned, Ralph stared at him, not knowing what to say. Had he walked into a trap?

Ralph swallowed hard and found his tongue. 'Who are you and what do you want with me?'

Holding out his hand to shake Ralph's, the man said, 'My

name is Carlos and it seems I am your Italian cousin. That is my money you have in your pocket.' He smiled.

Shocked at this revelation, Ralph paused for a moment and gathered his thoughts. He wasn't sure what to say to this man. He turned and looked out of the window and then back at him.

'So, what do you want? If it's guns you're after, I'm afraid I won't be able to get my hands on any more for you.'

'No need to worry. I'm just curious and I like to make a habit of eventually meeting the people I do business with.' Neither man was smiling and the car was full of nervous tension. They were playing cat and mouse, skirting around what they actually wanted to say.

Ralph cleared his throat. 'So, what do you want and how did you know I would be here? I kept my word and delivered your goods and you paid me for them. What more is there to say, Carlos?' Ralph made a point of calling him by his name, using the same familiarity the man had used with him.

'Of course you would come back after the delivery date to see if your money was here, or else there would be no point in dropping the goods off, would there? Although, I admire you coming in such a state. It looks as though you have been in a battle. It must have been one hell of a fight if you look like that and won. I have had my man watch the van for the last couple of days, waiting for you. I have also done my homework and found out a lot about you. It seems you have upset a lot of people, but others speak well of you and say you're a fair man.'

Ralph had almost forgotten what he looked like with his black eyes and fat lips. He rubbed his face and looked down at his grazed knuckles. No wonder some people were casting the odd glance at him. Although this Carlos seemed friendly enough, Ralph felt nervous. Carlos seemed very educated and suave. He wore a friendly manner as a mask, but even Ralph realised under that mask lay a very deadly opponent, or else why did he want guns in such huge quantities?

'Tell me what happened, Ralph. Why did you leave my men to clear up your mess? Were you hoping we would be found with it? Is that what you intended?'

'No! No way. That was never my intention. Things just got out of hand and I had promised delivery. I never even expected to get my money. Thinking about it now, it was stupid. I suppose I only came back here today out of curiosity.' Ralph just wanted to leave. Enough had been said.

'Why don't we find somewhere to go for a drink? It seems all this talking is thirsty work. Leave the car parked here; my man there will drop us off outside of the airport.'

Ralph felt uneasy, as though he didn't really have a choice. He wasn't being asked, he was being told. Getting out and getting into the back of the car alongside Carlos, Ralph felt his palms going sweaty. For the first time in a long time, he felt frightened.

All seemed well as they went into a bar at the airport and Carlos ordered some whiskies. Ralph felt slightly embarrassed and uncomfortable, sitting there amongst all the smartly dressed people killing time before their flights were due.

'So, tell me what happened.'

'Look, Carlos, mate, I really don't think this is the place to discuss this, do you? Why not just get to the point and tell me what you want?'

'Very well. I like a man who keeps his word and I have done you a big favour, cleaning your mess up. That vehicle was one big clue to any member of the police force. As for this place...' Carlos looked around the bar and smiled. 'You will learn in time that this is the perfect place to talk. It's noisy and people are far too occupied checking the boards for their flights to pay any attention to you. I hear you are an explosives man?' Carlos suddenly made his point and looked into Ralph's eyes.

Ralph shook his head and downed his drink in one. 'You know what, mister. If there is one thing I regret, it's learning explosives. The moment people find out, they want you to blow something up. I don't kill innocent people and I'm not interested in going back to prison.' Pushing his chair back, Ralph was about to stand up to leave.

'Sit, Ralph, hear me out. Don't be too hasty.' Carlos smiled and proffered the chair. 'I am not killing innocent people. In fact, I am not killing anyone at all. What I want is a safe blown. Albeit a very big safe. My family and I are prepared to pay very well for your services. Plus, you owe me.' Carlos spoke the words slowly to emphasise the meaning. 'You left your jacket in that van, and there are bloodstained clothes from your victims. The odd shoe here and there, some torn clothing from where you had obviously pulled them out of the van. Just out of interest, what did you do with them?' Smugly, Carlos smiled.

Checkmate, Ralph thought to himself. This man had him firmly by the balls and he knew it. Just what else had he saved from the van? He cursed himself. He had totally forgotten about his jacket. Christ, he had left enough evidence to go behind bars for a very long time.

'Well, it seems you're calling the shots, then. There is fuck all I can do, is there? Just how many more times are you planning to blackmail me in the future? There is one thing I'm curious about, though.'

Frowning, Carlos looked at Ralph. 'And what is that?'

'You seem to have connections. I don't know what you're involved in, but we both know it's not legal. Surely you know an explosives expert?'

'Fair point. I do know people and I have connections. My

family are being closely watched now. That is why we are buying our supplies outside of Italy. We cannot make waves, so an outside, unknown man would be just the thing. We are not sure how the police are getting their information, but we'll find out. We always do. But this job has been planned for a long time and needs to be done at the time stated. You, Ralph, have fallen right into my lap.'

'You mean you want me to be a fall guy because I was stupid enough to keep my word and deliver your goods.'

Nonchalantly, Carlos shook his head. 'Not necessarily. That's up to you. If you do a shit job, you will be caught. That is the name of the game. Get it right and you walk away with a lot of money.'

'I would need to know more about it. I won't commit myself to anything, whether you're going to blackmail me or not. How long are you going to give me to think about it?'

'You will know more when you decide that you're doing it, and not before. And blackmail is an ugly word. Tut tut!' Carlos waved his finger at him. 'A month. That is my limit. If you're going to do it, you dial this number.' Carlos took a card out of his pocket and put it on the table. 'You ring and you say...' Carlos looked up at the ceiling, thinking, for a moment. 'You say "happy birthday". That is all. And then I will be in touch.'

'Is that it? And what if I don't want to wish you a happy birthday, then what? What about me?'

'Well, we will think about that when the time comes.' Carlos stood up, indicating the meeting was at an end. He waited for Ralph to pick up the card then walked out of the airport to the waiting car, with Ralph following along behind. They got back in and Ralph was dropped off at his car. No other words were spoken.

The long drive home gave Ralph time to think over what

Carlos had said. He decided to drop in to see how Paddy was getting on. For now, he would keep quiet about this strange encounter. After all, he had not even told Paddy about the Italians. He would keep it close to his chest for the time being.

Paddy was lounging on the sofa, eating a bowl of stew and dumplings. He waved Ralph in when he saw him step through the front door. 'Oh, thank God you're here,' he muttered, still eating, letting some of the gravy spill down his chin. 'My ma is driving me mad. You got any booze on you?'

'No, mate, afraid not. Do you actually want to swallow that mouthful before you speak again?' Ralph sat down opposite him. 'You look better than the last time I saw you.'

'I am. Bit weak, but my arm is healing – Ma has seen to that.' Pulling open his shirt, Paddy showed him the stitched-up wound. 'I am glad I took the bullet because you look worse than I do. Ma! Bring Ralph some tea.'

Within minutes, Millie came through with a cup and saucer in her hand. 'My, Ralph, it is good to see you looking so well.' She laughed. 'See, our Paddy here is doing okay. What about you, love?'

'I'm going to be okay, just a few bruises that will disappear in a few days. The main thing here is that Paddy is on the mend. Even though you betrayed me, Paddy.' Ralph's stern look said it all. He had not forgotten what Paddy had done. Ralph's piercing words were harsh and cold.

As far as he could see, this was all Paddy's fault, and he could have got his own mother killed in the process. He had been stupid and his stupidity had nearly cost them their lives.

'I didn't mean to. I'm sorry.' Looking up at his mother, Paddy apologised again. 'Sorry, Ma.' He turned back to Ralph. 'But they said they wouldn't hurt Ma if you did a little job for them. What difference would it have made? One little job!' Paddy pleaded his case, but Ralph was not impressed. 'They said they only wanted to talk to you. It was only when we got there that I realised there was going to be trouble. That's why I had to leave you and come back with the gun. A fist fight wasn't going to be enough. It was all or nothing.' Paddy was doing his best to get Ralph to see his side of things, but he could see it wasn't working. He knew he had done the unthinkable.

'We have to stick together,' he pleaded. 'They'll go bonkers if they think we killed their mates. They're like the musketeers, all for one and one for all. Don't turn your back on me. Not now.' His eyes were almost bulging with panic and fear as he reached out to him.

'I'm not turning my back on you, Paddy. As you say, we have to stick together and stick to our stories. But if I ever hear you shooting that mouth of yours off again to anybody that will bloody listen, I will kill you myself!' Ralph was angry, and Paddy's betrayal had sickened him. Yes, sure, he had gone to get the gun, but he only came back to find out about his mother, Ralph was sure of that. He could have been dead already for all Paddy knew. Ralph stood up to leave.

'Ralph, mate. We're okay, aren't we?'

Looking at Paddy and hearing his humbled, pathetic voice, Ralph nodded. There was nothing more to say now. He had said his piece. This was a learning curve. From now on, he would keep his business firmly to himself. Paddy would know only what he wanted him to know.

22

'Do you think it will work, boss?' Marco turned towards Carlos, questioningly. Now he had met Ralph he wasn't so sure. He seemed like his own man and wasn't afraid to ask questions. Carlos had already decided he wanted him onside. Looking at Ralph's life over the last few days, he felt that his family and Ireland held him back. Ralph was a man who wanted more. Why else would he risk so much?

'I know it will. Did you see the look in Ralph's eyes when we were in the car? He's already thinking our offer over. You can tell a lot by a man's eyes; that is why I wanted to meet him. The word on the street about him is good. I like that. Apart from his criminal record, he seems to be well thought of. Get the wheels in motion, Marcos.' Carlos gulped back his whisky and pulled his eyeshade over his eyes so the sun shining through the aeroplane window didn't disturb him.

* * *

Ralph went back to work. He was feeling a little better and wanted to keep things as normal as possible. Carlos's words kept spinning around in his head, but it was a big gamble and he knew it. Although this Carlos guy seemed to have everything under control.

At home, Ralph had agreed to keep the peace for now and let Irene have her way, but he resented her for this more than words could explain. To him, moving back to the place they had left behind meant failure.

Ralph felt trapped and now there was going to be another mouth to feed. It seemed the more he tried to please everyone, the more it was flung back in his face.

Ralph felt like a failure. He knew that was what people were thinking. He hadn't moved on; he had gone backwards. Each night, when Irene tried to cuddle up to him and tempt him with her body, he turned his back on her. Was that what she thought of him? That all it took was for her to offer sex and everything would be okay?

The new house Irene rented seemed poky in comparison to the one they'd been living in. And the only place Ralph could escape to was work. If nothing else, Paddy was happy about it.

* * *

A few days later, while at work, Ralph saw a police car drive up. They walked to the cabin where Ben was and Ralph saw him point towards him. His heart was in his mouth as he watched them walk over to him. *That bloody Italian*, he cursed to himself. He knew he had grassed him up.

'Mr Goldstein?' said one of the police officers.

'You know everyone calls me Ralph. What do you want?' Looking down at the dusty, rocky ground, he waited for them to accuse him of being at the warehouse and killing those men. Instead, they looked at him with pity, and then glanced at each other. 'Mr Goldstein, there has been an accident at your house. Some kind of explosion. I'm sorry to have to tell you that your wife and son are both dead.' They paused and waited for their words to sink in.

Rooted to the spot, Ralph could see their lips moving but he could not hear what they were saying. He felt numb and his head was spinning. 'My ma, you haven't mentioned her. Is she dead, too?' His dry throat could barely utter the words. He sat down on a rock and waited.

'No. She was at a neighbour's house. Can you think of anyone that would do this, sir?'

'Sir? Since when did I get a fucking knighthood? You must be wrong. Irene is having a baby; she can't be dead. And Shaun will be at school.' He wanted to lash out, but just rambled on about how impossible it was. Irene and Shaun, dead. That was impossible. Wasn't it? It couldn't be true.

'Come with us, sir... er, Ralph. Your ma is at the hospital and I am afraid you need to identify the bodies. The car is over there.' The police officers waited for Ralph to compose himself and follow them. He was dumbstruck.

Ben ran up to him. 'Ralph, are you okay?'

Ralph looked around. Already word was beginning to spread. They were all curious as to why the police were there and Ben had obviously told them. Nodding, Ralph followed the police officers to the car. It was the first time he had ever been in a police car without being handcuffed. He still couldn't take in what they had told him and sat in the back seat in silence. It felt like the world had ended and he didn't know how he was supposed to react.

At the hospital, standing over the bodies of his wife and son, he still couldn't quite take it in. Shaun was badly burnt and the police explained it was from the fire. His little boy, his beautiful little boy, was dead. Suddenly, the tears started rolling down his face and he couldn't control them. The police looked away, saving him from embarrassment.

'Take a moment, Ralph. We'll be outside.'

Turning around, he looked at Irene lying on the slab of cold metal, a sheet covering half of her body. Apart from the black smoke on her face, she looked almost asleep. Raising the sheet slightly, he could see that she was badly burnt from the waist down. Without thinking, he put his hand on her stomach. His new baby would never see the light of day. Sobs wracked his body uncontrollably. Wiping his arm across his face, he opened the door and went outside to where the police were standing waiting for him.

'Where's my ma?' His voice cracked as he spoke. He stood there, numb.

'She's in the main hospital, upstairs. Before you go to see her, Ralph, we have to tell you she's not in a good way.' The police officers exchanged glances and waited.

'What do you mean? I thought you said she wasn't in the house. You told me she was okay!' he shouted.

'No, Ralph. We told you she was alive. Now, calm down, and let's go upstairs to the main part of the hospital. She's in a side room.'

The lift seemed to take ages, but at last, the doors opened and the police led him down a corridor. Ralph felt cold, even though it was a warm day. He hadn't had a full explanation yet about what had happened. He felt dizzy and sick and couldn't control himself. Suddenly, he leant over and vomited all over the floor. A nurse rushed forward to help him, but all he could do was apologise and wipe his mouth with the tissue she gave him. He offered to clean it up but she waved her hand at him and shook her head.

As though in a trance, he looked up and carried on following the police. Eventually they stopped at a door and turned the handle. Seeing them, a doctor holding a clipboard followed them in. Ralph's mother was lying in bed, asleep.

As he walked up to her, Ralph noticed her face was an odd shape. 'What's wrong with her face?' he asked.

'She's had a bad stroke, Mr Goldstein,' the doctor said. 'We have had to give her something to help her sleep. She's also in shock.'

'You know she has the palsy shakes?' Ralph looked up at the doctor and then back at his mother. Taking her hand in his, he squeezed it tight. She was surrounded by all kinds of monitors and tubes.

'The palsy shakes?' The doctor didn't understand, until Ralph went into more detail.

'Ah, yes, you mean Parkinson's disease. Yes, I did see that when we got a summary from her doctor. It seems she has had it for a while. We've been in touch with her GP. But Parkinson's wouldn't cause a stroke. This is just one of those things. There are no answers. Trauma, possibly.'

'A while?' How had she had it for a while without him seeing it?

'I'm afraid so. About a year or so.' The doctor looked puzzled.

Stunned, Ralph looked around the room for answers. He didn't know what to say. A million questions he wanted to ask danced around his head, making it spin. His mother had been ill for a year and he didn't know anything about it?

'Her stroke will have probably been brought on by the shock of... recent events.' The doctor looked across at the police officers, biting his tongue in case he had said too much.

'I know my wife and son are dead. You don't have to hide it. Will my ma get better?'

'Time will tell. We won't know anything until she wakes up. We'll run more tests and do a scan then.' Hanging his clipboard on the bottom of the bed, the doctor gave a weak smile and walked out.

'How did this happen? You said there'd been an explosion.' Ralph looked up at the police officers. They had not told him much and now he wanted to know the truth.

'We're not a hundred per cent sure. The fire brigade is still at your house. We don't know if it was a gas explosion or something else, but the whole house just blew up. Do you have somewhere to stay, or anyone you would like us to contact?' They were very business-like and matter-of-fact.

'I'll stay here, if you don't mind. I don't want to leave my ma on her own just in case she wakes up.' Looking down, he stroked her hair.

'Are you sure you don't want a lift anywhere?' the police officer asked. 'The doctor said she would be asleep for some time.'

'No. I'll just sit here.' Ralph pulled up a chair to his mother's bedside, sat down and took her hand, then buried his head in the blanket covering her body. He cried. 'Wake up, Ma. Please wake up,' he begged. How could this have happened? An explosion? He felt all cried out and then a thought crossed his mind. Dear God! This was revenge. Paddy had said friends of the men they had killed would come looking for them. Was this their revenge, to kill a woman and a child?

Was this what he had brought upon his family? His wife, son and their unborn child, dead, and his mother lying in a hospital bed? His heart was breaking, and no matter how many beatings he had taken in the past, he had never felt pain like this. He felt weak.

'Ralph! Bloody hell, I've been looking all over for you. I just heard what happened.' Paddy rushed into the room. Ralph's puffy red face looked up at Paddy. Tentatively, he walked over to the bedside. 'She'll be okay. She's a fighter, your ma.' At a loss for words, he looked around and saw a chair, placed it on the opposite side of the bed from Ralph and sat down.

You could have cut the tension with a knife. It was Ralph who eventually broke the silence. 'This is revenge, Paddy. An eye for an eye. I have murdered my wife and son.'

'Are they both dead?' Paddy's hushed whisper was barely audible.

'Yes. Did I tell you she was pregnant? Oh, Paddy, I hadn't been kind to her lately, what with this move and everything. I was angry, hurt. She threw everything back in my face. I was right, though. If we had never moved, she would still be alive.' Never once moving his eyes from his mother, Ralph carried on airing his thoughts, and worst of all, his guilt. 'I even told her I wished she was dead. What kind of a man does that make me? Be careful what you wish for. You might just get it.'

'You don't know this was revenge. It could've been the gas, couldn't it? Things like that happen all the time, especially in them old houses.' Paddy realised he did not have any answers. He just hoped he was right. 'Right, no arguments: you're going to stay with me and Ma.' As an afterthought, Paddy looked up at Ralph curiously. 'Have you seen your house? It's a pile of rubble. Only the stairs are left.' Paddy thought it was weird.

Empty, not quite taking Paddy's words in, Ralph nodded. He wanted to see the house. He would know if it was gas. He would also know if it was anything else.

'Have you got the car outside?' Licking his lips to moisten them, Ralph stood up.

'I have. Why? Do you want to go somewhere?'

Nodding, Ralph's face turned to stone. 'Too bloody right, I do. I want to see that house.' Ralph poked himself in the chest angrily. 'I will bloody well know if someone blew up my house intentionally or not. Come on.' Picking up his coat, he flung the door open and walked into the corridor, with Paddy hot on his heels.

Paddy parked as close as he could. The police were not letting people down the street. Ralph could see the gas company van parked down there. There were still a few of the houses occupied. His eyes roamed the street until they stopped at his own house – what was left of it. It was taped off, with warning signs to stay away. It seemed to him was there was only a roof left, and it sagged alarmingly at the front. The front of the house was completely blown away. There was no door and no windows. The bricks were black from the smoke from the fire. Everything was wet from the firefighters' hoses. Remnants of his furniture were on the pavement. He almost laughed when he saw Irene's beloved Hoover laid amongst the rubble and bricks.

'I need to get in, Paddy. Distract those coppers for me. I need to see for myself.'

'Bloody hell, there's loads of them. What am I supposed to do?'

'I don't care. Just do it. I need to see inside that house for my own peace of mind.'

Paddy walked over to the police and stood at the front of the house. 'Jesus Christ, lads, this is a state of affairs. What the hell happened here?' Paddy lit a roll-up and stood there, bored to death, while the couple of coppers guarding the door told him what had happened.

Ralph had gone around the back alley and through the remains of the back door. He wasn't sure what he was looking for. He needed to detect where the explosion had started. Everything was soaking and his feet were wet. It was a state. The television was face down in a pool of water. Scrambling about, Ralph noticed the fireplace. The black smoke seemed thicker there. Curious, he stepped forward.

The street was illuminated by the lights from the gas company van and he only had the outside streetlight to see by. The mantelpiece and surround were blown to pieces. Bending down onto his knees and carefully brushing away the rubble of bricks and plaster, Ralph looked up the chimneystack. Bricks were dismantled and coming away but, reaching his hand up further, he found what he was looking for. Mentally he closed his eyes and imagined it.

A bomb had been placed up the chimney. It was a light-triggered bomb: very clever. Even the slightest bit of light would detonate it. Sighing and reaching further up the chimney, he found what he was looking for. He felt bits of a wire. Yes, it had been put there on purpose, and when Irene had knelt down to light the fire, she had ignited it. It would have been one hell of an explosion. She wouldn't have stood a chance. He could only presume that Shaun had been standing close by.

He had been right; it was revenge. That bomb had been put there on purpose. And the purpose was to kill his family, and possibly himself.

Wiping his hands on his shirt, Ralph stood up. He had seen enough. Climbing over the furniture, he left through the back door and made his way back to the car at the top of the street.

'Well, did you find what you were looking for?' Seeing the state of Ralph and his clothing, Paddy presumed he had.

'It was done on purpose. I will fucking kill them. Take me to where those friends of yours go drinking. I'm going to kill every last one of them!' Ralph screamed out.

'No, Ralph, wait. Just wait and listen to me. I know you're upset, but—' It was too late; Ralph had already punched him in the face.

'I blame you, you bastard. You brought this shit to my doorstep!'

Paddy shook his head from his dazed state and started the car. 'We're going to my fucking ma's and you are going to be cleaned up. We're not going on some witch-hunt. Not tonight, you're not thinking straight.'

'Do as you're fucking told. I'm in no mood for your games. If you won't take me, then I will find them myself.' Ralph opened the car door and was about to jump out, when Paddy reached out and pulled at his shirtsleeve, dragging him back in.

'Get in and shut the door, you crazy bastard. Are you trying to kill yourself as well?' Paddy was shouting at the top of his voice. He pulled over and stopped the car; they were both breathless. He knew Ralph needed someone to lash out at. Tempers were high. 'For God's sake. I'm sorry. It's hard, but there is nothing you can do about it. Okay, you take revenge now, then they take revenge, and then it is your turn again... next time it could be your ma or yourself. For fuck's sake, Ralph, how long is this going to go on for? Until you're dead, and then what?' Paddy was all shouted out. They were both breathing heavily.

Ralph turned to Paddy. 'What am I going to do?'

Paddy hugged Ralph as he broke down in tears. 'We're going to my ma's house. We are going to get you cleaned up and fed. Then, in the morning, we're going back to the hospital to see how your ma is getting on.'

* * *

The next day, Ralph arrived at the hospital with carrier bags full of clean clothes and other goods for his ma. He crossed his fingers and hoped she would be awake when he opened the door. But she wasn't. The doctor followed him in almost immediately. 'Mr Goldstein. We've had little progress. We have sedated her again; it is for the best for now. When she eventually leaves the hospital, we will send her to a rehabilitation home. They will help her with speech therapy and so on.'

'Will she get better? Will she be like her old self again?'

The doctor exhaled heavily and shook his head. 'After a shock like this, it is hard to say, but I doubt it.' The doctor let his words sink in. He could see Ralph's mind was elsewhere.

Nodding, Ralph thanked him. 'I appreciate you talking straight, Doc.'

Later that day, the police turned up to inform him that there had been a small investigation into the blast, and there would be an inquest, but it looked like the house had been bombed. They were taking it seriously and would keep him informed. In the meantime, if he would like to arrange a funeral, he could go ahead. These things would need taking care of. It was all very matter-of-fact and as much as Ralph was listening politely, he just wanted them to leave him alone. Whatever they did now wouldn't bring his family back. It was time to move on. He was sick of Ireland. Sick of his way of life. Each day he went one step forward and two back. It was time to move on and it just so happened he had an idea. After all, what did he have to lose?

23

THE ITALIAN JOB

'Hello, it's me. I just wanted to wish you a happy birthday,' Ralph said to the voice on the other end of the telephone. A few minutes later, he went back to Paddy's and packed a bag. He had his instructions and as far as he was concerned, the sooner he left, the better.

The church was full of Irene's family and friends. Ralph felt almost embarrassed. He'd watched her family rake over the burnt ruins of the house, trying to retrieve anything that they could re-use or sell. They were like cockroaches coming out of the wood-work and they disgusted him.

'What's with the bag? What do you need it for?' asked Paddy.

'I'm leaving right after the funeral. I need to get away for a while. My ma is going to be in hospital for a while yet. She's stable and they say when she does come out, she'll go to one of those rehabilitation places. Keep an eye on her for me; I'll be in touch. Here, take this.' Ralph took some money out of his wallet and handed it over. 'The wake is paid for but keep them supplied with alcohol. That's all everyone is coming for.' His words were bitter and harsh as he picked up the coffin with the other pall-bearers and they carried it into the church.

He had been told to meet Carlos at 'the usual place' and the only place he could think of was the airport. He walked into the airport pub, sat on a stool at the bar and ordered a drink. No sooner had he taken a sip than a man in a suit and tie sat beside him.

'Happy birthday, Ralph.'

He was waiting for this code, although he was surprised that it wasn't delivered by Carlos himself. Eyeing the man suspiciously, Ralph wondered who he was as the well-dressed man handed Ralph a brown envelope.

Ralph could see the bar staff were busy and no one was paying any attention to him, so he ripped open the envelope. Inside was a passport, driving licence and birth certificate. Frowning, he opened them all and then looked at the man. 'It says Gold, Ralph Gold. My name is Goldstein. And who is the photo in the passport of?'

'Gold, Goldstein, what do you care? Perhaps the forger cannot spell. As for the photo, look closely. That passport is five years old. The photo is of a dark-haired young man. No one looks like their passport photos. I've done my bit. You had better go; you have a plane to catch. Here's your ticket.' The man stood up to leave.

'You know what my name is. What's yours?' Ralph asked out of curiosity.

'That's on a need-to-know basis and you don't need to know.' With that, he walked out of the bar and disappeared into a throng of people all rushing to catch their flights.

Over the loudspeaker system, Ralph heard the call announcing the flight to Italy. *Well*, he thought, *that is what it says on the ticket; I'd better leave.*

It was Ralph's first time on an aeroplane and he thoroughly enjoyed it. Rising above the clouds, he felt on top of the world. On arrival, he was met at the airport by another well-dressed man holding up a card with his name on. This was becoming a habit. Before long he was sitting in the back of a car being driven to God alone knew where.

The driver didn't speak so, taking the hint, neither did Ralph. The only thing he regretted was his heavy clothing. It was far too thick for this hot, sunny climate. He could already feel the sweat on his back. As they pulled into a large, gravelled driveway, then parked outside a huge mansion, Ralph's jaw dropped. He had never seen anything like it. Did people really live like this?

Carlos came out to greet him. 'Ralph, I hope you had a good journey. Come in, have something to drink.'

Shaking his hand, Ralph gave him a weak smile. He felt out of his depth. It seemed unbelievable that just a few hours ago, he was in Ireland burying his wife and son, and now here he was standing on a marbled floor, in the cool hallway of a mansion that was covered in vines on the outside. It was like Hollywood!

'You need to meet my father first,' said Carlos, leading the way down the hallway. Ralph almost lost track of direction, the house was so big. Eventually, he stood with Carlos in front of two large, well-varnished, wooden doors. Carlos knocked, then opened them. A large desk dominated the room. There were three or four men going through paperwork and discussing things. They all stopped when they saw Carlos and Ralph.

'Papa, this is Ralph Gold.' Carlos saw the stocky, white-haired man with the suntanned face frown at him. 'The man I told you about from Ireland,' Carlos persisted.

'Ah, yes, my boy. Sorry, it's been a busy day.' The domineering figure sitting at the desk looked past Carlos to Ralph, then lowered his gold-rimmed glasses and looked over the top of them to see him better. 'Come in, Ralph Gold. You are most welcome.' Turning to everyone else in the room, he waved his hand in the air. 'Leave me now, I wish to speak to Mr Gold alone. You too, Carlos.'

Ralph swallowed hard and felt uneasy. His palms were sweaty. All of this pomp and ceremony was far above the streets of Ireland. He couldn't understand why he was there. Once the room was empty and the door was shut behind them, Carlos's father beckoned Ralph closer. Unlike Carlos, the father still spoke with an Italian accent, although his English was good.

'You must be wondering why we have invited you here. I can see that you feel uneasy. Sit down, make yourself comfortable. You tell me. Why have you come here?'

Ralph felt it was a fair question and filled the man in on recent events, while he poured them each a whisky out of the huge crystal decanter on his desk. He listened carefully to Ralph, nodding in all of the right places and offering his condolences for his loss. Ralph was glad of the whisky; his throat was dry from talking. He had told this stranger much more than he had intended to, but once he'd started, he couldn't stop. Maybe it was true what they said about it being easier to talk to strangers.

'Carlos hasn't filled you in on the details?' He waited for Ralph to shake his head. 'He is a hot-headed young man. I have a large family. Not everything we do is legal.' He paused and waited for Ralph's reaction. When there wasn't one, he carried on. 'We have arranged a job in a well-known bank, far away from here. There are huge vaults and they need opening. To do this we would need someone who knows explosives and a little about safes, vaults, whatever.' He shrugged and threw his hands in the air. 'We already had one lined up, but sadly, he is an informer. My family are being put under pressure because of his accusations and our affairs are being looked into because of this. It will come to nothing.' The nonchalant air with which he dismissed it made Ralph feel uneasy. 'I'm sorry to say it, but Carlos has a twisted streak and has taken it upon himself to silence the man you're replacing.'

'Wait!' Ralph held up his hand to stop him from talking. 'I may not be the man you are looking for. I know nothing about it, or you, come to that. I appreciate your honesty but I have not agreed to anything.' Ralph was determined to get his point across. This was Mafia country. What did they need him for – plain old Ralph Goldstein? It didn't make sense. Nothing made sense these days.

'It is enough that you are here. I want you to enjoy my hospitality, Mr Gold. Take in some sunshine. Breathe in the clean air. It will do you good. I want you to have a clear head if you are going to work for me. Relax, take some time for yourself.'

The soothing voice of this elderly, supposedly concerned man made Ralph relax slightly. Maybe this was how things were done over here.

* * *

Carlos was sitting with Ricky in the drawing room. 'Are you sure about this, Carlos? We hardly know anything about him. If he ever finds out that it was you who had his wife and child killed, he will go crazy. He hardly speaks, but he watches everything you do, taking it all in.'

'Not everyone shoots their mouth off the way you do, Ricky. Remember, my dear brother. You buy loyalty, but you earn respect. We are the only friends he has at the moment. Papa was right, His wife would have held him back. I can see in his eyes he wants more from life, but he would never have agreed to come with her clinging to him. Those men he killed in Ireland gave us a golden opportunity. He knows, or rather he thinks he does, that it was a revenge attack. That covers our tracks.' Changing the subject, a smile appeared on Carlos's face. 'That other explosives man. Is he dead yet?'

'No. They are still torturing him in the cellars, as you ordered. You said to make it slow and painful. He doesn't have a finger or toenail left. They have pulled them out one by one.' Ricky cringed at the thought.

'Good! The police should have kept him in for safekeeping.' He laughed aloud, slapping Ricky on the back. 'But they didn't because we own the police. Where are they now to help him? Ralph knows his stuff and we're on a deadline. To Mrs Gold!' Carlos chinked his glass against Ricky's. 'May she rest in peace.'

* * *

After a few days relaxing in the sunshine and enjoying the full hospitality of Carlos and his family, Ralph felt like a new man. He had decided to do this job, so he thought he'd better tell them and find out what it entailed.

Carlos's father was known as 'the Don'. Walking into his office, Ralph was swept away by the scale of this operation. This was big time. They had a full-scale model of a bank set up on the table. Trying hard not to show amazement and shock, he stood beside Carlos.

'These are the underground vaults. This is where you come in. We want the vaults blown, but not enough to make a huge blast. We don't want anyone knowing we're in there. We want to be in and out and let them find out the day after. Everything else is in place.'

'You do realise there will be some system of tripwires that trigger the alarms? Banks don't just have one alarm, they have two or three, and back-up generators. They will alert the local police.' Ralph's interest grew more by the minute. 'What you need is an electronic magnetic source. That would interfere with their electronics. It can slow down the performance of a circuit or shut it down completely.'

Carlos looked at Ralph, who was concentrating on the model as he spoke, then turned to his father and smiled. They definitely had the right man. Carlos's instincts about Ralph had just been proved right.

'Are you saying we can just interfere with their frequency and that would shut the bank down?' Carlos folded his arms and listened with interest.

'For a while, but they will have a generator that will start up after a couple of minutes once the problem is detected. It's like jamming an illegal radio station to stop it from working, only bigger.'

'And this generator, what about that?'

'A wire here and a wire there.' Ralph smiled. 'It will all be in their maintenance room, underground. If you can get a security guard's pass, that would help.' Standing around the table, everyone smiled and followed Carlos's lead in giving Ralph a round of applause.

'It will take a bit longer to get all of your money, Ralph; we need to launder it first. Possibly another month. But during that month there will be another job and so the circle carries on.' Carlos's grin was wide and smug.

'That is one thing that has never been mentioned.' Ralph coughed to clear his throat. Everything else had been discussed and planned, but no one had said how much he would be paid.

Everyone in the room turned and looked at each other. Their curious, puzzled looks as they stared at him made Ralph feel uneasy. He knew he'd said the wrong thing.

'Gentlemen never discuss money. Don't worry. Your share is big enough.' Carlos smiled.

As far as Ralph could see, asking about money seemed like an insult. But he still wanted to know how much he was being paid. After all, that was why he was doing it.

* * *

Tonight was the night. The target was a huge well-known Swiss bank. They were all staying at different locations and the plan was to meet at 3 a.m. on the dot. When they got to a side door of the bank, where the staff came and left, a security guard opened the doors for them.

'It's up to you now, Ralph,' Carlos whispered through his balaclava. They were all dressed in black, five of them in all. Remembering the model of the bank, Ralph immediately left Carlos and walked down the corridor where he knew the main electricity system was. The two security guards who had let them in stood at the reception desk and ignored the proceedings.

The small room Ralph walked into had a central mains box and was the hub of the bank. Lights were flashing intermittently on the mains boxes, showing Ralph everything was working. The hardest thing about this job was the timescale. After four minutes, once the laser circuit was broken or interrupted, the bank would go into lockdown. There would be no escape until the police arrived. The sweat poured down Ralph's face underneath his balaclava, making it stick to his skin.

He had gone over the layout of the place and the model with a fine-tooth comb. However, now he was here and it was all on a bigger scale, he felt nervous. His hands trembled as he opened his rucksack. He needed to concentrate. The wires could not be cut; that would bring the whole system to a close and a second generator was set in place in case of power cuts. Everything had to appear as normal.

Firstly, he set his EMI in place to interfere with the system. Ralph looked along the wall, illuminating it with the torch, which he held in his mouth. Taking out his wire cutters, he held the wires, took a deep breath and cut them. This would stop all the monitors for a few seconds.

Next was the main fuse box. This controlled everything. It was a huge trunking full of multicoloured wires running across the ceiling and down the walls. He knew over a thousand volts would be running through it and it scared him. He had never seen anything so big. Working quickly and precisely, he set about disconnecting the wiring and connecting it up again to different systems. The last cut made a huge roar of a noise as the electricity turned off. Ralph waited. He half expected the alarms to ring, but after what seemed a lifetime, the generator started up, lighting up the room in a dull green. He had done it!

The door flung wide open and Carlos ran in. 'What have you done?' he yelled. 'The electrics are going crazy. The lift doors keep opening and closing and the cash registers are spilling out loads of receipts. It's like bloody robots gone crazy out there.'

'Just joined up the wires to different ones. It will be a little crazy out there, but we're not staying long!'

They all got into the side delivery lift that was used to transport the money down to the vaults. Once they had closed the gates, it seemed to go deep into the very core of the earth. Eventually it stopped and they looked around, then opened the gates. Surrounding them were vaults, safes and deposit boxes. Ralph had made his own explosives. He had used his favourite recipe of fertiliser paste.

Placing the doughy paste on the doors and setting up his

detonator, he blew the vault doors. In minutes, they were holding the huge, long handle and opening the double doors.

The vault was full of everything imaginable: gold, money, and papers that represented shares in different companies. It was like Aladdin's cave.

Carlos started pulling at the blocks of money. Two of the other men entered the room with long delivery trollies. They were stacked high with money, then they disappeared; they were filling the delivery lift and coming back for more. After three trips, two of the men got into the lift with their trolley and went up to the main floor of the bank. Without Ralph's knowledge, there was another army of men creating a chain, emptying the stash into the backs of security vans parked around the back. Then they had gone back to empty the rest of the trollies Carlos had loaded. 'Enough!' Carlos raised his hand. 'It's time to leave. Come on.'

Ralph was shattered; his clothing was wet through. He stood back, wiped his brow, and then looked around the huge vault. Even though they had taken trolley loads, it was still full to the brim.

'Come on, Ralph, we have eight minutes to leave. Let's live to fight another day, eh?' shouted Carlos.

Out the back, the security vans were pulling out and driving away. Ralph was amazed when Carlos stripped his clothes off. Underneath his black jumper, he wore a white shirt and tie. Opening his bag, he took out a police hat and jacket and put them on. Walking to the far end of the yard, he got into a police van. Looking over at Ralph, he smiled and said, 'Get in the back.'

Carlos started the engine. He and Ricky were both dressed in police uniforms, with their suspect, Ralph, in the back of the van. It was a masterstroke! Who was going to stop a police van with its siren on?

Within half an hour, Ralph was back in his hotel room, pouring himself a large whisky. He sat on the side of the bed. He could not believe it had all gone like clockwork.

The sound of knocking woke Ralph. Rubbing his face, he sat up on the bed and looked at his watch. Christ, he had only been asleep for two hours! He had been exhausted; the drop in adrenalin had almost wiped him out. Hearing the knocking again, he tentatively walked towards the bedroom door, then realised it was not his door that was being knocked on. Opening it slightly, he saw a drunk man banging on a bedroom door two doors down, begging his wife to let him in. Rubbing his face again, Ralph looked around the room. In a few hours' time, the shit was going to hit the fan. A bank had been robbed; there would be mayhem. Coppers would be crawling all over the place. Suddenly, it struck him. He had done his part of the job, and apart from a few quid in expenses he had nothing to show for it. What a bloody fool he was. He was Carlos's fall guy. He convinced himself that, even though he had worn gloves, the police would pin something on him. He had a criminal record! It was time to make a hasty retreat.

Picking up his bag, he walked out of the hotel and hailed a taxi. He did not know how far it was to the airport but it didn't matter. When he got to the enquiries desk, he asked for the first aeroplane out to Ireland. He didn't really want to go back there. Not so soon, anyway. Questions would be asked about his whereabouts and he wasn't prepared for that.

'There isn't one to Ireland, sir. All we have at the moment is a flight to London.' The woman on the desk was doing her best to find something immediately and that was all she had available.

Frowning, Ralph thought about it. Then the more he thought about it, the better it sounded. *London? Isn't that where everyone goes to get lost?* Maybe fate had handed him a lifeline. 'Okay,' he said, 'I'll take that.'

* * *

Heathrow Airport was enormous. He had no idea where he was going. Walking out, he saw a line of black taxis. 'Take me to a cheap hotel,' he said, climbing in the back. He was dropped off at one of a famous chain of cheap hotels. In the early morning light, he had looked out of the windows at some of the famous sights as they passed them. The last twenty-four hours had been a lifetime of adventure.

Ralph had seen the newspapers over the last couple of days; the Swiss bank heist was all over the front pages and the television. Everyone was talking about it. His money was running out fast and he probably wouldn't have enough to pay for the hotel.

The reception staff at the hotel had eyed him curiously when he turned up with hardly any luggage, but they had given him a room. After a long walk around London, killing time, he planned how he would make a run for it. As he walked into the hotel, the receptionist called him over. 'Mr Gold, there is a letter and a package for you.' He was as surprised as she was. Who was sending him letters? Walking over, he picked them both up and went up to his room to open them. They were from Carlos! The package had over a thousand pounds in it. The letter was brief:

Greetings. The Hilton Hotel, 8 p.m. Room 109.
    Carlos

* * *

The Hilton was very different from his own hotel, Ralph thought, as he knocked on the door of Carlos's room. Entering, he was surprised at Carlos's immediate wrath.

'You're a hard man to find, Ralph Gold. Did you think we had dumped you? We are men of honour, God damn you! How dare you go against our well-laid plans.' In his anger, he changed to speaking Italian. Ralph did not need to know the language to understand he was pretty pissed off.

'I'm sorry, I panicked! A whole city of police would be up in arms searching for strangers and I wasn't going to sit and wait around for them.' Ralph could see that Carlos was accepting his apology and his reasons. He hadn't lied and made up all kind of excuses without an apology.

Waving to one of the other men by his side, Carlos indicated he was to pour them drinks. 'I am glad you came to London. It is more central than Ireland. I, too, have business here.'

'How did you find me?' Ralph was curious how, within a few days, he had been tracked down.

'We have our spies, and you will be glad we do. It was better that we split up. You understand that... *capeesh?*'

Ralph didn't know what it meant, but he went along with it. '*Capeesh.*'

'We have another job to do soon and I think you will like it. It is what you are good at. Guns. We need some guns. Do you have any contacts here?'

'I'm not sure. I have a number, but I'm not sure it's a good contact.'

'Come with me.'

Ralph watched as Carlos and Ricky picked up their jackets, gulped down their drinks and made for the lift.

Ralph was amazed how quickly Carlos's mood changed, but

he was relieved that Carlos had contacted him. Maybe he would make some money out of this after all.

When they arrived at a funeral parlour, Ralph was even more puzzled. 'Has a friend of yours died?'

'Something like that. Come on.' Smiling and half laughing, Carlos slapped him on the back, gave him a wink and led the way around the back. A side door was opened and they were all ushered in by two men who obviously worked there, given their white coats. After walking what seemed like miles in this maze of a place, they stopped and opened a door.

In front of them was what seemed like a great big oven. Stunned, Ralph turned to Carlos and Ricky for answers. 'We have the jewellery, Ralph, and a buyer waiting for it. Open up!' Carlos barked at the two workers in the white coats.

Still puzzled by it all, Ralph watched as the door of the cremation oven was opened. He half turned his head, not sure of what he would see. He stood rooted to the spot while Carlos looked inside and grinned. 'Get the brushes, boys.' The two men in turn picked up large sweeping brushes and started to sweep at the ashes in the oven, pushing them towards the open door at the back of it. Walking around the back, Carlos beckoned Ralph. The glint in his eye and the smile on his face was more than Ralph could bear. Then he heard a *chink*. Curious, he joined Carlos and Ricky. Buried in the ashes were diamond necklaces, bracelets and all kinds of jewellery that Ralph recognised from the robbery. His jaw dropped.

'You had the jewellery brought back to England in ashes?'

Shaking his head and laughing aloud, almost hysterical, Carlos stood back. 'No, Ralph. However, the two security men at the bank would have broken their promise soon enough and spilt the beans. Therefore, we killed them and organised a very good funeral director known to us that had been pre-arranged to clear out the bodies and fill them with all these goods. Then we had the bodies flown over to England. To this place. Diamonds do not burn, and while the oven will melt gold fillings, it does not get hot enough to melt twenty-four carat gold. My good friends here have burnt the bodies and, a few hours later, hey presto!' Carlos put his hands to his lips and made a smacking sound, blowing a kiss in the air. Ralph's blood almost turned cold. He had never seen or heard anything like it!

'No stone left unturned, eh?' Nonchalantly, Carlos picked up a diamond necklace from amongst the ashes and stood admiring it.

Ralph looked on, lost for words. This man was crazy!

Once everything was packed away, Carlos and Ricky checked the ashes to make sure nothing was left over, then left with their holdall full of jewellery.

'We have to take these to get cleaned up now and deliver them to the buyer. You sort out your gun contacts and we will be in touch. We will drop you off at your hotel first.' Carlos beckoned him to the boot of the car. 'Here, this is yours. Don't you ever fucking doubt me again, you mad Irishman.' He pointed his finger at him angrily as he handed over a black briefcase. 'You will have to wait until the rest is laundered properly.'

Ralph took the case and said nothing. He knew better than to upset Carlos. He had already decided he was a psychopath who enjoyed his work.

Back in his hotel room, Ralph put the case on the bed. He wasn't sure what to expect. The combination and his name were on a ticket on the handle. Turning the numbers, he heard the click as the briefcase opened and he marvelled at what it held. It was full of money!

He sat and counted it into piles of thousands. He was sweating as he handled the bundle of notes. He could feel his hands shaking and his heart pounding in his chest. The final count was fifty thousand pounds. He stood there looking at it laid out on his bed in awe. He had never seen so much money in his life. This was more than he had ever imagined. Reaching down and touching the money lovingly, Ralph kissed it and threw it in the air. Finally, he was rich!

24

A CHANCE ENCOUNTER

Time passed, and as hard as Julie tried, she couldn't stop visiting the street corner where Frankie stood with a group of women under the streetlamp, night and day, all drugged up to the eyeballs and not caring what happened to them. Their safety was of no concern to anyone and Julie was thankful when she heard that Frankie had been arrested for soliciting and spent the night in the cells. Support groups had tried to rehabilitate her, knowing she was an addict, but you have to want to stop for it to work, and after a week or so spent in prison, she'd simply run away and never turned up for her appointment at the doctor's.

Marching across the road, Julie grabbed Frankie's arm. 'You're coming with me, Frankie, now! I've had enough of this shit.' Looking up, she saw Frankie's pimp was hot on her heels. 'You can fuck off as well, Ian. I am in no mood for you.' Lashing out, Julie slapped him hard and hit him with her handbag, which she just happened to have put a brick in, knowing this moment would come.

'You fucking bitch. You will pay for that. What the fuck have you got in there?' He stood back, rubbing his head, dazed.

'Frankie, get back to work and tell that fucking witch to leave you alone.' He lunged at Julie, grabbed her hair and yanked her backwards. 'Don't push me. You won't like it, I promise you.' Spit dribbled out of his mouth and he spat at her as he spoke. His sneering face bent over her own as she was bent backwards.

Julie shouted towards all of the women standing on the corner. 'You really think this prick gives a damn about you? And you' – she turned towards Frankie – 'I've had enough of your crap. You're coming with me.'

'No, she's not.' Toying with Julie, he reached his hand in his pocket and took out a silver foil wrap. 'Frankie, who would you rather be with, my beautiful girl: that horrid sister of yours, who is jealous of our love, or me? You are my best girl, you know that. I love you.' His charming voice floated through the air and Frankie's eyes lit up when she saw the packet in his hand. Julie's heart sank. How could her beloved sister resort to being a lapdog over a piece of silver foil? It was probably empty anyway. However, this time she was prepared for it. Opening her handbag, she waved her own foil in the air towards Frankie, then she took out another one.

'You see, Frankie, love, I have that shit you need, too. It's not hard to come by. He only has one. I have two.' Sarcasm dripped from her mouth as she looked towards Ian. She hated him. He was a stupid bastard, full of shit, preying on drug addicts for his own ends.

'Where did you get that, you bitch? I've told everyone not to supply you with any. Who gave it to you?' He was angry and his face grew redder as he shouted at Julie. Without thinking, he lashed out at Frankie and punched her in the face, knocking her backwards onto the pavement.

Julie rushed to her aid, but Ian was behind her and snatched the foil out of her hands. 'Let's see what is in this, shall we.'

Licking his finger, he dipped it into the open foil. 'Baking soda.' He grinned and turned towards his friend and laughed. 'This stupid bitch thinks she can screw me over with baking soda!' He emptied the wrap of powder onto the pavement.

Disheartened, Julie vowed vengeance on this bully. No one would sell her anything; he had made sure of that. She had tried everywhere. The doctors would not give her methadone unless Frankie attended meetings or admitted herself into a rehabilitation clinic. It was futile, but she wouldn't give up.

'I'm sick of you hanging around here all these months. If you like it so much and you want to look after Frankie, there is one way to do it.' That slimy grin crossed his face again. Julie did not answer; she waited for the punchline.

'You could take her place on the corner.' Turning towards all the other women on the corner, he held up his open palms.

'You can fuck off. I would never work for you.'

'Okay, no offence taken. Let me put it another way. I don't care what happens to either of you as long as I get my money. You give me the amount she earns each week and you can fucking take her with you. Miss one payment, though, and I will be back to collect my property.'

Stunned at this offer, Julie thought about it. It was an option, for now. If she did it for a while it might just give her enough time to get Frankie cleaned up. Once she was clean from the drugs, she would see this fat pimp for what he was. Swallowing hard and looking him directly in the face, she asked the question. 'How much is that, exactly?'

'I want a hundred pounds every week.'

Julie knew that was a sum he had picked out of the air. There was no way Frankie was earning him that kind of money: she looked like shit. Looking at Frankie's thin, sparrow-like frame and matted hair, she felt sick. She was wearing a thin, long-sleeved cardigan over the low-cut, short dress she wore in all weathers to cover the bruises and cigarette burns on her arms.

'I'll give you fifty.' Julie stuck out her chin defiantly. 'Fifty pounds is better than nothing. And look at her; eventually people won't be choosing her and she won't be worth anything to you.'

'Fifty it is, then. But she will be back.' Pushing Frankie towards Julie, he walked away. 'I want fifty tomorrow and then the same every week.' And with that, he walked into the corner pub, which he used as his knocking shop in the rain.

'Come on, Frankie, you're coming home with me.'

Slurring and half dazed, Frankie turned towards the pub. 'What about Ian?'

Sick at her concern, Julie helped her sister across the road and hailed a taxi. Fifty pounds? She secretly wished she had gone lower. That meant she would have to work twice as hard. The money at the escort agency was decent, but she had rent to pay and food to buy. However, this was an option to make things right with Frankie.

After she had put her sister to bed, she went and telephoned the doctor. She had called him so many times lately he knew her by name. 'I need help, doctor. My sister is at home with me. I need to get her off the drugs. Please come,' she begged. She was desperate. He'd already gone through the rules. He couldn't discuss a patient without consent from the patient. She had heard it all. Blah blah blah.

But a few hours later, the doctor turned up and gave her a prescription for Frankie. He could see she was in a bad way and he wanted to call an ambulance. She was starting to sweat and was in and out of consciousness, complaining of stomach cramps.

'No. I can look after her. Just give me the stuff, please,' Julie begged.

Thankfully he had taken pity on her and agreed to pop in the next day.

It was obvious that Frankie was overdue her next fix. She was moaning and curling up on the bed, holding her stomach. Julie had to go to work otherwise she wouldn't have Ian's money. Frankie was in no fit state to travel elsewhere. Locking her in her room with a bucket at her bedside, Julie felt horrible as she walked out leaving Frankie behind, but there was no other choice.

* * *

Three weeks into this arrangement, Julie realised she was struggling. She was robbing Peter to pay Paul. She had missed the rent. Thankfully, Sumatra was easy-going, but she still wanted double the next week. It seemed to Julie that the more she earnt, the less she had.

Frankie whined night and day, begging for more of the medicine. The room smelt of disinfectant where Julie had constantly cleaned up her vomit. The doctor had called it 'cold turkey' and eventually Julie had agreed to his requests and let him put Frankie into a clinic for addicts. She was drained and welcomed the respite.

That was, until she telephoned the clinic to see how Frankie was and was told she had discharged herself. Julie felt sick. Panic-stricken, she went to the clinic demanding answers. She wanted to know why they had let Frankie leave and they explained that they could not stop her. They couldn't hold her against her will.

There was only one place that Julie could think of where Frankie would go: Ian. He had won. He had taken her money and he had won. Angrily, she went to him. He denied all knowledge of seeing Frankie, but Julie knew he was lying. Julie had no choice but to go to the police and report her as a missing person.

Months passed without a word, and Julie thought her sister was probably dead. She had passed by the street corner many times but Frankie wasn't anywhere to be seen. She knew Ian had sent her somewhere out of the way or worse, but the police assured Julie that there had been no unidentified bodies turned up recently. Julie felt devastated.

Tonight, she had to go to work. There was a group of men staying at a hotel. It seemed a woman had been booked for all ten of them. Maybe there would be more money to be had. After all, if it was businessmen, they had money to burn.

She knocked on the door and a dark-haired man in a tuxedo answered it.

'Hi, gorgeous. It's call-girl time,' she said, and laughed. She had made a special effort tonight. If she played her cards right it could be a real money-spinner. She knew the numbers of the other rooms the girls were going to and thought she might just pop by later and take a chance.

'Who are you?' The man looked at the young blonde woman with the long overcoat on.

'Well, I'm not your fairy godmother, am I?' Julie walked past him and sat on the edge of the bed. Looking at the glass in his hand, she nodded. 'You got a spare one of those?'

Nodding, he went over to the bar and poured her a drink. 'What's your name?'

'Whatever. What's your favourite name, honey?' Flashing her best smile through her red lipstick, she waited.

'I said, what is your name?' he asked again, handing her over the glass.

'Julie. You can call me Julie. Personally, I hate it. So you can call me what you like. What's your name?' Her Liverpool accent floated around the room, making the man smile.

'Ralph. My name is Ralph Gold. Nice to meet you, Julie.' He put out his hand to shake hers, which she thought was very odd. No one had ever shaken her hand before.

'Well, I bet you took some stick as a kid.' She laughed and kicked off her shoes. 'Well, Goldy, we have an hour – or rather, less than an hour. Shall we get on with it? It's all paid for; your friends have seen to that.' As it was a bulk job and a surprise for their guests, the hosts had paid the agency in advance.

'Well, you had better take off that coat, and take your knickers off as well, seeing as you're here.' He chuckled. Although beautiful, Ralph found her a breath of fresh air from all the business meetings he'd had of recent times. But she looked vaguely familiar to him. He couldn't quite put his finger on it.

'That is a little awkward, Goldy, love. I'm afraid I can't do that.' Tapping her chin playfully with her fingers, she saw the twinkle in his eye and the puzzled look on his face.

'So, why are you here?' Putting down his glass, he walked to the door to open it. 'Well, Julie, it's been very nice meeting you, but I'm not up to company tonight. So, if you don't mind...'

'I can't take my knickers off because I'm not wearing any.' Standing up, Julie unbuttoned her coat and let it drop to the floor. She was wearing a short, black chiffon baby doll nightie edged with fur. 'It seems to me that you're the only one wearing pants around here.'

Ralph shut the door again. He wanted to laugh, but composed himself. Whoever this Julie was, she was funny. Walking up to him, she started to undo his belt.

'Stop right there.' He grabbed her hand. 'I didn't order you. And I can find my own women, thank you.'

'Okay. It's no skin off my nose. I've been paid for the hour.' She picked up her black mac and put it on again. 'Nice to meet you, Goldy.' Kissing him on his cheek, she reached for the door handle. She couldn't believe it. This was the easiest money she had made.

'You haven't finished your drink.' Ralph didn't know what made him do it, but he stopped her leaving. It was a brief meeting but there was something about this sassy, young blonde that he liked.

'You're right, and it would be a shame to waste it. Is it the good stuff?'

Ralph cocked his head to one side and gave her a knowing look. She was cocky and brash and he doubted she would not know the good stuff from the bad. She was unlike any other woman he had met before and a far cry from Irene.

'Well, I'll have this drink. You obviously want to talk. So spill the beans. I take it you're married and on a business trip. Are you a salesman, then? Pass me one of those cigarettes, will you?'

Ralph couldn't help himself. This time he laughed aloud. 'Do you always ask so many questions?' he said, while handing her the packet of cigarettes and his lighter. He watched her light one and then offer him one; when he nodded, she lit it and handed the cigarette to him. He also noticed how she put his gold lighter in her coat pocket.

'Only when I'm not in bed. Usually I would have your dick in my mouth by now and I couldn't ask anything. So, go on then, Goldy. Talk away. And while you're talking you can fill this up.' Handing him her brandy glass for a refill, she looked properly at this Ralph Gold while he poured her drink.

He was dark-haired, swarthy, possibly some foreign blood. He had big dark eyes and a pleasant face. His body was muscly and filled out his jacket well. He looked very smart in his black tuxedo. He was a good ten years older than her, she presumed.

However, he was handsome. He was nice, he hadn't pounced on her as so many men had in the past. He was a gentleman and she hadn't come across many of those.

Ralph found himself answering Julie's questions, which was unusual for him because he kept his private life very close to his chest. 'Well, Julie. My name is Ralph Gold. I am here on business, but I am not a travelling salesman, although I am in the export business. I'm no longer married. Does that satisfy you?'

Making herself comfortable on the bed and plumping up the pillows behind her so she could sit up and have her drink, she carried on. 'Are you foreign?'

Again, Ralph laughed. She was blunt and to the point and he liked that. 'I'm half-Jewish, which accounts for the black hair, if that's what you mean. I'm also half-Irish. I've been abroad for a while so that is why I have a suntan.'

'Mm. I thought you had an accent. So, are you in Liverpool long?' While sitting there with her feet up, having her drink, it dawned on Julie this was the longest decent conversation she had had with a man in a long time. It was normally the preliminary dirty talk and then down to basic sex. Or an argument, like the ones she frequently had with Ian or some client that tried short-changing her. This was different, and this Ralph bloke had not attempted to make a grab for her.

'I've got an accent? Have you heard yours?' He laughed. 'No, I'm here for a couple of days and then going home to London. What about you? You know my life story. What is yours?' This gorgeous blonde woman lounging on the bed making herself at home intrigued him.

Julie blushed slightly. She had never really thought about her Liverpool accent. Nobody had ever mentioned it before. 'My name is Julie. I live here in Liverpool. I'm not married. I don't have a pimp, but I am a prostitute. I work for this escort agency.'

Reaching in her coat pocket, she took out one of the agency cards and held it towards him. She always carried agency cards and would leave them on the bedside tables with her name on the back in the hotel rooms.

Taking it, Ralph looked at it for a moment and put it on the table beside his chair. He liked what he saw. He felt a deep stirring within him. He'd been far too busy lately to form any kind of relationship. 'You forgot to say that you're also a thief.' Ralph pointed to her coat pocket and held out his hand for his lighter. He knew he had taken her off her guard by the sheepish look she gave him when she handed it back.

'Sorry about that, I didn't realise. It looks just like mine,' she lied. She had never owned anything more than a box of matches and she got the feeling that this man knew it. He was going to be a hard nut to crack.

Ralph loosened his tie and undid the top button of his shirt, then gulped back his drink. 'What would you say if I was to join you up there on the bed?'

'Well, Goldy.' Julie grinned. She noticed the look in Ralph's eyes. It was a familiar look Julie had come to know well. 'I can see your sap is rising, honey, there's that lusty look in your eyes, but I would also say your time is up. This chat has been very nice and all, but you have about...' Pausing, Julie made a big deal about looking at her watch. 'I'd say two and a half minutes to get down to business. Can you be that quick?' she teased, and winked at him. Laughing aloud, she sprawled on the bed. Now she knew she was on more familiar territory. He fancied her and she knew it.

Standing up, Ralph walked to the bed and sat on the edge of it. 'What if you were to stay another hour?' Moistening his lips, he moved closer to her and bent his head to kiss her.

Holding her hand up, stopping his lips coming any closer, she raised her eyebrows. 'That depends on what your wallet says – can you afford it? I don't come cheap, you know.' Julie had lowered her voice to a hushed whisper and was looking him directly in the eyes. They were almost nose to nose. They stared at each other for a moment, although it seemed like a lifetime.

Stopping himself short, Ralph stood up. This Julie was like a serpent with hypnotising eyes. She drew you in and toyed with you, like a cat with a mouse. He picked up his wallet and opened it. He wanted her and his poker face had dropped, showing his desire. She knew it. They both knew it.

'What's the going rate?'

'Fifty pounds for the hour. One minute into the next hour, and I want another whole hour's money. No arguments. Wait here, I'll get my alarm clock out of my bag. We need to agree on the timing.'

'Don't bother with your clock. It will take as long as it takes.' Ralph threw his wallet on the bedside table and pulled her roughly towards him. Glancing at it, Julie could see it was thick with money. Maybe she had struck gold after all!

* * *

Unexpectedly, this calm, calculating man had been more passionate than Julie had presumed. Unlike other clients, he had given as well as taken, rousing something in her that had been dormant for years. She had surprised herself when she realised she wasn't faking it. Looking at the clock on the bedside table, she saw that it was nearly 5 a.m. She had been there hours.

Slowly moving herself out of the bed so as not to disturb the snoring man beside her, she reached for her coat in the darkened room and put it on. Then she tiptoed to the bathroom. When she came back through, she went to the bedside table and, adjusting her eyes to the dark, looked for his wallet and picked it up.

'You don't need to sneak off like a thief in the night.'

The voice in the dark startled her and she looked at the figure in the bed. 'Bloody hell, you made me jump. I'm not sneaking off. My work here is done; it's time to go home. Go back to sleep.'

Yawning, Ralph sat up and rubbed his eyes. 'I will when I see how much you're going to take from my wallet.' He held out his hand and waited until Julie handed it over to him.

'Only what is owed, Goldy,' she snapped, back in business mode. She angrily held out her hand for her money. She hoped he wasn't going to argue the toss over the price now. 'Now pay up, honey, and then I can leave.'

Ralph handed over five hundred pounds, more than was necessary. 'Do you want to have dinner with me tonight?'

She snatched the money out of his hands and stuffed it in her pocket before he changed his mind, then frowned. She wasn't sure she had heard him properly. 'Dinner? You want to buy me dinner? Or is that just a nice way of saying "same time, same place tonight"?'

'No, it means dinner, and then we'll see. I'll pay you for your time. You're an escort, aren't you? So, escort me.'

Nonchalantly, hiding her surprise, Julie drummed her fingers on her chin while looking at the ceiling, deep in thought. 'I will have to check my diary. I'm not sure what I have booked in tonight.' She was damned sure she would meet him tonight but she didn't want to seem too eager. Treat them mean and keep them keen. Isn't that what they said?

He smiled at the performance especially for him, then shrugged and yawned. Matching her matter-of-fact ways with his own, he said, 'Well, if I am lucky enough for you to have a free slot in your diary, meet me at the hotel restaurant at eight.' With that, Ralph yawned and turned over, faking sleep.

Julie stood for a moment, confused, looking at his back. She didn't know what to say. She moved to the door and opened it, then stared at his back again, waiting for him to turn over and say something. But he didn't.

Once she'd gone, Ralph sat up and lit a cigarette. 'You will be there, Julie. I just know you will,' he said to the door. He grinned, had his smoke, then went back to sleep.

25

A FINE ROMANCE

Over the past two years, Ralph had flourished. He was now a wealthy businessman with wealthy friends. It always amazed him how money attracted money. Carlos had laundered the money from the bank job and Ralph had been given a cool million. Carlos had advised Ralph to get a stockbroker and invest it and had introduced him to his accountant. God knows how this crooked accountant had worked his magic, but many of the shares in companies they had stolen from the Swiss bank were transferred into their names.

Mixing in Carlos's circle of friends, Ralph was surprised that most of them were high-ranking officials, or lords and ladies who, it seemed, had the title but no money. They were always wanting to borrow money so they could maintain their standard of living.

Once Carlos had given him the nod to go along with this, he realised why. These senators, members of parliament and celebrities didn't have a penny to scratch their arses with, but what they did have was influence. They paid you back by introducing you to other influential people. You became part of the elite and were invited to join men's clubs and go to parties where there was always a deal to be made. It seemed the higher up these men were, the more crooked they were. Some owed their very heart and soul to Carlos's father and the family, and he could call upon those favours that were owed at any time. So, taking the Don's lead, Ralph became a loan shark for the rich and famous, and in return they opened doors for him beyond his wildest dreams.

This was a life he had always dreamt of; it seemed impossible that only a few years ago he had worked in a quarry and lived in a backstreet, rented house. Although, he realised, he had paid a high price for all of his ambitions. He'd lost his family.

Ralph missed his son and thought about him often, and how much he could have given him now. He wanted to spoil his mother and dress her up in diamonds, but he couldn't. All he could do now was make her comfortable. He thought about Irene a lot. Would she have liked this life? He doubted it. He had paid a big price for all those times he had wished for better things. It was true what they said: when God gives with one hand, he takes away with the other. Either that or, as his mother would have said when he was younger, 'Be careful what you wish for!'

Sitting at his table in the hotel restaurant, Ralph waited to see if Julie turned up. *Of course she will*, he argued with himself. After all, she was a businesswoman and this was business. Looking at his watch again, he felt as if everyone else was staring and gossiping about him; he looked like a man that had been stood up.

Forty-five minutes late, and just as he was about to leave, he looked up and there she was, floating through the room in her black mackintosh, leaving a trail of perfume in her wake. Her blonde hair was flowing and her red lips and nails were painted to perfection. 'Evening, Goldy. As you can see, I had a cancellation.' Her charming, girlish smile washed away all the anger he felt.

So, he thought to himself, *she was late on purpose to prove a point and make me wait.*

The waiter stood behind her to take her coat, and in a slow, seductive way she undid the buttons as he watched. He caught his breath when he saw what she was wearing but remained stony-faced. She had come with the shock factor in mind.

She had on a short, white, halter-neck dress and it was more than apparent she was wearing nothing underneath it. As the dim lights in the restaurant glowed, you could see every curve and anything else, for that matter. Glancing at the tables around them, Ralph wanted to laugh. The men were drooling and the women were disgusted! Their gossip had now changed. He wasn't a dumped man. He was a man with a beautiful woman at his table who had no shame.

'Do you like my dress?' Julie leant provocatively over the table towards him.

'Mm hm.' Ralph picked up his drink and took a sip, while waving the waiter over to order one for Julie. Letting out a dramatic sigh, he looked at her again, as though inspecting her from all angles. 'I do find it a shame, though.'

Julie sat back in her chair and looked down at herself. 'What do you mean?' she snapped.

'Well, it's a shame they didn't have one in your size.' There was a moment's pause as they looked at each other over the candlelit table, then Julie erupted into laughter.

'Don't you think it would look better on your bedroom floor?' she said teasingly, loud enough for everyone to hear.

'I doubt I would even notice the difference. Here's the menu. Time to order.'

Julie took the menu and, pretending to look at all the options, glanced over the top at Ralph. She wanted to pinch herself to bring her back to reality. This wasn't real. This was work, but she liked bantering with this man. He was fun.

'Is that it?' Julie looked at her steak, with its two potatoes beside it and a very small selection of vegetables. 'Are you paying a fortune for this meagre offering? Bloody hell, I hope you get a doggy bag!'

'Tell me, Julie. Does the fork actually get to your mouth before you drop something down your cleavage? There might not be a lot of it, but most of it has gone down your dress. You are like a walking picnic table. Would you like a spoon?'

'Personally, I would prefer a plate of scouse. At least that fills you up.'

'Scouse?' Now Ralph was confused. He had never heard of it but, as Julie never stopped talking, he knew he would find out.

Julie wiped the top of her dress with her napkin, then fished a piece of carrot out of her cleavage and put it back on the plate. She frowned at him, as if he had said the most stupid thing ever. 'Scouse? It's a Liverpool stew. Something to put fire in your veins.'

'And where do you get this scouse of yours?' Ralph sipped at the champagne Julie had ordered. Apparently, she never drank anything else.

'What, you daft bugger, in Liverpool? Just about every café in town. Wherever you go they sell it.'

'I came to Liverpool a few years ago. I met a woman who hit me hard on the head with her handbag. She was stunning and I can tell you, I have thought of her every day since'. Suddenly Ralph realised who she was. This was his black rose. He had been too occupied last night to notice, but now, as her dress lifted as she sat down, he saw it: the rose tattoo.

Julie paled, and looked at him closely. He'd looked familiar and he had treated her with respect. Yes, this was the Irishman who had given her the money when her bedsit had burnt down.

'You. You brought the beer barrels.' Her mind was thinking back as she spoke. She had liked him then and now fate had thrown him into her path again.

'Yes, do you remember. A lot has happened since then.'

'You don't speak so Irish any more. You were very kind to me and I'm sorry about you getting in the way of my handbag. It's good to meet you again, after all of these years.' For once Julie was genuine. This man had only ever treated her with respect and kindness. She had never known his name but had often wondered about him when she saw the brewery trucks drive down the roads. 'You look very different to the last time I saw you. What have you done – robbed a bank?'

The irony of that joke made Ralph smile. Reaching out his hand, he held hers. 'It's good to see you again, my black rose.' His voice was husky as he bent to kiss her hand. The chemistry across the table seemed almost electric as they both remembered their last meetings.

'Would you like dessert, madam, sir?' the waiter enquired.

'Yes, I'll have the chocolate mousse, and make sure it's a proper portion, will you?' said Julie, looking up at him with a pout.

'Give her two portions,' Ralph instructed the waiter, who wasn't sure how to answer Julie and was glad to make a hasty retreat.

'So.' Now that the plates had been removed, Julie moved forward, put her elbows on the table and, using her forearms, pushed her breasts up even higher, giving Ralph full view of them. 'Do you fancy me, then?' She winked at him.

'You'll do.' Ralph wanted to laugh as he watched her face drop. That wasn't the answer she'd expected.

Ignoring his slight, Julie changed the subject. 'When do you have to go back to London?'

'Tomorrow. I leave at lunchtime.' He put his cigar in his mouth and waited for the waiter to rush forward to light it. He did, and another brought Julie her chocolate mousse. Blowing the smoke in the air during this awkward silence, he waited while she plunged her spoon into the large glass of chocolate mousse.

'Oh, I see. Well, you had to go home sometime, I suppose. It's a shame. I was just getting used to you.'

'After one night? I doubt it. But it's been an experience. One I have dreamt of many times.'

Grinning widely, Julie cocked her head to one side. She liked this man, but he was going soon. It had been such a nice experience for once in her life to be treated like a woman on a date. Ralph exhaled cigar smoke into the air.

'Have you ever had chocolate mousse poured on your naked body and licked off?'

'Not lately,' Ralph lied, blushing slightly.

The loud guffaw that left Julie's mouth left nothing to the imagination. 'No, you haven't, not ever! You're just a big fibber, Ralph Gold, with an erection. Would you like to order some up to your room and we could try it?'

Now it was Ralph's turn to lean forward over the table. 'And you, Miss Julie, are one sexy, cheeky little minx. Let's order some.' With that, he reached forward and pinched her nipple. As they stood up to leave the table, it seemed everyone in the restaurant knew what was next on the agenda.

'Here. Now. Ralph, take me here.' Julie leant backwards to the wall of the lift and held her hand out to his crotch. 'A hard man is good to find and that has real potential.' Putting her arms around his neck, she pulled him closer. Ralph did not need asking twice. He was more than ready, almost to boiling point. Julie had teased and flaunted her wares before him, and he wanted her. He wanted all of her, now. Undoing his trousers and letting them fall to the floor, he pushed her back, lifted her slightly and roughly plunged himself into her. It was mad, crazy passion, then suddenly the lift doors opened and, looking over Ralph's shoulder, Julie saw an elderly couple about to get in the lift.

'Hey, you two, can't you see we're going up?' she said.

Ralph half turned and saw the shocked looks on the couple's faces as the doors of the lift closed again.

'What have you stopped for? Come on, concentrate.' It was over all too soon. But this was just the beginning of a long night.

Sweeping Julie up in his arms and putting her over one shoulder, Ralph walked down the corridor to his room. His shirt was open and, although he had pulled his trousers up, they were still undone at the waist. There was a trolley outside the room and Ralph lifted the top of the dish that was on it. Inside was a glass dish containing the chocolate mousse they had ordered.

Reaching out her finger, Julie skimmed the top of it and licked her finger. 'Looks like I'm going to get my just desserts, honey.' They both laughed as Ralph carried her into the room, pushing the trolley ahead of them, then threw her on the bed.

Their night was one passionate encounter after another. After being covered in chocolate mousse, they had bathed together. This was a whole new experience for Ralph. He had never bathed up to his neck in scented bath oils with a woman before. He realised his sex skills were straightforward and not half as adventurous as Julie's.

As the dawn light shone through the windows, Julie woke up. She was surprised to see Ralph already awake, lying on his back smoking a cigarette, his other arm around her. He seemed to be staring at the ceiling, deep in thought.

'Do I get a drag of your cigarette?'

Ralph held it to her lips. 'You do realise they are going to charge me extra for the sheets stained with all that chocolate. It's even on the wallpaper.'

'Yes.' She exhaled cigarette smoke. 'Well, I didn't realise I was having sex with Phileas Fogg. Once you get in your stride, you do like to travel.' She laughed. 'I don't think there is a piece of furniture in this room you haven't had me bent over or stood up against. But you don't get a discount for dry cleaning.' She sighed. 'I'd better get up – things to do, people to see.'

'Like who?' Ralph snapped. 'Who have you got to see?' He felt jealous that she was leaving and had things to do. He wanted her to stay and didn't care what it cost; he knew he was lost forever in those eyes of hers. He thought he had done everything, but the one thing he hadn't done was feel like this over a woman leaving him. He felt sick but didn't want to show it. How did he know if she liked him? It was all a game to her.

Putting her finger on his lips, she smiled. 'Time for me to go, Ralph. All good things come to an end.' Kissing her finger, she pressed it against his. She suddenly felt sad.

26

Disappointed that he hadn't asked her to stay or made arrangements to see her again, Julie got into a taxi outside of the hotel and went home. Looking in her bag at the amount of money Ralph had given her, she could see he had been more than generous. She told herself it had just been another job, but even so, she couldn't remember anyone ever holding her or kissing her like that in her life. He had treated her like a lady, not a prostitute. And he was a gentleman. With a huge sigh, she paid the driver and walked up to her bedsit.

There was a woman sitting on the concrete doorstep of the house. It had begun to rain and Julie could see she was wet through. Her thin, blue dress was stuck to her skin. Shivering, the woman looked up at the sound of Julie approaching. 'Julie. Don't you recognise me?'

Stunned with disbelief, Julie stood rooted to the spot looking at the woman. No, she didn't recognise her, but she knew that voice. 'Frankie?'

'It's me. I've escaped. It's been horrible.' Frankie looked up at Julie pitifully. The silence was deafening as Julie looked at her sister. She wasn't sure if this was a dream. Frankie looked much older than her years. Haggard, in fact. Her eyes were sunk deep into her thin face, with dark rings around them. Her arms and legs were covered in bruises and she was wearing only a thin dress and flip-flops.

The thunder broke her thoughts. Julie looked up at the sky. The heavens had opened and now the rain was pelting down so hard, it was bouncing off the pavement. 'Come on. Let me help you up. Come inside.' Reaching for Frankie's arm to help her up, Julie got another surprise: Frankie was pregnant! Looking at her swollen stomach and glancing at Frankie, neither of them spoke. First things first, she had to get her warm and dry; the questions would come later.

As they walked in the door of the bedsit, Julie started stripping the sopping wet dress from Frankie and went and got her dressing gown. Wrapping it around her, she sat her near the electric fire, then put the kettle on.

As Frankie sat by the fire, Julie could not take her eyes off her. She looked skeletal, apart from her swollen stomach. The living dead.

'I've been sat outside all night. Where have you been?' Her voice was slow and slurred. She could barely speak properly through all the sores on her lips. Getting a towel, Julie started to dry her hair. That was when she saw that she was crawling with lice. She wrapped the towel around her head like a turban to soak up the rain.

Julie sat beside Frankie and spoke soothingly, as though to a child. Frankie looked traumatised and frightened. 'Where have you been, love? I've looked for you everywhere. I didn't know what had happened to you when you left the clinic.'

'I didn't leave the clinic. Ian came. He said you had sent him to bring me home. He took me to Bradford and then put me in a house with some other women. We were locked in. It was worse than the camp, Julie.'

It was worse than Julie had presumed; Frankie had almost lost her mind and Julie could not bear to think of the horrors she had suffered. Tears rolled down Julie's face as she stroked Frankie's hand.

'Day and night, men came. Every day. They were allowed to beat us up while Ian's friends looked on.' Suddenly, Frankie stood up as though in a daze. Her eyes were lost in that world of horror, remembering. She started to scream hysterically and shake. Pulling her into her arms, Julie held her tightly. She needed Frankie to calm down.

'It's okay, love. It's okay, Frankie. You're safe now, Julie's here.' Pulling away from her for a moment, Julie looked her in the face. 'Listen to me. You are going to be okay.' Julie emphasised her words as much as possible, hoping they would penetrate her damaged brain. At last, she felt her relax and slump in her arms, sobbing.

'Do you know who the father of the baby is?' Julie knew that was a stupid question, but it was something to say. There were so many unanswered questions. Frankie just shrugged. It was as though she didn't even realise she was pregnant.

'How did you escape?'

'We were being moved on to another house. I don't know where. They moved us around a lot. Ian likes to change the girls around so his friends don't get bored with the same ones and the police can't track them down.'

Julie remained calm, outwardly, at least, even though her heart was pounding and her very nerves were stretched. She wanted to kill that bastard!

'He must have forgotten about me, because when I woke up, they had gone. I went outside and couldn't see anyone and then a lorry driver stopped and picked me up. I told him I was coming to Liverpool to see you and he was driving near here so he dropped me off and I walked the rest of the way.'

Julie's mind was racing. She could see right through this story. They had left her behind on purpose, hoping she would starve to death or something. They didn't want a heavily pregnant woman on their hands. After everything that had happened, they had dumped her! Julie couldn't bear to hear any more. She could see Frankie was exhausted. 'Come on, darling. Let's get you tucked up in bed. You need your rest.' Like a baby, Frankie did as she was told. Julie wrapped her up and let her drift off to sleep.

Julie was angry. She wanted to go to that street corner and torture that evil bastard. He had sold her sister on and passed her around like an unwanted toy and now she was pregnant.

For now, she had to keep it low-key. No one knew Frankie was here and that was for the best. At last, she had her sister back. She did not want to inform the police. She knew it would not do any good. Frankie could hardly remember her own name and she wouldn't make a very good witness in court. Her mind spun around while Frankie slept. She wanted to do all kinds of things, but there was nothing she could do. Julie was troubled and heartbroken. She felt helpless. There was no one to turn to.

It seemed like Frankie slept for days. Every few hours Julie would wake her, spoon some soup into her mouth then let her go back to sleep again. She had some lotion for her hair and the doctor had visited. Seeing the state Frankie was in, he wanted her to go to hospital, but Julie had begged him not to send her there. The last time Frankie had gone to a clinic, she had disappeared.

The doctor had listened to the sorry story and given Julie a prescription for the sores around Frankie's mouth. He had checked up on the baby and told Julie that Frankie had malnutrition. She wouldn't be able to stomach large amounts of food and so he prescribed yogurts and baby food. He also gave her some methadone, because he warned Julie that when the exhaustion wore off, she would crave heroin again. That was going to be the worst fight of all. Getting her clean and keeping her clean!

Two weeks later, Julie was pulling her hair out. The doctor had been right: Frankie was craving her drugs again. Julie argued it was bad for the baby and she had the methadone to help her. A district nurse came daily and gave her the dose, checked on Frankie and the baby and left.

With money even tighter, Julie knew she'd have to go back out to work to support them all. The arrangement was that she telephoned the agency every morning around ten. This morning, when Julie called, they told her someone had enquired if she would go to London to spend a couple of days with him. The client was a Mr Gold. He'd left a contact number for her to arrange travelling and dates. Trying to hide her excitement, she had taken it in her stride and not given any information to the agency. She knew they would double their commission.

As soon as she put the telephone down, she rang the number for Ralph. Yet again, she wanted to play it cool. She didn't want him to know that he had crossed her mind on more than one occasion. 'Hello, is that Mr Gold?' The formality in her voice showed no recognition of who he was; she was stifling her excitement.

Hearing the blandness in her voice, Ralph stammered a little. He'd been busy over the last couple of weeks, but each time he saw a chocolate mousse on a menu, she came to mind. Now he felt a little silly. It was obvious she didn't remember him.

'Yes, is that you, Julie? We met in Liverpool when I was on business there...' He waited but there was no response, so he carried on. 'I'm not sure you remember me, but I'm at a loose end for a couple of days and I wondered if you would like to join me.'

There, he had said it. He felt like some silly schoolboy asking for a date. This was a bad, impulsive idea.

'Aren't there any prostitutes in London? I thought there was loads of them.' Biting her tongue to stop herself from laughing, she waited. Then she heard the sigh on the other end of the telephone.

'You're right, of course. I'm sorry to bother you.' Embarrassed, Ralph was about to put the telephone down.

'Oh, for God's sake, Goldy, can't you take a joke? Of course I remember you. You're like one of those Heineken lagers. You reach parts others don't.' She let out a large cackle of laughter, nearly deafening poor Ralph on the other end. He was relieved that she had remembered him and smiled at her comment. He should have known better than to expect her to sound pleased that he had called.

'You do realise you are paying all the expenses and the price will be higher because you have me on call, 24/7? I won't be able to work around you. Oh.' A sudden thought crossed her mind. 'I'd also like a room of my own.'

'Really?'

Hearing the surprise in his voice at this, she carried on. 'Well, if I am going to look my best for you, I want some space to put my makeup on without you looking over my shoulder, and somewhere to fart and shave my legs in peace. Okay?' She was relieved when she heard his warm laughter at the other end of the phone, and he agreed.

Ralph could not help smiling at this woman and her crude jokes.

Once all the arrangements had been made, Julie knew she had to act fast. There was no way she could turn this golden goose down. And, to be fair, she wouldn't mind seeing him again. But she couldn't leave Frankie on her own. She would have to take her with her. Hence, her own room. It wouldn't be easy but she could go back and forth to check on things. Blimey, surely she was entitled to a lunch break!

Frankie was in a better state to travel, although she still had night terrors and woke up screaming. The only downside was there would be no methadone. They would not give Julie the bottle but told her to go to a doctor near to where she was staying and they would supply it.

Instead, Frankie had begged her to get her some heroin. She complained of cramps and illness and broke out in sweats. Julie was at her wits' end. 'Just for those couple of days, Julie, to help me. Please,' Frankie had begged. But they had come too far to turn back now. Surely Frankie could manage for a couple of days? All she had to do was stay in the room and sleep. She was no juggler, but Julie felt like one now. She had so many balls in the air, she was afraid she could not catch them all.

They arrived at the hotel much earlier than Ralph expected them. To Julie's relief, the receptionist confirmed that he had already booked the extra room; all she had to do now was get up there with Frankie. She had drummed into Frankie throughout the train journey that she had to keep quiet and no one could know she was there. She would order food to be brought to the room. All she had to do was keep a low profile.

'Well, well, well. If it isn't that handsome man I met in Liverpool.' Julie waltzed into the bar, where she had agreed to meet Ralph, and put on her best performance. She needed to make this meeting go well. Not only did she need the money for her and Frankie, but she hoped this Ralph person would be a regular thing. In addition, secretly she could not deny that she was pleased to see him. She didn't realise how much she had missed him until she saw him.

'It's good to see you, Julie. I hope I haven't inconvenienced you too much. Thank you for coming.' Leaning forward, Ralph kissed her on the cheek, then pulled up a bar stool for her and ordered champagne. She reminded him of the very beautiful actress Mae West, who was known for her witty remarks. Yes, that was his Julie. And he liked the idea of that. 'His Julie.' He wanted her to be his.

'You know what they say, Goldy. Behind every man is a good woman and behind her is his wife!' She laughed and charmed her way through the evening. 'I thought you would have invited me to your house. After all, you did say you weren't married. Or were you fibbing?'

'No. I live here. It has cooked food, a laundry service and all the amenities I require.'

'You live in a hotel?' Shocked by his answer, she pressed further. 'This must cost a fortune. You must earn a lot of money to live in a place like this.' Again, Ralph just nodded and shrugged. She knew he wasn't going to fill in the gaps so she stopped asking.

'Shall we retire?' Ralph hadn't realised how much he had missed her. She made him laugh, something he had not done properly in a very long time. He felt relaxed with her.

'No. I'm too young to retire, but if you mean shall we go to bed and have amazing sex, then I'm up for that.' She liked the way Ralph blushed slightly and looked around the room. This made her want to tease him even more.

They were both taken by surprise when, alone in the bedroom, their ardent passion for each other took over. Over the last few weeks their feelings, which they didn't realise they had for each other, had been suppressed by other matters. But now they were alone, the chemistry in the room was electric. They couldn't get enough of each other. Their kisses seemed to last forever, leading up to a peak of lovemaking that neither of them had experienced before. When they were satiated and lying in each other's arms, Ralph was the first to speak. 'I have to go out first thing in the morning, but I will be back around lunchtime. Can you amuse yourself until then? Take some money and have a look at the sights. Is that okay?'

It was more than okay for Julie. She could spend the day trying to find an emergency doctor for Frankie. Maybe they could give her some methadone?

'So, where are you going, then?' Julie sat up in the lamplit room, lit two cigarettes and handed one to Ralph.

'Are you always this nosey?' He smiled, taking the cigarette from her. She was beautiful. Her blonde hair, although he could see it was out of a bottle, hung around her shoulders and her cheeky grin lit up her face, showing a row of white teeth. Reaching up, he touched a length of her hair and toyed with it. 'I work with my friend, Carlos. We export and import things.'

'Go on,' she coaxed. 'It's okay, Goldy, I'm a prostitute; we're like priests. We hear everything and say nothing. Go on, I'm interested.'

Much to his surprise, Ralph found himself telling her more than he had ever told anyone. He told her about the gun-running.

'What, and you work with an Italian guy called Carlos?' Wide-eyed, she sat up and stared at him. 'Oh, my God, that's Mafia country. Be careful, mate, you'll end up with a horse's head in your bed. I've seen the movie.' She laughed.

'There is no such thing as the Mafia, apparently. That is only a name the newspapers use. They like the word "family".' He wagged his finger in her face. 'And you could be the one with the horse's head in your bed if you repeat any of this, okay?'

Ignoring his warning, Julie carried on. 'Actually, you look a bit like that Marlon Brando guy, with your black hair slicked back. Although you need to mumble more.'

He smiled and took her cigarette from her and stubbed them both out in the ashtray beside him. 'Enough talk.' He reached out for her and they made love again, this time much slower and without the urgency.

* * *

Afterwards, as Ralph lay sleeping, Julie checked on Frankie in the room next door. But to her horror, she wasn't there. Running into the bathroom, she searched it, but Frankie was nowhere to be found. Where could she have gone? Then Julie noticed her bag on the dressing table was open and her purse was gone. Damn! Julie had no idea where to start looking for her.

Walking outside of the hotel, she looked around the streets and the Tube station. It was a wild goose chase and all Julie could do was wait for Frankie to turn up again – hopefully still alive.

After two brain-numbing hours, Frankie floated through the hotel door. She was shocked to see Julie and smiled.

'Where the hell have you been and where is my purse?' snapped Julie. She had been so worried she didn't know whether to slap her or hug her.

'Here's your purse.' Dropping it playfully back into Julie's bag, Frankie came and sat beside her on the bed. 'I went for a walk, that's all, and I feel better for it.'

Realising the signs and the change in mood, Julie's heart sank. 'What have you taken and where did you get it from?'

'Oh for God's sake. You're having a ball down there with Mr Goldfinger and I am cooped up in here. I was bored! I just went for a walk!'

'Don't lie to me – I know you've taken something.' Angry and upset, Julie was in no mood for lies. Ralph would be back soon and the last thing she needed was a full-on confrontation with Frankie in front of him.

'Okay, okay. I went to that Soho place – you can get anything around there. So I went and asked around. It's bloody expensive, but it will help me while I am cooped up here and don't have my methadone. I just needed a little pick-me-up. We're going home soon and then everything will be okay.'

'Do you have any more surprises up your sleeve? Couldn't you have left a note or something?' Julie snapped. There was no point in going around in circles; it was done and she couldn't do anything to change it now.

'Well, I did buy a little extra just in case you stayed longer. They don't give you needles but they gave me some light bulbs.'

'Light bulbs?' Julie's ignorance of drugs shone through like a light beam.

'Yes, you twist off the metal bit that you put into the socket, like this.' Mesmerised, Julie watched how easily Frankie knew these tricks of the trade. She took off the end and took out her silver foil packet and dropped some into the light bulb, then lit it with her lighter and put her mouth around the end, inhaling in the mixture. Julie's jaw almost dropped. She had never seen anything like it in her life.

'Stop it! Stop it now. God, it could be rat poison for all you know!' Disgusted and angry, Julie looked at the clock and realised it was time to meet Ralph again. After quickly getting herself ready, she ran back to Ralph's room. She had slipped into a black basque and stockings. She ordered some champagne and waited for him. Within a few minutes, he had arrived and they were lounging on the bed together, drinking champagne, and she was pouring it over her body for him to lick off. But although she enjoyed her time with Ralph, the events with Frankie had left Julie shattered.

* * *

Ralph felt something was missing from Julie this time. She was always popping to her own room, claiming she had forgotten something. If he went to the bathroom, off she went. When they turned off the light that night, he feigned sleep and watched her creep silently out of the bedroom, and then back in an hour later. He said nothing. A horrible thought suddenly struck him. Who was in the other room? Had she brought her pimp with her? Exactly who was he providing a hotel room for? It was time to find out.

He waited until she had made another excuse to go out for something the next morning, gave it a couple of minutes and then went to the room. He knocked on the door; Julie answered, and then tried shutting it in his face. Pushing it open, he stormed in past her. The sight before him stopped him in his tracks and he looked at Julie for answers. There was a pregnant woman lying on top of the bed. This was not what he had expected to find.

'Look, just fuck off, will you? This is none of your business!' Julie shouted at him.

'What is going on? Who is she?' Walking closer to the bed, he could see the woman was half asleep. She hadn't roused, even with all the noise.

'She's my sister, not that it's any of your business. I didn't want to leave her alone. You got what you paid for. What's your problem?' Julie spat at him, embarrassed at being caught out. She felt stupid, humiliated.

'If you wanted to bring your sister, all you had to do was ask. It's not a big deal. Why all the sneaking around?' Ralph tried reasoning with her. He sat on the edge of the bed. 'Is she okay? She doesn't look too well.' His concern was genuine, but Julie wasn't having any of it.

'Just get out of here. I'll be in to perform later. Now just fucking leave us alone, will you?' After another few minutes arguing, Julie almost pushed Ralph out of the room. He thought it was best to leave and let her calm down.

A couple of whiskies and an hour later, Ralph decided to return to the room. He had half expected Julie to come to him and explain, but she hadn't. When he got there, he realised his biggest mistake. It seemed no sooner had he left than she had packed up and left the hotel without so much as a goodbye. There was no note at reception. In addition, the porter who had let him in the room to look around confirmed he had seen two women, one pregnant, leave about an hour ago. Julie had gone.

On arriving back in Liverpool, Julie went to get a taxi and left Frankie standing outside of the train station. She had only been gone a couple of minutes when she saw Ian, standing beside Frankie, laughing in a casual manner. He greeted Julie with the usual contempt but kept smiling. This place was too busy for him to cause a scene and he knew it. Police officers were walking around the station and there were far too many witnesses around for his usual outburst.

'You can fuck off. I know what you did to her. Kidnapping her and dumping a pregnant woman. Now just fuck off and leave us alone.' Julie picked up her case, linked arms with Frankie and bundled her into the taxi. 'What the hell are you talking to him for?' Julie was angry. She could not believe Frankie had been so stupid.

'I didn't realise until he was there. He just said hello and asked how I am and then you came back.'

'Well, it's just as well I did. God knows where you would be by now. What is that in your hand?' Grabbing open Frankie's palm, Julie could see the familiar foil. 'For fuck's sake, will you never learn? He just gave you that, didn't he?'

As usual, Frankie turned on the tears when she had no words. 'He just asked if I needed a little pick-me-up. That's all, Julie.'

Angry and breathing heavily, Julie opened the taxi window and threw it out, much to Frankie's dismay. Julie couldn't believe how stupid she had been this last couple of days. More to the point, it had all been in vain. She hadn't even got her money from Ralph Gold, she had left in such a hurry. What a bloody waste of time!

Once indoors, Julie went to the coin-operated telephone that was in the hallway of the house. She needed to find work. Fuck Frankie, and fuck Ralph Gold. She needed some money. She rang the agency and was surprised to hear that Ralph had paid his bill. He had called the agency and transferred the money into their account to pay Julie. She was almost taken aback at this. It was very unexpected, considering how she had spoken to him last. *He's a gentleman*, she argued with herself. No other client would have done that. She still had the telephone number he had given her in her purse; she didn't know why. She thought she should call him and thank him, but there was nothing really to say.

* * *

Two weeks later, Julie came home in the early hours of the morning and found the room empty. There was no sign of Frankie and her first instincts were there was something wrong with the baby. Running down the hallway, she telephoned the hospital. No one had been admitted. Searching around the bedsit for a note or anything from Frankie, she saw the old tell-tale signs of Frankie's addiction.

Damn it! Julie felt like disowning Frankie. After everything she had done for her! But she was still her sister. She knew where she would be... that famous street corner under the streetlamp.

When Julie got there, she felt sick to her stomach. She was right. There, in the early morning light, was a group of scantily clad women, rubbing their arms to try to warm themselves up, and in the middle of them was a very pregnant Frankie.

'What the fuck are you doing here? Don't you realise you're pregnant!' Julie was shouting and dragging Frankie away by the arm. 'How dare you betray me after everything I've done for you?' All her pent-up anger came flooding out and she slapped Frankie across the face. She was tired of all this.

'I'm sorry. I didn't mean to upset you.' Frankie was crying. Neither of them noticed Ian coming out of the café opposite.

'Oi, bitch. She's come back to me of her own accord, now beat it!' The punch in the face Ian swung at her knocked Julie to the ground. He started kicking her while she was down, and all she could do was curl up in a ball until he was finished. Dragging Frankie by the arm, he bundled her into the back of his car and drove off. Julie lay in the middle of the road with her coat wrapped around her, crying. Her face was red with blood; it was oozing into her blonde hair and her body was wracked with pain. No one came to her aid, even though everyone there had witnessed what had happened. Desperate and alone, she picked herself up, wiped her nose and began to walk home.

As she passed a telephone box, a thought occurred to her; she went inside and dialled Ralph Gold's number. 'Ralph, is that you?'

'Yes. Who's that?'

She heaved a sob when she heard his voice. 'It's me, Julie. I'm sorry about London.' Her voice broke and she began to cry.

'Where are you?' Ignoring her crying, Ralph asked for more details.

Without caring, Julie told him the complete story and what had just happened to her. She was terrified because she did not know where Frankie was or where Ian would take her.

'Is there somewhere you can go until I get there? I'll be a couple of hours. Give me an address to meet you.' His authoritative voice brought her back to reality. He was going to come and help her, though God knows what he could do. But she was tired of fighting alone.

After giving Ralph the address of a pub on the other side of town, Julie put the telephone down. She felt better. It felt good to have someone to pour all of her troubles out to. It was always the other way around; everyone expected strong Julie to sort their problems out.

She went home first. She was still wearing only a camisole under her coat. In addition, she was covered in blood. Her face and lips felt swollen and she was tired. But when she got there, the door of her room was ajar. Tentatively pushing it open, it was obvious the place had been ransacked. Clothing was thrown all over the place, drawers had been pulled out and emptied, and spray-painted across the wall, it said:

LOSER BITCH.

Julie didn't have much money stashed away, or many possessions, but everything was gone. She went to the bathroom to wash her face; she was still shaking when she looked into the mirror. She hardly recognised herself. Her face was already changing colours where the bruising was coming through. Her head was cut where she had fallen and her nose looked twice the size, and bloody. Gently washing away the blood with a damp flannel, she searched around for something to wear. Some of the clothing was damp and when she smelt it, she realised they had urinated all over it. Bracing herself, she found a mismatched tracksuit and put it on. She had no more tears left in her as she shut the door and left to go and wait for the only person who might help her: Ralph Gold.

27

A KNIGHT IN SHINING ARMOUR

Getting out of his car, Ralph looked around the outside of the pub where Julie had said she would meet him. The rain didn't help. When he had told Carlos he had to go out on personal business, he'd insisted Ralph told him what it was and also made him take Joe and Alex along in case he needed back-up. Ralph never needed back-up, but it crossed his mind Carlos must have presumed he was doing some secret deal on the side and wanted to keep an eye on him. He was becoming very paranoid lately.

Stunned, Ralph turned as he heard his name. Emerging from a side alley, shaking and half frozen, was a very different Julie. Her hair was tied back in a ponytail. It was pink with blood. Her bruised, swollen face made him wince and the baggy, wet tracksuit told him a story all of its own. She had said she was in trouble, but he had never expected this.

Opening the car door, Ralph waited until she got in. When she saw Joe and Alex in the back, she halted. 'It's okay, get in,' he said. It was clear to him she was frightened of her own shadow now. Handing her a cigarette and putting the heater on in the car, he waited until she composed herself.

'He has my sister.' Panicking, she grabbed at his shirt and almost shouted. Her hands were shaking as she tried lighting her cigarette. Bit by bit, the three men listened to Julie's story. She could see them exchange glances now and again and her heart sank.

'Okay, show me this street corner.' Ralph started to drive off, waiting for instructions.

'Do not cross him, Ralph; you don't know what kind of a person he is, or what he will do to Frankie.'

'Is that him?' Ralph parked the car and looked across the road. It seemed he had come at the right moment. In the midst of a crowd of women were two men, taking money from them and arguing.

Wide-eyed with panic, Julie nodded. 'The big one on the right.' She pointed. 'That's him.'

Ralph got out of the car and walked up to them all. Ian turned; he obviously thought this well-dressed man wanted 'business' and smiled when he saw him.

'Take your pick, mate. You pay me. Not them.' He grinned, proud of his pimp status.

Ralph's arm flew at Ian and hit him in the face, knocking him flying backwards. Standing over him, Ralph grabbed hold of Ian by the throat and dragged him upwards, bringing his knee up hard into the pimp's crotch. Julie sat there in shock; she had never expected this. With his gentlemanly persona, Ralph did not seem like the kind of man who could have a street fight with a bunch of thugs and win. Julie sat there wide-eyed, watching how easily he crushed Ian. Ian was helpless and begging Ralph to stop, holding his hands up in submission. He looked like a rag doll in Ralph's hands. 'You women-beaters and bullies are all the fucking same: cowards, the lot of you. Now, where is Frankie?' Ralph was breathing hard while he stood there, hands on hips, watching Ian howl with pain on the ground.

'Wouldn't you like to know, you bastard!' Ian shouted. Grabbing Ian by the throat again, Ralph punched and punched until blood spurted out all over the place. Ian went limp as he lost consciousness and he fell to the ground when Ralph let go of him. Ralph's shirt and hands were covered in blood. Julie couldn't believe what she was seeing. Her Ralph was an animal!

Turning to Ian's friend, who was sitting on the pavement rubbing his head, watching the fight, he said, 'Are you going to tell me where she is, or do you want to take his place?' Ralph's voice was very steady, although his words were staggered with his heavy breathing.

'I'm not getting my head kicked in because of those old slags. She is at Razor's place. He's having some sort of stag party there. Try to ruin it, though, and he won't be happy.'

'Where is this place?' Ralph looked across at the waiting car. 'Better still, you piece of shit, you can show us and introduce us to Razor yourself.'

'No way! No fucking way, he'll slit my throat.'

'Fair point. He will slit your throat if you do and I will slit your throat if you don't. I'd personally say you have a better chance begging him for mercy than me.' The pair of them were soaking wet from the rain. Ralph grabbed his arm and frogmarched him to the car, almost lifting him off his feet.

Alex and Joe moved up in the back of the car as the sodden man, dressed in cheap denims, T-shirt and leather jacket, sat beside them.

They arrived at a third-storey flat on a local estate. Ralph, who had now found out the man's name was Steve, pushed him forward and made him knock at the door. Instead, he shouted for Razor through the letter box and then put his hand inside and pulled out a long piece of string. On the end of it was a key. Steve put the key in the lock and turned it. Turning to Ralph, he said, 'He can't be in or he would have answered. Look, I've brought you here, mate, I'm leaving now.'

Ralph grabbed the shoulder of his jacket. 'All you have brought me to, Stevie boy, is a shithole of a flat that is obviously empty. You go first.'

Steve's face dropped. He gave a huge sigh and stepped through the door. Ralph looked over the balcony down at the car. He held up his hands and displayed five fingers. It meant give it five minutes, then come up. He saw Joe nod through the window. Maybe he would need some help after all. God knows what was waiting for him inside this place.

Ralph had seen many things in his lifetime, but nothing could have prepared him for this. Frankie was gagged and handcuffed to a table; the pitiful look in her eyes pleaded with him for help. She looked like she was in labour. Steve scarpered as soon as possible.

After removing the tape from her mouth and getting her out of the handcuffs, he carried her as best as he could to the waiting car downstairs. 'Get her to the hospital. Julie, tell them where to go,' he instructed. Panic-stricken and trying to soothe Frankie, Julie pointed Joe in the direction of the hospital.

Seeing the state Frankie was in, the hospital took her straight down to surgery and gave her an emergency caesarean. It was their only chance of saving the baby. Within minutes, her small son was put into an incubator on life support. Frankie was in a bad way and the doctors told Julie to prepare herself for the worst; the next twenty-four hours were critical.

Ralph wanted to stay with Julie. The doctors had fussed over her and said they wanted to check her injuries, but she brushed them off, not wanting to leave Frankie for a moment.

'Thank you, Ralph. You don't have to stay; you have done more than enough.' She was trying to gather her thoughts and compose herself, and she didn't know what else to say.

'I'm staying with you as long as it takes. You rang me for help and that is what you are going to get. Come here.'

She fell into his arms and cried while he held her.

* * *

Day after day, Julie sat beside Frankie, but eventually her weak body gave up and she died, leaving Julie devastated, hysterically shouting at the doctors and stopping them from taking Frankie to the morgue until Ralph intervened and calmed her down.

The baby, who they had named Josh, had been quickly baptised and was a fighter. He was holding his own but the doctors warned Julie they would not know what damage Frankie's addiction had caused until they ran more tests. She blocked out as much as she could and concentrated on Josh in his incubator.

'You smell nearly as bad as I do, Goldy,' she said. Julie looked down at herself. Apart from the change of tracksuit, she hadn't changed or washed in over a week. Her own bruises had turned yellow and black, but she didn't care.

'Well, at least we won't offend each other with the smell,' said Ralph, trying making light of it. 'Listen, serious talk now. I will pay for Frankie's funeral.' Julie opened her mouth to speak but Ralph held his hand up. 'No arguments, we're both too tired for that.'

Julie had been about to argue the point and refuse, but she accepted gracefully. The last thing she wanted was a pauper's funeral for her sister. 'What is that going to cost me? What do you want from me? Why should you do this? I am nothing to you.'

'You're my friend. That's what friends do. They help each other.'

She nodded, and when Ralph reached for her hand and squeezed it, she gave him a weak smile in return. She wasn't sure if he meant it, but she hoped so. Time would tell.

'I have some business to attend to in London but I'll come back and sort things out with you, okay?' Ralph was loath to leave Julie, but he had a gun-running export to deal with for Carlos, and there was some other problem Carlos wouldn't discuss over the telephone. He couldn't stay away any longer.

Again, Julie nodded as he stood up to leave. Sighing to herself and looking around the room, she shrugged. That would be the last she would see of him. Nevertheless, she would be eternally grateful.

* * *

'Where is Carlos?' Ralph was surprised that he was not at his hotel, where he'd said he would be.

'He's had to go home. The Don has been shot. Carlos wants to see you. I'll book you a flight for tonight if that's okay.' Joe didn't give any more information, even though Ralph pressed him. He was shattered. All he wanted to do was have a bath and sleep. The last thing he wanted was a flight to Italy.

When he arrived at the Don's mansion, it seemed everyone was in mourning. Ralph presumed he was dead. Carlos greeted him but seemed on his guard. 'What's happened, Carlos? Who shot the Don? Why didn't you tell me this over the telephone, for God's sake?'

'Because I wanted to see your face, Ralph.' Sitting calmly in his chair, dressed in a black suit and tie, Carlos picked up his glass of whisky and sipped it. His eyes bored into Ralph and his face was set in stone.

'My face?' Ralph was confused. 'What has my face got to do with it? Look, I'm tired. If you have something to say, spit it out.'

'Andreas,' said Carlos, and he took another sip of his drink while looking over the glass at Ralph, who stood in front of his desk. He didn't invite Ralph to sit, nor did he offer him a drink. Their meeting was very hostile, which Ralph felt was unusual.

Puzzled, and with his own anger rising, Ralph said, 'Andreas? What the bloody hell is that supposed to mean? What are you talking about?'

Nodding and satisfied with Ralph's answer, Carlos pushed the whisky decanter forward. 'Sit down.'

Ralph poured himself a drink and sat down.

'You and Ricky are the only two people, apart from myself, who knew that my father was going to Sicily to see my mother's grave. That is where he was shot. At my mother's graveside. Andreas is not a "he", it is a family, much like our own. They are our rivals and someone gave them information as to my father's whereabouts. I needed to see your face, your body language, to make sure it wasn't you. I now know that it wasn't.' As Carlos spoke, his face showed no emotion. His voice was calm, although it sounded hate-filled.

'You really suspected me? Shit, Carlos, I can't believe that. I thought we were friends of sorts.'

'Do you really think I wanted to know it was my *brother*? I wish it was you, Ralph, but my apologies. Ricky wants to be don around here. Head operator, as it were. God knows what promises and bullshit the Andreas family have given him.' With one sweep of his arm, Carlos cleared everything from the surface of the desk onto the floor. He was angry and he was shouting now. 'Our family have been betrayed by our own kin.'

'Calm down. Have you spoken to Ricky?' Ralph was trying to appease the madman who was now storming around the office, smashing things and throwing furniture around. Carlos was going berserk!

'No, I fucking haven't. Because now I have to kill my own fucking brother. I will make that bastard eat dirt. He has been lying and cheating. He has betrayed the family!'

Trying to play devil's advocate again, Ralph tried to get Carlos to see reason. 'Speak to him. You could be wrong. Anyone could have found out where your father was. Do not do anything you could regret. Find out the truth.'

'Oh, I intend to. I have fed Ricky a line that we're doing a gun run tonight. The lorries are full and outside. Even you didn't know that, did you?' He smirked.

Perplexed, Ralph picked up a chair that had fallen over and sat on it. Christ, he had only been away a few days and the world had gone mad!

'But really the lorries are empty, but padlocked securely. I bet you those lorries will be ambushed tonight. That snake will have told his new friends. God, I cannot even speak his name.'

'How long have you known all of this? You've had your suspicions for a long time, haven't you?'

Carlos ignored the question, but Ralph did not need him to respond. The information answered all his questions.

'I am to be married soon, Ralph. Don Leo always made it a rule that he wouldn't do business with an unmarried man... silly, I know.' He smiled. 'But wives cannot testify. In addition, having a wife and children provides a good respectable front. Being a married man can open many doors. Remember that in the future.'

'Well, you're full of shocks today. I didn't know you were serious about anyone.'

'If...' Carlos faltered and started again. 'No, *when* my father dies, as he is only hanging on by a thread, I will have to be sworn in by the other gangland bosses. Agreed by the Mafioso to do business with each other. An initiation, if you like. Maria is the beautiful daughter of one of the Sicilian bosses. It makes good business that we should be joined by marriage.' Carlos tried his best to explain things to a very confused Ralph, who felt this conversation had taken a strange turn. 'But first we find out if my brother is a traitor.'

* * *

Just as Carlos had predicted, gunmen stopped the empty lorries. The two innocent drivers were shot. Carlos had called that collateral damage.

Don Leo finally died, leaving Carlos to organise a massive funeral. People flew in from all over the world to pay their respects. Ricky had cried at Carlos's side and worn dark glasses to hide his grief. Carlos said nothing.

Next was Carlos's initiation, which was for Italians only. Ralph was not invited. The wedding was to be announced after a respectful grieving period.

This all happened in just a few short weeks. Ralph had tried calling Julie at the hospital and hoped they would pass on the messages that he left. He was due to fly back to London in a couple of days. And he couldn't wait to see her again.

28

A CHANGE OF LUCK

No sooner had Ralph touched English soil than he was arrested. The police arrived at his hotel, mob-handed and handcuffed him. He was charged with the murders of the two security guards back in Ireland over two years ago. Apparently, the wife of one of the security guards had been on her way to take her husband his lunch box when she saw Ralph leaving. He was immediately taken back to Ireland to face the music.

Paddy went to visit Ralph, at his request. Sitting across the table from him, in the prison visiting room, Ralph said, 'I'm innocent, Paddy. Someone has set me up. I never killed those people; when I left they were alive and well. And why is it that this wife has decided to speak up now – two years later? I smell one hell of a rat.'

Paddy looked Ralph up and down. He looked tanned and well. The prison uniform didn't take the shine away from him. 'Where have you been? I know you said you had been travelling around, but you look really well.' Paddy's jealousy was apparent and the way he avoided Ralph's questions suggested he knew more about the investigation than he was letting on.

'I had a stroke of luck, gambling. I came into a bit of money.' Ralph thought about his dealings in Italy and London. 'In fact, I have quite a bit left over. I want you to buy up some of the pubs in Ireland. Buy some of the houses, too.'

Paddy's eyes lit up. 'Christ! How much did you win?'

'As I say, quite a bit. Are you still collecting from the pubs?' Ralph whispered so the guards could barely hear.

'Yes, and those couple of friends of yours that came over as a bit of muscle have helped. Thanks for that; you know me, always like a bit of muscle around.' Paddy laughed. 'Yes, sure, I can buy up the property you need.'

'Thanks. I'm no stranger to prison, and if I'm going to spend the next thirty years behind bars, I may as well make the interest on the property.' Managing not to divulge too much, Ralph gave Paddy his instructions. 'Oh, by the way. One more favour. There is a woman I want you to contact for me.'

Paddy's eyes lit up and a large grin crossed his face. 'A woman, Ralph, mate. Well, you are a dark horse. You kept that one quiet.' Paddy laughed, slapping Ralph on the shoulder, much to the guards' disapproval.

Ralph gave Paddy the number of the hospital and told him to tell Julie what had happened to him, and that he would fulfil his promise.

'That's all?' Paddy looked half disgusted at Ralph's message. 'Don't you want me to tell her that you love her or something?' Paddy winked. Again, he looked disappointed when Ralph shook his head.

Three days later, Ralph was told he had a visitor. When he got to the room, he was surprised to see Julie. Now the tables were turned. Here he was in prison uniform and there was Julie, looking like he always remembered her: full makeup, cocky smile and properly dressed for a change.

'Well, you always have to go one better, Goldy. You're accused of killing two people. Most people only ever kill one!' Julie sat down and looked around her, smiling at the other men who had visitors.

'I didn't kill anyone. I know they all say that, but I'm telling you the truth. Why are you here?'

'That daft Irishman called me. Paddy. Fucking weirdo.' She shook her head and rolled her eyes at the ceiling. 'He told me about this. God, I cannot understand a bloody word he says. He's like a tit in a trance.'

Despite the situation, Ralph could not help but laugh. Julie always made him smile. She had not met Paddy before, but she had the full measure of him. 'What about Josh?' he persisted. 'How is he?'

'He's doing okay. They think he might have mental problems because of Frankie's addiction. I don't want to think about it. Tell me about you.' Looking up, Julie could see one of the warders standing close by. 'Oi, fuckface. Can't I talk dirty without you getting excited? Piss off,' she snapped.

'Julie, behave. They can easily end this visit,' Ralph warned. He was enjoying the visit and didn't want Julie's hot temper to ruin it.

'Yes, okay, sorry, officer.' Julie's voice dripped sarcasm. 'So, what's happening here, when do you go to court?'

'Bloody hell, give me a break. The case hasn't even been put together yet and you have the hangman out. There's no evidence I was there, but they have found an eyewitness. The wife of one of the victims. She has pointed me out in a line-up. All they have to do is build a case around it. It's not the first time I've been in prison, so don't worry about it. I'll sort you out, as promised, even if it's only through Paddy.'

'I know first-hand that you have friends in high places.' She moved in closer to Ralph to avoid being heard. 'Couldn't they get the wife to change her mind?'

'No, this Chief Inspector Connor has got her under some kind of witness protection because she's afraid for her life. This inspector wants to wind it up quickly, I think.'

Stunned, Julie looked at Ralph. A thought crossed her mind. Could it be? No way. Connor was a common name. 'Is this copper local?'

'Don't think so. Why?'

'No reason. Just me being nosey. Does this Carlos bloke know you're here, then? Where is he?'

'Yes, he does, and he will probably be staying as far away as possible. Actually, let me give you his number at the hotel he stays at. Carlos will see you right in my absence.'

'Oh, forget the sodding money, Ralph. You're not bound to your promise. All the same, I will take that number, just in case you do come up trumps.' She cackled and took out a pen and paper from her handbag. Her mind was working overtime. She wanted to get out of there. Instead, she filled Ralph in on how Josh was doing and where she was living now. 'Apparently, they found Ian's body floating in the sea,' she said. 'Oh, and I remembered you telling me about that old ladies' home your mother is in. Well, I called them before I got here and said you had to go away for a while and asked how she was doing, and she's doing okay.'

Ralph burst out laughing; she was a breath of fresh air, and despite the circumstances, she made him laugh aloud. 'It's not an old ladies' home! But thank you for enquiring about her.' Ralph had to admit he was smitten with Julie. It was a shame he was facing a thirty-year-plus prison sentence. 'If you're ever passing by, come and see me again, if you have time.' He didn't want to push her, but he thought he would ask.

'Oh, believe it. I'm like bad luck. I always turn up unexpected.' As the warder called time, Julie blew him a kiss and winked.

Julie had left Paddy waiting outside for her in the car. 'Take me to the airport, Paddy, mate. I need civilisation.'

Once at the airport, Julie telephoned the number Ralph had given her. She felt nervous and didn't know what kind of reception she would get. 'Can I speak to Carlos, please,' she said, when a man instantly answered the telephone.

'Who wants him?' The voice on the other end was crisp and articulate.

'A friend of Ralph's.' She didn't know what else to say. They did not know who she was.

'Carlos speaking. What do you want?' he said flippantly.

'I'm in Ireland, on my way to London. Can I come and see you? Will you meet me at the airport?' Julie was hopeful, but the disinterested voice on the other end didn't inspire her.

'I will not. However, I will see that someone does. What time is your flight?'

After fumbling in her bag for her ticket, Julie read out her arrival time. Then the line went dead.

Arriving at the terminal, Julie looked around. Everyone was picking up their cases from the carousel and meeting their loved ones. She had no idea if anyone would turn up to meet her. She saw a dark-haired man in a black suit and tie and, even though it didn't particularly look sunny, he was wearing sunglasses. He was holding a piece of cardboard with 'GOLD' written on it. It was so small if she had blinked, she would have missed it.

'Are you waiting for me?' She smiled, to no avail.

'If you say so. Come on.' He did not introduce himself and he didn't offer to pick up her bag. He just turned and walked ahead and waited for Julie to catch up with him.

Once in the back of the car, she tried making conversation, but he turned the radio up. For once in her life she felt it was better that she just played his game and said nothing. When they arrived at the hotel, the man got out and threw his car keys to one of the staff and pulled her along behind him.

'Okay, mate, I'm coming. I'm not as tall as you; I've got little legs. Get off me!'

Releasing her arm, he walked ahead of her. Looking up at the great big hotel that nearly reached the clouds astounded her. International flags from all over the world were on the top of it. It was an amazing sight.

The lift seemed to take forever to reach their floor, then at last it stopped and Julie walked through the door. Looking around the large room, she could not believe her eyes. She did not know hotels could look like this. This whole room resembled someone's lounge. It had sofas, a bar and coffee tables. It also had about half a dozen men dressed like the one who'd picked her up. Some were sitting on one of the sofas having a drink, talking in Italian. Others were busying themselves getting a drink. Either way, Julie felt uncomfortable.

One put his hand out and indicated that she should sit down, then walked away. Sitting nervously on the edge of the sofa, she tightly held on to her bag on her knee. She could feel her palms sweating and she was thirsty. She could not remember the last time she had been in a hotel room with a group of people with her clothes on. After looking at the lavish surroundings and the well-dressed men, Julie looked down at her own clothes. She felt common.

'Any chance of a drink?' Pouting stubbornly, she looked across at them. Without a word, one got up, poured her a drink, and put some ice in it. She did not care what it was; she was thirsty and needed some Dutch courage.

* * *

'Is she here, Marco? Let's make her sweat. What can she possibly want apart from money?'

Carlos had showered and was getting dressed. The telephone call from Julie had intrigued him.

'I could give her a few pounds and tell her to piss off, boss. God, she's Ralph's prostitute; why are you giving her the time of day?' Marco was disgusted that this cheap woman with her cheap clothes had come.

Slapping his face hard, Carlos gripped Marco's chin. 'You're a prostitute too. You offer your service and you get paid. We all have to do what we can in life to get by. Now, hold your fucking tongue. Ralph has told me all about her. If I didn't know better I would say he's sweet on her, so for his sake, be polite.'

* * *

Julie had been there for the best part of an hour when suddenly she was beckoned to another room. Walking in, she saw a lone man sitting at a desk. His face showed no emotion.

'Are you Carlos?'

'I am. Thank you for waiting, Julie. Can I offer you a drink?' His charming smile put her at ease. She could not help but notice what a handsome man he was. Typical Italian: dark hair, pleasant smile and that naughty twinkle in his eye. Julie accepted another drink and then she and Carlos were left in the room alone together.

'So, what can I do for you? You have made a long journey, visiting Ireland and then coming here.'

'I think I might be able to help Ralph. He mentioned the inspector on his case is called Connor. I think it might be the same one I know... or knew, anyway,' she stammered. Carlos's eyes burnt into her. His face did not move. He waved his hand in the air for her to continue her story and sipped his drink while he listened. For the first time since that awful night, she blurted out what had happened to Donna. She could see she had taken him off guard. He had not expected a story like this.

'So. What do you think you can do to help Ralph? You know he is charged with two counts of murder.'

'Well, at least I am trying to do something! Not sitting on my arse like you, with laughing boy out there,' she snapped. She had had enough of this game. She had tried and failed. It was all going to blow up in her face. It probably wasn't even the same copper. On the aeroplane, rehearsing her speech, it had made sense. Now, it all sounded silly.

Ignoring her sarcasm, Carlos carried on. 'My lawyers will help Ralph as best as they can. However, they have a witness and they are protecting her in a hotel around here somewhere. She is guarded night and day. So I'll ask you again, how do you think you can help Ralph?'

Her nerves were getting the better of her, but she carried on. 'I want you to confirm it's the right policeman that is looking after this witness and then...' She faltered, feeling embarrassed. She could feel the blood rushing to her face. 'And then... I want a gun! Ralph Gold has been very good to me and I owe him.'

Carlos exploded with laughter. He could not believe his ears. 'You want me to hand over a gun to you. This is not Tesco; you do not just get one over the counter. Tell me, why would I give a gun to someone like you?'

'What do you know about me?' Breaking into a big grin, Julie laughed. 'Oh, I see, the prostitute is on the take, is she? You think I have come here with my begging bowl? Well, fuck you, Mr whatever your name is and fuck those well-dressed statues out there. Bollocks to the lot of you!' Picking up her bag, Julie walked angrily towards the door.

'Stop!' shouted Carlos. 'Sit down, Julie.' His commanding voice stopped her in her tracks and she turned. 'Please, sit down.'

Julie walked back to the desk and sat down opposite him. Her face was flushed with anger and her eyes threw daggers at him.

'Let's start again. It seems we have got off on the wrong foot.' His crisp, cultured voice floated in the air and she nodded.

'Marcos will book you into a hotel where you can eat and sleep.' She was about to butt in to tell him she couldn't afford it when he held his hand up. 'My treat, of course.' Seeing her body relax, he carried on. 'I will be in touch.'

'What about Ralph?'

Raising one eyebrow, Carlos grinned. 'Well, he's not going anywhere, is he? He told me you were a feisty one. Your profession has nothing to do with me. Never be too proud to accept money or help, my father always said.'

'Talking of that,' Julie interrupted. Her stomach was doing somersaults and she felt sick. However, Ralph had told her to ask. 'Ralph was going to help with my sister's funeral costs. He told me in Ireland to ask you—'

'Of course, make whatever arrangements you want. Ralph told me about you and your sister. My condolences.' Sorrowfully, Carlos explained he had recently lost his father. 'Also, the baby. How is he doing?'

Surprised, Julie smiled. 'He's a fighter, but very small. He will have problems.'

'In that case, we shall have him moved to a private baby unit and you can sort out things for your sister.' Looking at the beautiful blonde woman before him, Carlos could see the attraction. She was hot-tempered, but funny. If things were different, he wouldn't mind spending an hour or so with her himself. He soon dismissed the thought. Ralph obviously had a very soft spot for this woman – or a hard one!

'Marco,' he barked. 'Take Julie here to the hotel. She is my guest.'

Picking up her bag, she was about to leave when Carlos held out his hand to shake hers. 'It's been very nice meeting you.' The squeeze of his handshake seemed to get tighter. 'I don't play games, Julie. Bye.'

The threats in those sweet undertones made her blood run cold. She nodded and left.

Her own room was just as glamorous. As she spied the king-sized bed, the minibar and the large Jacuzzi bath, she ran around the room, smiling. Jesus! This was living like movie stars. Picking up the telephone, she ordered room service. Everything on the menu looked fantastic and she couldn't resist ordering all of those fabulous-looking desserts. She ran the bath and poured all of the free samples of bubble bath into it, watching the soapsuds rise. Pressing one of the many buttons, she saw the Jacuzzi start to flow. The smile on her face couldn't have been wider.

* * *

Wrapped in a fluffy white towelling robe and full to the brim with all the food, she had fallen asleep on top of the bed. She was woken by knocking. Still half asleep and dazed, she went to the door. A porter stood there with an enormous bouquet of flowers for her. It was obvious he was waiting for a tip but she just thanked him and shut the door. God, he probably earnt more money than she did, working in a place like this!

She could not help grinning to herself that maybe that Carlos had taken a fancy to her... and why not? Going into the bathroom, she opened the box at the bottom to let the flowers breathe. To her surprise, she saw a plastic bag inside it. There was no water, as presumed.

Feeling more awake, she curiously opened the plastic bag. Inside was the gun she had requested. There was another bag beside it. She was not sure what it was, but fiddling around with it, she saw that it screwed onto the end of the gun. A silencer! She had seen them in the movies and recognised it. Surely Carlos would not send her an empty gun. Shit! What if it was loaded? In her panic she nearly dropped it, and then came to her senses. Inspecting it closer, she saw a button which pressed in and out. It was obviously a safety catch. She needed to try it. Going over to the bed, she curled up one of the thick luxurious pillows and fired the gun at it. Instantly feathers flew in the air and there was hardly any noise. Her heart was beating fast and she had to sit down for a moment. Her hand was shaking. Putting the safety catch back on, she gingerly put the gun down and went back into the bathroom.

Inspecting the flowers again, she saw a small envelope with a card inside. It read: 'The ball is now in your court.' It also had the room number where Chief Inspector Connor was staying and the name of the hotel.

Julie sat on the edge of the bed, covered in the feathers that had flown into the air, and stared at the gun on the bedside table. She trembled at the sight of it. Maybe she had been too impulsive, saying she could do this. Doubts were creeping in and she was afraid. However, it was too late now. Carlos had warned her: no games.

Tonight, Julie the escort was going to get some justice for Donna. Poor Donna: she had been so kind to her. She was the one that had taken pity on her and introduced her to Carrie at the brothel. God knows where Carrie had ended up. The more she thought about it, all her fears and doubts left her. Not only had she lost a good friend, but also, through this copper, she had lost her home and her job. That bastard didn't deserve pity!

Julie took a walk around the West End, near Soho. The place was buzzing and the smell of restaurants and their delicacies filled the air. London was an amazing place. Walking past a shop window, a thought occurred to her. Tonight, she intended to kill a man. Was she really going to go to his hotel room dressed as herself?

Looking again at the wig shop, she decided to go in. The assistant came to help her and Julie told her she was just browsing. Then she saw a long, black wig with a fringe. Trying it on with the help of the assistant, she looked into the mirror and was immediately transformed. The fringe was thick and straight, and the rest hung down her back. It was lovely, almost silky. There was nothing cheap about it. When she asked the assistant how much it was, she nearly had a heart attack.

The assistant explained it was real hair, which was why it didn't look cheap. Altering it again, Julie bit her lip. She did have an option. She'd seen it in the movies and thought it was worth a try. 'Do you do accounts or deliver to hotels?'

'We do, madam, where are you staying?' When Julie told

her the name of the hotel, the assistant nodded. 'Oh yes, madam, we can deliver there. They will put it on your hotel bill.'

Staggered by this, but trying to keep composed, Julie looked around the shop. 'Send that black fedora as well, will you? Oh, and these.' The assistant took her room number and smiled. She had obviously done this before. This would all go on Carlos's bill. Julie gave the assistant a five-pound tip for helping her, which was a lot more than she could afford. However, she had to act out the part. Nonchalantly waltzing out of the shop, Julie was elated. She could get used to this life.

At midnight, she packed everything into a plastic bag, including the gun. She had asked the receptionist not to put any calls through to her room and to give her an early call in the morning. She said she did not feel well and was going to have an early night. After putting the 'Do not disturb' sign on the door, she caught the Tube and went to the hotel she knew Chief Inspector Connor was staying in.

After working in many hotels, Julie knew the layout like the back of her hand. Once she had the right floor, she walked along the corridor to the toilet. Every corridor had one, and they were a great place to change in.

Nervous and summoning up all her courage, Julie went into autopilot escort mode. She had done this a thousand times. Why should tonight be any different?

She knocked on Connor's door and a police officer opened it slightly. Seeing Julie standing there with her long, black hair, the black fedora balanced jauntily and provocatively over one eye, he gaped. Her lips were bright red, in contrast with the blackness of her hair. She stood with her mackintosh wide open, showing a red basque and black stockings, her voluptuous bosom nearly spilling over the cups.

Lowering her voice to a husky tone, she smiled and said, 'Hi, honey. I have a present for Chief Inspector Connor.'

Confused, the police officer looked at her and then turned behind him. 'Sir, there is someone to see you.' Almost embarrassed, he shut the door in her face.

'Well, that's not the greeting I had hoped for,' she muttered to herself. A minute later, the door opened again and Julie pushed past the officer and walked into the hotel room. It was obvious there was more than one person staying there. It was a pigsty. The ashtrays were overflowing. There was half-eaten food on dishes that had not been taken away yet.

'Hey, lady.' Chief Inspector Connor grabbed her arm and pulled her back sharply. 'You have the wrong room. Now, get back under the stone you just crawled out from and get out!' Just as she remembered, he was a horrible man, still pushing women around. Another uniformed police officer came out of the bathroom. 'Is everything alright, sir?' he asked, looking at Julie.

It was obvious to them that she was no threat. She was a prostitute who had the wrong room. 'Look, off you go and find the room you're looking for. We don't need any whores here. Go now and we won't have you arrested.' Chief Inspector Connor stubbed out his cigarette and reached for his coat. 'Get rid of her.'

Trying to think on her feet, Julie blurted out, 'How's your wife, Janet? I haven't seen her in a while. The last time I saw her was with Donna. Do you remember Donna? Oh, by the way, I have a present for you, here.' Julie opened a small plastic bag and waited until the inspector looked inside. The colour drained from his face. 'I was in the area and just thought I would pop in for a drink, see if you might need some company.' She winked.

She had seen some handcuffs in the shop when she bought the wig and had bought them, too. How would this man know they weren't the ones she had taken as insurance? They had done the trick and he was shitting himself. She was doing her best to brave it out, even though inside she was shaking. She hadn't thought there would be three of them. 'Why don't we all have a little party,' Julie purred. She grinned, licked her lips and let her hands run over the chief inspector's shoulders.

Chief Inspector Connor put his coat down and turned to the two police officers. 'Look, why don't you guys take a break. I just need a moment,' he said. He could see the look in the police officers' eyes. This was good gossip.

'Actually, boys, would you mind if I had a bathroom break first?' Before she went any further, she wanted to know if the woman they were supposed to be protecting was here. Seeing as it was so late, she presumed she must be in bed. Time to go and look.

The two police officers gave her a wry smile; they knew why the inspector wanted them out of the room for a while. They raised their eyebrows at each other and said they would just have a walk down the corridor to check things out.

'Thanks, boys. Five minutes, eh. And not a word, okay?' the chief inspector warned.

Julie lounged on the chair, showing her stockinged legs and high heels, revealing she was not wearing any knickers. 'This won't take long. Go and have a coffee or something. There's good boys.' She winked provocatively and waved at them, then licked her lips.

'What the fuck do you want? Money? Is that it?' he snapped at her the moment they were alone.

Slowly taking off her hat and then pulling off her wig, Julie straightened her own blonde hair into place. 'You do remember me, then?'

'Look, we had a deal. What do you want and why are you here?' He was angry, standing with his hands on his hips.

Looking at him with distaste, her smile dropped and all the bitterness and hate she felt for him surfaced. 'Oh, I thought you might want to spend some time with me. I heard you were here and my "date" has just passed out on me. What do you say, Chief Inspector? Fancy some fun?'

She saw him lick his lips and his attitude changed. 'What? You're up for a good time?'

Julie saw that old familiar glint in his eye that she had seen in a million men's eyes before. Shifting position on the chair, she opened her legs wider to give him a better view. 'Where's your wallet, honey?'

Reaching for his coat, he fumbled around and pulled his wallet out of the pocket. 'Here it is.' Opening it, he took out some notes. 'This enough?'

'That'll do nicely. Why don't you crawl towards me on those knees of yours and bury your head right here, between my thighs.' Purring like a seductive kitten, she beckoned him forward. Watching him bend down and crawl towards her made her cringe. She felt sick as he crawled between her thighs. Pulling the back of his head even closer towards her, she closed her eyes while he licked her stocking tops and further.

Her plastic bag was at her side; she squirmed and moved around excitedly, egging him on as she reached for her gun. The silencer was already on and the safety catch was off. Rubbing his head and shoulders, she pointed the gun at the top of his head and pulled the trigger. There was just a low thudding noise as the bullet entered his brain and then he fell, lifeless, to the floor. Sitting there for a moment, she looked at his body. It had been a direct hit. There was just a hole in his head.

Pulling herself together, she went into the bedroom that was in darkness. Only the light from the other room shone in, showing Julie the bed. Running her hands along it, she felt a body. Picking up her gun, she shot two bullets into the body in the bed. Putting on the bedside lamp, she pulled the covers back. It was a woman and she was most certainly dead. Walking into the bathroom, she ran a flannel under the tap, walked back into the bedroom and wiped the lamp. She had watched enough movies and cop shows to know that you had to clean away your fingerprints. Good old Lieutenant Columbo!

Julie could hear someone outside of the door. Damn it. It was those two coppers coming back. Quickly running to the door, she stood with her back against it and started bumping her bum against it and moaning with excitement, imitating sex. She felt the handle release and she could hear them laughing together as they walked away. Letting out a sigh of relief, Julie ran around the room, cleaning up as she went. She pushed her wig and hat into the plastic bag and pulled on her coat. Cautiously opening the door, she looked both ways along the corridor. There was no one around.

She ran to the end of the corridor and down the fire exit stairs. No one had seen a blonde come in and as she reached the quiet reception area, no one would notice her leave. Flushed and breathing heavily, she walked as quickly as possible to the doors and pushed them open, breathing in the cold night air.

She was sweating and shaking. Only now was what she had done sinking in. She had just killed two people. She needed to get away fast. 'Rest in peace, Donna, love. I'm sorry I betrayed you. I love you,' she mumbled, as tears rolled down her cheeks and she looked back on that awful night when she had been helpless to do anything. Now she had rectified that. That evil bastard copper was dead now and he had died easier than Donna had. Poor Donna had been murdered and discarded like rubbish without a second thought. How Julie had hated herself for that. She took off her shoes then ran as fast as she could away from there.

It had been easier than she thought getting back into her own hotel. It was nearly 2 a.m. and no one took any notice of her as she got into the lift and went back to her room.

She opened the minibar and took out a small bottle of whisky, then gulped it back. Unexpected tears ran down her cheeks. This wasn't the first time she had murdered, and she was glad she had killed Connor. He had thought he was above the law and he'd had the cheek to want to put Ralph behind bars. Well, hopefully, Ralph would now be released. Without a witness, there was not a lot they could do. This was one murder Ralph could not be accused of.

30

REFLECTION

The morning air felt crisp and new as Ralph shook the prison warder's hand and left the building through a side door. Standing outside of the jail, Ralph took a deep breath and filled his lungs with fresh air. It was good to be out. He'd had a lot of time to think, lying on his bunk bed at night in the dark and he had vowed he would never go back inside; this was the very last time.

He had made a lot of money by many means and it was time to build up a secure future. Throwing his bag over his back, he walked away from the prison along the long road. He had not told anyone he was being released today. He wanted time to get things in order in his mind.

The sun was beginning to rise and the warmth felt good on his back; it showed the promise of a good day. Yawning, he walked on and saw a lorry in the distance. He stuck out his thumb and was surprised when the lorry actually stopped. It was obvious to anyone where he had just come from. The prison was the only place in the area.

Ralph had continued working out in the gym and he was lean and muscly. He had a long day ahead of him. First, he would go and see Paddy. It was time to set the record straight. Paddy had been to see him a few times to keep him updated on the property he thought worth buying. He also knew that Paddy had betrayed him... again.

Secondly, he would go and see his mother. She was still very ill and in a rehabilitation home. Then, he would go and see Carlos. He would know that he was out of prison. He had been his wingman through all of this, sending his fancy lawyers to fight his corner. Again, his mind wandered off. It was strange how you met people. His ma would call it fate; he just called it chance.

The rehabilitation home pleased Ralph. He had not been sure what to expect. This place was bright, airy and friendly. It did not look like a clinic or an institution and there were no uniforms as such, just the district nurse on a brief visit. He was told his mother was sitting in the lounge. Again, he was pleasantly surprised. It was a beautiful lounge with a television and chairs. The manager walked ahead of him, then stopped beside one of the high-backed chairs.

'Diana, your son has come to see you. Ralph's here. Isn't that lovely?' The manager knelt down beside the chair and smiled.

Ralph could not believe his eyes. His mother had aged considerably. He thought he saw a glimmer of a smile on his mother's face, but he was not sure. Half of her face had dropped and she was a shell of her former self.

'How are you doing, Ma?' Sitting down in a chair beside her, he reached out and held her weak, feeble hand. Feeling a lump in his throat, he coughed. He could not remember the last time he'd cried, but he could feel tears brimming. 'It's me, Ma – Ralph.'

There was no response.

A trolley came round and the manager gave Ralph a cup of tea. He didn't once take his eyes from his mother.

This was what those bombers had done to her. Not only had

they killed his wife and son: they had turned his mother into a vegetable. All he could do was make her as comfortable as possible.

Next, Ralph turned up at Millie's house, opening the door as usual. He knew Paddy would be there at this time of day.

'Ralph! You're out. Why didn't you tell me? I could have come and picked you up!' Paddy was talking around a mouthful of sausage sandwich and spitting bits out as he spoke. He shoved the last of the sandwich in his mouth then rushed towards Ralph, putting his arms around him. 'Ma, put the kettle on, our Ralph's home,' he shouted towards the kitchen.

Millie poked her head through her multi-coloured strip blinds from the kitchen and smiled.

Paddy went on and on about different properties he had seen and the breweries he had contacted about buying up some of the pubs. It seemed some of the breweries were more than happy to get rid of those pubs that were not making money.

Ralph could not hold his tongue any longer. 'You know who set me up, don't you, Paddy?'

Crushed, Paddy's excitement stopped and he shrugged. 'I think so. I did warn you that those guys would want some kind of revenge. We killed all of their men and it wasn't the first time you had insulted them.'

'So, how come they haven't set you up? You're as guilty as I am. You were there as well. So I find this all kind of strange, that nothing has happened to you.' Poker-faced, sitting on the sofa opposite Paddy, Ralph looked right through him and for the first time saw him through new eyes. He knew Paddy was a double agent and the only person he cared about was himself. Money always spoke volumes to Paddy and Ralph would buy his loyalty, if that was what it took.

'I don't know. Maybe the luck of the Irish, eh?' The weak smile on Paddy's face said it all to Ralph. 'I fucked up when they were asking about you, okay? Yes, I fucked up and told them where you were staying. You, Ralph Goldstein, in his fancy suits, flying around the world. What about me? We're supposed to be mates.' Paddy was on his feet, shouting, and the jealous venom he spat out confirmed Ralph's suspicions.

Paddy's face was red with anger and he was pacing around the room.

'All I want to know...' Ralph's calm, emotionless voice stopped Paddy ranting. 'Was the wife of the security guard really there? Had she seen me?'

Paddy sat down and put his head in his hands. 'No.' He shook his head. 'She was never there. She didn't know you. They made her say that. I don't know how they threatened her.' His voice dropped almost to a whisper. 'I had to give them a photo of you so she could identify you. They wanted you to rot in jail, but at least you would be alive and in your hometown. They were threatening both our mas, and God knows what they were going to do to me. I had no choice. Sorry.' Paddy started crying. He looked like a child who had been caught with his hand in the cookie jar.

Ralph stood up to leave. 'That's all I needed to know.'

'Wait! What about us?' Paddy wiped his snotty nose and tears on his sleeve and ran to the door to stop Ralph leaving.

'Nothing has changed. Carry on with your arrangements with the breweries. When the pubs are bought, we put the rent up. It's up to the managers whether they want to stay there or not. If not, we will put another manager in. You have the two men I sent to help you. Well, I'll be sending another one, so you'll have plenty of back-up.'

Wide-eyed with hope, Paddy could not believe his luck. 'So we're okay, Ralph? We're still partners?' The smile appeared back on his face and he held out his hand to shake Ralph's.

'No, Paddy. We're not partners.' The cold, stern look on Ralph's face showed Paddy there was no changing his mind. This time, Ralph had grown up. He'd seen how different things were in other parts of the world. 'It's my money and I own them. You'll get your share. Just do your job.'

Paddy's face dropped. 'Why don't we go for a drink, and talk things over properly?'

'I have to be somewhere. I've had enough of Ireland. Just keep things ticking over and I'll be back soon.' Ralph shook his hand and left, leaving a very forlorn Paddy in his wake.

Waiting at the airport before his flight, Ralph realised he had not eaten yet. He was hungry. He had already had a long day and he had a feeling it was going to get even longer. Sitting in a café with a great big fry-up of eggs, sausage and beans, along with fried bread, he had to admit it was the best food he had tasted in a long time. No sooner had he finished eating than his flight was called. Pleased with his day so far, he mentally ticked things off his to-do list. Now there was Carlos to go and see.

* * *

Ralph knocked on the door of Carlos's penthouse suite at the hotel, not knowing what to expect. So much had changed since the last time they had met. Carlos was now Don Carlos, head of the Mafia family.

Some new 'soldiers', as they were known, answered the door. He had seen these men before with Don Leo, Carlos's father.

'I'm here to see Carlos,' he said. No one moved, however; they still barred Ralph's way. 'Is there a problem?'

The two men in black suits took off their sunglasses in unison and raised their eyebrows. 'Who do you want to see, Mr Gold?'

Realisation dawned on Ralph. Of course. He was no longer

'Carlos' and Ralph had to show respect. 'Sorry, boys, it's been a long flight. I meant Don Carlos. Does the don have time to see me?'

'*Sì*, come in.'

The room was full of similar men. Some raised their heads and nodded or waved to Ralph as he was being led through the lounge towards another room, which Carlos used as a study.

Rising from his chair, Carlos offered a warm Italian greeting, which made Ralph feel on firmer ground. 'Ralph. It is good to see you,' he said. The men hugged. 'Leave us,' he told the others. Once alone, they greeted each other as friends.

'You seem to have increased your entourage, Don Carlos.'

'Of course, it is official now. I am Don Carlos, although not when chatting with an old friend. You look well. I am sorry I could not do more. Here, let's have some drinks. We have lots to talk about.'

'Well, whatever you did, I am most grateful. Though how you did it I don't want to know.' Ralph laughed.

Carlos filled two tumblers with whisky. Ralph took a sip and waited. 'What do you want to talk about? Prison food?'

Ralph made a face. 'I'm no stranger to it.'

'I wish I could have done more. I would have made your life comfortable if you had been convicted and then we could have appealed. You have a good friend in Julie.'

'Julie? What do you mean, Julie?' Looking at Carlos's reaction, he couldn't fathom who was more surprised. He took a large gulp of his drink.

Carlos sat down. He eyed Ralph suspiciously. 'Have you seen her?'

'No.' Ralph laughed. 'She came to the prison, once. I asked my friend to let her know where I was. That is it. That is the last time I saw her. Not even a bloody postcard!'

The disbelieving look on Carlos's face surprised Ralph. He had never seen him at such a loss for words.

'*Mamma mia*, Rafael. You really don't know, do you?' Carlos rolled his eyes up at the ceiling and then looked back at Ralph with a sigh. 'Let's have another drink. I think you might need it.' Once the drinks were sorted, Carlos spoke. 'As much as I would like to take the credit, I fear I cannot. It was Julie, with a little help from myself, who went to that hotel room.' He looked into Ralph's eyes and waited. 'You understand what I am saying, don't you?'

Puzzled and taken completely aback, Ralph hardly dared speak the words. 'Are you telling me that Julie murdered that woman and the chief inspector?' He lowered his voice, almost to a hushed whisper. He could hardly believe his ears.

'I presumed you knew.' Carlos let out a huge sigh and fell back in his chair. 'Yes, she has helped you enormously. At my expense, of course!' It was the first time Carlos laughed; he was remembering his meetings with Julie. 'You know, she actually said she would buy me dinner in the hotel while we talked. It was only a couple of days later I realised she had put it on my hotel bill. She is a scorpion! The very devil in disguise.' Carlos laughed long and loud; it was plain to Ralph that Julie's exploits amused him. 'Why, even the men here are terrified of her. Whenever I say she is coming, they all make an excuse to leave the room!' Carlos thought this was hilarious, the way Julie and her sarcastic comments had belittled his men more than once and put them in their place. Ralph sat listening to Carlos's tales about how Julie had cheated him, scared his men and constantly reversed the charges when she called his private number!

Ralph looked down at the floor and said, tentatively, 'Have you been seeing a lot of her, then?'

'Far more than I would like. Why, she treats this place like her own.' Carlos waved his arms around the room, then paused and shook his finger as the penny dropped. 'We have only talked business and money. Nothing else. You are a good, loyal man, one of the best I have had the pleasure to work with, and we are friends. I would never touch your woman, if that is what you're thinking.'

'Well, she is not officially my woman. Our paths just seemed to have crossed a lot. I can only presume whatever she has done, she has done out of gratitude for her sister. Naturally, I will reimburse you what is owed.'

'Don't worry about it. It has been worth it in entertainment value. She is a very funny, determined, beautiful woman. However, I would not trust her as far as I could throw her. She is your problem and I pity you.'

Still bemused by this revelation, Ralph spoke up again. 'She's not my girlfriend, Carlos.'

'What is it that stops you? You have been a widower for some time.'

'I'm a good ten years older than her.' Ralph felt embarrassed having this heart-to-heart with Carlos. 'We have only met through her line of work. We hardly know each other. I appreciate everything she has done and, of course, I appreciate your help in these matters. However, I feel she thinks we are even now. She knows I am out of prison and that will be the end of it. So, what other things do you wish to talk about?'

Carlos let the matter drop. 'We have a couple of things I wish to discuss. Firstly, I can now make plans for Ricky to get his just desserts.' Carlos banged the table with his fist. The very thought of it made him angry. 'The other families have agreed to it. In fact, sadly, they insist on it. They do not trust him.' After a sharp intake of breath, Carlos carried on. 'And secondly, on a lighter note, that job we talked about is still on.'

'What do you mean, that Arab king or whatever is still going to bring all his jewels and stuff to the London exhibition?'

'That's exactly what I mean. They are coming straight from Las Vegas to England. All his family's jewels and ornaments will be on display for the public, and we are going to take the lot!' Carlos's enthusiasm and excitement shone in his eyes. Ralph knew he did not need the money; he just loved the preparation and the chase. 'This has been a year in the planning, and I already have buyers set up to take them from here as soon as we have them.' An afterthought came to Carlos and he looked perturbed. 'There is something missing from the plan, however, and maybe you could help there.'

'If I can, I will, you know that. What is it?'

'We may need someone small enough to get into a side panel. All of his jewels will be under laser alarms, but there is a side panel, not far from the reception area, that a smaller person could get through. Maybe even charm the security guards. Once in, they could switch the lasers off.'

'A side panel? Who do you suggest we get to do this? I don't know of anyone.' Ralph shook his head; he was all out of ideas.

'Julie. Julie could do it. She has guts, she can think on her feet. In addition, I would want her to stay in the exhibition room when they closed for the evening. She could easily hide in that side panel and let us in at the right moment. Then you could switch off the alarms.'

'For God's sake, Carlos. Can you hear yourself? Why would Julie do it?' Ralph laughed, exasperated and amazed at the mere suggestion of Julie being their inside man.

The serious look on Carlos's face stopped Ralph mid-chuckle. 'Firstly, as you have experienced, I only do business when I have insurance, and I have insurance against Julie. She is a cold-blooded cop-killer and I have proof in the receipts from the shop that she bought her wig and accessories from as well as which hotel she stayed at. A word in the right ear of one of our commissioner friends would soon put the search out for a female killer, posing as a prostitute. They might even find the gun, which she threw into the Thames.' The smug, satisfied grin on his face turned Ralph's stomach. 'I also think she would very much like the money.'

'I thought you said you liked her. One minute you are praising her and now you're talking about blackmailing her. Make up your mind.'

'I had insurance over you once, but it didn't mean I didn't admire you. You have proved your loyalty and we are friends. Well, I hope we are. I think you should be the one to put this plan to Julie.' Getting out of his chair, Carlos walked over to the window and looked out at the view. 'I want you to kill Ricky for me, Ralph. I cannot kill my own brother, but it needs to be done. You will do it quickly.' Carlos's voice broke slightly as he spoke. 'I trust you. Also, Ricky has acquired some property in the West End of London. A club, or something.' Carlos shrugged nonchalantly. 'It is a small-time club, but the land is worth a fortune. You can have it.'

Staring across the room at Carlos's back, Ralph knew he did not want to show any emotion. The thought of killing his brother cut him deeply, but the thought of what Ricky had done angered him more.

Thinking about it, Ralph drummed his fingers on his chin. 'I'll get on to that right away.'

Turning swiftly, Carlos shouted across the room, 'No! First, you must see Julie. Go there and get her on board.'

'Can't you do it? I don't think she's very eager to see me.'

'You are cut from the same cloth, whether you like it or not. She didn't contact you so that there would be no paper trail from her to you. She has been clever. But she has also visited your mother and had flowers sent to her – on my bill, of course. God, now I think of it, does she ever spend any money of her own?' When Ralph remained silent, Carlos sighed. 'Tell me, what are you after? You ask me if I know what she does for a living. Yes, I do. So what of it? You want my blessing, is that it?' Wide-eyed, Carlos turned to look at him.

Looking down and playing with his hands, slightly embarrassed, Ralph said, 'I suppose I would like your blessing. We're friends. I have thought about her a lot, though, and no, not just physically... she's funny and she makes me laugh. I have never felt like that before...' Ralph trailed off. He felt like a silly teenager rambling on. He had often thought about Julie, wondering what she was doing and more to the point who she was with. It tortured him, thinking of her laughing and joking with another man in her bed.

'You have my blessing. She has looked after all your affairs while you were away, and I have a feeling she would have done it for the next thirty years, if you had stayed in prison... at a price, of course. Go and see her, you coward. If the chemistry is right, it makes no difference. I bless you but I pity you. She is going to run rings around you. In fact, God help us all.' Carlos looked up at the ceiling in despair. 'Apart, the two of you are ruthless. Together, you will be merciless. I am very glad you are both on my side. Seriously, now, Ralph.' Carlos sat down and the smile disappeared from his face. 'That other matter I asked you to handle for me, can you do it soon? Ricky will be waiting for you outside to take you wherever you want to go.' That done, the smile reappeared on his face and Carlos came forward, slapped Ralph on the back, hugged him and planted a kiss on each cheek. 'We'll speak soon. Off you go to Liverpool, and keep your eye on your wallet!'

* * *

Ralph went into the other room and saw Ricky slouched on a seat. 'Ricky, good to see you. I need to speak to you privately.' Moving in a bit closer, he whispered, 'I need some tools. Why don't you drive me to the train station?'

As they got into the car, Ralph explained he was heading up to Liverpool and needed a gun. He knew Ricky was always tooled up.

'There is one in the back with a silencer. Are you expecting trouble in Liverpool?'

'Who knows? Better to be on the safe side. I'll get in the back with my bag and take a look, if you don't mind.'

Shrugging, Ricky got into the front and started to drive to the train station.

'Park over the back, there,' Ralph said when they got there, 'then no one will see us. I want to talk to you.'

Again, Ricky nodded his head and drove to a remote part of the car park. Once he had turned the ignition off, Ralph shot him through the back of the head. His death was instant. Ralph grabbed Ricky's hair and pulled his head back onto the headrest of the car seat. 'Sorry, Ricky, but now here comes the shitty part.' Thankful it was dusk, Ralph followed Carlos's instructions. Once done, he took Ricky's briefcase over to one of the black cab drivers waiting outside of the station.

'Here's thirty pounds. Will you take this case to this address?' Seeing the worried look on the taxi driver's face, Ralph smiled. 'Don't worry; it's not a bomb or anything. Just deliver it to reception; if I go back I'll miss my train.' He handed the taxi driver the piece of paper he had written Carlos's name and hotel on and watched as he pulled away from the rank. Once he knew the package was on its way, he left the station to do some shopping before he caught his train.

* * *

'Don Carlos, a porter has brought something for you.' Joe looked at the briefcase oddly. He knew it was Ricky's.

'Good. Open it. And let this be a lesson for you all.' Don Carlos stood with his hands on his hips and looked around at the men in the room. 'This is what the other families have demanded for Ricky's loose, disrespectful tongue.'

Joe opened the case slowly. Everyone else stopped what they were doing and waited on tenterhooks, glancing over at each other.

'Oh, my God! Santa Maria!' Joe ran towards the bathroom, holding his mouth so that the vomit did not fall on the floor, while the others looked on in horror. Inside the briefcase was Ricky's tongue, which Ralph had cut out, as requested.

Satisfied with Ralph's swift job, Carlos nodded. 'Ricky's loose tongue will be no good to him now that he is dead. Parcel it up and send it to Don Alfredo. Our promise is fulfilled.'

31

LIVERPOOL LASS

After a few stops on the way, the train reached Liverpool. Ralph's thoughts were anguished. Would Julie be pleased to see him? Or was that just him being a silly old fool? They hadn't known each other long and their meetings had been brief. So why was she constantly on his mind? Normally, he would have driven there in his new black Jaguar, but he wanted time to think. To get everything he wanted to say straight in his mind.

'For God's sake, why does it always rain in Liverpool?' he shouted at the taxi driver, outside of the train station. Holding his newspaper over his head, he opened the back door and got in. 'It must be the wettest place in Britain.' Ralph handed him a slip of paper. 'I need to go here.'

The driver shrugged, but did as Ralph requested.

After paying the driver and getting out of the taxi, Ralph checked the door number. The chipped, wooden front door looked even worse in the rain. Taking a breath, he knocked. While waiting for an answer, a thought popped into his mind. Maybe he should have brought flowers. When there was no answer, he knocked again. He was sodden and the rain was dripping off the end of his nose. Not exactly what he had envisioned all those times in his prison cell when he'd imagined them meeting again. At last, the door opened and he saw a young man in his twenties with shoulder-length hair. Ralph's heart sank. 'Yeah, mate. What do you want?' The youth stood before him, dressed in denim jeans and a T-shirt.

'I'm looking for Julie. I believe she lives here.'

'You one of the bizzies?' The young man yawned and scratched his crotch. When he saw the confused look on Ralph's face he started again. 'You know, bizzies, police?'

'Oh no, no, I'm not the police, I'm an old friend just looking her up.'

'Come and stand in the hallway, mate, you can drip-dry on the mat. Julie!' he shouted at maximum volume up the staircase. 'There's some bloke here for you.' He turned back to Ralph. 'She's on the second floor, mate.' The young man scratched his head, then disappeared into one of the ground-floor rooms.

Standing alone in the hallway, Ralph looked around. The paint was peeling and he could hear music blaring from one of the rooms. Then he heard footsteps and looked up the stairs. Julie stood on the landing, with her curlers in, no makeup on and wearing a dressing gown. Not exactly Romeo and Juliet. 'Goldy! What are you doing here? Come upstairs; you look like a drowned rat. Have you got any fifty pences on you?'

Ralph put his hand in his pocket and pulled out some loose change. 'Here's two.'

'Good, then we can put them in the meter and dry your clothes by the fire. Come on, I'll put the kettle on.' Following her fluffy slippers up the stairs, Ralph felt stupid, but he had to smile. Carlos was right. Did she ever spend any money of her own? He had only been there five minutes and already she'd had a pound off him!

'Well, strip, then! You're not sitting on my chair with that wet arse. Don't worry, I've seen it all before.' Letting out a loud cackle, she went and got a towel and threw it at him. Slowly he took off his coat and started undoing his tie. His shirt was almost stuck to his skin. He could hear her putting the money in the meter and he dried himself with the towel she had given him. Sitting there in his underwear, he squirmed. The warmth of the electric fire was welcome, but inside he really felt like a prat.

'Here you go, Goldy, get this down you to warm yourself up.' Julie handed over a mug of tea and sat on a worn chair at the other side of the fire with her hands wrapped around her own mug. 'So, what brings you here? If you're hoping for a quickie just cos you've been inside, be warned.' She wagged her finger in his face. 'I don't do discounts for ex-cons and I don't do buy one get one free.' Again, she laughed.

Ralph looked at her at the other side of the fire. The warm glow from the two-bar electric fire seemed to highlight her face. 'Why don't we go out to eat somewhere?'

'What, in those wet clothes of yours? Tell you what, give us a fiver and I'll get young Jimmy downstairs to get some fish and chips. Actually, make it a tenner, then he can get some for himself... come on, Goldy, cough up.'

Reaching for his wallet, standing only in his boxer shorts, he grinned and shook his head. She really was Dick Turpin in a G-string. God, he hadn't been here long and already she had her hand in his wallet!

'Jimmy! Oi, you lazy bastard, Jimmy! Go and get us both some fish and chips, and get yourself something as well.' Wrapping up the money into a ball, she threw it down the stairs at the young man Ralph had met when he arrived, then shut the door. 'Now, where were we? How are you?'

'Well, I was a lot richer till I got here.' He smiled and gave her a wink. 'I'm sorry I missed Frankie's funeral. I take it everything went well?' He waited, but Julie didn't answer. She turned her head and looked at the fire. 'How's Josh doing?' He felt this was a lighter note and one that would get a response.

'He's out of intensive care. Poor little bastard had to go cold turkey; he was so full of heroin. However, he's doing okay. They think he should be out in a few weeks.' She smiled hopefully at the prospect. She looked almost excited. 'Listen, Ralph.' Julie's tone turned serious and she looked him directly in the face. 'What's done is done. I don't want you to mention Frankie again. Part of me went in that box with her. I should have looked after her better.'

It was as though Julie was deep in thought and talking to the fire. All her words came tumbling out and her eyes filled with tears.

'So, what are you here for?' As though coming out of a dream, she painted that familiar smile on her face.

'Well.' Ralph put his mug down on the hearth. 'Carlos has sent me to ask you something. It's not great, but it might bring some money in for you and little Josh. Carlos likes insurance. He also likes blackmail, and he feels he has both with you. I hear that it was you that got me off the charges.' Ralph skirted around the truth, not wanting to say the words.

'Did I? I'm not sure what you mean. What kind of insurance are we talking about?' she snapped. 'Anyway, whatever you and Carlos think I've done or not done is irrelevant. We're even, now, Ralph. You helped me when I needed you and maybe, just maybe, I helped you. That clears me of all debt to you. Therefore, what does Carlos want? Fucking mad Italian git. His mood changes quicker than the weather. He's fucking nuts!'

Not quite knowing how to put it, Ralph paused. 'What can I say? Carlos knows what you did and he wants you to do a little job for him. If you refuse, he will hand you over to his police friends. He did the same to me. He also admires you. He thinks you have real guts. He speaks very highly of you,' Ralph lied.

'So, that little shit is going to grass me up, is he? Is that what you're telling me? Well, I think I should go and see him and tell him what I think of him. Bloody hell, you cannot trust anyone. Anyway...' Julie paused. 'Apart from you, I had my own reasons for seeing that copper take his last breath. Yes.' She pointed to her chest. Her eyes were blazing with anger and she spilt her tea all over the floor. 'I murdered the bastards. And for your information it wasn't the first time!'

'Calm down, Julie, calm down. We're both murdering bastards, right? And Carlos, well, I have lost count of the people he's seen take their last breath. But this job could be very lucrative. He's a generous man; you would get your share. How do you think I became so wealthy?' He could see that his words were penetrating her brain, although her face was flushed.

'So, what does he want me to do?'

Ralph explained about the exhibition that was to come to England. He didn't have the full facts, but he told her exactly what Carlos had told him. They needed someone smaller. Someone with guts who could think on their feet, should the need arise.

Ralph could see that she was interested. 'Carlos always works out his alibis before the job. Think about it. I have passed the message on; now it's time for me to leave.'

'You're going? So soon?' She could not hide the disappointment from her voice. Then she looked at the clothes airer and grinned. 'Even though your trousers are scorched from the fire.'

Sighing, Ralph shook his head and looked at the scorch mark. Then they both looked at each other and burst out laughing. Without thinking, Ralph pulled her to her feet. 'Come here, woman. I've wanted to do this for a long time.' Pulling her head closer, he kissed her. He was surprised when she did not push him away, but kissed him back just as passionately. As they were both half naked anyway, Julie pulled him down to the floor, on top of her. Their frenzied passion released the unspoken words of how they felt about each other, shouting out with each thrust of his body.

* * *

The next couple of days rolled into one as they spent it making love on Julie's bed settee before the fire, as the condensation dripped from the windows. Between breaks they would talk and laugh and Julie would shout down to one of the students to go and get them some food, drinks and cigarettes, while throwing Ralph's money at them.

Interrupted by the knock on the door, Julie reached for her dressing gown and answered it. It was Tom, one of the students who lived downstairs. Ralph waited to see what delight Julie had ordered to ruin his digestive system this time. He looked around at the poky bedsit, with mould at the side of the windows. He couldn't help smiling as he sat up with his arms at the back of his head. This was the happiest he could ever remember being. It was true what they said: it wasn't the surroundings; it was who you were with.

'What the hell is that?' Ralph looked down at the foil cartons swimming with gravy and potatoes.

'It's scouse. You'll love it. Come on, eat up, you need your strength,' she said, holding out a spoon.

Tasting it, Ralph laughed. 'It's a stew.'

'Ahh, but it's not just any stew. It's Liverpool stew. The stuff the Beatles were made of.'

Sitting up on the bed settee with their stew and mugs of cheap wine seemed like the most romantic, natural thing in the world to Ralph. He felt now he had softened her up; it was time to put his plan into action. He had definitely made his mind up.

Fully satiated with the food, Ralph lay back. 'I'm not a well man, Julie. It's my heart.'

Instantly he saw the frown and worried look on her face. 'Surely the doctors can do something. There are all kinds of treatments these days.' Putting down her own carton of food, she reached out and held his hand. 'What have the doctors said?'

Nonchalantly, ignoring her worried face, he sighed and looked up at the ceiling. 'There might be a slim chance for me. It depends. That is why I am thinking of getting married. I'm sick at heart.'

Julie sat there, stunned. His words were like a knife to her heart. For a moment, she was speechless, then she said, 'I didn't realise you were seeing someone. You never said.' Her voice cracked and became a hushed whisper as she fought back the tears. This man had played her and she had fallen for it. She felt foolish. 'Well, don't forget the meter's running. These last couple of days will cost you dearly,' she snapped, as she pulled back the covers and reached for her dressing gown. Getting up, she turned her back to him and switched on the kettle. She needed a moment to gather her thoughts and compose herself.

'Yes.' Ralph carried on talking to her back. 'She is lovely. I have never been in love before, so I presume this is what they mean.'

Julie brushed away a tear that had fallen on her cheek as the words floated in the air. The lump in her throat rose as Ralph, her Goldy, spoke of his love for another woman. She wanted to lash out and scream at him, but instead she went into defence mode. After all, this wasn't the first married man she'd had in her bed.

She could hear him moving around behind her, but didn't turn around. She concentrated on making the mugs of tea. She was hurt but didn't want to show it in front of this customer.

'Here, drink this before you go.' Her voice had hardened and she could barely look at him.

Taking the hot tea from her, Ralph grinned. He knew she really wanted to throw it at him. She was fiery and impulsive. And he could tell by her tone that she was angry. He couldn't remember being so happy as he was now. These last couple of days in this bedsit, lying in the arms of the woman he loved, would last forever in his heart.

'Swap you.' Taking her mug from her and placing it on the floor, he reached underneath the bedding, took out a small leather box and handed it to her.

Confused, Julie stared at it for a moment, not knowing what to say. 'What's that?' she asked, although she could see it was a ring box.

'Open it.' He smiled. 'I told you the doctors said I had a slim chance to get over my heart sickness.'

Opening it, Julie saw a small diamond solitaire ring.

'Is this a diamond ring, or just a ring with a very small diamond in it? What happened, Ralph? Was Woolworths having a sale?'

'I like it, personally, but when I was shopping, I thought about you. Then I thought you might prefer this one. It reminded me of that hot temper of yours.' He was holding out another ring box. Julie took it and opened it, and a smile crossed her face. It was a huge ruby surrounded by diamonds. Relief and disbelief washed over her. Was he asking her to marry him? She wasn't sure. Julie didn't like games and she felt this was one. Handing him back the box, she nodded. 'Well, I'm sure whoever she is, she will like it. Not bad, if you like that sort of thing.'

'Well, what about this one?' Again, he handed her another box. Opening it, her jaw nearly dropped. It was the largest sapphire she had ever seen, surrounded by diamonds. She couldn't resist trying it on. 'Is it real?' Trying to hide her emotions, Julie looked at the rings.

'I wouldn't buy you anything else. I'm surprised you haven't got your eyeglass out to check for the hallmark.' He laughed. 'They are for you. That is, if you want them.' Realising he had played this game long enough, he explained, 'I'm a lot older than you, but I would like to look after you and little Josh. You annoy me, but I love you for it. Do you like me?' he asked, hopefully.

Still stunned, waiting for the punchline, she nodded. 'Let's just say I like you more than any other man I have ever known, and coming from me that is a lot. I respect you, because you're the only person who has ever helped me without any strings attached and you've treated me like a lady.'

Ralph nodded, deep in thought. It was a better answer than he had expected. He was halfway there. He had never expected Julie to wear her heart on her sleeve and tell him she loved him. She showed that in the tenderness of her kisses and the way she held him. They were comfortable with each other. They were survivors. They understood each other, and she had been the best wingman he could ever have hoped for. She would never betray him and would always fight his corner. What more could he ask?

'I'm not living in a fucking hotel, though,' Julie snapped, and she laid down her rules. 'I've seen enough of hotels. I want a house. A big house, furnished to the hilt with expensive furniture. I'm going to learn to drive and have a big car. And I want a credit card with no limits.'

'A done deal, Mrs Gold. Is that a "yes", then?' Ralph held out his hand to shake hers and, satisfied, he lay back down again. He had what he'd come for. The rest was immaterial. He could afford everything she wanted and more.

'You bastard, Ralph Gold! You are going to pay dearly for that stunt you've just pulled. A bloody handshake? I would ask you to go down on one knee but you're so old you would probably never get up again!' Julie was skipping for joy inside. There were butterflies flying around her stomach. Her heart was pounding and she could not help smiling. She liked this man very much. Yes, she probably loved him, but would never admit it to him... not yet, anyway.

Wrapping the bed sheet around him to cover his nakedness, Ralph went down on one knee before her and proffered the three ring boxes. 'I love you, Julie. I know I'll regret it and you will cause mayhem and chaos in my life, but I love you. Will you marry me?'

Smiling, she reached out and ran her hands through his black hair. 'Go on then,' she said, slipping each one of the rings on her fingers. Ralph cocked his head to one side and raised one eyebrow.

'So, when do we do this jewel heist at this Arab's exhibition? I'm game if you are. One of those jewels might just slip around my neck. That will fuck that Carlos up!'

Reaching her hand out to pull him up, Julie put her arms around his neck and kissed him. Doing so, she opened one eye to peer over his shoulder at the three dazzling rings on her fingers. 'Just for future reference, I have five fingers, not three. You will have to make up the difference. Yes, I will marry you and make you proud.' Kissing him again, Julie couldn't help but move her hand around behind his neck and marvel at the stones. It was true what they said. All that glitters is not gold!

ACKNOWLEDGMENTS

Thanks to Avril and Sue for putting up with me while writing this... real besties.

Many thanks to the UK crime book club and all the other book clubs for their support.

To all the lovely readers and their support.

Many thanks to everyone at Boldwood publishers – a really great team.

MORE FROM GILLIAN GODDEN

We hope you enjoyed reading *Gold Digger*. If you did, please leave a review.

If you'd like to gift a copy, this book is also available as an ebook, digital audio download and audiobook CD.

Sign up to Gillian Godden's mailing list for news, competitions and updates on future books.

http://bit.ly/GillianGoddenNewsletter

ABOUT THE AUTHOR

Gillian Godden is a Northern-born medical secretary for NHS England. She spent thirty years of her life in the East End of London, hearing stories about the local striptease pubs. Now in Yorkshire, she is an avid reader who lives with her dog, Susie.

Follow Gillian on social media:

facebook.com/gilliangoddenauthor

twitter.com/GGodden

ABOUT BOLDWOOD BOOKS

Boldwood Books is a fiction publishing company seeking out the best stories from around the world.

Find out more at www.boldwoodbooks.com

Sign up to the Book and Tonic newsletter for news, offers and competitions from Boldwood Books!

http://www.bit.ly/bookandtonic

We'd love to hear from you, follow us on social media:

facebook.com/BookandTonic

twitter.com/BoldwoodBooks

instagram.com/BookandTonic

Printed in Great Britain
by Amazon

51901916R00194